ALSO BY JENNI OGDEN

FICTION

A Drop in the Ocean: A Novel

NONFICTION

Fractured Minds: A Case Study Approach to Clinical Neuropsychology

Trouble In Mind: Stories from a Neuropsychologist's Casebook

THE MOON IS MISSING

A NOVEL

JENNI OGDEN

A catalogue record for this book is available from the National Library of New Zealand.

First Edition: August, 2020

ISBN 978-0-473-53197-3 (Paperback)

ISBN 978-0-473-53199-7 (Kindle)

ISBN 978-0-473-53198-0 (E-book)

ISBN 978-0-473-53201-7 (Audiobook)

Published by Sea Dragon Press

www.jenniogden.com

Cover by *Julie Metz Design*

 Created with Vellum

CONTENTS

"Readers will enjoy this novel of second chances, not only at love but at life, reminiscent of Terry McMillan's *How Stella Got Her Groove Back*"
—**Booklist**

"A novel about turtles, the fragility of life, and the complexity of love . . . a story to savor, discuss, and share."
—**Barbara Claypole White**, best-selling author of *The Perfect Son* & *The Promise Between Us*

"A quietly majestic book, taking on quests for identity, for connection, for love, for self . . . a book to lose oneself in—and then share, enthusiastically, right away.")
— **Robin Black**, bestselling author of *Life Drawing*

"A complicated, deep and passionate love affair that transcends stereotypes. . . . Ogden brought the island to life with her words. . . But the book's real treasure is how island life changes Anna. . . ."
—**Story Circle Book Reviews**

"…Life, love, and loss are strong themes that will lure readers back to this beautifully woven journey of second chances…a powerful read that I highly recommend."
—**Readers' Favorite**

"Evocative and thought-provoking, *A Drop In The Ocean* is a story about belonging—and the ripples that can flow from the family we choose to the family that chooses us."
—**Anita Heiss**, Best-selling author of *Tiddas* & *Barbed Wire and Cherry Blossoms*

"Jenni Ogden is a natural storyteller who writes characters to care about."
—**Nicky Pellegrino**, author of *One Summer In Venice*

THE MOON IS MISSING: A NOVEL

"Jenni Ogden is a beautiful writer. In her newest, a tale of domestic suspense, she tells the story of a neurosurgeon bedeviled by her own sophisticated brain and the memories of a long-ago tragedy that still has the power to destroy her and her family. Pick up *The Moon is Missing*. You won't put it down."
— **Jacquelyn Mitchard**, #1 New York Times bestselling author of *The Deep End of the Ocean* and *My Only*

"With gripping scenes set during Hurricane Katrina and on a remote New Zealand island, this tightly-woven family drama —fueled by long-buried secrets and a daughter's desperate need to answer the question, 'Who am I?' —is ripe for book club discussion."
—**Barbara Claypole White**, bestselling author of *A Perfect Son* & *The Promise Between Us*

"Jenni Ogden's powerful novel, *The Moon is Missing*, is a mother-daughter coming of age story exploring a woman physician's passion-driven work, the terrible mistakes and long-held family secrets that haunt her life, and the power of loving connections to heal. The evocative settings on three continents are an added bonus!"
—**Barbara Stark-Nemon**, author of *Even in Darkness* & *Hard Cider*

"...Beautifully written ... characters were immensely believable...Ogden did not shy away from the harsh realities of

what can happen when someone in a family is experiencing panic attacks and trauma from the past. Katrina was a tragedy… the novel really paid homage to the medical staff who worked tirelessly to make sure people were evacuated….a must-read for anyone who is a fan of women's fiction, especially harkening back to the old greats such as Fern Michaels."
—**Readers' Favorite**, *5 star review*

A DROP IN THE OCEAN: A NOVEL

AWARDS

GOLD: Nautilus Book Award for Best Fiction, Large Publisher (2016)

GOLD: Sarton Women's Book Award for Contemporary Fiction (2015–2016)

GOLD: Independent Publisher Book Award (IPPY) for Best Regional Fiction, Australia and New Zealand (2016)

SILVER: Reader's Favorite Book Award for Women's Fiction (2016)

PRAISE

"In *A Drop in the Ocean,* protagonist Anna Fergusson learns that love is about letting go. Jenni Ogden takes us on a sweeping journey, rich with unique characters and places, moving backward and forward in time, to reach this poignant and heartfelt lesson."

—**Ann Hood**, *New York Times* best-Selling author of *The Knitting Circle* & *The Book That Matters Most*

"Reading *A Drop in the Ocean* was everything a reading experience should be, endearing and enduring, time spent with characters who seem to be people I already knew."

—**Jacquelyn Mitchard**, #1 *New York Times* best-selling author Of *The Deep End Of The Ocean*

PART I

GEORGIA

London, March 2005

CHAPTER 1

"$\mathcal{W}$ho am I? *Who bloody am I?*"

The bubble of Sunday-gardening bliss floating in my chest deflated as I took a step back from my furious daughter. *This is just a teenage thing. Treat it with gentle humor.* I reached out and put my fingers under Lara's chin, turning her head first to the left and then the right. "You *look* like my daughter, Lara Aroha Grayson. Have I got that wrong?"

Lara pushed my hand away, her mass of dark red curls sparking like the ends of cut wires around her flushed and frowning face. "Stop patronizing me. I'm not one of your awestruck interns." Her eyes, greener than usual, pinned me to the wall, her face even more arresting than when she was in her usual happy mode. "I want to know who I am, where I come from, what bloody genes lurk inside me, make up every tiny cell in my body, make me horrible at math, give me my *passion* for music."

My pulse took off, ricocheting between my heart and throat. I focused on keeping my expression mildly concerned and forced my damn body to at least act relaxed. Not exactly easy, as my carefully controlled world teetered on the edge of implosion. "Where has all this come from?" I asked, my voice hopefully sounding calmer than I felt.

Lara glared at me, the creases marring her smooth forehead as clear as a red flag to a bull. An image of her in full tantrum, aged about three, flashed in my head, and for a second the corners of my mouth twitched dangerously near a smile. I swallowed it and pulled myself reluctantly back to what was happening right now; the showdown I'd always known must happen one day.

"Have you not noticed? Have you not caught on to the small fact that I have a Social Studies assignment due in one week, and it's worth thirty percent of the entire year's internal assessment mark? What did you think I was doing stuck in my room all bloody weekend while you and Dad and Finbar were frolicking in the garden, basking in the first hint of sun we've had this year, picking fucking daffodils?"

"Mind the language, Lara. And calm down; you look as if you're about to burst into flames."

"Well, at least I've got your attention at last. I cannot, *cannot* find an entire half of who I am. And it is *your* fault. You refuse to tell me anything about my father, let alone who his parents and grandparents and great grandparents and brothers and sisters were. Are, I suppose, unless they're all tragically dead too."

"What has this to do with an assignment on—what is the topic exactly?"

"Who am I. Who—am—I? Get it? It's about genealogy. Who do you think you are. All that shit. How my ancestors' characteristics and lifestyle and social circumstances and mad choices and where they came from gave me the *blueprint* for who I am and how I am different and why that might be and blah blah." Lara's voice rose even higher. "So get this. I don't want to be a neurosurgeon or any sort of doctor or scientist, so that gene of yours didn't make it into me. You can barely sing in tune so I'm making a wild guess that I got my singing voice from my father, like my hair. But what else did I get from him? You've never even shown me a photo of him. How is that even remotely fair?"

"Lara, please lower your voice. You'll disturb the entire neighborhood. This is not a conversation to have when you're upset. We'll sit quietly after dinner and talk about it. I'm not sure what I can tell you that will help though. I haven't any photos of Danny, and I know almost nothing about his family. So apart from his hair and his musical genius… Mind you, my father also has a beautiful voice, so you could have inherited that from him."

"I know Granddad can sing, but what about my other granddad? My father's father? My father's mother for that matter. Could they sing? Were they shit at math? Were they from America, from New Zealand, from England, from Russia, from Timbuktu? Are they even alive? Why don't they want to know me? Why don't they want to know *who I am*?"

"We'll talk about it later. In the meantime, think about how nurture as well as nature makes you who you are. More so in my opinion. You've incorporated into your being many more qualities and values from Adam than from a man who by a twist of fate was your biological father and died months before you were born." *Shit, I sound like a patronizing prune.* But I couldn't seem to stop. "Adam's your real dad and he got many of his personality traits and values from his parents and grandparents, and you know all about them and about my background. You can complete your assignment without even mentioning your biological father if you want to; the teacher doesn't even need to know."

"That, mother dear, is not the point, but thank you for the lecture. The *point* is for me to think about who I am, and I am *half blank*. I don't want to be half blank. I know lots of good stuff comes from Dad and I've already written about that, but it isn't complete. *I'm* not complete." Lara sniffed and swiped her arm across her nose, her face now blotched with tears.

"Oh sweetheart, come here." My eyes were threatening to well up as they always did when almost anyone cried, but especially my own two usually uncrying kids. I opened my arms and felt my tears escape as Lara allowed me to fold her in a close hug, her curls wiry and precious against my damp cheek.

DINNER WAS TENSE, FINBAR THE ONLY ONE WHO SEEMED oblivious to Lara's mood and Adam and my stilted attempts to behave as if the perfectly roasted New Zealand-born Sunday lamb, bought as a special treat to celebrate this glorious and rare London promise-of-spring weekend, was as delicious as I'd planned. It was the first weekend in a month that I hadn't been on call. Since Peter—the Director of the Neurosurgery Department—had been laid low by old age and cardiac problems, my workload had escalated. This weekend was Jim Mason's turn on call. Over the past month, he and I, as the next two most senior neurosurgeons in the hallowed hierarchy of our large London hospital neurosurgery department, had taken turns practicing for the Directorship role. Near the end of the year, when Peter was officially to retire, we'd both be up for the job, along with who knows how many outside candidates. Just another ever-present stress to add to my mess of anxieties, a state-of-mind I was well attuned to and mostly successful at keeping to myself. Or at least keeping firmly at home, away from Jim bloody Mason's sleazy little eyes.

Adam's hand grazed mine as he reached for some more potatoes. He'd been looking tired lately. Hardly surprising given that he was the one who bore the brunt of my anxiety attacks. For years I'd been suffering only one or two restless nights a fortnight, but lately sleep refused to come, or stay when it did come, night after night. I smiled at Adam, hoping I was beaming my thank you for his valiant efforts to support my crazy work schedule. On top of that, now he'd have to pretend that Lara's sudden desire to find out more about Danny and his genes did not spear him through his heart. He who'd been her father in every way since she was three years old.

I'd managed to catch him alone before dinner to warn him about Lara's mood and the talk I'd promised her once dinner was over. Adam obviously took it for granted he'd be part of any discussion; we'd always believed that sticking together was the best policy. None of this allowing the kids to pit one parent against the other in an unsubtle tactic designed to get the best deal. Not that it always worked.

I snuck a glance at Lara, stabbing at her tender lamb slices as if they were made of leather. Shit, how the hell was I going to convince Adam that Lara wasn't rejecting him; that this was merely another hormonally charged fifteen-year-old's over-reaction? Cross fingers that within a day of handing in her assignment Danny and his mysterious genes would be over-shadowed by the next crisis in Lara's full-on life.

Finbar, bless his sunny socks, was babbling on about the book he was currently engrossed in. At least he was indu-bitably Adam's son with his thick tawny hair and dark choco-late eyes. *Should have been a girly*, as his sister was apt to remark of her brother. Perhaps she was right. Our youngest was endowed with a generous nature that was as conciliatory and non-confrontational as his sister's was boisterous and loud. And poised at that lovely age of eleven. Old enough to be funny and interesting and young enough to still want to cuddle his parents.

LARA WAS SITTING SO NEAR THE EDGE OF HER CHAIR I thought she might slide off any second and land unceremoni-ously on the floor. That wouldn't add anything positive to the aura of calm Adam and I were trying to project into the tense space between us and our daughter.

"Stop going on about a tragic accident," Lara said, clearly through gritted teeth. "Of course it was tragic. All accidents that kill people are tragic. That tells me nothing. I want details. People don't just casually fall off cliffs. Was he drunk or stoned? Is that what the big secret is?" She bunched the ball of damp tissues clasped in her hands even more tightly.

"No, he wasn't drunk or stoned. That I do know. But I can't tell you much more because I don't know myself. All I can remember is that we were at our holiday house on Great Barrier Island and there was a massive storm. Danny had been away visiting his parents in the South Island and had just come back and we had an argument about something; probably I was mad about him being away so long and not contacting me. It's fuzzy. The next memory I have is …" My voice stopped working and I stared down at my hands gripped knuckle-white in my lap— "The police found him at the bottom of the cliff. It's a sheer drop from the top of the Pa, sixty meters probably, straight onto the rocks and the sea." I shuddered. "Danny was caught on a ledge of rock. Just above…" — I closed my eyes as the sea thundered in my head — "…just above the surf. It was massive that night; pounding, crashing on the boulders."

I forced my eyes open and saw Lara's wide-eyed gaze. Adam's hand was rubbing my back and I fought away the rising panic, staring at the carpet, willing myself to breathe, willing myself not to throw up. I clenched my hands tightly over my mouth, my whole head jittering, my body a swamp of pulsing fear held in by desperation.

"Deep breaths, come on Georgia, slowly now: in, out, in, out."

I clung to Adam's voice, forcing myself to do as he said.

"Don't cry Mum. Please don't cry." Lara's small voice called me back and I closed my eyelids over my tears and thought about relaxing my arms, my fists, my legs, my body. I was floating, absorbing the aroma of Adam's slightly sweaty scent, my face buried in the safety of his chest. I felt a smooth warm hand on my arm and opened my eyes on Lara's red hair. She was kneeling at my feet, stroking my arm, her voice crooning, sobbing. "I'm sorry Mums, I didn't mean to upset you. I'm sorry. Please don't cry. It's all right. I don't need any of that stuff for my stupid assignment. Please don't cry."

CHAPTER 2

$\mathcal{M}$onday morning came as it always did after the weekend and I had to become the calm, together woman all my colleagues thought I was. And I bloody was, most of the time. Only Adam knew my other self. Occasional other self. Before we got up—me still dozy from the sleeping pill I'd taken in the wee small hours in a last ditch attempt to get some sleep—Adam did his best to jolly me along, send me, superwoman, back to my other world where I strode with confidence through the antiseptic, male-dominated corridors of medical power.

Apparently last night after I'd had been 'packed off to bed' as Adam put it, he and Lara had talked for a long time.

"What did you tell her?" I asked, the nausea back home in my throat.

"I was worried that I was talking out of turn, but Lara was beside herself. She's not used to seeing you crying and so terribly upset. You're an expert at hiding those feelings from the kids. So I didn't think I had any other option but to tell her what I knew about Danny."

"I *have* told her quite a lot about him. She knows that an old school friend of mine suggested I look him up when I was on holiday in New Orleans. I've told her he was a jazz singer in a nightclub. Actually, I think that's what intrigues her most. She's romanticized it."

Adam turned me over to face him. "Yes, sweet, I know she knows all those things. You've no need to be defensive. I'm talking about the things she doesn't know."

"I know Lara's never seen a photo but I've tried to give her some idea of him. I've told her that he was charming, funny, and charismatic, and that he had a mop of curly red hair exactly like hers. I even told her he had a crooked grin. She knows that the only family of his I ever met was his grandmother in New Orleans, that his parents lived in New Zealand, and that after Danny died they refused to ever meet me or let me contact them."

"Calm down. I'm on your side here. Perhaps we'll be able to locate Danny's family somehow; it's a different world now. They're probably on bloody Facebook."

"I have no idea where they live. Mum and Dad thought they'd gone back to New Orleans because that's where Danny's father came from. I don't know. For all I know they might be back in New Zealand. I don't know and I don't want to know. They didn't want anything to do with me. They probably blamed me for his death. They didn't care about me or what his death did to me. They didn't care about their own grandchild." I scrabbled under my pillow for a tissue and blew my nose.

"You told me they didn't even know you were pregnant."

"They didn't, but they didn't want to know, did they? They didn't deserve to know."

"Come on Georgia, that's a bit harsh. They were hurting as much as you. More probably. They'd just lost their son."

"And I'd lost the man I loved and the father of my baby."

"OK. Enough of this. It's pointless. It was sixteen years ago. The important person now is Lara, and how we're going to help her come to terms with all this. She seems to be in the early throws of what my clinical colleagues call an identity crisis." Adam placed a finger in each corner of my mouth and pulled it up into a smile. "You must have known this would come to a head some day."

"But what more can I tell her? Do you want me to make something up about why he died?"

"No, of course not. Lara deserves as much of the truth as we can give her. All I did was explain why you couldn't tell her much more because of how you were affected by his accident."

"What did you tell her?"

"The truth. That after Danny's terrible death you were lost for months in a fog of depression. I told her you were traumatized and that when someone is traumatized like that their memory shuts down to protect them until they are in a space where it is safe to bring those memories back."

"Oh, no. She didn't need to know all that. What good will it do?"

"It might help her understand. I told her that having a baby inside you was what saved you and gave you the strength to pull yourself through the nightmares and start to live again. It's important for her to know that she, baby Lara, gave you everything to live for, and that by keeping those traumatic memories of whatever happened that night when Danny died locked safely away, you were able to go on with your life and be a good mother.

"Do you think she understood?" I whispered.

"I imagine so. She has an emotional IQ as high as the sky. It might take a while for her to digest it and the two of you might need a few heart-to-hearts."

"Did you tell her anything else?"

"Only that having a baby to love made you so strong that you were able to go back to your studies and eighteen months later pass your Neurosurgery Fellowship exams." Adam cupped my face in his hands and forced me to look into his eyes. "Damn it Georgia, you were one of the few women to do so, especially back then. Be proud of that."

I gently patted beneath his eyes, pools of dark, shimmering a little. "Is that what you really think?"

He moved his hand over mine and kissed my palm, sending little shivers scuttling up my spine. "It is what I think. You're the most courageous and wonderful person I know. And sometimes toxic memories are best kept firmly in a box."

"Did you tell Lara I was in a psychiatric hospital for two months?"

"I did not. That's for you to tell her if and when you're ready. It's enough that she knows you were in a terrible state for a long time, and that's why you haven't been able to tell her more about Danny's accident. I hope she understands now that it's not that you *want* to keep what you know from her, but that you don't know it yourself."

SHIT HAPPENS. THAT WAS ABOUT THE BEST DESCRIPTION OF A long gray Monday that I could come up. Days when I wasn't in theater were always second best, especially now I had to stand in for Peter. Tedious meetings about budgets and how to cut staff and facilities and operate on more patients. No gap for lunch. Straight into my outpatient clinic. Patients in the door, out the door, no time for anything resembling bedside manner, or whatever the variety is when the patient is fully clothed and sitting in a chair. But at least I had a chance to finish up by five-thirty and make it home in time for dinner. That almost never happened on theater days.

Not today though. Too many patients I'd given just another five measly minutes to while they got themselves together after being told something that no one ever wanted to hear. Then the very last appointment, and a new patient walked in. Faded jeans and a brilliant emerald-green silk shirt that seemed almost the color of his eyes. And that hair—dark red, messy loose curls, his hand reaching up again and again to flick them out of his eyes. Not a care in the world. A brave front to protect him from the bad news he knew lurked in the brain scans he carried with him. New patients always took longer, but Alfie Juvnik took longer than most.

I staggered from the hospital close to seven o'clock. Great, I was on track to be late home as usual. Not that I'd be able to enjoy the leftover lamb and salad that was our standard gastronomic delight following a Sunday roast. The nauseating lump of worry and apprehension sitting low in my stomach would see to that—it was waiting until around two in the morning when it would rise up and choke me. Another night like last night to look forward to.

My thoughts continued to bumble around my aching head as I stepped onto the 7.10pm train to Maida Vale. Why did Alfie come to see me? Why bloody me? Today of all days when my head was already weighed down with Lara's questions? The clinic secretary could have scheduled him for any of the other clinics on any other day but Monday; a choice of six neurosurgeons.

He didn't look like Danny, not really. Not that I had much of a picture of the details of how Danny looked after sixteen photo-free years, but the hair and the eyes were enough. Those I'd never forget—and Alfie had them. And now I'd have to clip his aneurysms. I should have discouraged him. Bloody truth is, if we left them be and kept a close eye on them, gave Alfie an MRI every year to check that they weren't getting too big, he'd probably die of old age at ninety-nine, his aneurysms happily intact. Why couldn't I have made that his only option? Oh, for the olden, golden days when doctors didn't have to tell their patients everything and then expect them to make such impossible decisions. What will it be today sir? Would you prefer a brain operation that carries its own risks, however minor, however unlikely, or would you prefer to live with the knowledge that some small flaw in your makeup might kill you one day when you're least expecting it? Or might not.

Why was I being so flippant? Christ, if we knew all the possible ways any one of us might die, we'd all be screaming wrecks. The sooner we got the message that all these expensive screening tests were double-edged swords, the better.

I suddenly wanted to be home, right now, with my normal healthy family. At least a day at the office put our trivial problems into perspective. How to organize transport to cricket and netball practices and working out how to pacify a daughter who wants to know who she is.

Thank heaven for Adam, my voice of reason. Where would I be without him to talk to? We discussed our kids, the books we were reading, our friends' problems, our own problems, my patients, Adam's students, my operations, his experiments, the hospital, the university, our childhoods, our dreams for the future. I shivered, and pulled my coat closer. But my ghastly past? Not for years. Danny had been safer locked away in the compartment in my head where I kept the emotions I didn't have the guts to deal with.

I almost ran the dark moonless streets from the Maida Vale train station to our house. Perhaps Lara would leave it alone now after Adam's chat with her. I stopped outside our gate, trying to catch my breath. Not forever she wouldn't. This was it. The end of fooling myself that I could keep Lara happy without her knowing the truth about why, how, her father had died. And those were questions I couldn't answer.

"SORRY, SORRY. I HAD A CLINIC THAT WENT ON AND ON."

Adam opened his arms and I collapsed into him, my head buried in his familiar smell, sudden tired tears threatening to overflow.

"Hey, it's OK." Adam pulled away a little but kept his arms around my back. "You look exhausted. What you need is some stunningly delicious and soul-warming food and a very large glass of wine." He grinned, and my wobbly head cleared.

"It's a special concoction of left-over lamb slow simmered with all sorts of herbs and healthy greens. And I can have it on the table in a jiffy. But why don't you go and have a nice deep bath first, and I'll bring you your pre-dinner drink?"

"Mmm, sounds perfect. Are the kids upstairs?"

"Angels the both of them, heads immersed in their home-work. They fed their faces early, poor starving mites. It's a wonder there's anything left for us. Now scram, and I'll bring in the crystal goblet of Aussie red on a silver tray. Perhaps a nice cracker and Stilton as well."

I dumped my coat and bag in our bedroom, stuck my head around first Lara then Finbar's bedroom doors and blew them each a kiss, and ran my bath. Bliss.

Glowing and perhaps ever so slightly tipsy—the crystal glass had been over-full—I floated to the dining table and discovered that I was ravenous.

"Has Lara been OK?" I asked, when we were on to the ice cream.

"Subdued. But she'll be fine. She's tired, like you, and likely feeling a bit churned up after yesterday."

"I feel terrible. It must have been scary for her to see me break down like that. Should I talk to her about it tonight? Or leave it a few days?"

"You're her mum. You know best what to do."

"I'll at least see if she wants to talk or ask me anything. I hate to think of her bottling things up. "

"Off you go then, but don't get into too long a thing. You both need a decent night's sleep." Adam began collecting our plates.

"I'll clean up when I come back down. That was a beautiful dinner. I feel like a new woman."

"You do look a tad better than when you staggered in the door. Now go. I'll clean up."

LARA HAD MOVED FROM HER DESK AND WAS HALF LYING, HALF sitting on her bed, pajamas on, her headphones clamped to her ears, nose in a book. She looked up when I knocked on her open bedroom door and managed a very small smile. Taking it as an invitation, I perched on the edge of her bed, my hand automatically covering her's with its long fingers and clean pretty nails. She pulled off her headphones with her free hand and looked up, tiny furrows in her forehead. "Hi Mums. Wussup? You OK?"

I nodded, words suddenly stuck in my throat. I leaned forward and Lara sat up and then we were chest to chest, my dark hair pressed against her red curls.

"Oh, Mum," Lara muttered. "I was scared last night when I made you so upset."

"Sweetheart, I'm sorry. It wasn't your fault, it was mine. I don't know why that happened. I suppose I've been waiting for the day you'd want to know more about Danny and what happened to him and dreading it, and then when it happened I went to pieces." I was mumbling into Lara's hair, my eyes screwed tight.

Lara made a sound that might have been a sob or a sniff. She pulled back, her beautiful eyes holding mine. They were Danny's eyes, exactly. Green pools captured in a circle of dark gray.

"Ask me anything and I'll tell you whatever I can," I said, while my heart broke.

"Dad told me how you lost your memory after the accident because you were totally traumatized. Hasn't anything come back, ever?"

"I only remember that Danny and I were both upset, but I don't know why. A car picked me up really early the next morning. I was a mess, wandering along the road in a daze. Apparently I was hysterical and covered in scratches and grazes, and soaking wet. The man who picked me up was a farmer from up the road. Back then that road would only have had about one vehicle every two hours along it. Perhaps it's still like that. So I suppose I was lucky he found me so early. He took me into the doctor in Claris; I think we got him out of bed. I don't remember much about it but then the police came—there was only one policeman on the island—and I think the doctor gave me something to calm me down and I suppose the police collected some of the locals and set up a search. They found Danny's body on a ledge near the bottom of the Pa. He could have been swept away and never been found. I couldn't remember how I got to the road, or why I was soaked to the skin until weeks later after I'd been in the hospital having therapy and hypnosis and probably being drugged up to the eyeballs. I have only the vaguest memories of all that." I shuddered, the cold green hospital walls closing in on me.

Lara was rubbing my hand and crying, and I stopped trying to talk and breathed: in, out, in, out.

"It's OK, Mum. Don't tell me any more just now."

I took a strand of Lara's hair and tucked it behind her ear. My hand was trembling. "This is crazy. It's so frustrating. After all this time I still can't think about that night without shattering. Thank you, sweetie, for understanding."

"I'm not sure if I understand really, but whatever happened must have been terrible to do this to you." Lara squeezed my hand. "Perhaps you could try therapy again? It might work better now that it's so long ago."

"You might be right. I'll think about it, I promise." I bent over and kissed her forehead. "Have you finished your home-work? Because I think it's time I tucked you in and sent you to dreamland."

"You haven't tucked me in since I was about ten." Lara snuggled down in her bed and put her arms around my neck. I breathed in her sweet scent. Still a hint of the little-girl-after-her-bath smell.

"Sweet dreams, Lara-my-Lara. Mind the bugs don't bite." I backed towards the door and gave a little wave.

"Do you think Danny…" Lara stopped, and I could see her eyes shining.

"What?" I asked.

"Do you think he wanted me?" Her voice was almost a whisper.

"Oh Lara, he would have wanted you. He would have wanted you so so much."

$\mathcal{I}$ stood motionless in the scrub room adjacent to Theater Eight, my mass of black hair concealed beneath a cap, and a mask covering my nose and face. It was ten days since Alfie Juvnik had walked into my outpatient clinic, and my hardest task right now was to clear my mind of everything other than the technical processes of the operation I was about to perform. With eyes closed I imagined a string attached to the top of my head pulling me straight and tall. Inside my calmed mind I visualized a brain—not just any brain, but the very individual brain of the young man now prepped and waiting for me. Alfie's brain was transparent, and I could see the cage of his arteries, almost glowing as they pulsated with oxygen-rich blood. I focused on the aneurysms —two of them—one protruding off the left middle cerebral artery and the other at the bifurcation of the middle and anterior arteries. Luckily they weren't large and I concentrated on rotating the brain, first this way then that, so I could see more clearly exactly where and how each aneurysm was attached. I'd clip the more difficult one first, and then, all going well, the second. Detailed angiograms and MRI scans would be displayed on the theater monitor throughout the operation, but I'd found that, however straightforward or complicated the operation was, committing the dynamic 3D image to memory gave me the calmness and focus I needed.

The ritualized scrubbing of my arms and hands completed, I backed through the doors into the cool air of the theater, my fingers tingling and my senses savoring the sights, smells and sounds of an operation about to begin.

Gowned and gloved, I settled myself on the high stool at the head of the operating table. All I could see of the patient was a square on the left side of his shaven head. I made my first incision, slicing the blade cleanly along the blue line already drawn on his scalp by David, my neurosurgical registrar.

"Where's our music?" I kept my eyes on the scalpel.

"What do you fancy? The patient gave me a CD of Joe Cocker's to play." The anesthetist chuckled. "Probably too raw for your taste. Do you want some jazz?"

I hesitated for a second. "It would be bad karma not to play Alfie's choice. He's the important one here, and if he likes Joe Cocker, Joe Cocker is who we'll have. Put him on."

The anesthetist flicked the play button on the CD player remote and the singer's gritty voice echoed around the theater. I blinked as an image of Alfie's face imprinted itself on the drapes surrounding the bloodstained operating site. As his face vanished I puffed out a quiet sigh. I didn't need reminding that this healthy young man was putting a lot on the line. I almost wished I hadn't met his anxious wife and two seriously cute kids yesterday.

I wriggled my backside. A sharp splinter was trying to separate the ball in my hip from its socket. I eased my buttock off the stool and gingerly put it back down again. *Ignore it.* Glancing up, I grinned behind my mask at the house officer's steamed-up glasses. Tension and excitement oozed out of him. Observing an aneurysm clipping for the first time was a big deal.

"Carl, come closer. You'll never see anything from there. This should be a smooth operation—our patient's young, he's got a nice clean, healthy brain, and clipping off those two unruptured aneurysms will prevent them from bursting in the future."

Carl peered over my shoulder. "How long will he take to recover from the operation?"

"He might have a few days of headache and he won't be able drive a car for six months because of the craniotomy, but other than that he should be right as rain in a few weeks with no more worry about those two little time bombs lurking in his head."

I held my hand out for the drill, then the saw, and within thirty minutes I'd fashioned a window in Alfie's skull and cut through the membranes enclosing the soft brain, peeling them back to reveal the fat, pink coils. I gently inserted retractors into a deep fissure, pulling apart the temporal and frontal lobes.

Time disappeared, the sounds of the respirator and the clicks of the anesthesia equipment enclosing me in a familiar bubble. Maneuvering the operating microscope into place, I commenced the delicate work of exposing the middle cerebral artery, cautiously dissecting my way along it to the point where the rogue aneurysm, still intact, ballooned off its surface. David stood at my side, cauterizing bleeding points as small vessels were cut.

Joe Cocker was singing 'Have A Little Faith In Me' by the time the aneurysm was visible. Even magnified by the operating microscope it looked innocuous; a small protrusion pulsating quietly off the healthy-looking artery. The nurse placed the instrument holding the tiny spring-loaded titanium clip into my outstretched hand. The most delicate part of the procedure was positioning the clip across the aneurysm neck, taking care not to puncture the large artery in the process.

The neck was wide and in an awkward position and my

first two attempts failed. Before trying again I withdrew the clip, sat back from the microscope, and flexed my hands and back. It wasn't particularly unusual to have to make more than one attempt to place a clip securely, and I was prepared to take as long as needed to ensure that it was completely across the aneurysm neck before closing it. I returned my eyes to the microscope and had just begun to insert the clip once more into the deep hole when a jet of blood exploded from the brain, splashing my gown and rapidly turning my field of view red.

"Shit, it's ruptured. Suction, hurry." I dropped the instruments onto the trolley and, using my fingers, tried to feel my way to the source of the bleed. The brain was flooding with blood pumping out faster than David could suction it up and the theater nurse was pushing a second suction pump past my fingers into the blood-filled hole.

"I can't see anything. Quick, another clip." My pulse thundered in my head. Gluing my eyes to the microscope I held my hand out to the theater nurse, muttering for Carl's sake that I'd have to put a temporary clip on the artery to stop the bleeding.

It was another ninety seconds before I succeeded and the pulsing blood finally ceased. The theater had become a bomb-site. The anesthetist was fighting to keep Alfie stable and his blood was now spattered over David, the theater nurse, and me, across the concrete floor and onto my white gumboots. I desperately tried again to position a clip across the neck of the now flaccid aneurysm so that the temporary clip blocking off the artery could be safely removed. If it was blocked for more than a few minutes Alfie was in danger of a stroke to the left side of his brain—on top of the brain hemorrhage he shouldn't have had.

"Five minutes," said the anesthetist, his tone screaming that it was too long.

"I think it's clipped off," I mumbled, rapidly releasing the temporary clip. I watched the blood fill the large artery and flow past the secured neck of the aneurysm without leaking, and breathed again. And then Joe Cocker's plaintive voice splintered my focus. *Georgia, Georgia…*

"Turn that off. I can't stand that song." My voice was too loud. I lowered it. "Let's have some quiet so I can concentrate."

Georgia on my mi… Then grim silence as we all worked to put Alfie back together again. Two hours later he was in Critical Care, intubated and ventilated and in a deep coma.

I CHANGED OUT OF MY SCRUBS AND TOOK THE LIFT TO THE ward to break the news to Alfie's wife. No one had yet told her there'd been any complications— that was my job. And it was never easy. Without a word being spoken, somehow families knew.

As I entered Alfie's small room, the tiny woman sitting on his neatly made bed took one look at me and dropped her head in her hands. "Oh no, please no," she whispered. "Something's gone wrong, hasn't it?"

My hip screeching like a rat caught in a trap, I lowered myself onto the chair beside the bed. "Celia, I'm sorry. I'm afraid there were some problems. We're going to have to take good care of Alfie for a while." Celia's face—so white that the freckles scattered across her upturned nose looked like spots of blood—filled my vision.

"But I thought it was a straightforward operation?" Celia whispered. "You said there was hardly any risk."

"I know. But there's always some risk and unfortunately we can never exclude all possibility of complications. The aneurysm was in an awkward position and before I was able to clip it off, it ruptured. I wasn't even touching it at the time." I looked past the fear in Celia's eyes to the dark clouds that filled the window behind her. I swallowed and faced her again. "We'll know more when we do a brain scan later today. But I'm afraid Alfie had a significant hemorrhage and he's in a coma, probably because of that."

"Isn't a rupture what you were trying to prevent? He was so healthy and happy before you operated" —Celia's voice broke— "and now he's in a coma?" Her face crumpled, her eyes lost in tears.

I breathed in, breathed out, but Alfie's blood-smeared face stayed put in my brain. Leaning over I covered Celia's hand—icy cold—with my own warm one. "I know it's hard to take in. Alfie's in Critical Care and everything possible is being done for him. We have to hold onto the hope that he'll be OK; I just can't tell you yet. Celia, I'm so very sorry."

"Can I see him?" She sounded desperate, almost as if she thought she'd be kept from him.

"I'll take you down now. So that he can be properly treated all his functions have been taken over, so he's on a ventilator."

Celia took in a shaky breath and tried to wipe away the tears that were streaming down her cheeks. I leaned over and pulled a handful of tissues from the box on the bedside table, closing Celia's hand around them.

"Will he be in pain?" she hiccupped. Her silent plea that Alfie be spared that at least throbbed in the air between us and I swiveled my gaze to a picture of a vase of flowers on the wall, willing the prickle behind my eyes to disappear. Blinking hard, I forced my eyes back to Celia's anguished face.

"No, he's not conscious yet so he won't feel any pain or discomfort. But I'm sure he'll know you're there."

I took Celia to Critical Care and introduced her to Maddie, who, thank goodness, was the charge nurse on duty. She'd had more experience taking care of bewildered and distraught families than anyone else in the hospital. How she stayed so calm and warm and comforting day after tragic day was a bloody miracle.

By seven next morning I was back in the Critical Care Unit. I stood behind the glass in the dimly lit Nurses' Station, my eyes on the patient tethered to the bed closest to the window—the bed reserved for the sickest of the sick. Caught in the glaring overhead light, Alfie's hair blazed red against the deathly white of his face, tubes invading and distorting his mouth and nose, gurgling and panting like live things as they snaked their way to the whirring machines. Celia was there beside him, tears coursing unheeded down her face, her love in every stroke of the brush as she pulled it repeatedly through the remains of Alfie's wild hair.

Closing my eyes I saw again the pale scalp where the rest of his hair used to be; the raw, nearly circular wound, contained but not diminished by the neat row of stitches and now blessedly hidden from his wife's eyes by a thick bandage. I shook my head to dispel the image and looked at Alfie's medical file open on the bench in front of me, seeing my own indecipherable scrawl relating the facts about the surgery, the bald facts about the 'complications.' The writing blurred and morphed before my tired eyes and my words seemed to read, 'The worst that could happen, did.'

"It's so sad. What will happen to him?" The nurse was whispering, the break in her voice revealing her youth, her inexperience.

I turned to answer and realized she wasn't speaking to me, but to a junior doctor. Screwing up my eyes against a stabbing pain in my left temple, I tried to blot out the young doctor's reply.

"It's tough seeing families go through this. You never really get used to it. He might make it, but as what? The grim truth is he'll be lucky if he dies."

My stomach turned and like a coward I fled and made for the staff cafeteria. I needed my morning caffeine before talking to Celia. The cafe was almost empty and I sat alone at a corner table and gulped a mouthful of black coffee, wincing as it burnt my throat. The young doctor's words echoed in my head. *Lucky to die. Celia, your beautiful young husband will be lucky to die.*

I rubbed my eyes but the image of Celia's haunted expression stayed put. The poor woman would be clinging to a desperate belief that a miracle would happen and Alfie would wake up and smile at her. How could she begin to comprehend that her exuberant husband had been destroyed in a few disastrous minutes. That if he did survive he'd probably be paralyzed, unable to speak coherently, unable to understand, depressed, frustrated, with no idea who his children were or who she was, his spark extinguished forever.

"Georgia, are you OK?"

I started and looked up at David, standing on the other side of the table. The cafeteria was buzzing with activity, the sun was streaming through the long windows, and my coffee was cold. "I've felt better." I glanced at my watch. "Holy cow, it's almost eight. I must have dozed off."

"It can happen to the best of us. It's been a rough couple of days. I bet you're not getting your eight hours sleep." David was giving me a strange look.

"I can't remember when I last had more than six hours in one stretch. Probably before I went to Med School." I flexed my neck and shoulders. "I'll finish this coffee and then we'd better get up to the ward for the morning round."

"Yep, that's why I came to find you. Do you want to check on Alfie Juvnik first?"

"No, we'll do that later when we've seen our other

patients. Right now, the very thought of Critical Care turns my stomach."

"Perhaps a fresh coffee would help," David said. "I'll get you another. That cold one looks past its best."

I focused on my other patients—the ones I could still do something for—while I waited for David to return. But his first words as he parked himself in the chair opposite plunged me back into gloom.

"Are you still beating yourself up over the aneurysm disaster?" David's tone was sympathetic.

I felt the saliva thickening in my mouth and tried to swallow. "I feel terrible about it. I should have referred him to one of the other consultants."

"Whatever for? They would have made the same decision and probably had the same outcome."

"It's not that. Do you know how his aneurysms were discovered?"

"I thought he was in some psychology experiment at the university—looking at language or something using functional MRI. The researchers found his two aneurysms when they did the imaging."

"Adam was one of the researchers for that study."

"Adam? Your Adam, you mean?"

"Of course that's who I mean." I glanced at David. "Sorry, I'm a bit uptight."

"No worries. Poor Adam. I bet he's a bit shattered. It's going to happen though, with all these experimental imaging studies being done these days."

"He is upset, but luckily he wasn't the researcher running the study on the day Alfie was being tested, so it was his colleague who had to explain to Alfie that the radiologist needed to talk to him about his scan."

David frowned. "I can see that the connection with Adam's research would have been a bit of a shock, but it's hardly a reason for you to have referred Alfie on."

A spear of pain shot behind my eyes and I screwed them shut and kneaded my forehead. The pain abated and I cracked open my eyes and took a few mouthfuls of the coffee David shoved towards me. His long face was looking even more worried than usual.

Perhaps if I talk about it, it will stop haunting me. I picked up my coffee and put it down again. "The connection with Adam wasn't the only thing. Alfie reminded me of an old boyfriend of mine. Same eyes, hair, build. Even his voice and the cool way he reacted when I explained the risks of the surgery reminded me of Danny."

"I know that feeling. When I was on my last rotation, a woman who was a dead ringer for my mum was admitted with a meningioma. Luckily I was not the surgeon and was only assisting, because I had a hard enough time prepping her and shaving her head. When she was back on the ward, every time we did a ward round I half expected her to tell me off about my dirty shoes."

I forced a smile.

"But I thought by the time I reached your age I'd have gotten over all that," David went on.

"Thanks. I hadn't realized 44 was that old."

"You know what I mean. You've had years of experience. You must see patients who remind you of people you know quite often. Obviously you can't refuse to operate every time that happens."

"It was more the outcome I suppose. If the operation had been successful, I probably wouldn't have given Alfie's likeness to Danny another thought."

"The poor fellow was simply horribly unlucky. He was the perfect candidate for an aneurysm clipping. If you ask me, he made the right decision. If I'd been Alfie, I'd have opted for the surgery too. He probably didn't want to spend the rest of his life wondering if one of his aneurysms was going to explode at any minute and kill him."

My mobile beeped and I pulled it from my pocket.

"Dr. Grayson. Not good news I'm afraid. Alfie Juvnik had another massive hemorrhage, presumably from that second unclipped aneurysm. We had no hope of saving him."

I closed my eyes, Alfie's face filling my head. I sighed. "I didn't think he'd make it. What a dreadful outcome. Makes me think again about clipping unruptured aneurysms in healthy young people. Does his wife know?"

"Yes. She's in the family room. She was with him when he died, poor woman."

"I'll come now."

CELIA STUMBLED TO HER FEET WHEN SHE SAW ME. WE STOOD silent, our eyes locked. I couldn't begin to imagine what she was feeling. Then I collected myself and managed to produce some inadequate words. "I'm so sorry, Celia. I'd give anything to be able to go back and advise Alfie not to have that operation."

"I can't believe I'll never see him again. I can't."

The raw grief etched on Celia's face was too much, and I looked away.

"I'm sorry. I can't think straight." Celia's voice faltered and she pressed her lips together and stared blindly past my shoulder. She swayed and I reached out and steadied her, helping her into a chair. After a long few minutes she spoke again, her voice a river of tears. "I wanted to see you to thank you for doing what you thought would be best for Alfie."

"Celia, thank you. That's very generous." I sat on the chair beside her, my arms aching to hold her but knowing I couldn't.

"I don't blame you for what happened. Alfie made his own decision to have the operation. We knew the risks and we decided to go ahead. It's no one's fault that we lost him."

Then her face seemed to dissolve and she covered it with shaking hands. "What are we going to do without him? How can I tell the children?"

"Oh Celia, I know, I know. Is there someone I can call for you? Has the nurse spoken to you about talking with someone; a social worker perhaps or a minister or priest—I don't know if that would help?"

Celia didn't seem to hear. "Alfie's parents are at our place with the children. Chrissie is only two; she won't understand why her daddy doesn't come home." She wiped the back of her hand over her eyes and face, but her tears kept coming. "Our dog died last month and Jack was so upset. He's only five. Alfie's his hero. He got Jack a guitar for his birthday and he's already learned some chords. I can't even play the guitar. How will he learn now without his daddy?"

My hand was rubbing Celia's stooped back. *What can I do?*

"I want my Mummy and Daddy."

The childish names hung in the air and my arm tightened around her; almost a hug. "Where are they?" I asked, my fingers crossed behind Celia's back. *Please make them still be alive and on their way to their daughter's side.*

"Their plane arrives tonight. They live in Sydney. All my family live in Sydney. I feel so alone here and now I don't even have Alfie."

"I know what that's like, to miss home. My parents and brother live in New Zealand. But your parents will soon be here; it will be easier then."

Celia raised a blotchy face. "We knew you were a Kiwi. You've still got a bit of an accent. I know it's silly but that's why I was really happy you were doing Alfie's operation. We're family really, Aussies and Kiwis, aren't we? When things go wrong." She lurched towards me and I opened both arms and held her.

BACK IN THE CORRIDOR I HURRIED TOWARDS THE escalator, head down, wanting only to get out. As the door slid open another doctor followed me in and I stifled a groan. The last person I needed to see right now was Jim Mason.

"Georgia. Sorry about that young patient of yours. I was in the observation room when he died. His poor wife was in a bad way so I had a bit of a chat to her. Tried to explain that these operations always carry a risk and it was simply bad luck."

"I've just been talking to her. She seemed to understand." I sighed. "It's a terrible outcome."

"I should e-mail you the reference to that latest paper on incidental aneurysms. It seems pretty clear that they shouldn't be clipped when they are that small. It's a shame you hadn't read it before you made that call."

"His aneurysms weren't as small as those in that study. I did give Mr. Juvnik all the options."

"Lighten up, Georgia. I know it's been a struggle for you taking on some of Peter's load. Perhaps you should take a few days off and I can cover for you. It's one of the advantages of being single and not having kids. I get some quality sleep from time to time."

"I thought you were divorced?"

"That's what I said. Single." He winked at me.

"My family make my job easier, not harder. At least I can understand how Celia must feel as a mother."

"Touché." He grinned. "I don't think you were at that seminar a couple of weeks ago when that American researcher was talking about her study on why patients sue their doctors?"

"No. I was covering for Peter at a Department Heads' meeting. As you well know."

"Bummer. Well you missed an interesting talk. Right up your alley."

I kept silent and waited for the door to open so I could escape.

"She found that patients whose surgery had been stuffed up were less likely to sue their doctor if they liked him—or her — than if her bedside manner wasn't too good. Didn't matter if the doctor was blatantly incompetent and caused massive unnecessary damage."

"How unsurprising."

"So, you'll be fine. One thing you have is a nice touchy-feely way with your patients."

"I can only hope such groundbreaking research gave you some insight into your own inadequacies," I said, willing the door to slide open. It heard my plea and Jim splayed one hand towards me, ushering me out. I narrowed my eyes at him and received a wink back.

"My bedside manner is more than adequate. I can provide plenty of references should you request them, madam."

"Creep," I muttered, as I walked away from him as quickly as I could without actually running. "Next time I'll say it to your bloody face."

THAT NIGHT, I DREAMED OF DANNY. IT WAS THE SAME nightmare that had robbed me of sleep, again and again, in that first empty year after he was gone. In my dream he was holding me close as we danced across the moonlit beach. And then he slipped from my arms and I was clutching only a tangled mass of red seaweed, its lifeblood seeping in a thin stream into the white sand.

I woke, clammy with fear, and lay still for a moment while the dream receded and the warmth of Adam's body, curled around mine, calmed my pounding heart. His arms tightened around me and I turned in his embrace. In the harsh yellow streetlight filtering through the small window above our bed I could see him looking at me with sleepy dark eyes. I inched my mouth across the gap between us and kissed his warm lips, his familiar soapy smell rescuing me from my past.

"You OK?" he mumbled drowsily.

"Just a dream. Go back to sleep."

"I hope you're not still stressing out over Mason's nasty comments."

"Why? Do you think he's right?"

"Mason's a sexist bully. But he might have a point about the crazy workload you've taken on given you have to deal with all of us as well."

"So you think he'd be a better director because he doesn't have a family to care about?"

"Personally I don't give a toss about Mason, and from what I know of him he'd be a bloody terrible director. He's got the empathy of a shark. But that has nothing to do with whether you should take such a massive role on. Lara and Finbar miss you."

"Miss me? I'm always here for them."

"I know you try to be, but more often than not you don't get home until after dinner and by then they're stuck in their rooms doing their homework. Not to mention all the weekends you've been on call."

"Don't you want me to apply? Is that what you're saying?"

"No, it is not. I'm simply saying you shouldn't rush into it. Lara seems fine now, but she's still mulling over the Danny mystery. It's not going to go away. And Finbar asked me the other day if I thought you might be able to be one of the parents who goes on their school camp in June."

"Why didn't he just ask me?"

"Because he's a sweet kid and he didn't want to pressure you. He knows you have zero spare time."

"Oh, Adam."

"He'll be fine. He's proud of you. We all are. But you do

need to take better care of yourself. Which means it's time to stop worrying and go to sleep."

Adam pulled me close and I snuggled into his bare chest, my tense muscles gradually relaxing as his breathing deepened. But my mind was still revolving, thinking now about Lara and Finbar and how lucky I was to have them, and worrying about Celia and her children, bereft of the man they loved, his death warrant signed by me the day he walked into my clinic.

CHAPTER 4

*E*aster came at just the right time. I had four days off and we escaped to a holiday cottage on the Devon coast. Warmish weather, long walks, and fires on the beach. By the time we got back to London on Monday evening, I felt almost ready for the hospital again.

But on Tuesday morning I didn't feel quite so keen and lingered over breakfast, reluctant to leave my family. Finbar sitting in the sunny window seat, eating an overflowing bowl of muesli, engrossed in his book as usual. And Lara back to her old self. Today she was handing in her 'Who Am I' assignment, which, she said, was based on a certain degree of deceit. Her latest ploy was trying to guilt-trip me into taking the family to New Orleans. "We could go in the summer holidays; it could be my sixteenth birthday present. It'd be so awesome to find the club where Danny sang. And we could track down my grandparents and perhaps even my great-grandmother. Please?"

I'd fobbed her off with a "We'll see," and hoped she'd forget it. But of course she wouldn't. New Orleans. All that amazing music. Lara would be in heaven.

She was singing right now, standing at the bench,

buttering her toast. Even at this ridiculous hour of the morning her voice was rich and soulful. I was so lucky. Kids with deep passions. Books and music. Both passions of mine too, even music, in spite of Lara's unkind comments about my inability to sing in tune. I wasn't that bad, and being able to sing wasn't a prerequisite for loving music. I'd grown up with it; part of the weft of our daily lives. An integral part of my dad's Maori heritage. Sometimes putting on headphones at the end of a long day and losing myself in sound was the best thing I could do for my sanity. The right music could sweep away the sadness and helplessness that churned me up when I'd had an overload of other folk's sickness and pain.

Perhaps we could take a week off in late July and go to New Orleans. It was Adam's university break as well as the kids' school holidays, and sixteen *was* a special birthday. When Peter returned to work and I didn't have to do half of his job as well as my own, I'd find a quiet space to talk to Adam about it. Get a week off, let Jim bloody Mason cover for me. Surely I could cope with going back there after all this time, and we could make a project out of it to see if we could track down Danny's grandmother. If she's even still alive. But how would I tell her that she has a great granddaughter? She might have a heart attack. What if she didn't want to know? What if she blamed me for Danny's death, like his parents did? Wouldn't that be worse for Lara than never trying to find them? Simply getting on with her life like I have done? Huh. Some role model I've been lately.

I looked over at her as she sat opposite me eating her toast, her nose in a magazine. Sweet sixteen soon. And never been kissed? Her boyish body had blossomed into curves over the past year. Testosterone-ravaged young men were probably already lusting after her. I grinned, and Lara caught it as she got up from the table. She raised her shapely eyebrows. "What are you smiling at? Have I got jam on my nose?"

"Just feeling happy, that's all."

Lara grinned back. "That's what I like to hear mother dear. Keep it up."

Below the table I crossed my fingers. Hopefully our feisty daughter's total lack of flirtatious behavior would keep her safe from creeps and premature sex. She was more likely to flatten an admirer's ego with a well-placed witticism or a flying tackle better fitted to a rugby field than flatter him with fluttering eyelashes and sweet nothings. A beautiful woman in the making though. Danny's eyes and hair, but thankfully not his —or my—pale skin. Lara turned brown the second the sun peeked out. Another Maori gene sneaking in from Dad. When I was a kid I'd sizzled to a cinder every summer, growing up in New Zealand's burning sun. I uncrossed my fingers and held my white hand up, wriggling my long fingers with their closely clipped nails.

"'Morning, early birds. What's with the hand exercises, Sapphire Eyes?"

I flexed my fingers vigorously. "One of the downsides of being a surgeon—a daily finger workout." I raised my face for Adam's kiss, then leaned back and looked at him, arching my left eyebrow, a trick I'd perfected by the time I was sixteen. *Sexy man.* No way did he look forty-six. Jeans and worn black turtle-necked sweater, his hair sticking up in messy spikes. Obviously wasn't giving any lectures today—on those days he dressed up in a shirt he'd painstakingly ironed the night before. Clueless. Didn't realize that his doting female students would dote even more if he wore his scruffy look. Not my place to tell him.

I glanced up at the wall clock. "I'd better get my skids on or I'll miss my train. Unlike some I could mention, I have to show up at work before eight." I stashed my dishes in the dishwasher and turned to Adam for my goodbye hug, wrinkling my nose when he slid both hands down to squeeze my butt.

"Wench. Behave yourself with all those sex-crazed young doctors."

I returned his buttock squeeze. "They're only interested in young nurses, not old married women, and especially not if she's their senior and better. Shame really."

"Well then, give bully-boy Mason a good knee in the balls for me."

"Yes sir. With pleasure."

Adam kissed my nose. "This is going to be a good week."

"Yes, it is." I kissed him back, waved to the kids, and stepped outside into a misty rain.

SQUASHED BETWEEN COMMUTERS IN THE CROWDED CARRIAGE of the Maida Vale train, I closed my eyes and focused on the operations scheduled for today. I'd purposefully put surgery for a prolapsed cervical disc in the morning slot, leaving a clipping for a ruptured aneurysm for the afternoon. I tried to ignore the hollow sensation in my gut as I thought about the aneurysm. At least this one had ruptured and really had to be clipped. The patient, a sixty-year-old woman, had been admitted, confused and disoriented, over Easter. I'd talked to David last night and he was satisfied that she was stable enough for surgery today. She'd been a heavy smoker most of her life and David said she looked nearer to eighty than sixty. So it might not be the easiest operation if her arteries were as worn as her face.

As I emerged from Russell Square station my heart squeezed as the hospital loomed up in front of me and Celia's anguished face was back in my head. Five days since Alfie died. What would Celia do now? Alfie was the Londoner, not her. How could London feel like home without him? *Go home Celia. Go home to Australia where your parents can help you, and all the London reminders of your life with Alfie are gone.*

I still had the post-mortem report to take on board, and then I'd have to sit through a dissection of the case at the monthly Morbidity and Mortality conference. What would their reaction be if I told them that perhaps it wasn't just one of those rare complications that would have happened whoever was the surgeon? That I couldn't entirely rule out the possibility that I'd allowed my own feelings to influence my performance? Jim would love that. Even if Peter decided to let it go—*forget it, Georgia, every one of us has bad days*—it would hover as a question mark over my suitability to lead a department of egotistic male surgeons.

Damn them, they needed someone who wasn't always so wary of showing any feelings. I sighed, and saw the startled look on the face of a young doctor in a white coat, scurrying beside me up the hospital steps. The wheels of propriety would drag on; it would probably be months before the coroner's report appeared, bringing it all back again. Hardly a new scenario for me, but it was never easy. A professional attitude was essential if we were to learn from our errors, but it never did mask the personal—that while we moved on in our professional lives, lessons learned, somewhere out there a family—Alfie's family— remained devastated by grief. Something I knew about from the inside.

My morning operation had gone well. Bad backs were such a bugger to fix. It often seemed a case of the operation being a success yet the patient continuing to suffer. The nice young man I'd operated on this morning was fit and motivated, so with some good physiotherapy and a dollop of luck his pain would disappear in due course. He mightn't get back to rugby, but hopefully he'd find some other less punishing sport. And now for the aneurysm. No doubt I'd cope. As soon as I began, everything but the brain under my hands would vanish from my mind.

I felt the familiar surge of adrenalin as I accepted the scalpel from the theater nurse and made the first firm incision along the blue line on the patient's scalp. I was feeling good, good to be back. The theater was silent except for the sounds of the respirator, suction, and the occasional slap and clink of instruments. No Georgia on my Mind in my theater today, thank you. Time disappeared as I concentrated, and now I could see the aneurysm pulsing off the artery, David's diligent suctioning and cauterizing clearing my field of view.

Without warning an image of the patient's face appeared, white with fear under the bloody mush in her open skull. I turned my head away from the microscope, blinking hard, but when I clamped my eyes back on the eyepieces, all I could see was a blur of grey and red and the cold glitter of the point of the scalpel. I could hear my breathing loud and fast in the echoing theater, my heart was racing and cold sweat was pouring off my forehead. I jerked back from the microscope and carefully moved my hand, still holding the scalpel, away from the brain. I sat shaking, it seemed, for minutes, as I struggled for breath against the vice that was tightening across my chest. *Dear god, I'm having a cardiac arrest.* I concentrated my whole being on trying to calm my breathing. But the pain was engulfing me and I couldn't stop it. Someone took the scalpel from me and hands were pulling me off the stool and holding me up as I stumbled across the theater and through the heavy swing doors.

Out in the annex I collapsed on the padded bench. A hand forced my head between my knees and a voice told me to breathe slowly. Then my head was lifted up and a paper bag thrust into my hand.

"Georgia, listen to me. Breathe into this bag. You're hyperventilating."

I pushed the hand away. The pain in my chest was making me dizzy. "My heart. I think I'm having an arrest," I gasped.

"It's OK, Georgia, we'll check that out, but try breathing into the paper bag to see if that helps." The voice was losing its calmness. Strong hands gripped my head and held the bag firmly in place. I gave up and breathed in and out, in and out. The bag made a smacking sound with each breath and the dizziness began to recede. I could feel the blood creeping back into my head and the vice on my chest loosened its grip. I shrugged away the hands holding me and leaned back, saturated with sweat, eyes closed, heart still pounding but slowing now.

"Better?" Jackie asked quietly.

I opened my eyes and looked up at her. Other gowned figures were crowded into the small room. A glass of water was pushed into my hand and I gulped it down.

"It was so stifling in there. I don't know what happened. I think I might have had an arrest." I was almost whispering, my face hot, as Jackie shooed the others away.

"Christ, what's happened to the patient?" I began to stand but Jackie pushed me down again.

"It's OK. David has taken over and it's all going well. You need to sit quietly and rest a while. Can't have you arresting over the operating table," she said, smiling at me.

I wiped my hands across my damp face, pushing off my paper cap. "Sorry, Jackie. I haven't been sleeping too well lately. Not that that's any excuse."

"I think you might have started over-breathing. Perhaps it was brought on by your being too hot in there." Jackie sat beside me and covered my clammy hand with her warm dry one. "It can happen to anyone. I really don't think it was your heart, but get it checked out if you're worried."

"I feel so stupid. Everyone must think I'm a right basket-case." My face was still burning.

"Everyone is thinking no such thing. Only Gina and Polly were here and they're not going to turn it into some juicy gossip, even if you do want to be in the limelight for a change." Jackie grinned at me and I tried to grin back.

"Seemed like the room was full of people."

"Well it wasn't. That's just an embellishment by your fertile little mind. Only we three gals were here and we ain't talking, so stop worrying."

"I need to scrub up again and get into theater to give David a hand."

"No way. David's a big boy now; he doesn't need you in there nursing him. And truly Georgia, don't stress over this. I had a panic attack once and I thought I was dying, so I know how frightening it is."

My pulse was thundering in my head again. "Perhaps I did get into some hyperventilation, but that's not the same as a panic attack."

"Of course not. I just meant that it could happen to anyone— hyperventilation I mean. Doesn't have to be anything to do with panic. Even if it were, it's no big deal. I only had that one and it's never happened again."

I looked at her, her usually bright expression clouded with concern. "Thanks Jackie. I'll be fine."

"What about having a chat to Simon Armstrong? I know him a little and he's a good psychiatrist. A sweet guy too. I think if something like this happens we staff are meant to at least check in with him."

"Shit. I know that. Do you think it's necessary just for this?"

"Come on Georgia, you know I have to report it. It would be better if you saw Simon now and didn't wait. Looks better that way and Simon will treat it in confidence, you know that. The longer you wait the more likely the gossip machine will get hold of it and turn it into goodness knows what."

"Sprung. Just try and keep it from Jim Mason. Wouldn't he just love it." I tried to keep my voice light and gaily unconcerned.

"No one will hear anything from me, and I'll make sure Gina and Polly understand that they mustn't get into any talk about this."

"Thanks Jackie. And can you please tell David I'll phone him tonight?"

CHAPTER 5

Thirty minutes later I was in Simon Armstrong's office. He was talking to me about taking a break from surgery and seeing a psychologist who specialized in therapy for panic attacks. Like a zombie I heard myself agreeing with everything, and taking a referral letter for a therapist that Simon had written on the spot, and a prescription for Valium and even some sleeping pills. I was damned if I was going to tell him I already used them occasionally.

Now he was being reassuring. "You'll be fine after a few weeks of therapy and back operating in no time. Probably the result of overwork and job stress," he said, as calmly as if he told neurosurgeons this every day. "Burnout, we call it. You're fortunate to get this warning symptom so you can sort it out before it gets too serious. If you ignore symptoms of burnout, you risk losing your career for good."

Cheerful fellow. I'd known Simon for years, although not that well. He was always pleasant and he had a good reputation. He was still prattling on.

"Don't worry about what your colleagues and Admin will think. No one needs to know you had a panic attack. We'll tell them you'd been overworking and you need some time out from surgery. You can continue with other aspects of your work if you feel up to it."

"Some of my colleagues will know what happened. They saw me in theater."

"Come on Georgia, they're not going to talk. I know Jackie, she's one of the best theater charge nurses in the hospital, and she was right to send you to me. She'll make sure her theater team keep this confidential."

"I know she'll try at least. Anyway, I've got more to worry about than a bit of gossip; like whether I'm going crazy."

"I hope that's your poor attempt at humor. I know that you neurosurgeons think the mind is only a theoretical concept, but I trust you realize that it takes more than a panic attack to make you crazy."

"Yes, Simon, I'm aware of that." *And I'm not telling you why.*

"There must be something worrying you that has precipitated this. That's why you need to see a psychologist, to find out why it happened. Then you can work on ways to prevent it happening again."

"And if I can't, I'll never be able to operate again." I could taste my fear.

"Don't even think that. The chances that you won't get over this quickly are almost nil I'd say, as long as you're willing to look seriously at why this panic attack happened. Sarah Waring is an outstanding therapist—the best in the field." Simon's look was sympathetic. "I'll call her later today and let her know you'll be in touch."

"Even if therapy is any use, I don't see how I can possibly find time for it. Even if I'm not operating I still have a full schedule."

"Georgia, you know you're already finding excuses not to work on this, but you can't go back to surgery until you have a clean bill of health from me, and you won't get that until Sarah tells me you're OK."

"So it's not quite so voluntary after all. This is an ultimatum." My fingernails dug into the palm of my hand.

"There's no need to think about it like that. You know you can't operate safely until you've sorted this; you don't need any ultimatums from me."

I looked away, blinking hard to prevent my eyes from watering. Simon sat quietly. I leaned over and pulled a tissue from the box on the table between us and blew my nose while I got myself together. "I know. I know I have to deal with this. It's just a bit hard to take on board."

"I can imagine. If it helps, come and see me any time."

"Thanks, Simon. Here's hoping your therapist friend can sort me out and next time you see me I'll be back to normal."

I snuck out of his room and ignoring the elevator took the stairs up to my office, my head averted from the people coming down. What had happened to the poor woman I'd left mid-way through surgery? What about the tumor removal I'd scheduled for later this afternoon? I looked at my wrist but my watch wasn't there. I was still dressed in my blue scrubs. At least I'd changed my gumboots for clogs. Retracing my steps I pressed in the digits on the security pad that opened the hallowed operating suite doors and walked rapidly towards the change rooms, hoping I wouldn't see anyone. I glanced through the window in Theater Eight as I passed and saw David's tall form crouched over the microscope, intent on the brain beneath his hands. Bile surged into the back of my throat. *Shit, shit, shit.*

WHEN ADAM ARRIVED HOME FROM THE UNIVERSITY I HAD A roasting chicken in the oven and the gas fire warming the big open living space. The table was set, complete with wine glasses and candles, and Lara and Finbar were in the family room watching something loud on the TV.

"Mmm. Smells good." Adam's face shone with pleasure as he bent to kiss me. "How come you're home so early on a Tuesday night?"

"I wanted to surprise you and I didn't have any ops this afternoon." I ignored the turmoil in my stomach.

"It's a lovely surprise." Adam kissed me again, his lips cool from his walk from the station in the crisp evening.

The kids were in high spirits over dinner, Lara in top form as she recounted the latest in a series of stories about her French teacher, a particularly disgusting male—if Lara could be believed—with a habit of spraying the front row of students with saliva as he lisped and stuttered through the French verbs. I felt for him, the constant butt of teenage girls' jokes. Still, I couldn't help chuckling at Lara's clever imperson-ations of the luckless fellow, and for a few seconds it felt as if everything were normal.

After the dinner dishes were stacked in the dishwasher and the kids had gone upstairs to do their homework, I cornered Adam.

"Adam, we need to talk."

"We do? Why, what's the matter?" The anxious look that flickered in his eyes shook me. He was still on tenterhooks about what I was going to do next.

I lowered myself onto the couch and pulled Adam down beside me. I screwed my eyes shut. "I've really messed up now." I opened my eyes and forced myself to look at him.

"Messed up? What do you mean?" Adam asked, and I could hear the plea in his voice —*you forgot to pay the rates, missed a dental appointment…*

"I had an anxiety attack halfway through an aneurysm clipping this morning."

"Sweetheart, that's awful. What happened? Is the patient all right? Are you all right?" Adam laid his hand on my cheek.

"Yes, of course the patient's all right."

Adam dropped his hand.

I touched his arm. "Sorry. I'm just upset. David took over the operation and the patient's fine."

"But what about you?" Adam asked, the look in his dark eyes bringing me to instant tears.

"I'm, I don't know. I had to see Simon Armstrong. I think you've met him; he's one of the psychiatrists. He's nice enough but it was pretty difficult..." My voice tailed off and we sat silent, looking at each other.

"You've exhausted yourself, that's the reason for this." Adam sounded almost angry. "What did Armstrong say?"

"He seemed to think that it was a panic attack. He thinks I should see a psychologist. He can't see me professionally as he's a colleague."

"Did he refer you to someone?"

"He recommended Sarah Waring. Have you heard of her?"

"Her name sounds vaguely familiar. I could ask Frank. He knows many of the clinical psychologists in London I imagine, because he has to organize all the placements for the clinical students," Adam said.

"God no, don't ask anyone at the university. I don't want everyone knowing."

"OK, OK. But you know it's nothing to be ashamed of. Did you tell Simon about your history?"

"My history?" I felt my eyebrows go up.

"Georgia, don't be like that."

"No, I didn't tell him about *my history*. He's not my therapist, he's a work colleague. He might feel he has to report back to Peter, especially when the department directorship is being decided."

"Perhaps you should rethink that. It's not long since you had that meltdown when Lara wanted to find out more about Danny. Don't you think your body is trying to tell you something?"

"You're not my therapist either, so stop trying to analyze

me. You know how hard I've worked for this. And I don't want anyone to know; at least not just yet, not even the kids."

"I won't tell anyone until you're OK with it. You've been pushing yourself too hard, that's all."

I winced. His tone was the one he used when he was trying to placate me. "That's not the worst of it. I've been banned from doing any surgery until the psychologist gives me a clearance, so that's going to look awfully strange to everyone."

"Oh love, that's hard. But it's sensible to stop surgery for a bit," Adam said. "Are you on sick leave or something?"

"Mental health leave, you mean." I looked up and saw Adam's concerned expression. "Sorry, I'm just so mad at myself. I'm still allowed to do everything else, just no surgery. David will have to cover all that, poor man."

"He'll revel in it. It'll give him heaps more experience, and you've always said that he's a good surgeon."

"He is, I suppose. He'll only be able to do the basic stuff though. A lot of my caseload will fall on the other consultants, as if they weren't stretched enough. Christ, Jim Mason will be crowing. He'll have to take over all of Peter's ops and I'll be left with all his admin jobs. I may as well forget about applying for the Directorship." Standing up, I began to pace, pushing my hands through my hair and letting its weight slither through my fingers.

"You're getting way ahead of yourself. I'm betting you'll only need a couple of therapy sessions and you'll be fine. You know how to control panic attacks; all you need is a refresher course. So the sooner you see this psychologist and start therapy the better."

"What if it gets out that I have a history of them? That'll be the end of my entire career."

"Bollocks. Peter knows that you had some issues years ago, doesn't he?"

"Yes, but only because he was on the selection committee when I first got the consultancy. Once he retires, the next Director mightn't be so understanding. Not if it's Jim Mason. Once he sees my full record, that'll be me, history. "

"Come on Georgia, it's only April. There's months to go before the Directorship is decided. You'll be back to normal long before that. No one will even know that your time off surgery was any more than what it is; a sensible precaution while you sort this out. And surely doing all the Directorship admin will be a plus if you do decide to apply for the position? You'll have really proved how good you are at that side of things." He grinned. "All those powerhouse meetings; come on, you love 'em."

I stopped pacing and stuck my tongue out at him.

"And bonus, at least you'll be able to spend more time with us, Sapphire Eyes." Adam stood up and pushed me down on the couch. "Now sit there. I'm getting out the whisky. I think we deserve a dram or two."

ON SATURDAY NIGHT WE'D BEEN INVITED TO A DINNER PARTY at Sonja and Mike's posh Notting Hill home and Adam insisted that we go, in spite of my glum mood. I'd finally got up the courage to phone Sarah Waring and my first appointment was on Monday at one o'clock, so until then there seemed nothing much I could do. David had phoned me on Wednesday, and although our conversation was awkward I felt relieved afterwards. He was obviously fully aware of the situation and was genuinely concerned about me; either that or he was a bloody good actor. He managed to stutter out that he and the other theater staff who knew something of what had happened would be discreet. Not that I was entirely convinced. Who didn't enjoy gossiping? Even if hospital staff knew they shouldn't. Not about patients of course, but doctors were delicious targets. And good old Jim would be in there, boots and all, with his unsubtle barbs. I could almost hear him. *"Poor Georgia, she's having a rough time. That stuff-up with the young chap with the aneurysms knocked her around. All the extra work-load is simply too much for her to handle. I heard that she's feeling guilty about never being there for her kids, too, and that doesn't help. We'll all need to pitch in and support her."*

AT SONJA AND MIKE'S WARM HOUSE I BEGAN TO RELAX, THE strong G & T Mike thrust into my hand no doubt helping. The other six guests were an eclectic mix of old and new faces. Our oldest and dearest London friends were the perfect hosts and as always seated their guests strategically at the long antique dinner table in their glorious conservatory—Mike and Sonja at opposite ends and boy, girl, boy, girl along each side with partners carefully separated. Everyone had guests on either side of them, chosen by our hosts on the grounds that stimulating repartee would be almost inevitable. At mine and Adam's rare dinner parties, where everyone sat was entirely random as I never seemed to have time to think it through in advance, and the rice was usually boiling over and the fish burning around the time everyone was flocking to the table. Giggles aside, Sonja's seating arrangements did seem to enhance everyone's pleasure, and as always she took great care to avoid pairings that might cause friction between partners.

The table glowed with elegant silver candles and clusters of sparkling glasses at every place setting, and as I ate my way through the four perfectly plated courses served on dramatically colored hand-painted Italian dishes, each with a different pattern, I realized I was enjoying myself. There was something to be said for having lots of loot and being happy to share it.

I smiled at the slightly balding man seated on my left, introduced as Will. Adam was diagonally across from me, sitting next to Will's wife. I gathered from Mike's remarks that Julia was some sort of big shot criminal lawyer from Dublin, in London for six months to advise about some major policy changes in criminal court procedures. She looked ridiculously young for such a role. But she was probably not much younger than Adam and I; early forties perhaps? Good for her. Adam was being very attentive. She did have a rather lovely Irish accent.

Will—who had a marked Yorkshire accent—turned out to be quite a charmer himself. He and the talented Julia had two children, and, inevitably, a nanny, though their kids were twelve and ten. Our own nanny had been vanquished the minute Finbar turned three and deemed old enough to spend all day at preschool.

Will was also a lawyer of some sort when in Dublin, but seemingly part-time to allow his involvement in all manner of arty charity things, including being on the board of a major Dublin art gallery. I got the impression that he also spent considerable time and money on renovating their country house and extending their ten-acre garden. He seemed fascinated by the idea of neurosurgery, and I started raving on about the amazing technological advances that had revolutionized our surgery equipment and techniques over the last few years, and explaining how some of these had developed out of the NASA space program. Good old Will managed to stay awake.

Adam and Julia were obviously finding a lot to talk about as well. I caught fragments of their conversation over the general hum of enthusiastic chatter. They seemed to be deeply into dissections of the human psyche, I suppose an obvious topic for a criminal lawyer and a psychologist. I tried to catch Adam's eye, but he was too wrapped up in his tête-à-tête. On occasions like this he became the flirt I remembered from our own early days. He knew that I knew that he knew I wasn't really worried. I usually rather enjoyed the fact that everyone —women especially, but men too—loved being around Adam. It felt a bit too bloody much tonight though.

When everyone else moved into the adjoining lounge for coffee and liqueurs, Adam and Julia remained seated at the table, engrossed in their mutual revelations. A niggle of irritation distracted me whenever I glanced in their direction. *Heaven forbid, surely I'm not jealous?* I'd lost Will in the move to the lounge and was stuck with Sonja's grumpy retelling of the latest problems teachers had to put up with in the state secondary school system. I snuck a glance at my watch, but it was only ten o'clock.

When, almost an hour after everyone else, Adam and his new girlfriend finally rose from the table, I watched Adam's expression as they found two chairs close enough together to enable them to continue their cozy chat. I had a perfectly good empty space beside me on the couch. *Damn him, he knows how low I'm feeling. How dare he ignore me.* I stuck it out for a bit longer then made the first move, telling Sonja we'd promised Lara and Finbar we'd be home by midnight. Of course everyone stood up then, kissing us goodbye as if they were our lifelong friends. Adam left Julia until last and I almost dragged him out the door, knowing I was embarrassing him but too angry to stop myself.

It was bitter outside on the street and not a vehicle of any sort in sight. "Well, are you going to phone for a taxi?" I asked. "I'm bloody freezing standing here."

"I thought you'd phoned for one when we were in the house?"

"No, I didn't."

"Well, why did you drag me out here? If you'd phoned ahead we could have waited in the warm until it arrived."

"So you could continue gazing into what's-her-name's eyes?"

"For heaven's sake, Georgia. You've had too much wine."

"I have not…"

"You two still here?" called a male voice and I swung around to see Will and Julia walking down the steps, Julia in what looked like a genuine mink coat. *Animal murderer.*

"Hasn't your taxi arrived yet?" Julia asked, brushing against Adam with her mink.

"We haven't called one yet," Adam said, his voice making it clear he was pissed off. "I'm just about to."

"Well, looks like this one's ours then," Will said, as a taxi cruised around the corner.

"Why don't you share it with us?" Julia's voice was so husky I could barely hear her. "We're not far from here and then you can take it on to your place. In fact, why don't you come in for a nightcap first?" She turned to me. "You'll love the apartment we've rented. It's the penthouse suite and it has a view to die for."

"No thanks. We'll get our own taxi. We need to get back as soon as we can. We don't have a live-in nanny to mind our children."

Adam grabbed my arm. "Sorry, Julia, she's had a few too many wines. I should get her home. But thanks for the offer."

"Too many wines. The mark of a great evening," Will smiled at me. "Come on old girl," he said to Julia. "In the cab with you."

As Will practically shoved her through the door Julia turned her head. "We'll be in touch to organize a lovely quiet dinner, just the four of us."

Not even when hell freezes over. I wished I had the nerve to say it aloud. Adam pulled out his mobile and jabbed in the cab number.

In the taxi he slumped in the seat, head turned towards his window, leather jacket pulled tight around him. I stared out my own window and watched the lighted buildings stream past and couples walking hand-in-hand on their way home after a night out. Bringing my hand to my mouth I felt the hard curve of Adam's gold band on my lips. My eyes and nose stinging, I closed my eyes and gave into the creeping darkness.

CHAPTER 6

aking a deep breath I obeyed the command 'Please enter' on the red door below a sign announcing 'Sarah Waring, Clinical Psychologist.' The small waiting room was empty and I sat on a low couch covered with a bright throw. Quashing a flashback to the vomit-green psychiatric ward at Auckland Hospital, I breathed in the private clinic ambiance: high ceilings; one dark red wall and three cream ones; old-fashioned windows letting in the pale autumn light; a Turkish rug on the dark polished wood floor; various large tubs with erupting greenery; three prints of English scenery. I'd never understood why some famous folk seemed to find their endless psychoanalysis pleasurable, but perhaps today was the day. That thought almost made me smile, but not quite.

A low coffee table was covered with a jumble of magazines, *National Geographic* and *The English Home* being two that I recognized. *Psychology Today* did not seem to be present, at least in the top layer. Another door stood closed, presumably with Sarah herself behind it, so I sat back and waited, willing my churning stomach to behave like a grown-up. I'd spent sixteen years trying to put those agonizing, painful months in therapy behind me and here I was, back again.

There seemed to be no bell to ring, and I could hear a murmur of voices from behind the door. Then it opened and two middle-aged-plus women emerged, saying goodbye. The woman with the handbag didn't seem to notice me as she walked past. I stood up as the second woman came towards me, her hand outstretched. "Georgia, glad you found me. I'm Sarah. Come right in." Her handshake was warm and strong and her voice low-pitched and lilting.

Is she Welsh? My nausea dissolved as I returned her direct gaze. Brown eyes almost disappearing when she smiled and a sweet face with soft, finely creased skin, clean of makeup. Even her hair was just right—she obviously didn't provide financial support to the hairdressing salon below her rooms— it was iron grey and pulled back from her face in a thick plait, wisps floating freely around her face and neck.

I glanced around the therapy room. A cozy family room with comfortable chairs and a couch pulled around a coffee table, walls lined with bookcases, and a large desk in one corner. Not in the least way reminiscent of the over-heated claustrophobic closet with its straight-backed chairs where I'd spent endless hours with the gaunt, white-coated, Dr. Rhodes.

"Get as comfortable as you can on this couch. No need to lie down. I do most of my therapy with the client sitting upright." Sarah grinned, and sat in the chair facing me.

I smiled back. *Thank goodness she's not twenty. Or a man.*

"Simon told me you'd experienced a panic attack when you were operating. I'd like to hear more about it, but first we should get to know each other a little," Sarah said. "I'll begin."

I didn't really take in the list of qualifications Sarah sped through; Simon wouldn't have referred me to a quack. But I listened more closely as she explained the psychological models she worked in.

"I use cognitive behavior therapy for helping my clients take control of their panic attacks and narrative and talking therapy to help them explore the underlying issues." Her infectious grin flashed. "And I don't usually talk as much as this."

Familiar territory and it hadn't worked last time. But from my mad Googling over the past few nights I knew it was the therapist and not the therapy model that made the difference. "It sounds as if it mightn't take too long?" I said, hearing the plea in my tone.

"I hope not." Sarah's smile returned. "Do I detect a touch of New Zealand in your accent? One of my favorite places. I spent a year there in my twenties, back-packing. Never will I forget that spectacular Milky Way and watching the moon rise out of the sea."

"Oh, don't. You'll make me homesick. Adam and I are both Kiwis. We moved to London eleven years ago, a year after we were married. I was thirty-four and a few months pregnant with Finbar. Lara was three. I was a single mum when I met Adam and he adopted Lara when we married."

"So why London? That's a big change from New Zealand."

I smiled. "The moon here doesn't have quite the same magic, even on the rare occasions it can even be seen. But there are compensations. I'd managed to get a consultant position at the hospital and Adam got a research assistant post at the university where he's a senior lecturer now. Luckily he was able to go part-time when Finbar was born. I'd only been working there a few months before Finbar's birth, so I had to return to work full time when he was three months old."

"No plans to return to New Zealand?"

I shook my head. "It's nice to go back when we can afford it so our kids can get to know their grandparents and cousins, but London's home now." I looked down at my hands, gripped together like drowning souls. "Although if I can't sort out this"—*panic attack, say it*—"this panic attack, I can't see how we can stay in London. The NHS can't afford to continue to pay a surgeon who can't operate."

"We should get started then. Are you ready?"

I nodded, my voice stuck in my throat. Sarah's eyes held mine. I forced some words out. "It seems it's my only option."

"Therapy is certainly not for everyone, but even skeptics sometimes find it useful."

"Sorry. I didn't mean to sound so dismal," I said.

"I was taking a punt that you mightn't have much faith in therapy, based entirely on my stereotype of neurosurgeons."

"I don't think I could be classified as a stereotypical neuro-surgeon. The truth is, I had a serious anxiety disorder when I was pregnant with Lara, panic attacks and all. I spent months in therapy. But I hadn't had a full blown panic attack since we left New Zealand."

"You must be gutted. It's so disheartening when something triggers an old disorder again. But it happens pretty often I'm afraid. You've done well to keep the panic attacks at bay for so long."

"But why now? It couldn't have picked a worse time. Our director is on sick leave and I'm covering half his clinical and administrative work as well as my own. If you can sort me out so I can get back to operating, I'll bury all my prejudices about therapy."

"Truth is, even I have some doubts about therapy. It's no picnic. Emotionally draining, damn hard work and you have to keep working on yourself even outside this room. You've probably heard this before, but if you aren't doing at least fifty percent of the work while we're together then the therapy is doomed to fail. The paradox is that you do most of the work but I'm the one who gets paid."

"I know it will be difficult, but it can't be harder than what I'm going through now."

"Perhaps not, but from my experience, the pain gets worse

before it gets better," countered Sarah, her voice gentle. "And as you know from your last therapy experience, emotional pain can affect every aspect of your life and the lives of those you love. So it's a courageous step to take."

"I think I understand that, and I'm willing to do whatever I have to." I looked steadily at Sarah, trying to believe myself.

"What are you feeling when you say that?"

"I'm feeling OK."

"Too quick. I want you to take the time to look inside at your feelings. Perhaps you can't put a label on them but you might be able to describe bodily sensations."

I closed my eyes. "I think I feel apprehensive and anxious, but not as much as before I came in," I said, realizing it was true. I opened my eyes. "I'm feeling more hopeful that you can help me. I don't think I'll find it too hard to talk to you and that's a relief. I've been feeling so out of my depth over this."

"That's a good start."

"It's so important in my job to be in control that I've got used to it, at least when I'm working. Not being in control terrifies me."

"We'll work on helping you feel less uncomfortable when you can't control every aspect of your life and your feelings. That will give you the courage to look at what's happening inside you, with the knowledge that you can regain control when you need to. You clearly learned some techniques to help you take control of your panic attacks the last time you had them so I think you'll learn quickly how to stop them in their tracks once again."

"How do I do that? Feel comfortable about being out of control, I mean?"

"Not needing to be in control all the time is a better way of thinking about it. It comes with time, and as we build up a trusting relationship. Then you can begin by trusting that I won't let you experience painful feelings too deeply before you're ready. That's my job, to take care of you while you get to know yourself at a level that you haven't reached before."

"I don't think I ever got near that point last time." I gazed out the window at the gray sky.

"Meanings take time to understand, and feeling apprehensive and wanting to avoid therapy is normal, and often accompanies a journey into one's psyche. But I'm confident you won't avoid the hard issues. A woman bold enough to dissect the living human brain is surely bold enough to dissect her own feelings."

I took a deep breath. "If dissecting my feelings is what it takes, I'll do my best. I have to for my family's sake. Lara and Finbar don't deserve a mother who can't keep it together. And I need be able to operate again."

"Both those parts of your life are precious."

I nodded, trying to swallow the lump in my throat.

"Let your feelings happen. You're safe here."

"I'll try." I swallowed again. "How do I start?"

"You start by telling me about yourself. Who are you, what makes you tick, who do you love, why are you a neurosurgeon and not a pediatrician or lawyer or psychologist, what do you do for relaxation?"

"But that will take most of our session."

"It probably will, but trust me, it's the right place to begin."

I soon discovered what Sarah meant when she warned me that therapy was hard work. And talking to Adam about my sessions was the most difficult thing of all. He didn't push me, but after my third therapy session he cornered me in my study.

"Sweetheart," he began. "Why don't you tell me a bit about your therapy? It might help to talk about it."

"I'm still too confused myself about what's going on. I'm not sure I'd make any sense." Suddenly hot, I pushed my hands through my hair, lifting it off the back of my neck.

"You're miserable. Perhaps the therapy's not helping?"

I pressed my lips together, fighting back tears. The silence seemed to go on for a long while before I found the courage to speak. "I'd forgotten how soul destroying therapy could be. It's… it's …" My voice gave out again and Adam pulled me into the soft blue wool of his jersey.

"It's OK, OK," he whispered, one hand stroking the back of my head, the other keeping me safe.

"Do you think I should stop therapy?" I'd calmed down and was sitting as close to Adam as I could get, my hands around a hot mug.

"I want to say yes, but I don't really know. What will happen if you stop?"

"With my ban from operating, do you mean?"

"I suppose so, but I really mean what will happen to you now everything has been stirred up. Is it important to get through this bad part and hope it will soon be easier?"

"That's what Sarah says. But that's not what happened when I was young. It never got better."

"In some ways it did from what you've told me. You went from someone who was almost mute with anguish to becoming the best mother and passing your neurosurgery exams. How can you think it didn't work?"

"I don't know. I suppose learning how to control my anxiety and learn not to worry about whatever horrible things I'd buried, keep them buried… I suppose that was progress. Perhaps that's all I need now too. I simply need to relearn how to control my panic attacks and get on with life."

"Is Sarah OK with that?"

I shook my head.

"Why not? Does everyone have to remember everything? Sounds like psychobabble to me."

"It's not really Sarah, it's me. I feel a responsibility to Lara, now she's old enough to know what happened to Danny."

"She does know. He fell off a cliff and died."

"She needs to know why. I need to know why."

"Georgia, the police investigation concluded that it was an accident. Danny slipped on the steep wet grass, that's what happened."

"That doesn't answer the real question. Why was he up there in the first place in the middle of the night and what did it have to do with me? Was I there? How did I know where to look for him?"

"You need to stop blaming yourself. Isn't that called survivor guilt? Whatever the reason he was up there, he slipped, and that's terrible, but it's not your fault."

"I don't really know that. Inside, somewhere I know the truth. I can sense it sitting just out of my grasp, in my head somewhere, and it's terrifying. If I don't remember, these panic attacks won't stop. I can feel it."

Then Adam was holding me close against his jersey again. I breathed in the wool scent and it smelt like the sea. The thunder of the surf was inside my head, the sting of salt in my eyes. Rocking, rocking, to and fro.

"Hush now. It's all right. You're safe here with me. Shhh, shhh."

CHAPTER 7

In our fourth session Sarah went straight for the jugular. "Tell me everything about you and Danny." She settled back in her chair and waited.

"What's the point? I see the connection. Lara needed to find out about Danny and I couldn't help her. Then Alfie turned up with his Danny hair and I stuffed up and he died too. No wonder I went to pieces."

"Humor me. Where did you and Danny meet?"

"How on earth can that help? I simply want to learn how to stop these damn panic attacks and get back to surgery."

"Have you some sort of plan on how to go about that?"

I glanced at Sarah, but she remained tranquil. "You're meant to be the expert. That's why I'm here."

"I can't promise any miracles, Georgia, but I suspect you'll get nowhere until you can talk about Danny. I know it's hard, but aren't we comfortable enough with each other for you to give it a try?"

"What's the point? Heavens Sarah, it was sixteen, seventeen years ago. Could you remember everything about a relationship you had when you were in your twenties?"

"It would depend on how important the relationship had

been to me. Tell me honestly, have you thought about Danny since our last session?"

"Mmm. I wondered when you'd revert to that old line. Have you ever had a client who did nothing between sessions? What happened then?"

"Their therapy took much longer. If you haven't thought about Danny over the last few days, have you any idea how you avoided it?"

I shook my head.

"Tell me about him. When did you meet?"

I groaned. I was catching on to Sarah's pitbull side. "In 1988. I was twenty-nine and near the end of a two-year stint as a neurosurgery resident at Massachusetts General Hospital. I was with Harry, a friend of mine—he was an orthopedic resident there. We had a three-day break and decided to go to New Orleans. I hadn't been before."

"So how did you meet Danny? By chance?"

"No. When I knew I was going to New Orleans I phoned an old school friend of mine in New Zealand. Judy had been full of New Orleans after she'd been there for a holiday a couple of years before, so I thought she might have some good recommendations for restaurants and music. She told me I *had* to meet Danny. He'd stayed for a few days on Great Barrier Island with Judy's grandmother when he was a teenager, and they'd kept in touch. I think knowing him was one of the main reasons she went to New Orleans on her big American trip."

"Ah, so by the look on your face, Danny was a good recommendation. "

I wiped away my goofy smile. "Well, that's what I thought back then. Judy was convinced we'd like each other. She gave me the name of the club he sang at and instructed me to show up there unannounced and introduce myself."

"Georgia, I think it will help you to go back there—experience it again—if I take you through that relaxation exercise we've been practicing. Are you game?"

"I suppose so."

"Good. Now make yourself comfortable on the couch, feet up, and close your eyes."

Usually we ended our sessions with relaxation and I'd become a dab hand at following Sarah's voice and relaxing my muscle groups one by one. It was the only part of therapy I actually looked forward to, welcoming the warmth as it filled my body and emptied my mind.

Sarah's voice was warm and low. "New Orleans. Feel it on your skin—hot, steamy. Look around you. What do you see? Colors? Is it day or night? Can you smell the muddy Mississippi? Can you see it, hear it, hear the riverboats, hear people laughing? Perhaps you can hear music. Is it jazz, blues? Listen."

I'm hot, so hot. From my shelter in the dense shade of the verandah, Bourbon Street is blindingly bright. Wonderful old buildings with their high balconies strung with hanging baskets, overflowing with brilliant colors and long dangling greenery. I want to stop on every corner and absorb the musicians and dancers and clowns and jugglers and pavement artists. I take another gulp of the icy-cold drink from a giant-sized paper cup. A Hurricane minus the rum. Too early for the real thing.

Peering into dark shops filled with color and shiny junk, I'm jostled down the street with happy people of every shape, hue, and age, all in love with New Orleans. I take in a deep breath of the muddy, fishy, slightly oily smell that wafts through the humid air. I can't yet see the great river slithering and sliding, hidden behind the buildings, but I can sense it.

"Georgia, is Danny there?" Sarah's words floated through my head.

Still hot, but dark now. Danny's Piano Bar. I follow Harry through the blue door with the poster advertising Danny Leaumont into the dim, steamy, smoky club. We sit at a table right by the dais. The three-man-band begin to play, their voices smooth and melting, almost seeming out of place in a blues club. Then from the side, a flash of green as a man in a billowing sea-green shirt steps onto the dais and pads across the boards in his bare feet. He sits down at the battered baby grand, his dark red hair blazing in the spotlight—a thick messy halo around his arresting face. I catch a sudden movement in his throat as he swallows, and then the tip of his tongue glistens as he moistens his lips. Pulling the microphone attached to the piano to his mouth, he closes his eyes, slides his hands across the keys in a bluesy contrast to his band, and begins to sing.

"Listen Georgia, listen to his song, hear the words." Sarah's voice might have been a dream.

'Georgia, Georgia….' I shiver as his gritty voice reaches inside me. 'Georgia on my mind'—Danny's hand is drawing me towards him. I can see the sheen on his skin, feel his heat as he comes closer.

We're holding hands, walking along by the dark river, spangled with the reflected lights from the silent paddle steamers and riverboats. We sit on a bench on the paved pedestrian walkway. I can feel the slight breeze coming off the water and whispering over my hot body, and Danny's gentle hand stroking my back, exposed by my summer dress.

My thighs tensed against the heat in my groin and a shiver scurried through me. I was back there, in Danny's arms. He was teasing me about my blue eyes and I was flirting back at him like a sixteen-year-old.

"You can talk. I've never seen eyes as green as yours." I smooth the tiny crinkles at the corners of his eyes, his skin feeling hot under my cool fingertips.

"Cat's eyes," Danny says, enclosing my hands with his.

"Judy said I'd fall for you, Cat's Eyes," I murmur. "Fancy you meeting her on Great Barrier Island. What are the chances?"

Danny slides my right hand to his mouth and kisses my palm. "What? That you were at school on the island when you were small and I spent five days there years later? I don't suppose it's that unusual for surf-crazy guys traveling around New Zealand to go to Great Barrier. Especially as I was about to come back to New Orleans where finding surf would be pretty much a non-event."

"But to stay with Judy's grandmother. How come? Most surfers stay in the backpackers."

"Rachel was some distant cousin of Mom's. She came to stay with us once when we lived in New Zealand, not long after we shifted there. I

must have been about thirteen. I thought she was seriously cool with her dreadlocks and no shoes, even in Queenstown in the winter."

I grin. "I remember her. She ran the shop in Tryphena, and always had those dreadlocks and bare feet. Not that that's anything out of the ordinary for the Barrier."

"Mmm." He weaves a hank of my hair through his fingers. "Glad you didn't torture these gorgeous tresses with dread locking." He kisses me again.

After some time I manage to pull away. "I haven't snogged in a public place like this since I was a teenager. Thank goodness no one here knows me. Hardly appropriate behavior for a neurosurgeon."

Danny's eyebrows zip skywards. "Really? Aren't the best neurosurgeons risk-takers?"

"Definitely not. So, how long did you live in New Zealand? You don't have much of a Kiwi accent. In fact you don't have any Kiwi accent."

"Nope. 'Fraid not Ma'am. I'm a Mississippi boy, born and raised. But Mom came from New Zealand and we went back there when her dad got sick. I went to high school in Queenstown."

"Lucky you. I love Queenstown. It must be one of the most beautiful places on earth."

"Sleepy though, back then, once the tourists left. As soon as I finished school I came back home to New Orleans. Mainly because I wanted a music career. I've never wanted to do anything but bang the ivories and wail, and I figured I could wind my grandmother around my pinky." He grinned. "Actually, that's when I went to Great Barrier, on my way back here. Thank the good Lord for that!"

My whole body was throbbing.

Pulling my hand to his chest he holds it there. I can feel his heart beating and the heat in my face as he smiles at me and then carries on talking as if I haven't just melted in a puddle in his lap.

"Gran— Dad's mother—owns a few nightclubs here so I got a head start. She bought 'Danny's Piano Bar' as soon as I got back, and for some crazy reason, named it for me."

"Your own nightclub! Danny Leaumont, you're disgustingly spoilt!"

"Guilty." A white tooth flashes, and I catch the twinkle in his eyes.

"Gran bought it because she didn't want her innocent eighteen year old grandson singing in her real clubs full of drug dealers and loose women."

"I'd like to meet your Gran."

"Tomorrow you shall. Savannah Leaumont, the doyenne of jazz dives; she's something else. For my sins I still live with her in the Garden District."

"Did you meet his grandmother, Georgia? Can you see her? Does she look like her grandson?" Sarah's voice was in my head, taking me deeper.

I stand at the end of a short wide path lined on each side by a waist-high clipped hedge and gaze at the white, two-story house raised on low brick piles. Four white columns span both floors, each with a covered gallery fronted by a black iron balustrade. The twin double doors opening off each gallery are framed with green shutters.

Danny is standing beside me. His faded denim jeans have been replaced with faded denim shorts, cut off just above his knees and revealing muscular legs, surprisingly brown, given his red hair. With one arm he pulls me close to his washed-out pink T-shirt, its New Orleans Jazz Fest banner barely visible. In his bare feet he is only a few inches taller than me, and I can feel his grin as our lips meet. I lean back and smile into his wicked green eyes.

"'Morning gorgeous," he murmurs and kisses me again. "Come and meet Gran." He takes my hand and leads me up the path and into the cool dim entrance hall.

"Hey Gran, my New Zealander is here," he hollers.

Savannah Leaumont sweeps down the grand staircase, a tall and elegant woman, her thick black hair streaked with silver and arranged in a coil on the top of her aristocratic head. Her smooth skin is the color of milky coffee, and her eyes, under straight dark brows, are so dark they're almost black. She wears a knee-length denim skirt and a soft white shirt, and her long shapely legs are those of a young woman. She smiles and holds out a slim hand sparkling with rings. Her handshake is firm.

"It's always lovely to meet New Zealanders. My son, Leroy, loves New Zealand, and he's forever trying to get me to visit."

"Yes, Gran, and you should go. You'd love it," Danny said.

"One thing at a time, my boy. First you have to get yourself properly established here as a musician and then perhaps we can take time off for world tours."

Sarah's voice washed over Savannah's cultured Southern drawl. "And soon, Georgia, you must return to your hospital in Boston. Did you see Danny again?"

I smiled, lying on the couch in Sarah's room. Moistening my dry lips I taste the sea. And now I could smell it; crisp, sea-saturated air—late October on Cape Cod. Harry's thirtieth birthday, and Danny and his trio were singing. They'd all kept it from me. My surprise. I was back there, standing on the verandah of the big house, Danny's gravelly voice throbbing through the cool air, drawing me back into the room, hot with entangled bodies swaying to the sultry rhythm in the semi-darkness.

Bathed in the soft lights left burning at the far end of the large room, Danny stands, his head on one side, his eyes closed, the microphone in one hand. The guitarist and bass player on either side of him disappear in his glow and I can see only him. I shiver as he opens his eyes and looks across the room into my very soul. Singing the last words of 'Georgia On My Mind,' he moves across the room towards me and the dancing couples make a corridor for him. Still singing, he takes my hand and keeps moving, outside and down the steps. I pause to slip off my sandals and they dangle from my free hand as we walk into the sand dunes. In the distance I can hear new music beginning, and as it grows fainter Danny stops, takes my sandals from me, and drops them in the sand.

There was something heavy pressing on my chest and I desperately pushed it away. I tried to scream but couldn't make a sound.

"It's OK, it's OK. Georgia, look at me."

My heart pounding I cracked open my eyes. Sarah's face filled my vision. Swiping at the clammy sweat on my face I struggled to sit up, but fell back, my breath rasping in my throat.

"Think about your breathing; slow it down." Sarah leaned over and pressed her hand against my chest. "You're starting to hyperventilate. Breathe from your diaphragm, not using your chest muscles." Her voice was soothing.

I closed my eyes and took in a long shuddering breath.

"That's better. Remember what to do. Count your inhalations and think 'relax' as you exhale."

Gradually my breathing slowed and calmed. Sarah pushed the box of tissues towards me and I mopped the cold perspiration from my face and neck. "How did that happen so quickly? Heavens, am I going to have these all the time?"

"No, you're not. You've learned to recognize the early signs; as soon as you start that fast breathing you need to tell yourself to sl-o-o-o-w down, and you can take control before the panic takes hold."

"I could feel that terror coming again, thinking I could die."

"No one has ever died of a panic attack. But I know it feels as if you will."

"Before I lost it, was I hypnotized? It felt like a dream, only more logical. And I can remember it all."

"I don't think I hypnotized you, just helped you go into a deep state of relaxation and feel safe enough to remember things that have for so long been too painful to think about."

"Did I talk? It didn't feel like I did. I vaguely recall your voice asking me things, but it's all very hazy."

"You talked enough for me to understand something of what you went through and how you felt back then. The most important thing is that you were able to re-experience it."

"Until I got to the bad bit."

"Your subconscious knows when it's time to bow out. I won't take you back there yet, but you might be able to talk about what happened next, simply as something that happened in your past, almost as if you were telling a story that happened to someone else."

I heard a noise that sounded like a cow in the final stages of giving birth. It was coming from me. I grabbed the glass of water Sarah was holding out and took a gulp. Spluttering, I wiped my mouth and sat up properly before trying again. This time I emptied the glass before setting it on the coffee table. I felt about 80 years old.

"OK?"

I nodded.

"You and Danny, what happened?"

Shivering, I wrapped my arms around myself. "I thought we were in love." I shook my head. "Deep down I must have known our relationship was doomed to fail. Why on earth I thought that Danny could become a neurosurgeon's husband in backwoods New Zealand is beyond me. But I was bewitched by him. He had a charisma that was more than just a stage presence. It radiated from every pore, even when he was with his family. And his voice was soul warming. Joe Cocker, Randy Newman, that sort of gutsy, sexy sound. And for some unfathomable reason, he fell for me."

I found myself over at the window, surprised to see the light was still bright and the traffic still zoomed back and forth below as if it were a normal day. "Perhaps it would have been different if I could have stayed in the States, but that was impossible. Danny had dual citizenship and could live in either country. We promised each other that we would be sensible, do the trial run first. If it worked out—although we both thought it was love forever—I would try and get a consultant position either in the US or even in the UK, where Danny could still have a singing career." I stopped, my eyes suddenly stinging.

"Go on," Sarah said, bringing me back to the room.

"I had to pass my fellowship exams first, and that was looking more unlikely by the minute. When I arrived back in New Zealand it was late November and my parents were in Australia—my brother Andrew lived there back then and he and his wife had just had twins. Mum and Dad were planning to stay with them until March. I went straight to Great Barrier Island. Our family has a holiday house there. The Barrier is wild and remote; about a hundred kilometers off the coast north of Auckland. Perfect for studying, at least until Danny joined me."

My eyes lost focus and I was back there, hearing in the muffled traffic noise the lull of the sea. "I loved Great Barrier. It was always home to me. Both Andrew and I were born there and we didn't move to Auckland until I was nine. Dad was a fisherman, and Mum was the island rural nurse. I was never sure why they decided to leave, but I think Mum found it pretty isolating."

Sarah coughed behind me and I turned around. "I hated Auckland at first; I was dropped into a city school mid-way through the year. I came in for a lot of teasing; nothing too terrible really—bush baby, dumbo—that sort of thing. Our Barrier school had eighteen pupils, and the new one had about five hundred. The girls in my class were into Barbie dolls and spent most of their time changing their nail polish color, at nine years old! I never liked dolls and even at that age the very idea of sitting about painting nails bored me to tears." I looked at my short clean nails and made an attempt at a laugh, but it came out as a snort. "Who knows, perhaps that was why I decided to become a neurosurgeon, so I'd have an excuse to leave my nails alone."

Turning back to the window I gazed down at the street. "I don't think Dad liked Auckland much either. He established a successful little building business there but deep down, he's still a fisherman." I started as a red London bus rumbled by and realized I was twisting my long hair round and round my fingers. "He phoned last night. Dad I mean. He asked me to think about bringing the family home to New Zealand next January for Mum's 75th birthday; he's planning a big family occasion on the island. We go back to New Zealand quite often but the kids have never been to Great Barrier Island. They would love it, but I've always found an excuse not to take them. I haven't been back since Danny and I were together there."

"Tell me about it."

I lent my forehead against the cold glass of the window and searched for some words to describe how I felt when Danny joined me on the island. *No, why go there? I'll tell her the bare facts.*

"Once Danny arrived that was the end of any studying. The rest of the story is pretty straightforward. He came, he had fun, and he died." I thumped the window and the glass quivered.

"You're angry."

"Apparently. Not that I'd noticed it until I started seeing you."

"Or until Alfie died."

"That was the killer. Not the best word I suppose. I should never have operated on him." I returned to the couch and sat down, my head in my hands.

"So why did you? If you knew you shouldn't."

I sighed and looked up. "I didn't become a good neurosurgeon by listening to my heart. There were no objective indications to warn me off. Alfie was the perfect candidate for a straightforward operation."

"Why do you think your heart and not your head was telling you the truth in this case?" Sarah's voice was gentle.

"It wasn't. His aneurysm rupture was coincidence; nothing to do with my feelings about him. I can only assume the aneurysm must have been weakened to the point of rupture when the university researchers got Alfie's MRI done and discovered it. It would probably have ruptured soon, spontaneously, even if I hadn't operated. In most cases when an unruptured aneurysm is accidentally discovered, the aneurysm is not even close to rupture, but unfortunately there's no way of telling. My messing about trying to get the clip on probably weakened it further, and then the hemorrhage put strain on his second aneurysm. When that ruptured the following day, he had no chance."

"Do you think it's reasonable to feel guilty?"

"No, not logically. Upset, disappointed, but not guilty of any surgical misconduct or even poor decision making."

"And that's what the Hospital Morbidity and Mortality Committee decided?"

I nodded.

"So why the panic attack and this ongoing anxiety?"

"You tell me."

"It all goes back to your daughter, doesn't it? Her desire, her need—even perhaps her right—to know more about Danny. It all goes back to Danny and your heart. "

CHAPTER 8

I woke before dawn on Saturday morning and lay still, watching the dark curtains dissolving to blue. The rain stopped and the silence was taken up by the melodic tune of the resident blackbird, always the first to begin the dawn chorus. I listened to the swelling orchestra of whistling and chattering as the birds of London woke, and hearing a little snuffle from a still sleeping Adam, yearned to snuggle into his arms and stay there forever. But he seemed as far away in the bed as he could get, his back turned against me.

My eyelids were being held open by barbed wire. I blinked hard, and they scratched across my dry eyes. It was weeks— months even—since going to bed had been something I looked forward to; now I almost dreaded it, knowing that, with or without a sleeping pill, I was destined to journey through hell.

As suddenly as it began the morning chorus stopped, and in its place another heavy shower marched across the roof. Now the full force of the rain was pounding the house, yet over that I could hear the delicate plop of individual spears as they hit the eaves and disappeared into the guttering, already half blocked by rotting spring blossoms. Then the sweet clear sound of the blackbird rose again and I imagined the sleek black shape braving the rain and proclaiming his right to be king.

Hauling myself out of bed and down the stairs into the cold kitchen I collected the morning newspaper. But it lay on the table unread as I slurped down two cups of coffee. Last night Adam and I had again failed to talk about anything important. He had almost given up trying. I knew it was my fault but I was so bloody exhausted by my misery and the emotions therapy stirred up that it was easier to shut Adam out. Even when I saw the hurt in his eyes. And Lara was being a toad; my fault too I suppose. Rude, and more often than not, late home from school. Yesterday her form teacher called, asking for a meeting. I thought she might be keeping it together at school at least, but apparently not. And poor Finbar. He adored Lara, even though he always pretended he found her a pain, but all they did now was fight. Tonight Lara was out with her friends yet again, leaving Finbar to put up with our problems all by himself. Last night he'd made such a gallant effort to chat over dinner, and Adam, his face gray with fatigue, had done his best to join in. I'd done nothing to help. After dinner the three of us sat dumbly and watched a murder mystery on the box, goodness knows what about.

I shook my head delicately but the barbed wire—inside my head now—didn't budge. I had to get out of the house.

Gulping in the cold air, I raised my aching head to the drenching rain and closed my eyes as it ran down my face and seeped in the sides of my anorak hood, licking long strands of escaping hair. Then I walked, head down and hands deep in my anorak pockets, one suburban street to the next, making no attempt to avoid the occasional wall of water that plastered my cold jeans to my calves every time a car swished through the deep puddles spilling from overflowing gutters.

I have to stop this therapy. All it's doing is destroying our family. It sure as hell isn't getting Danny out of my head or clearing up what happened that night. Sarah had probably got the message that it wasn't working—I'd missed my last two sessions and she'd left two messages for me, rescheduling for Monday. I'll tell Sarah then. There has got to be an easier way to get over these cursed panic attacks.

Therapists were nothing but voyeurs. Sixteen years. How can I possibly be expected to remember with any sort of accuracy what happened so long ago? I unclenched my hands and pulled them from my pockets. Back then, I'd been stupidly naive about relationships, in spite of being twenty-nine. Too long locked up in universities and hospitals. No wonder I'd been snared by Danny's charm.

I looked up as a plane flew low over the city, headed for Heathrow. I cupped my cold wet hands over my mouth and blew on them. No stopping the rest of my body shaking. My teeth were practically rattling in their sockets. At least it had been a lot warmer on that November morning so long ago, when the small plane I was waiting for landed on the island.

DANNY JUMPED OUT OF THE DOOR ONTO THE GRASS RUNWAY, his hair vivid red against the white of the plane, his grin lighting up my world. The late afternoon light was still bright as we drove north along the spectacular coast, Danny's exuberance spilling in pools around him.

"Hey, Georgie-girl, I can't believe I'm finally back here," he said, again and again. "You look good enough to swallow whole—you've even got a smidgeon of color on that alabaster skin of yours."

I laughed at him and he put his hand on mine as I steered the big vehicle around the next bend.

"Mmm, and you look pretty delectable yourself, sir. You certainly don't look as if you've just spent eighteen sleepless hours traveling. How do you do it?"

"Thinking of you-o-o-o" he sang. "I've spent the whole dang journey with a hard on."

My face flared. "Stop it. You haven't even seen our beach and our house and everything yet."

"Slow down, you're goin' too fast," sang Danny. "Sorry sweets, I want to see it all."

"Look out there," I said, pulling my hand from under his and pointing out the open window. "I don't believe it. Only for you."

"Man! That is something else."

And out in the surf a pod of dolphins danced along the waves.

I LIT THE CANDLES IN THEIR GLASS JARS AND SAT THEM ON THE wooden table on the deck. I'd already laid it with chunky blue and green pottery plates and my mother's old silver cutlery, a treasured wedding present left in the house when we moved from the island. With a flourish I placed a blue vase filled with grasses and wild flowers I'd picked earlier that day in the center of the table.

"Hungry?" I murmured, leaning over the hammock and kissing Danny's warm lips.

"Mmm, it smells phenomenal," Danny said sleepily. "But you might have to drag me to the table."

"My pleasure, sir," I said, kissing him again.

"Stop it woman," Danny groaned. "That's if you don't want to waste your bloody fabulous smelling dinner."

"DID YOU EVER SEE THAT OLD MOVIE, *TOM JONES*?" DANNY said. "Starring Albert Finney?" We were using our teeth to pull the last of the fragrant white flesh from the crayfish.

I nodded.

Danny's eyes sparked in the candlelight. "D'you remember that scene where Tom and his mistress were eating chicken legs?"

I licked my fingers. "I do, I definitely do."

"Crayfish makes chicken seem like child's play."

"Hmmm." I reached over and lifted Danny's hand to my mouth. Kissing his palm, I bit the soft swelling at the base of his thumb, and then taking it in my mouth I began to suck on it, making a soft sound like a baby. Danny closed his eyes as I swirled my tongue around the tip, and slowly he slid it out and stroked it across my lower lip, buttery from the crayfish.

"I think I've had enough seafood," he croaked, moving around the table and pulling me into his arms. "Time for dessert." Kissing off the buttery remnants, he lifted me and walked backwards through the French doors. Then we were in the bedroom, filled with light from the bright half moon sailing in the sky, and he was laying me on the patchwork quilt and kissing my ears and my neck as he pulled the straps of my summer top from my shoulders. I closed my eyes as he undressed me, biting back moans as his mobile lips explored me, his warm hands moving me like a rag doll. I heard my cries becoming more urgent until he finally pulled away and moved over me. I captured him with my legs and felt him deep within me; my Danny, here with me on my island.

FLOATING IN A BUBBLE OF HAPPINESS, WE LAZED, AND SWAM, and cooked, and ate, and drank, and made love, and slept in each other's arms in the moonlight. We even explored the island, as far as the roads, tracks, and our legs would take us. Three days before Christmas we cut down a wilding pine and decorated it with hand-made angels and stars that Andrew and I had made as kids, and we raided Dad's shed and borrowed his drill and the finest drill bit and made holes in shells we'd collected from the beach and strung them and draped them around the tree. I painted sea urchin cases gold and silver with paint that still worked after a good stir, and we hung those too. Perched precariously on the highest rung of a step ladder that should have been retired twenty years earlier, Danny tied the star—a stunning creation of tiny red, yellow and white shells stuck on a star shape I'd cut from heavy cardboard—to the top of the tree.

On Christmas Day we packed cold crayfish and bread and cheese and wine into our backpacks and climbed to the saddle of the Pa at the north end of the beach. From there, sitting in a sunny hollow, on one side we could see the estuary and its stream winding along the beach and into the hills, and below us on the seaward side, the flax-covered hillside sloped down to a jewel of a cove with water such a clear green that we could see fish swimming about. Above us the Pa stood out against the deep blue of a perfect day.

"Let's climb up there," Danny said, when we'd woken from our nap after too much crayfish and wine.

A faint track led steeply up through the grass and flax to an enormous egg-shaped rock perched on the very top.

I shook my head. "No, it's tapu."

"Tapu?"

"Sacred, forbidden. Maori for taboo. The highest point of the Pa is where ancient Maori would have placed the bones of their chiefs before their final burial, so their wairua—their spirits—could fly free. Dad would never let us climb further than here."

"Shame. It must be an incredible view from the top. Obviously some people climb up there. Perhaps it would be OK for me to go? I'm not Maori."

"That would be worse, silly. If you went up there from this side the spirits might throw you off, and you'd be swept into the wild sea and never be found. We can go back down to the beach and get around to the other side of the Pa. It's dramatic. A steep cliff face straight into the sea."

"Charming. Has anyone ever fallen off?"

I shuddered and nodded. "Some teenagers were up there years ago, drinking probably, and one of them slipped and fell. His body was washed back onto the beach days later. The divers had given up ever finding him."

ON A DARK NIGHT, TWO NIGHTS PAST CHRISTMAS DAY, WE dragged an old mattress and some blankets onto the beach and lay gazing up at the brilliant wash of stars saturating the Milky Way, arching across the sky. The Southern Cross hung low over the dunes to the south, marking this as home. As the moon rose, a great orange orb coming out of the sea, Danny gently stroked my hair from my face and kissed me so very very softly.

"Marry me, my Georgia."

"Oh Danny, yes, yes, I'll marry you." I felt the tears trickle down my cheeks.

"Why the tears?" Danny whispered, wiping them away with his fingers.

"Tears of pure, over-the-top happiness, silly," I sniffled, laughing at the same time. "Are you sure you're really OK about giving up New Orleans and your spoilt-boy Blues club? Giving up that offer from RCA?"

"Oh, yes, yes. This is what I want. *You* are what I want. I can sing here, anyway. I don't need N'Orleans for that."

"I don't want my career to sink yours. I promise that once I'm qualified and get some consultant experience, I'll look for a position in a big city where you can become disgustingly famous—New Orleans, New York, Chicago, or even London or Sydney. Almost anywhere would be better for your career than staying in New Zealand."

"Fiddle-de-de, I do declare you're serious," teased Danny in his best falsetto Southern Belle accent. "You could get a little ole job as a noo-rosurgeon in dem cotton fields an' makes us pots o'gold, so's I can sing dem ole blues while I'se livin' in our ole plantation mansion wit' our five comely chil'un."

"Five? Ten, by the time I'm done with you, you crazy crooner, dropping your blue jeans for any noo-rosurgeon who grovels at your feet," I laughed, as Danny wriggled out of my arms and waving his hands crazily in the air, shimmied naked down the beach.

CHAPTER 9

The house was silent when I arrived back cold and wet. Stripping off my dripping clothes I deposited them in the laundry before standing under the downstairs shower for five minutes. Dry and warm, at least on the outside, I made Adam a cup of tea and took it upstairs. The bed was empty.

Finbar, still in his pajamas, was gazing at the contents of the fridge when I returned to the kitchen. "Hi sweetheart. Checking out the breakfast options?" I tousled his already tousled hair.

Finbar jerked under my touch. "Don't."

"Sorry, Fin. I keep forgetting you're almost twelve. Where's your dad?"

Finbar pulled the butter out of the fridge and slammed the door. "He's gone to the university."

"It's Saturday. Do you think he got his days mixed up?"

"Nah. He said he had stuff to do." He dumped himself down at the breakfast bar, his back to me.

"He left you here alone?"

"Lara's here. Not that she's any use, sleeping all morning. Dad said to phone him if you didn't come home soon."

"Oh. Well, I need a jolly big breakfast. I've walked miles. Let's have a feed of bacon and eggs"—I peered in the fridge—"and potato patties with the mashed spuds left over from last night."

Finbar's hunched shoulders straightened a little. "OK. I'll have some. I'll make some toast."

"Thanks sweetheart. The aroma of bacon will soon flush Lara out of bed."

"Not likely. She won't eat fried stuff."

"Since when was Lara so picky?"

"Since ages. She thinks she'll get fat or get zits or something."

"Really? I thought she had more sense. Perhaps Adam will get home soon and he can eat Lara's share."

"Yep, whatever." Finbar turned around and my heart ached. His face was so pale. My baby, usually so happy. I reached out and drew him close and felt him soften against my breasts. "Oh Finnie," I said, his baby name escaping before I could stop it. "I'm sorry it's been so miserable around here lately."

Finbar sniffed and his body tensed. "It's OK, Mum, it's not your fault." His voice was so muffled I had to strain to make out his words.

"It *is* my fault, and I'd do anything to sort it out and get back to normal." I hugged him closer but he pulled away and looked up at me, a hunk of hair falling over his forehead.

"What's the matter with you anyway? Why aren't you operating anymore?"

"A young patient of mine died after I clipped his aneurysm and for some reason I lost my nerve after that." I struggled to sound calm.

"But you've had patients die before. You're a neurosurgeon; that's what happens. Patients sometimes die. What's so different about this patient?"

"He was a healthy young father and he didn't need to have

the aneurysm clipped at all because it had never bled. It was to prevent it from rupturing in the future. I feel bad about encouraging him to have the surgery and now there are two small children without a father." Through blurred eyes, I could see Finbar struggling not to cry.

"It'll be all right, Mum. I should have been more helpful. It must be awful. You'll get over it; you have to. You can't just not operate any more, can you?" He kicked the table leg.

My throat tightened. "You're right, sweetheart. I can't." I pulled him close again and whispered into his hair. "I'll come right soon, I promise." Reluctantly releasing him, I held his narrow shoulders. "I *am* still doing all the rest of my job, you know, so they're not going to chuck me out. Don't you go worrying about that."

"Can't you take a pill or something?"

"Oh, for a pill that would solve my problems," I said, shaking my head. "Pills can help with anxiety problems like mine for a while, but they're not a cure. I've got to work out why I've got them and do something about the cause, or they'll just keep coming back."

"But what happens to you so you can't operate? Do your hands freeze up or something?"

"Anxiety can affect people in lots of different ways, but my problem is that I had this thing called a panic attack when I was operating. It's like I suddenly couldn't breathe and I did sort of freeze. I couldn't think straight for a few minutes and then I calmed down and the panic went away. So until I'm sure that I'm not ever going to have a panic attack again, it's simply not safe for me to operate."

Finbar's smooth brow furrowed. "That sounds pretty bad. I've heard of those before. Jamie's mum has panic attacks when she has to go outside so she just stays home all the time. That won't happen to you, will it?"

"Not a chance. In fact I've only had one when I've been in theater, so it's different from people like Jamie's mum who've had panic attacks for a very long time. You're not to worry your head about me; it's my worry, not yours and Lara's. If you can put up with my moods for a bit longer and try and cheer Dad up by being your happy self, then that will be a massive help."

"OK, Mum, I'll try." He put his arms around my waist and squeezed. "I love you," he muttered.

"I love you too, sweetheart. And you know what, I reckon that's enough serious stuff for one morning. Let's start frying."

ADAM DIDN'T COME HOME UNTIL FOUR, BRINGING WITH HIM A bottle of wine, a large bag of velvety purple grapes, and my favorite blue cheese.

"Thought it was time we had a quiet pre-dinner drink and snacks," he said, bending his head and brushing my cheek with his lips. "Sorry I deserted you today. I wanted to get Monday's lecture written." Walking over to the sink he filled a glass with water and took a long drink. He stood, back to me, looking out the kitchen window. He muttered something.

"Say again? I didn't catch that."

He turned around and leaned on the bench. "I said that I thought you might need some space away from me. Was that why you went off so early this morning without even a kiss?"

"You were asleep, and I didn't want to disturb you. I wasn't to know you'd be gone when I got back. You never said you were planning to go into the university today."

"I hadn't planned it. But I can't seem to work at home anymore. Too much on my mind. Fewer distractions at work, especially in the weekend when no one much is around."

"What if I'd had to go into the hospital? It would have been unfair to count on Lara staying in all day just to mind Finbar." I heard the irritation in my voice and tried to soften my tone. "You should have called me."

"You knew where I was; I asked Finbar to tell you. All you would have had to do was phone and I'd have come home. Although why would you have to go in when you don't do on-calls any more?"

"I do have other responsibilities that might require me to go in. I just wish you'd be more communicative about your plans so we could organize our schedules better."

"Got it. Here's what I'm doing tomorrow. Mac and I are taking off into the country for a day's walk. I checked with Lara and she's going to Amber's for the day, and I'll drop Finbar off at Jack's. You do remember he's been invited to go with Jack and his dad to the cricket?"

"Yes, of course I do. Where are you walking? Can I come?" I felt a smidgeon of warmth creeping through me. I felt suddenly desperate to be out of London.

Adam walked over to the glass-fronted cupboard and took out two wine glasses. Opening the wine, he poured two glasses and handed me one. "Actually we've decided we deserve a boys-only day. There are a few things we need to vent about, and we've spent no time outside of work together for months. I thought you'd rather like to have a day for yourself with no kids or husband around. Read a novel or muck about in the garden. It would do you good."

YESTERDAY'S RAIN HAD WASHED LONDON CLEAN, CREATING ONE of those rare and almost balmy late spring days. I considered working in the garden for two seconds before writing Adam and the kids a note and grabbing a bottle of water, an apple, and my car keys.

Once out of London I opened the car window and breathed in the scented Oxfordshire air. I felt almost happy, random thoughts flicking through my mind as I meandered down narrow country lanes and through timeless thatched villages. But I missed Adam. Why couldn't we have done this together? I couldn't remember when we'd last escaped on a weekend drive without the kids. I sighed. Perhaps I shouldn't blame all our problems on my therapy. Perhaps we'd been losing the romance long before that. Work pressures, teenagers, and now these horrible panic attacks.

Drawing up at a crooked, ivy-covered pub on a village green, I took my coffee and carrot cake to the only outside table not already occupied by lazy, happy, weekenders, some with children in tow. *Adam, we used to be these people.* What happened to our pledge to spend at least one day of every weekend I wasn't on call enjoying being a family and exploring some of the beautiful spots in and out of London?

Driving on as the sun swapped its warmth for a soft glow, I felt more hopeful. Of course Sarah's right. I'll find a way to remember what happened that night. I have to. That's the only way I'll get to the bottom of these panic attacks. And I owe it to Lara. Adam and Finbar as well. They're all suffering because of my fear. Why is it so hard to go deeper? It was all so long ago. It's not as if I'm a young woman whose lover has just died. Surely I'm secure enough now to deal with the truth, whatever it is? Adam and I have to find a way to talk again. Really talk. And being miles out of London on a Sunday evening isn't a good start.

I drew over and stopped on the side of the road and pulled out my mobile. Adam answered after the third ring.

"Adam here." He sounded grumpy.

"Hi love. Did you have a good day? I've had such a lovely drive, but it would have been more fun if you'd been with me."

" We had a magnificent walk. We're going to do it more often. We'd forgotten how much we enjoyed each other's company."

"Oh. That's great. Are the kids home?"

"It's seven o'clock, Georgia. Of course they're home. Where are you?"

"On my way. I'll be back in an hour at the most."

"If you're going to be that long, perhaps you'd better get yourself something to eat on the way. The kids and I are having dinner. We're all tired."

My eagerness to rush home and explain to Adam how much I loved him evaporated, and on the outskirts of London I found another pub and tried to bury my disappointment with a Caesar Salad and a small glass of wine. As the rumble of conversation and the patter of a TV sports commentator merged into the background, I forced myself to think about Danny and what happened that night. Perhaps if I prepared myself gradually, tomorrow I'd be able to talk to Sarah about it without risking another panic attack? Perhaps I'd finally remember what happened.

Neither Danny nor I had, as yet, told our families about our relationship. We figured we needed this time on Great Barrier to get to know each other first. All Danny's parents knew was that he was traveling around New Zealand's North Island before going to Queenstown.

Danny reckoned his folks would be over-the-moon about him marrying a Kiwi girl and staying in New Zealand. He booked his flight to Queenstown for January 3rd. He'd surprise them and then break the exciting news; tell them they were going to have a Kiwi daughter-in-law and he'd be staying in New Zealand. "Mum will love that," he said. "N'Orleans is too far away for her."

The plan was that when Danny returned to the island we'd call my parents—they weren't due back from Australia until March—and give them the happy news. About our marriage plans, that is, not about the baby, if my suspicions turned out to be right. I'd had sore boobs and some nausea for a week, and had finally checked my dates and realized I'd not had a period since our romantic roll in the sand on Cape Cod—the only time we'd indulged in unprotected sex, for heaven's sake. My periods had never been very regular and I'd been too crazily happy to worry. Just put it down to my stress levels at the end of my Mass General Residency. I was dying to tell Danny, but I wanted to be absolutely sure first. What if he thought it was too soon? It *was* too soon, but we'd manage. Danny would see that. The island doctor was away for Christmas and New Year, but I'd managed to make an appointment to see him the day he got back, a few days after Danny flew out. By the time he got back from seeing his parents I'd know for sure. That's when I'd tell him.

Danny's excitement at being back in Queenstown after so long away was palpable when I phoned him on the night he arrived—no easy task as the public phone box was a thirty minute walk away from our house.

"I haven't told them yet," he said, and my heart slowed down. "They're so excited to see me I thought I'd spin it out a bit. Tell them tomorrow after I make them pancakes for breakfast. Then I might come home early. I miss you already."

"Oh, I wish you could," I said. "But you have to stay a little longer; it would be unkind to leave so soon when your family hasn't seen you for so long. We'll have the rest of our lives to celebrate."

"The rest of our lives, oh oh the rest of our lives..." Danny crooned into the phone, and I enjoyed the little shiver of pleasure that flicked up my spine. Even when he was fooling around, his voice touched something sensual inside me.

But when I phoned the next night, my hands shaking a little as I dialed the number, there was no reply. Perhaps they'd all gone out to celebrate their son's forthcoming marriage? I tried again the next morning and again was too shy to leave a message. Finally, that evening, Danny's brother John answered. He told me that Danny had flown to Nelson to keep an old school friend company while he nursed his dying father. I stood in the phone box almost mute with disappointment. When I asked for Danny's friend's phone number, John was unable to oblige. Danny, he pointed out, was in the habit of not telling them where he was. Their parents, John added, had also gone away on a fishing trip. Obviously John had no clue about Danny and me. Had he even told his parents?

And now seven days had passed and still no word from him. I was having a hard time forgiving him for his silence. How could he be so thoughtless and not at least leave a phone contact? I felt some empathy with his parents being kept in the dark about his whereabouts when he was on Great Barrier Island.

ON THE ISLAND THE WEATHER WAS DRAINING. USUALLY WE didn't get this humid wild northeasterly weather until February, when cyclones haunted the Pacific. But this cyclone was early, hitting the Cook Islands, causing havoc there, and then whipping up the sea as far away as New Zealand. On Saturday, after two days of dense sea mist hanging low over the hills, it dropped its weather bomb, hitting Great Barrier Island with gale-force winds and torrential rain. According to the news on my temperamental battery-driven radio, nearly fifteen centimeters of water fell on the Barrier in forty-eight hours. I welcomed the storm; it fitted my mood just fine.

Late that afternoon I pulled on my running gear and took off along the beach. The rain had finally eased off, and the light drizzle and still strong winds cooled my hot skin as I ran in my bare feet, dodging the flotsam and jetsam that littered the sand, and exhilarated by the massive surf crashing onto the foam-covered shore. An hour later, wet with rain and sweat, I puffed back up the sand dunes. The house in its little hollow was bathed in a strange yellow glow as the sun, now low in the sky, tried to penetrate the racing storm clouds. As I reached the deck I heard a *creak, creak, creak,* that didn't seem part of the storm. Then I saw him, moving back and forth in the old rocking chair in the far dim corner of the deck, his red hair luminous in the eerie light.

I covered the distance between us in a millisecond. "Danny. Darling, thank heaven you're back. I've been out of my mind with worry. Why didn't you write or leave your phone number so I could call you?" Relief almost choking me, I dropped to my knees beside the chair and peered into Danny's face. Leaning over to kiss him I saw his eyes close and felt his cold lips on mine. Then I was falling back as his head jerked to the side and his hands pushed on my shoulders.

"No Georgia, don't," he rasped. "We have to talk."

I scrambled back to my knees, my heart pounding. "What's wrong? Are you hurt? Danny, you're saturated." I grabbed his cold hands. "Come inside, you're shivering. However did you get here in this storm?"

Danny didn't speak as I led him inside. Pulling off his sodden anorak, I wrapped a throw around his shaking shoulders as he sank on the couch. "What you need is a good fire and a hot drink," I said, trying to stifle the terror that was building in my chest. I could hear his teeth rattling as I laid paper and kindling haphazardly in the fireplace. The fire finally began crackling and I slid a kettle on the hob, and then sat close beside him. "Please Danny—darling, tell me what's wrong."

Danny shook his head and a strand of wet hair slapped my face. "I don't know how to tell you. Georgia, I'm sorry I've been off the radar. It's taken me so long to come because I didn't know how to tell you. And then of course I picked the worst weekend in living memory to get the ferry. It was so bloody rough even I was sick. Everyone was sick. I thought we'd never make it."

I put my hand on his and he shook it off, pulling the throw closer around him. "I managed to hitch a ride from the wharf across the island, but I got dropped off in Claris and had to slog the rest of the way in the pouring rain."

"Why didn't you let me know you were coming so I could pick you up?"

"How the hell could I do that? Mental telepathy?"

"Well, perhaps if you'd left a contact number for me to call, we could have stayed in touch."

"I wasn't in any fit state to talk to you, and I only got the guts up yesterday to come over here."

"What is it? What's happened?" My voice came out in a whisper.

"I'm sorry Georgia." Danny got up and moved away, his back to me.

"What? What are you sorry about?" My voice rose to a squeak.

"I think we should put off our marriage for a while," he said.

"What did you say?"

Danny turned around, his silhouette dark against the last of the light filtering through the window. "I can't…" His voice cracked, and I almost fell in my desperation to get to him. His hands went up, palms towards me. "Don't make it harder, Georgia. I've decided it's too soon for me. I need to be sure. I can't marry you, not yet."

CHAPTER 10

I looked over at the door, wishing I were on the other side of it. I glanced at my watch. "Looks like my time's almost up. You've given me a lot to think about."

Sarah got out of her chair and stretched. "This session has been tough, but you've come a long way."

"Doesn't seem like it. I feel as if I'm getting worse, not better."

"Today you talked about your painful breakup with Danny without any sign of a panic attack."

"Perhaps that's because I spent most of the weekend thinking about it."

"That's what I meant when I said a lot of the work of therapy is done between sessions. Having the courage to quietly walk yourself through part of that terrible night primed your memory so that today you were able to recall a little more. Before I see you again I hope you can go even further. You'll have extra time because I have to leave London and I won't be back until the middle of next week. I'm going to my granddaughter's birthday." Sarah smiled. "Turning five is pretty special."

"That'll be fun. Pin the tail on the donkey, pass the parcel.

I remember it well. Seems like a lifetime ago when our two were that age." I swallowed a sudden urge to weep.

"Wednesday next week then, same time. I'll give you a colleague's number in case you need an emergency session while I'm gone."

"I won't need that. I'm not about to bop myself off."

"I want you to have Jasmine's number anyway, for my own peace of mind. You have plenty of thinking to do before our next session, not least about why you find these sessions difficult to keep sometimes."

"I thought we'd covered that today? I won't cancel again."

"That's good to hear. Talk to Adam. Having his understanding and support is what you need before you can make peace with your past."

"Believe me, I'm going to do everything in my power to make it up to him and the kids. I can't live like this. None of us can."

FRIDAY, AND I FELT EMPTIED OUT. BENDING OVER BACKWARDS to please Adam hadn't worked. He seemed to think he could stay longer at the university now that I was able to spend more time at home. His excuse that he had an urgent research grant application to write on top of a heavy teaching load seemed to me just that, an excuse. The kids were lost as well without Adam's calming presence—Finbar shutting himself in his room as soon as he got home from school and Lara rarely home.

I made it out of the rain and into the door by five o'clock, with a weekend's worth of everyone's favorite food weighing me down: two varieties of pasta for Lara, spicy spare ribs for Finbar, and exorbitantly fresh scallops for Adam. The house felt forlorn. In the kitchen the only bright point was the light flashing on the phone. Just one message.

"Me here. I'm having a few drinks with some friends so I might be a bit late home tonight. Lara, you're in charge of Finbar 'til your mother gets home. If you need me for anything, call me on my mobile." That was it. No message of affection, even for his children. How the hell could I talk to him about my last session with Sarah if he was never home?

Dumping the groceries on the kitchen bench and my bag in the hallway, I dragged myself up the stairs. Lara's door was wide open, her unmade bed and a chair piled with clothes looking like props for a crime drama. No Lara. Even her computer looked despondent, sitting silently on her paper-strewn desk, its black face filmed by a layer of dust. I knocked on the opposite door, pushing it open to Finbar's grunt. He was crouched over his laptop like a little old man. I laid my hand on his back. "What are you working on? Stop stooping like that; you'll end up with a hunchback."

"Hi Mum." He straightened up. "I need a stand to sit my laptop on. Max has got one and it's ace. But then I'll need a separate keyboard and mouse as well." He let out a sigh worthy of a film contract.

He and Lara should join forces. They might come up with the next award-winning TV crime series. "That's an excellent idea," I managed, keeping the smile off my face. "How much will they cost do you think?"

"I dunno. A hundred bucks probably."

His gloomy tone made me want to laugh and weep at the same time. Still my kid. "Check it out. I'll pay for them. Cheaper than paying to have your spine straightened later."

Finbar twisted around, his grin transforming him into a junior version of Adam. I returned his High Five and felt a smidgeon better.

"Do you know where Lara is?"

"Nope. She hasn't come home while I've been here. I think she's got netball practice today."

"I'd forgotten. Shouldn't she be back by now?"

"Perhaps she's gone to Amber's. She probably told Dad."

I frowned. Damn Adam, leaving Finbar alone like this. "Didn't you hear the phone? Your father left a message on the answer machine to say he'd be late home. He'd obviously forgotten Lara wouldn't be straight home after school."

"Oh. I did hear it ring but by the time I get downstairs it always stops so I don't bother. Can we get pizza for dinner?"

"I've bought some scallops for a seafood pasta. Will that do?"

"Yum."

Finbar's grin worked its magic again, and I smiled. "Let's hope your dad gets home soon. Scallops are his top favorite."

Finbar's grin disappeared and a crease appeared between his fair eyebrows. "I could make an apple crumble for pudding if you like? Dad loves that."

"That's a lovely offer, sweetheart. Let's hope Lara appears soon." I bent over quickly so Finbar wouldn't spot the moisture in my eyes, and kissed the top of his head. The slightly sweaty smell of his thick hair tickled my nose and I straightened up, my tear ducts behaving themselves again.

"I quite like cooking actually," Finbar said, turning off his computer. "Lara's useless. All she can make is toast."

"I tell you what, if she appears in time to eat our efforts, she can clean up afterwards."

I EYED THE TABLE SET FOR FOUR, COMPLETE WITH FLOWERS and candles, their flickering lights sparking off our best crystal wine glasses. "Where are they? So much for our nice dinner. We'd better go ahead without them."

I jumped as the backdoor slammed and Lara burst into the room, her face flushed from the cold night air.

"Lara, thank goodness. Where have you been?" The ball

of tension in my chest shrunk a little. "Look at the time; it's almost eight o'clock."

"What's it to you? I'm not a kid. I don't have to get your permission just because I'm a bit later home than usual." Lara dropped her bag and jacket on the floor.

"If you don't want to be treated like a child, stop behaving like one. You know you should call home if you're going to be late. Why couldn't we get you on your mobile?"

"So the battery was flat; it does happen occasionally, you know."

My relief morphed into annoyance. "I've been phoning around your friends to try and track you down. I was beginning to think you must have been in an accident." I tried and failed to keep my voice level.

"Jeez, Mum, you're tragic. How could you? How totally embarrassing." Lara's pretty face was distorted with rage. "Where's Dad?"

"He's out with friends. He won't be very pleased when he finds out what time you got home."

"He won't care. He's probably out enjoying himself with his Irish girlfriend."

"Shut up Lara." Finbar glared at his sister.

"Shut up yourself you little snot. What would you know?"

"That's enough," I said, my words about as effective as my parenting skills.

"Julia, Julia," said Lara in a singsong voice.

"Lara," I warned, "Stop teasing Finbar. Adam's out with friends from work."

"Yeah, I bet. Julia was panting to go out with him when she was around here the other day."

"Don't take any notice of her, Mum," Finbar said, kicking the rocking chair and sending it into a frenzy. "Julia's a friend of Sonja and Mike's. She gave Dad a ride home from work, that's all. She came in to borrow a book from him." He stuck his tongue out at Lara. "She's nice."

"Just because she pretended to like your childish little computer game," Lara sneered.

"It is *not* childish." Finbar gave his sister a shove. "Lots of adults all over the world play it, so there."

"Enough," I snapped. "Quiet, the pair of you."

Lara collapsed into the rocking chair, and as Finbar turned away I saw his mouth wobbling.

"So where have you been, Lara?" I repeated. My head was swirling with images of Julia in her mink.

"Out with friends that you don't know. And there's no way you're going to know them either. I'm not having you phoning them every time I'm five minutes late." Lara narrowed her eyes as she stared at me.

I felt the blood drain from my face as I looked back at her, this stranger who vaguely resembled my daughter. "Don't speak to me like that, and apologize to Finbar for being so mean."

Lara got up and pushed past me, her face flushed. "I will not, and you can't make me."

"In that case, go to your room and stay there until you decide to apologize to both of us. And until you do, you can forget about going out in the weekend."

Lara flung herself around and screamed in my face, "Why should I apologize to you? You're the one who should be sorry." She stamped her foot. "I've had it up to here with you and Dad and your stupid problems. Why should I have to hang around and put up with your fucking moods?"

Jamming my hands in my pockets, I counted silently to ten before I dared speak. "I'm unhappy you feel like that, Lara, and I know things have been difficult around here. But that doesn't excuse your rudeness, and it doesn't mean that you can stay out whenever you want without our permission. Surely you can see you're only making things worse?"

"Since when did it matter what *I* did? It's not going to

make any difference to you and Dad, so why can't I get out of your hair and leave you to work out your own shit?"

"Perhaps you could show a little understanding. What we need from you now is love, not aggravation," I said, forcing my tone down a notch or two.

"Ha, ha. Don't see much understanding and love between you two. No wonder Dad doesn't want to hang around here anymore. If you're going to split up, I don't know why you don't get on with it and stop drawing out the agony."

A ball of nausea jammed in my throat. "Why do you say that? We're not splitting up."

"Why are you having therapy then?"

"You know why. I'm trying to get over some anxiety attacks."

"I thought Dad was a shit-hot psychologist? Why doesn't he sort you out?"

"This is getting us nowhere, Lara. I think you'd better go and cool off in your room. Finbar can bring you up some dinner."

"Yes, go on Lara. I'll bring you some tucker in a bit," Finbar said.

"Don't worry, I'm going. And forget the food—I couldn't eat it if it were the last meal on the planet," Lara hissed, disappearing up the stairs.

I sank down on the couch, my whole body shaking.

Finbar patted my arm. "You OK, Mum?"

"Not really, but thanks sweetheart." I covered his hand with mine. "I'm sorry you had to witness all that."

"Don't take any notice of Lara, Mum. It hasn't been as bad as all that. She's just a drama queen but she'll get over it."

"Perhaps, but it's not OK that she even *thinks* that things are so bad between us that we might split up. Do you think that as well?" I swallowed but it didn't sooth my need to vomit.

"No, not really, though how would I know? We're just not used to you two bickering and not talking about stuff."

"Oh Finnie, I'm sorry. I'll talk to Adam tonight. We've got to get past this; it's not fair on you two."

The phone shrilled and Finbar picked it up. I listened to his brief answers, my stomach churning.

"But Mum's made a special dinner and we're waiting for you." Silence while Adam said something else. "Are you sure you don't want to talk to Mum? She's right here." More silence. "OK. I'll tell her. Bye Dad."

Finbar's voice was gloomy. "Dad said he was sorry but something came up that he really had to deal with tonight, and he can't be home for dinner. He said not to wait up for him."

I sat very still, trying to compose myself. "Oh well, all the more for us! Where was he?"

"He didn't say, but I think he might have been in the car— his voice was breaking up a bit. He did sound a bit weird, though."

"What do you mean, weird?"

"I don't know; a bit upset, I suppose. Perhaps you could phone him back?"

"No, I don't think so," I said, my voice strangled by the ache in my throat. "I hope he's OK."

"He will be, Mum. He's probably got some old meeting or something. Can we eat now?"

"Yes, let's pig out!" I grinned at him, wondering how I would swallow even a scallop without choking.

I'D GIVEN UP TRYING TO READ HOURS AGO. SLUMPED IN THE big chair by the kitchen window I listened to the rain pouring down outside the dark room and fought my irrational thoughts of car crashes or affairs with Julia and her laughing

Irish eyes. The clock ticked towards midnight. Why hadn't he phoned?

When at last I heard his key in the lock I froze, my heart thumping, as Adam tiptoed into the kitchen, his shoes in his hand.

"Where have you been? I've been worried about you." My voice echoed harshly in the dark space.

Adam jumped, his shoes crashing to the floor. "Christ, you gave me a fright. What are you doing sitting in the dark?"

"Waiting for you."

"I left a message on the answer machine, *and* I phoned, so I don't know why you were worried," Adam shot back.

"You didn't bother to say who you went out with, so anything could have happened to you and we wouldn't know where to look or who to call."

"Come off it, Georgia. You just want to control everything I do. One rule for the goose and another for the gander. You are forever disappearing for hours without telling me, and if *I* question *you*, it's apparently me just hassling you again. Now you know what it feels like," Adam said, his low voice not disguising his fury.

I thought about getting up but my limbs were too heavy. "What am I meant to do; just go to bed and see you in the morning, all forgiven?"

"That's apparently what I'm meant to do, so why not you?" Adam said. "And what do you mean, forgiven? What do you have to forgive me for? *I've* done nothing wrong."

"Who *were* you with tonight?"

"What's that got to do with you?" Adam's voice rose.

"It's got everything to do with me, if you insist on keeping it a secret." Hauling my miserable body out of the chair I reached over to switch the light on. The glare was blinding and Adam's face loomed white, raindrops sparking off his hair and raincoat.

"I don't see that it's any of your business who my friends

are. I do have some friends of my own, you know," he said, two spots of red burnt into his cheeks.

I collapsed back in the chair. "Christ, Adam, let's stop this. Lara's being a nightmare. This tension between us isn't helping her or Finbar."

"Of course it's bloody not. But it's hardly my fault. You're the one who comes home from therapy looking like hell and pushing me away."

"I don't push you away. I've been trying to talk to you all week but you've been so distant I couldn't."

"Distant? What about you? We haven't made love in weeks. I can't remember the last time you actually kissed me. That feels as if you're pushing me away. And Lara is struggling with the whole Danny business. I overheard her talking on her phone to someone—one of her girlfriends I suppose— about him the other day; saying something about how she was thinking of leaving school and going to New Orleans to find her long-lost family."

"Oh god. What did you say to her?"

Adam looked at me, his face shadowed with something that looked almost like dislike. "Nothing. I didn't want her screaming at me about listening in on her private conversations. You need to talk to her. Tell her something, anything to give her some hope that you're on her side. That you haven't decided to keep her in the dark forever."

"Even in therapy it's hard to talk about what I'm remembering. Given the way Lara's behaving, how can I talk to her?" I gripped the arm of my chair. "I don't know what else I can do to help her understand that I'm doing my bloody best."

"Well, nor do I. But if you don't do something soon, I don't know what Lara will do. I wouldn't put it past her to leave school as soon as she can and go to New Orleans."

"Shit. Did you know that she thinks we're splitting up? How can she think that? Are we that bad?" I looked up at

Adam, still standing, still a long way from me. "Is that why you stayed out so late tonight?"

Adam was silent.

"Tell me. Is that why you were out so long? Because you can't stomach being here with me?"

"I'm lonely. I wanted to feel as if someone cared about me again." Adam's voice was too quiet.

"What do you mean? Who were you with?"

Adam moved over to the chair opposite me and sat down, his head in his hands.

"Tell me."

"It doesn't matter. I'm tired. I'm going to bed."

"You were out with Julia, weren't you?" My voice came out in a whisper, and at first I thought Adam hadn't heard me, but then he looked up and I saw his guilt.

"How could you? How could you?"

"It was nothing. Just a few drinks and dinner, that's all. I needed someone to talk to."

"But her? You know how I feel about her."

"You don't even know her. You've met her once. You refused to go to dinner at their place. You've refused to make any attempt to get to know her and Will. Christ, we don't see any of our friends any more. Julia is a nice person. She just wants to help. At least she cares about me."

"And I suppose Will is happy about that," I hissed, tears hot on my cheeks.

"Will had to go back to Ireland for a couple of weeks and Julia's lonely, that's all."

"I bet. She's been after you since the first moment she set eyes on you. Christ, it's after one in the morning, Adam. What have you really been doing? Dinner can't have lasted that long."

"We…we talked, that's all."

"Talked in bed you mean." My voice sounded as if it were

coming from someone else. Someone I didn't want to be. "How could you?"

"We talked, that's all." Adam's face crumpled and my anger was suddenly gone, replaced by a fatigue so dense I thought I might faint.

"I'm so miserable, Georgia. Nothing I do seems to help you. I want us to be like we were but I've almost given up hope. And all Lara wants is to find out about her real father. I'm no use to her either."

"Adam, I'm sorry. Lara loves you; you know that. Danny is nothing to do with that."

"That's not how it feels. I'm worried about her; she's like a different kid and I'm not sure you've even noticed."

"Don't be so cruel. I'm worried sick about her too. I'm doing my best to get through this. It's much harder on me than you. You've still got your job and your pride at least. I've got nothing left. Just guilt that everything is my fault."

Adam stood up and I looked up at him. His face was white. "That's what I mean. You're lost in self-pity. Poor you; no job, no pride. That's all that seems to matter to you. You can't stand the thought that people think you're a failure; that you're no longer the amazing neurosurgeon smashing through all the glass ceilings. Is that really what's most important to you? Try thinking about us for a change."

"Shush, keep your voice down." My face was hot. "The kids will hear us."

"Don't tell me to shush. You shush."

"I'm going to bed. Perhaps you'd better sleep in the guest room and we'll talk in the morning when we've calmed down." I got up, my heart hammering, and started for the door.

"I am attracted to Julia, damn it, and I'm beginning to wish I had slept with her."

I turned around, my legs shaking. "What are you saying?" I said, my voice rising.

"You don't want me and she does, that's what I'm saying. You don't want to make love any more and I'm bloody frustrated, that's what I'm saying. I'm surprised you even care."

"Of course I care. I love you, you stupid man. How can you think I don't?" I lost control of my voice as I flung myself at Adam, smashing my fists on his chest.

He grabbed my wrists and I stood still, my words ringing in my head. Adam's shoulders slumped and he let me go and turned towards the door. "When you've sorted yourself out and can see past your own self-pity, perhaps we'll be able to get through this. I don't know." He put his hand on the door handle and stumbled back as the door opened in his face.

Lara stood there, hunched in her coat, her red hair a tangle about her tear-streaked face, her complexion almost green in the harsh light. "Stop it, you two, stop it, stop it," she wailed, tears streaming from her swollen eyes. I collided with Adam as I rushed towards her. Lara waved us violently away, screaming in our faces. "How can you hate each other so much? Just shut up and stop fighting all the time. How do you think you make us feel? We're sick of it."

"Lara, sweetheart, I'm sorry," I said. "We'll stop, I promise. You know we love you; we didn't mean you to hear us fighting."

"You don't act like you love us and you don't love Dad any more, so don't try to tell me you do," Lara sobbed. "Finbar's locked himself in his room and won't let me in. I could hear him crying."

"I'll go and see him, sweetheart. I'm so sorry." I touched her arm. "We won't argue any more."

"Come on Lara, let's all calm down and talk about this," Adam said, pulling us both into the room.

Like a punch to my diaphragm, the panic started and I bent double, forcing myself to breathe slowly. I felt Adam's hand on my arm and desperately tried to ignore the pounding in my head. "It's my fault," I gasped. "We were fine before I started having therapy." I heard my own rasping breath and grabbed the doorframe. Lara was staring at me, eyes wide. I wanted so much to hold her, but the distance between us was too far.

"You've been like this for ever, Mum. Why don't you change your therapist? Find one who has some clues?" Lara swiped at her eyes. "I'm never going to find out what happened to my father, am I? He could have killed himself for all I know. He could have been murdered, and nobody cared. You don't care. Nobody cares."

My grasp on the doorframe weakened and I slid down until I was sitting on the floor. Adam's voice cut through me and I pulled myself back up.

"Lara, get a grip on yourself. That was cruel. If it weren't for your sudden great need to find out about Danny, your mother wouldn't be in the state she's in."

"Adam, please don't. It's not Lara's fault. She needs to know. I understand that. I just don't know how I'm going to get my bloody memory back. Not by having these stupid panic attacks, that's for sure." My head felt as if it was going to ignite, but my rapid heartbeat was anger now, not panic. Anger at myself.

Adam grabbed my arms and I winced. He loosened his grip, the color draining from his face. "I thought you were going to crash down again. I didn't mean to hurt you. I'm sorry love."

The endearment wiped out my anger and I closed my eyes. *Re-lax, re-lax, re-lax.* Sarah's lilting Welsh voice played in my head and my body slowly obeyed. A stray thought jumped into my head: *At least my damn therapy has been some use.*

Lara pushed past me and Adam grabbed her coat sleeve. "Come on Lara, lighten up. Let's all sit down and talk about this more calmly."

Lara shoved his hand away.

"You're freezing, and so am I. Go and get yourself back

into bed, and I'll make some hot chocolate for us all." His voice was pleading now.

"No, I'm out of here. I've had it with you two screaming at each other."

"Please Lara, have some sense," Adam said. "You can't go out at this time of night. And it's pouring with rain."

"Yes I can, and you can't stop me. I phoned Selina, and she and Tony are coming to pick me up, so there!" On cue a loud horn sounded. "That's them, so I'm gone." She flounced across the room, her frayed designer jeans sticking out from under her navy coat, laces on her sneakers undone, and her bag, stuffed full of something, slung over her shoulder.

"No Lara. This is ridiculous." Adam grasped at the air as she bolted for the door.

"Don't worry about me; I can take care of myself. I'm staying at Selina's tonight, so don't wait up." The door banged behind her and we heard her footsteps down the hall and the front door opening and slamming shut.

"Now what do we do?" Adam groaned. "Who the hell is Selina?"

"I think she's a girl she goes skating with. I've never met her, but I've heard Lara talking to her on the phone. I don't know who this Tony is though." I shuddered as I heard an engine roar into life and the screech of wheels on wet tarmac.

"Don't you even have a phone number for this Selina?"

"No, I don't. Do you?" I said, barely recognizing my own voice. "You could try ringing Lara on her mobile, but I doubt she'll answer. "

"I suppose it's all my fault that she's out tearing around in a hot rod, angry and upset, with kids we don't know and who are probably high or drunk or both?"

"Of course I don't think it's your fault. I'm sorry I yelled at you, but if you hadn't spent the night with bloody Julia then we wouldn't have got into this shouting match."

"I don't recall shouting. Perhaps you would like to go and

make sure our son's all right, and hasn't escaped out the window." Adam went over to the sink and filled a glass with water. "I'm going to bed."

I collapsed on the couch, burying my head in my hands. I felt Adam's hand on my shoulder.

"Come to bed, Georgia. We're too exhausted to sort anything out tonight."

I looked at him, unable for a moment to speak, my anger gone. I wanted to touch his face. "I'm sorry, sorry, sorry. I wish I'd never waited up for you." I screwed tight my eyes and then opened them again. "Did you sleep with Julia?"

"Oh Georgia, no, of course I didn't," Adam said. "We'll sort it out. Just let me in more."

"I will, I'll try. I'll be better, I promise. I can't keep putting us through this. Christ, Adam, Lara can't stand being near us. Our own daughter. How could we let it get to this? What if something happens to her tonight with this Tony?" I stared at Adam and saw a flash of my own fear reflected in his eyes. Then he shook his head.

"Lara will be fine, the little minx. You go and check on Finbar, and then let's get to bed. I think you need a long cuddle."

My eyes filled. "Yes please."

CHAPTER 11

I'm being stuffed into a dark place. A wooden coffin. Bang, bang, bang— my heart is pounding through me. Shrieking forms staring in, Adam and Lara above me, faces distorted, crying, screaming, pressing me down, down, into the deep hole. Dank wet smell, death, blood. My hands, forcing a body into the coffin. Falling onto two bodies, white and cold, their red hair flying in my face and wrapping around my arms, pulling me in. The lid closing over me, darkness, bang, bang, bang, nails driving into the coffin lid. Push on the lid, must have air, light, suffocating. Bang, bang, bang. Hands grabbing me, shaking me. Adam's voice.

My eyes snapped open and I sat up abruptly, my heart slowly slowing as I took in the familiar shapes of our bedroom. The rain was no longer drumming on the roof and I shook my head to drive out the nightmare.

Adam jerked beside me. "What's that? Hell, it's someone banging on the door."

I turned and saw his face in the streetlight glaring through a crack in the curtains. He was shoving the covers back and reaching for his dressing gown.

My voice came out in a whisper. "Who can it be? It's three

in the morning." The events of last night were vibrating in my head.

"It'll be Lara. She probably forgot her keys."

"Do you think so? Adam, be careful." I was still whispering. "What if it isn't?"

"A burglar is hardly going to knock on the door, silly." Adam was already out in the passage and stumbling down the stairs.

I knew this wasn't Lara returning, but something much worse. My heart hammering, I clung to the bannister as Adam flicked the hall light on and fumbled with the lock on the front door. The banging stopped as he pulled the door open and exposed two cops standing under the porch light. The thought flashed through my mind that we were in a cheap TV drama. The image intensified as the taller one whipped out his ID and held it up for Adam to inspect.

"We're the police." His voice was loud and he shoved his ID card out of sight. "Is this the Grayson residence?" he said, his voice lower.

"Come in," Adam said.

How normal he sounds.

"I'm Adam Grayson."

The cops entered, wiping their shoes vigorously on the doormat.

I was beside Adam. "What is it?" My voice was trembling. "It's Lara, isn't it? Something's happened to her."

The woman cop touched my arm. "Mrs. Grayson?"

I nodded, mute with fear.

"I'm PC Kathy Marsh, and this is PC Neville Mason. Let's all sit down. I'm afraid we have something to tell you."

I felt Adam's arm on my back, guiding me into the family room. My body shaking in my thin nightgown I sat down, grabbing Adam's hand as he sat beside me. As if from far away, I heard the man say, "Is Lara your daughter?"

I heard a gasp—my own—and Adam's nails bit into my

hand. I nodded again and concentrated on the cop's mouth, willing her to tell us that Lara had been taken into the station because she was drunk, or drugged, or had robbed a bank. Anything at all, as long as it wasn't what I knew it was, and had known since I first heard the banging on the door.

"Yes, yes, Lara is our daughter." Adam's voice sent shivers through me.

"I'm afraid she's been in an accident…"

My mind went blank as the officer continued, "She has a head injury and some other injuries, and she's been taken to City Hospital."

Finbar was beside me on the couch and I hugged him close with my other arm. Adam was shaking so hard the couch was trembling. "How bad is she?" I heard him ask. "Is she going to… to be all right?"

"I'm sorry, Mr. Grayson, we don't have any details. She was unconscious, but that doesn't mean anything much until they can check her over properly. We can take you to the hospital now, but you should get some clothes on and a coat. It's cold outside."

"Yes," said Adam. "Clothes and a coat."

"Mum, she'll wake up soon, won't she?"

I turned to Finbar, my hand coming up to stroke his cheek. *His skin looks almost green.* "She has to be all right, Finbar. You know Lara, she's a fighter." I concentrated on speaking calmly.

"But if she has a head injury, you'll be able to fix her. You know more about head injuries than anyone." Finbar's voice sounded doubtful.

I gave him a little push. "Go up and get dressed and Dad and I'll come up in a minute." I turned to the police, for a second my heart going out to them as they stood silent, bereft of the right words, watching another family struggle as their lives changed in a moment. How well I knew that feeling. Somehow seeing their stricken faces clicked me into another gear. "I'm a neurosurgeon at City Hospital, so the sooner I get there the better."

"That *is* good," said the woman cop—I had no idea what she'd said her name was. "You'll be able to find out what's happening much more quickly than most people could."

"Has she been taken to A & E?" I was in surgeon mode.

"I'm not sure. Would you like me to see if I can find out?"

"No. I'll phone in myself." I realized I was still holding Adam's hand and let it go. "Adam, come on, we need to get dressed and you can get the car out while I'm phoning the hospital."

"Would you like us to drive you, Doctor?"

"That would be good, I suppose. You might get there faster than we could." As I followed Adam to the stairs it occurred to me they hadn't said what sort of accident it was. I'd assumed it was a car accident, but is that what they'd actually said? Adam had disappeared into our bedroom. I turned back to the police. "Was it a car accident? Who was driving? Were there any others involved?"

"It was a head-on collision with a lamp-post. The car seems to have skidded out of control on a corner on these wet roads. Fortunately there wasn't another vehicle involved, but I'm afraid the driver didn't make it."

I sank down on the stairs, bile filling my mouth. "God, who was the driver, do you know?"

"I believe it was a young man called Tony Kerrigan. Did you know him?"

"No, but we knew Lara had gone out in a car with a Tony, and also a girl called Selina. Is she all right?" My voice was shaking again.

"It seems she has only a few bruises. She identified the others in the car. Your daughter was in the front passenger's seat, and with the head-on collision the two front seats took most of the impact."

"Did they have seat belts on? Airbags?" I was desperate for some magical mitigating factor that would save Lara's brain.

"Your daughter and the girl in the back were belted in, but the driver wasn't. And the car was an old one and didn't have airbags. This must be dreadful for you, Mrs. Gray… Dr. Grayson. Teenagers will be teenagers, but it doesn't make it any easier."

"I suppose they were drunk as well?" I said, already knowing the answer. *This is happening to us, to us.*

"We don't have that information yet. They'll test their blood-alcohol levels at the hospital."

And at post-mortem. I silently thanked the gods for Lara's unthinking action to belt up, ingrained into her from birth.

Adam and Finbar were coming down the stairs, coats on, and Adam was holding his mobile out to me.

"Hurry up and ring the hospital and get dressed. We have to go." His voice was under control but his hand shook as I took the phone.

AS WE PUSHED THROUGH THE MASSIVE DOUBLE DOORS THAT led into A & E, I saw a familiar figure striding along in front of us. Accelerating my already rapid pace, I caught up with the tall man who glanced at me in surprise, and, without slowing, spoke to me. "Georgia, what are you doing here?"

"Lara's been brought in; she was in a car accident and has a head injury. Is that why you're here?" My words came out in a rush.

"I didn't realize. Hell, Georgia, that's rough," said David. "I've only got here myself. I haven't seen her yet, but unless there's been another accident, I suppose it must be her."

"I haven't seen her either. I'm glad you're on, David. I would have called you in anyway if there were any problems. I don't want the A & E night shift messing around." I took Adam's arm as he and Finbar caught up with us.

"Hullo, Adam. Hi, Finbar," David said. "Try not to worry; Lara will probably be fine in no time."

"Why would they call you in if she is going to be fine? They only call in the neurosurgeon in the middle of the night for serious cases, surely?" Adam's voice was hoarse with fear.

"Not at all. The thing is that with a comatose patient it's difficult to tell how serious it is at first. She's probably already coming round." The usual hopeful platitudes tripped off David's tongue.

"She'll be all right, Dad, she has to be," said Finbar. Adam reached out for our son's hand, his knuckles white as he gripped it.

Three silent men occupied the waiting area, identifiable as motorbike riders by their black leather pants and jackets and the crash helmets by their chairs. I steered my own family towards a door marked STAFF ONLY off the public waiting room. "You'll be better in here. I'll go with David and see what's happening. I'll be back as soon as possible." I brushed Adam's cheek with my lips and smiled at my son, trying so hard to be brave. "Sweetheart, why don't you make a strong cup of tea for your dad, and you should have one too. The tea things are over on the trolley."

"OK, Mum, but hurry up and see Lara. Dad and I'll be all right."

"I know you will." I kissed the top of Finbar's head before following David, who had already disappeared through another door off the public waiting area, this one with an even more daunting sign, AUTHORIZED STAFF ONLY. A nurse came towards me, obviously alerted to my presence by David.

"Dr. Grayson, over here," she said, not attempting any niceties. "Your daughter has been stabilized and we're taking her down to CT in a minute." She pulled back the flowered curtain hiding a cubicle. Between the nurses and doctors surrounding the high bed I could see Lara's body stretched out on the hard surface of the orange plastic spinal board. My gut turned over as I looked at the scene before me—my daughter's head smattered with blood, clamped in a cervical collar, and her nose and mouth covered by an oxygen mask. I took in a shaky breath. *At least she hasn't been intubated.*

An intravenous line snaked from Lara's right arm to a drip, and an oximeter was attached to her finger. Stuck to her skin above the green drape covering her from her breasts—making such small bumps in the cloth—to her upper thighs, I could see the white circular sensors leading to the cardiac monitor, broadcasting reassuringly regular blips. Extending out from the lower end of the drape was a Foley catheter, emptying into a bag swinging below the bed. I felt a fleeting relief that there was no telltale sign of blood in her urine. Shifting my gaze to Lara's left arm lying taped to her chest at a strange angle, I saw the white bone protruding from where her elbow should be. I swallowed, pushing back the taste of panic. Lara's legs extending from the drapes were smeared with blood, and a young doctor was sitting on the far side of the bed, stapling up a gash in her left thigh.

Noticing Lara's sneakers, laces still trailing, peeking out from under a muddle of clothes dumped on the floor, I grabbed the curtain and hung on. I recognized Lara's blue jersey and her frayed designer jeans, soaked in blood now, with jagged edges denoting the path of the sharp scissors that had cut them from her slim frame. Beside them lay her bikini pants, cut open at the seams, looking ridiculously small and out of place on the cold green tiles, but thankfully with no crimson spattering their pure white.

Dragging my eyes back to the bed I watched as David checked Lara's pupils. The nurse was reciting her vitals: Pulse, BP, oxygen sat— I strained to hear but my head was buzzing and the numbers made no sense. I found myself beside David and managed to croak, "How is she?"

He didn't turn from his task but answered me calmly. "She's doing well; her pupils are a bit sluggish but reacting to light and there's no airway obstruction. Nurse, can you repeat her other vitals for Dr. Grayson?"

"Oxygen sat ninety-eight percent, BP one twelve over sixty-four, heart rate eighty-five, respiratory rate eighteen, and Glasgow Coma Scale improving," she recited rapidly, looking at her chart. "It was eight at the scene but it's ten now."

Lara suddenly groaned and her right arm moved up to push David's hand away.

"Good, she doesn't like that bright light in her eyes." He released her eyelid and Lara's eye closed. Pulling the oxygen mask off her face, he leaned close and said loudly, "Lara, open your eyes." She groaned again and said something unintelligible. David moved back from the bed and touched my arm. "You try."

I took her slender right hand in mine and leaned over, my heart in my mouth. "Lara, it's Mum. Squeeze my hand, darling." I pressed her hand gently and waited. Lara's hand lay still. "Lara, speak to me." I kept my voice steady. "Try hard and open your eyes. Dad and Finbar are waiting to see you. You've been in an accident, but you're going to be fine." I thought I saw her eyelids flicker. "Come on, Lara, open your eyes."

"Can't," Lara croaked. "Won't open."

"Yes," David almost shouted. "Good girl."

I tried again. "Now squeeze my hand when I squeeze yours, so we know you can hear us. Come on, you can do it." I felt the tiniest pressure on my hand and looked down, remembering that same feeling, that delicate pressure of baby Lara's much smaller hand holding mine. Her eyeballs moved below her almost transparent eyelids as she strained to open them.

"Come on, Lara, come on. Open your eyes."

For a brief moment she looked up at me, both eyes bloodshot, but a hint of green still visible. "Mummy?" she whispered. Her eyes closed.

I swallowed hard. "Darling, I'm right here." I bent and kissed her on her forehead, every cell in my body loving her.

"I hurt."

"I know, sweetheart, but the doctors are fixing you up as fast as possible." I looked at David who was fiddling with the intravenous drip.

"I've increased her pain relief. We should get her down to CT and X-Ray now," he said, his long face tense with relief.

The trauma doctor who had been working on the gash on her thigh moved to the bottom of the bed. I gave David a wobbly grin as Lara made it clear she could feel the doctor scraping her feet and pricking her legs, torso and arms. Then she managed to wriggle her toes on command.

The doctor looked at me, his expression pleased. "I think we can move her off this spinal board safely. Apart from the broken arm, there are no other bones broken as far as I can see, but we'll find out when we X-Ray her. And she has a scalp wound over her left temporal area with a possible fracture that we'll need to watch."

My smile disappeared. "Why didn't you tell me that before?"

David put a hand on my arm, stopping me from moving towards the head of the bed. "It's OK, Georgia. If there is a fracture, it's minor; we'll check it out properly after we get the CT scan and X-Rays. She probably won't need surgery." He looked towards the trauma doctor for his opinion.

"No, I don't think she will; it didn't look too bad," the doctor agreed.

"Sorry, I'm a bit uptight. You've done a good job."

"That's OK, Dr. Grayson. It's tough when it's your own family."

David was talking loudly to Lara again. "Do you remember being in the car?"

Tears squeezed from below Lara's closed eyelids and I moved quickly towards the head of the bed as David stepped out of the way. "Don't cry, sweetheart. If you can't remember, that's OK. It will take time." I tried to push away a strand of bloody hair that was clinging to Lara's eyelashes, but it was stuck fast. Her bloodshot eyes opened and her voice came out in a whisper. I bent low to hear her.

"I remember having a big fight, you and Dad." Her tears were flowing fast now; she sounded terrified. "Dad? Where's Dad? I want him, where is he?"

CHAPTER 12

It was six in the morning when we reluctantly left the hospital, leaving Lara, still confused and drowsy, in the neurosurgery ward. I knew she would be woken every thirty minutes until David was confident that she was completely out of danger. My concerns about Lara's skull fracture I kept to myself. The chances of it causing any problems were slight, but I wasn't happy about its location so close to the middle meningeal artery.

We'd barely walked in the door of the house when my mobile vibrated. As I flipped it open I saw Adam stiffen, his face etched with fear. "It's Lara," I told him, as soon as my conversation ended. "Her GCS has dropped from fourteen to thirteen, so she's been taken for another CT scan." I managed to keep my tone even.

"What do you mean? Is she in a coma again?"

"No, but she's become a lot more drowsy and confused. It sounds as if she might have developed a blood clot between her skull and her brain, and it's causing the pressure inside her head to rise."

"So you'll have to operate? Isn't that an emergency?"

I took Adam's hands in mine. "It's not good, love, but

David's alerted the theater staff just in case, and he'll start scrubbing up immediately. Lara will be all right."

"How can you possibly know that?"

"I know, because she's had this period of being fairly lucid. Her coma score was almost back to normal, and her CT looked good. That suggests that she didn't sustain significant brain damage from the accident, so if we remove the clot quickly, her brain won't suffer any damage."

"But why is she bleeding now? That must mean they missed something."

"It's a small risk when there is even a minor fracture over the middle meningeal artery; that's why she was being watched so closely."

"How can you be so calm about it?" Adam's face was white.

"Oh, love, I'm trying to be objective, that's all. I'm as scared as you, inside. But I've seen many cases like this, and she has a good chance of being fine. I've got to get back to the hospital. I'll phone you as soon as I know more." I started towards the door.

"I'm coming with you. I can't stay here while Lara's going through this."

"Phone Sonja and take Finbar over there first. He doesn't need to be there."

"Damn, no. I'll take him on my way to the hospital. Are you going to operate, or are you going to let David do it? He's not a consultant..." Adam's voice tailed off.

"David is perfectly capable of doing a straightforward burr-hole and evacuation. And you know I can't operate on my own daughter. Even if I could, have you forgotten I've been banned from operating?"

"What about getting Jim Mason to do it? This is our daughter we're talking about. I want a consultant, not a trainee."

"David isn't a trainee, you know that." I could feel my

tension escalating. "And I'll be in theater observing, so stop worrying. If I have any doubts at all, I'll call Andrew Wilson in. Mason's not going near our daughter."

"Get going then. Keep your mobile on. And call me straight away when you find out whether she's going to theater."

"Of course I will. Adam, try not to worry." I swallowed my fear as I looked into Adam's terrified eyes.

I WENT STRAIGHT TO THE IMAGING SUITE, BUT LARA HAD already been taken to theater. The CT had shown the telltale pale convexity between the skull and the brain, indicating a rapidly forming extradural hematoma. It was still small, but it was essential that it be evacuated without delay, as a further rise of pressure could be fatal. I considered phoning Andrew Wilson but decided I was being over-cautious. If David got into difficulty I would simply take over, ban or not. I wasn't going to let my daughter suffer because of some stupid rule. It was a straightforward procedure, for heaven's sake. Hardly like clipping an aneurysm.

Fifteen minutes later I was scrubbed up and in theater for the first time in weeks, but this time standing well back from the table. David hadn't looked too happy when I joined him in the scrub room, and had tried to discourage me from observing. I'd almost felt sorry for him. He'd clearly found it embarrassing attempting to keep his boss out of the operating room.

As the operation began, I tried, with increasing desperation, to focus on the technicalities of the procedure and ignore the body already covered in drapes before I'd entered the theater. The team worked silently, the only noise the bleep of the monitors and the regular *whoosh* of the respirator. I closed my eyes and tried to breathe normally as the high-pitched screaming of the drill began. The distinctive odor of burnt flesh and bone permeated the air as David ground a hole in Lara's skull so he could suction out the blood clot. The image of my daughter's face flashed before my eyelids and I shuddered.

Why can't you save our daughter? Adam's voice echoed in my head. Then the acrid taste of vomit was in my mouth. I clamped my lips shut and rushed to the door, pushing it open with my shoulders and running, almost falling, down the corridor. My mouth filled up, and choking and gagging, I made it to the bathroom before the mess exploded out of me into the toilet bowl.

After washing my clammy face and swilling out my rancid mouth, I dressed and left the operating suite, careful to avoid the glass porthole in the door of Theater Eight. I found Adam in the neurosurgery ward, sitting on Lara's empty bed. He leapt up as soon as he saw me, his fear palpable.

"She's still in theater, but everything is going well." I prayed I wasn't tempting fate.

"Thank heavens." Adam sat down abruptly. "Why aren't you there? I thought you were in theater with her. What's wrong?"

"Nothing's wrong. I just couldn't deal with it. I'm no good any longer, Adam. I can't even cope with observing a simple burr hole from the other side of the theater." I sank down beside him, my head in my hands.

For a while Adam sat in silence. Then, wearily, he spoke. "Don't be silly, Georgia. I should never have made you go into theater. I'm sure you would have been fine if it hadn't been Lara."

I didn't reply. As the light faded we sat mute and apart in our daughter's room.

The vibrating of my mobile jerked me out of my black thoughts, and I ripped it from my pocket. "David?"

"It went absolutely perfectly, Georgia. Lara is already coming around. I think she's going to be fine."

My eyes filled as I smiled shakily at Adam. "Thank you, David, thank you, thank you. I'm sorry I left so abruptly. Can we come down and see her, please?"

"You sure can. I'll see you in Recovery," said David, a smile in his voice.

Before Adam and I left her, Lara was awake and talking, drowsily recognizing us, and even asking where Finbar was.

TWO DAYS LATER SHE WAS SHIFTED FROM INTENSIVE CARE INTO a single room in the main ward. Her broken arm had been pinned and encased in plaster, and on a follow-up head CT, the shadow indicating the blood clot had vanished and her brain had expanded back to its normal circumference. Her memory for new events was still patchy but was improving rapidly. It was time to tell her about Tony.

I took her hand. "Sweetheart, we talked to Selina this morning and she said she'd be in to see you tomorrow."

"Thank goodness she's all right. I suppose being in the back of the car meant she didn't get hurt as badly as me." Lara's voice wavered.

I could hear the traffic on the road far below as I waited for Lara's next and inevitable question. But she averted her gaze and stared out the window, her shoulders shaking.

"How well did you know Tony, Pumpkin? Was he—is he —a special friend of yours, or is he more Selina's friend?" Adam's voice was gentle.

Lara turned her head and looked at us, her face pale under the purple bruises. Tears slid down her face. "He's my boyfriend. I didn't want you to know because you'd only stop me seeing him."

Her words punched me in the stomach. "Oh, Lara. How could you think that? We've always enjoyed meeting your friends."

"You've both been so shitty lately, and Tony has left school, and I knew you'd think he's too old for me." Lara scrubbed at her eyes with a sodden tissue.

"Darling, that makes me feel dreadful. I always want you to feel happy about bringing your friends home, whoever they are and however old they are." I tried to hug her but was shrugged away.

"I know it's been difficult at home lately, Pumpkin," Adam said. "I promise we'll be better. All we want is you home and well again."

Lara sniffed and blew her nose. Then in something close to a whimper she finally asked the question we'd been dreading. "What happened to Tony? No one talks about what happened to him." She tried to sit up. "You have to tell me. He's badly hurt, isn't he?"

I sat on the bed and brushed her hair from her face. "I'm sorry, sweetheart. His injuries were so bad that he didn't make it. He took the full impact when the car smashed into the lamppost. He didn't stand a chance."

"What do you mean, he didn't make it? You're lying. Don't lie to me." Her tears welled up again.

"I know it's hard to understand, and that you don't want to hear it, or believe it. I know how much it hurts," I said.

"He can't be dead, he can't be."

I pressed her close, trying to still her shaking body. "Hush, darling, hush," I murmured. I was weeping too as Adam closed his arms around us both.

TONY'S FUNERAL LOOMED. WITH LARA STILL IN HOSPITAL, Adam and I felt we must go, for her sake as well as for our own. We sat at the back of the church and listened to the heart-rending eulogies from Tony's friends and family. Selina was there, sitting near the front with a large group of young people, most of whom I didn't recognize. They looked so young and innocent, these friends of Tony's and Lara's, their shoulders shaking with grief for their dead friend. Then a young boy, no older than Finbar, his face so pale it was hard to distinguish it from his hair, walked to the front of the church and sang Ave Maria in a voice so pure it really could have been an angel. I looked down at the printed service I held in my hand and saw that he was called Billy and he was Tony's little brother. Billy's round blue eyes were the only dry ones in the church, but his tears glistened in every note of the beautiful song he sang. When the last notes had died away, the only sound in the church the rasping sobbing of a woman sitting in the front row, Billy went and sat beside her and she pulled him close. On her other side a man sat seemingly frozen.

My sadness for all these people who loved Tony—the young man who a few nights ago I was cursing as an irresponsible lout—was almost too much to bear. My guilt about our own good fortune to still have our daughter while Tony's parents stared into blackness, nearly sent me running out of the church, and it took all my strength to remain long enough after the service to murmur my condolences. I knew Adam felt the same. Tony's father bravely thanked us for our sympathy and asked after Lara, but his mother, her eyes swollen and the agony etched into her face making her look much older than I knew she must be, was bereft of speech. I was unable to imagine how I would cope in her place.

That night we collapsed, exhausted, into bed. As soon as Adam flicked off the bedside lamp I moved over to him and maneuvered his arm under my head. We lay still and quiet for a while, and then tentatively I gently stroked his chest, pushing aside his pajama jacket. My hand settled softly on his groin as my lips placed butterfly kisses along his chest and up to his chin, finally finding his mouth. He groaned, and I felt him responding to my hand, and I hungrily returned his kiss as he pushed up my nightgown. Our lovemaking was fast and intense and Adam spent himself quickly and collapsed on me, his head buried in my shoulder. We lay like that for many minutes, Adam's body heaving with dry sobs and my tears soaking the pillow.

"Hush, my darling," he whispered, when his body had stilled. "Hush. It's all over now. It's going to be all right."

I pushed on his chest and he lifted up from me. His face was soft.

"Oh, Adam, what have I done to you all?" I caught his frown before he rolled off me.

"If Lara hadn't heard us arguing and if I hadn't been dragging you through hell for all these weeks, she wouldn't have run out like that," I said. "You know she wouldn't. And she wouldn't be lying in hospital now with a head injury and broken bones."

"I was arguing as much as you," Adam said, and I heard the weariness in his voice. "Let's just be thankful that she's going to be OK. She could have died."

I shuddered. "I can't seem to stop hurting everyone I care about—Lara, you, Finbar... Alfie's death seemed to start it all off and it's because of me that poor Celia and those two little children have lost everything."

"Please stop it, Georgia. I don't know why you insist that Alfie's death was your fault. The Hospital Review Committee cleared you completely."

"I've remembered more about my argument with Danny that night. I tried to find a time to tell you after my last session with Sarah, but then Lara had her accident..." I sat up, pushing away the stifling bedclothes. "Danny told me he didn't want to marry me. It made no sense. His parents must have been against it. Perhaps they thought if he stayed in New Zealand that would be the end of his singing career. Married to some feminist neurosurgeon."

Stumbling to my feet I began to pace. "If Danny had loved me he wouldn't have taken any notice of his parents. I think he was scared. Marrying me, being stuck in New Zealand, well, that really would have stymied his career." I stopped and rubbed my throbbing head. "I should have told him I was pregnant. But I didn't. I didn't want him to stay with me because I was pregnant. If only I had, that might have changed his mind."

I sat down again on the edge of our bed. "Instead I was hysterical, accusing him of caring about his career more than me, screaming at him to get out of my house. Christ knows why I was so vehement. I'd been so worried and pissed off with him staying away so long and not even contacting me, and I suppose all those pregnancy hormones weren't helping my mood. Not much of an excuse. It was wild outside and pitch black by then. Our house was miles from anywhere. There was nowhere he could have found any shelter."

I forced myself to turn and look at Adam, every muscle in my body stinging with memories. "Adam, all that time Danny was away, not contacting me, part of me was thinking it would be better if I weren't pregnant so soon, give me the chance to complete my neurosurgical training, give us time to be together for a year or two without the extra stress of a baby. Perhaps that's why I was so angry with Danny when he wanted to get out of marrying me. I was feeling guilty about my own thoughts about having an abortion—perhaps even secretly, perhaps I wouldn't even tell Danny. He might have stopped me. I had no idea really what his reaction would be to a baby so soon." I dropped my face in my hands. "Adam, how am I going to tell Lara that I wasn't sure even about whether I should go ahead with the pregnancy? That I didn't want her enough? I promised I'd tell her if I remembered any more. I promised always to tell her the truth. How will I tell her that if I'd really wanted her and told Danny, he might not have died?"

"Give yourself some time, Georgia. It'll be ages before Lara is home and is herself again. Anyway, I can't see why you have to tell her. You didn't have an abortion. Kids don't need to know all their parent's secrets. And it's ridiculous to think it had anything to do with Danny falling off a cliff because he was crazy enough to go up there in a storm."

"He had to get away from me. Like Lara." My body was trembling so violently I could hear my teeth knocking between words. "Adam, what if I were up there too? What if I pushed him?"

Adam stared at me. "You're really being ridiculous now. You can't even stamp on an ant," he said, his voice hoarse. "You need to calm down or you'll have another panic attack. I'm so tired, Georgia. I can't take any more of this. I just want to go to sleep and not have to think about any of it."

"I need to talk about it. Don't shut me out."

"Shit Georgia, do you never listen? I don't want to talk about this anymore, not until Lara's better. She's what's important now. Your problems will have to wait. Make an appointment with your therapist; that's what she's for." Adam turned away from me and didn't move when I fumbled for my nightgown and stumbled down the stairs to the lonely guest room.

It was another eight days before Lara came home, a scarf concealing the prickly pale strip on the left side of her head where her hair was growing back around the scar. Our hope that she would cheer up once she was out of the hospital proved too optimistic. When she wasn't asleep she lay staring into space, her iPod silent and the books and magazines delivered by friends unread. Even tickets to a blues concert she would have once swooned over couldn't entice her out of bed. Nothing we could say or do seemed to help.

Selina came to see her once, but the visit didn't go well. When I asked her gently what was wrong, she replied that Lara didn't want to see her anymore because she reminded her too much of Tony. When Adam broached the idea that Lara see a psychologist, or her school counselor, she refused, telling him that no one could help her and talking wouldn't bring Tony back. I felt only empathy for her stance. After discussing our concerns with our family doctor we decided that if Lara's depression continued much longer we would encourage her to try a course of antidepressants. I shuddered at the thought; our extrovert, sunny daughter brought to this.

The post-mortem revealed that Tony's blood alcohol levels

had been high, and blood tests on Lara and Selina confirmed that they too had been 'under the influence.' The police report concluded that the crash had been caused by a combination of the driver's high alcohol levels, the wet, greasy, roads, and poor visibility from the heavy rain. Not wearing a seat belt had contributed to Tony's death as he'd been thrown from the car on impact, and Lara's survival was probably due to the fact that she was wearing hers. We had seen the car wreck, and could only agree.

I'd moved back into our bedroom for Finbar's sake; we didn't want to give him anything more to worry about. But we lay apart in the bed, a brief hand touch the best we could manage before saying goodnight. We were both floundering, afraid to risk stressing our fragile relationship with any real attempts at intimacy. We talked daily about how to help Lara and that at least gave us some connection. But I didn't bring up my demons again, and we remained painfully civil to each other, even when alone.

One evening Adam asked me if he could have one of my sleeping pills; he had an important research-funding interview the next morning and was desperate for a decent sleep. When I told him how worried I'd been by his constant exhaustion, he admitted he'd been plagued by a recurring nightmare— Lara's body catapulting from a car and exploding in a ball of fire, her severed head landing with a hollow thud by a shadowy figure that he knew was me. Shuddering, I'd reached over and covered his hand with mine, but he'd pulled away, leaving me stranded once more.

A constant stream of friends with casseroles, cakes, and offers of help only emphasized our own miserable existence, and I found the strain of trying to keep up the appearance of a loving couple almost unbearable. Even Finbar seemed complicit in our deception, smiling bravely for the friends who visited and making no comment to me, or, as far as I know to Adam, about our strained relationship. One day Julia appeared and foisted on us a fancy giant gourmet platter of cheeses, cold cuts, olives, dips, and high-end biscuits from Melrose and Morgan, with two bottles of white wine as an extra. Already chilled. As it was 6.30pm on a Friday—"on my way home after an *exhausting* day"— we had only one option. We sat on the patio out the back—it was, of course, a perfect evening—and picked at the platter. Adam consumed most of the wine and became increasingly tense with every glass; not, I suspect, his intention. I finally excused myself saying I had to get dinner ready, ignoring my mother's voice telling me it would be polite to invite Julia to join us.

Later, when Finbar had gone to bed, Adam managed to mutter that he was sorry. That pissed me off even more. "How did she even know about Lara?" I hissed. "Obviously you've still found time to see her."

"I assume she heard from Sonja. She's called me a couple of times, that's all."

"I bet. And I assume Will has decided to stay in Dublin. Can't blame him."

"Leave it, Georgia. I'm going to bed." And that was the end of that.

I RETURNED TO THERAPY AFTER TONY'S FUNERAL AND TALKING with Sarah gave me some release from my emotional isolation. Our focus had shifted from my past to my guilt and concerns about Lara, and the emotional distance between Adam and me. Obsessing about my culpability for Danny's death was at the bottom of my list.

A week after Lara was discharged from hospital, I decided therapy had become an indulgence and told Sarah I wanted to take a break until Lara was much better. Perhaps then I could find a way to talk to Adam about my past, and at that stage I could focus on how to accept what happened and move on. Sarah pointed out that until she was convinced I was unlikely to experience further panic attacks she couldn't recommend my surgical reinstatement, but agreed that without Adam's understanding, I couldn't get much further. She counseled me firmly to persist with my relaxation exercises and continue my daily symptom diary. Perhaps, she suggested, I could even experiment with writing down my thoughts and feelings in the form of a journal.

I wrote in it at night before I went to bed, and sometimes it helped and usually it didn't. Instead of calming me, whatever I'd been writing got stuck in my head, and I'd toss and turn until I gave in and took a sleeping pill. I hated that. So I decided to forget the journal. That evening I went to sleep quite quickly but woke up in the middle of the night, my nightgown saturated with sweat. I couldn't remember what I'd been dreaming, but then I saw the rocks at the bottom of the Pa as clearly as if I were standing on them, not lying in bed in London.

So cold, so wet. I'm in my shorts and singlet and my running shoes are squelching as I pull myself over the rocks. The waves keep breaking on my feet and I cling to the rock face above me, terrified I'm going to slip and be bashed to pieces. The face of the Pa is so steep and I can't see the top, only the dark sky. Rain is drowning my face but I have to keep going. My bare legs are grazed and stinging but I've got to get higher. My fingers grab a ledge above my head and I scrabble my feet to push me up. I put my other hand on the ledge and I slip back and start again. The rain stops suddenly and for a few seconds I can see the rock face in front of me. I look up and see dark clouds racing across the starless sky, the half moon appearing then disappearing then appearing again. I reach up for the ledge and scrabble until I find something solid to cling to. Now my other hand. My fingers touch something wet and slimy. Seaweed. I know it's seaweed. I pull myself higher and get my chest over the ledge and wriggle the rest of my body up and I'm on the ledge and he's lying there, on his back, his eyelids closed over his green eyes. I scream at him to wake up but the sea is too loud and he can't hear me. I stroke his hair back from his face; it's so white. He's so still. There's blood on my hands, he's not waking up, he's dead, he's dead, he's dead. I'll carry him home and make him warm again. Perhaps he's not dead, he's just knocked himself out. He's so heavy and stiff, I can't lift him, the sea is going to wash us away.

ON JULY 7TH, A MONTH AFTER LARA CAME HOME, TERRORISTS bombed London, and for a while we were distracted from our own problems. I called the hospital to see if I could come in and help deal with some of the minor injuries. "Thank you, Dr. Grayson, but there's no need. We're covered pretty well here," I was told.

Three days later, Lara appeared for dinner, dressed and with her hair clean and brushed. Sitting at the table she told us, her voice a little shaky, "I'm sorry I've been so miserable. I'm going to try harder. I've been upset about everything, all those poor people who were bombed right near where you work. It could have been one of you."

I looked over at Adam, seeing his eyes mist over. My own throat refused to work. Thank goodness for Finbar who leapt out of his chair and bounded around the table, his hug almost lifting Lara out of her seat. "Go, sis," he whooped. "Welcome back."

Lara hugged her brother with her good arm. "Thanks, little bro," she whispered. "Don't let me get so gloomy again." She had tears in her eyes as she looked across the table at Adam. "Sorry."

Adam reached over and took her hand. "I'm so happy you're on the mend, Pumpkin. You've had an awful time, and we've been so worried."

"Oh, darling," I said, "this house has been too quiet." Then I was behind Lara's chair, my hands on her shoulders. "It's tough to lose someone you care about, and in such a tragic way. We don't want you to feel so alone again, dealing with it all by yourself." I bent and kissed her curly head.

Lara looked down and I could almost hear the emotions fighting in her head. Then she shrugged my hands away and said flatly, "I'll come right. You did, after Danny died." Turning deliberately to Adam she smiled at him and I sat back at the table and pretended to eat. Closing my eyes I let myself sink into the white clouds of relief that were filling me up, swallowing the chilly air streaming off the window of ice that separated me from my daughter.

LARA CONTINUED TO IMPROVE BOTH PHYSICALLY AND emotionally, and I told myself she was forgiving me a little every day. One night I was in the kitchen plowing through a pile of bills when I heard hysterical laughter from the family room where Adam and the kids were watching TV. "What's so funny," I asked, poking my head around the door. Lara was in fits of giggles, literally rolling on the floor, and Adam was wiping tears from his eyes. Finbar raised his eyes to the ceiling, but he was chortling as well—more, it seemed, at Lara than at the source of her amusement. The TV was playing the credits of *The Vicar of Dibley*, and Adam flicked the mute and waited while Lara got herself under control.

"It was that silly end bit where the Vicar tells simple Alice a joke," Adam said, grinning. "Lara found it amusing."

"That would be putting it mildly. What was the joke?" I asked, coming into the room.

"Lara, you tell her," said Adam.

Lara fell back on the couch, still giggling. "There's this nun taking a bath and there's a knock on the bathroom door," she managed. "The nun calls out 'Who is it?' and a voice answers 'It's the blind man.' So the nun thinks for a minute and then calls back 'Oh, well OK then, come in.' The door opens and in comes a man…" Lara snorted, starting Finbar and Adam off again too.

"Come on Lara, get on with it," I said, laughing myself.

Lara took a deep breath. "The man comes in and looks at her and says, 'Nice pair of tits.' Then he points at the window and says 'Is that where you want me to hang the blinds?' "

Later that night when the kids were in bed and Adam and I were having a cup of tea, Adam began laughing.

"What's so amusing?" I asked.

"I was remembering the blind man. It was good seeing Lara like that, back to her old self. Giggling so much she practically wet herself." Adam stretched, still smiling. "It's amazing how wonderful a good guffaw can make you feel. Finbar and I were laughing more at Lara than the joke, but the joke was pretty funny too. I think I'll write to Dawn French and thank her for her Vicar of Dibley. If we had a vicar like her near here I'd bloody well turn religious."

"I'm sure I've read that laughing really is a good therapy. Probably why mine failed; I can't remember too many giggles," I said, smiling at Adam to show I was joking.

He moved over to the stove and lit the gas under the kettle again. "Georgia, do you want to tell me what else you've remembered?"

"Are you sure? You've been so happy tonight."

"That's why. I think I've got the strength to hear it now. Lara's turned a corner, and we have to make more of an effort too." He sat beside me. "I want to hear the truth, however painful it is."

I took a deep breath. "I still don't remember everything, but bits and pieces. After I told Danny to get out of the house, the next thing I remember is finding him near the bottom of the Pa. It's on a sort of peninsula that juts out into the sea at the other end of the beach from where our house is. It's at least a thirty-minute walk in good weather. And it was terrible weather: pitch black, with gale-force winds, and raining. I must have waded through the stream that separates the Pa from the beach and clambered around it to the seaward side." I swallowed and pushed onward. "I have no memory of getting there but I've finally remembered finding Danny's body. He was on a ledge almost at the bottom of the Pa. If he hadn't landed there he'd have been washed into the sea." I breathed: In out, in out. *Re-lax, re-lax.* "I don't remember getting back across the stream and all the way to the road. I must have been frozen. I still had my running gear on and I was saturated with rain and seawater when I was picked up. Even that's hazy, the drive to Claris and the police. But I've remembered more about being in the hospital and not knowing what happened to Danny or whether I still had a baby inside me, or if I'd lost it. Or perhaps I never had a baby, and there was no Danny, and I was locked in there because I was crazy and everything I thought was true was not."

Adam took my hands in both of his and unclenched my fingers.

"Later when I was home again with Mum and Dad, they told me about Danny's parents. They'd taken Danny's body back with them to Queenstown and they were too upset to ever see me. Danny's mother told Dad they were leaving New Zealand and never coming back." I took a large gulp of my tea.

"They didn't know about the baby. The psychiatrist didn't even tell Mum and Dad because of confidentiality. Apparently I wasn't crazy enough to be denied my rights. When my pregnancy became obvious after I'd been in hospital for weeks, Mum and Dad talked to me about having the baby adopted out; they thought I had enough to do to get properly well again. They even got a social worker to come in and talk to me. But I could never give her up. So I went home with Mum and Dad, and after Lara was born we stayed with them and of course they were wonderful."

We sat in silence, Adam holding my hand.

"Danny died because of me. That's the truth I can't tell Lara."

"But *he* broke off your relationship, not you," Adam said, and I finally managed to look at him. I shook my head.

"When he needed me to understand, I told him to get out of my life. So that's…" My voice petered out.

"It's a long time ago," Adam said. "You have to stop blaming yourself."

"So that's what he did. He must have been desperate to get away from me to climb up the Pa. He'd never been up to the top before. He knew it was tapu."

"How would Danny have known that?"

"I told him. When Andrew and I were kids we used to scramble to the flattish bit about halfway up, but we were too scared to go to the top. I know the police report concluded that Danny slipped on the wet grass at the top, and fell, but if I'd let him stay in the house until morning, he'd still be alive. Even if he'd gone back to the States and we'd never got back together again, he and Lara would know each other. Perhaps she would know his parents and his brother. Perhaps she would know Danny's grandmother. She would have loved Savannah. She would have her other family as well as us. She would know who she is."

MY CONFESSION MADE A HOLE IN THE WALL BETWEEN US AND little by little it expanded. Even Lara gave me a quick hug every so often, almost as if she was trying it out. Poor kid had a lot to deal with. She saw a psychologist every week and I knew how hard that was. We weren't let in on it, but hopefully it was helping her cope with her sadness and guilt about Tony. She continued to struggle with fatigue, a normal consequence of head injury, and neuropsychological tests showed that she still had problems with information processing and sustained attention. But the plan was to try her out at school, mornings only at first, when the new academic year began at the beginning of September. She was upset because she'd have to repeat Year 11; she'd missed too many classes as well as her GCSE exams. At least we'd managed to steer her away from leaving school altogether. She'd turned sixteen on the 15th July so officially she was an adult now—as she pointed out—and could legally leave school. We had convinced her to have two friends around for dinner to celebrate her birthday, and I think she enjoyed that, but she was exhausted the next day.

At the start of August I returned to work after nine weeks leave, but still banned from operating. The kids were on their summer break, Finbar spending every day at a cricket camp and three of Lara's girlfriends keen to act as 'baby sitters' as Lara put it, taking turns to hang out with her at our house while Adam and I were at work. Peter was also back at the hospital, but had retired himself from surgery. A neurosurgeon from Finland had been seconded for nine months, as even the amazing Jim Mason had struggled to cover my surgical list as well as Peter's.

Within days of my returning, Peter called me into his office and asked if I would stand in for him at the annual international neurosurgical training meeting, where training standards and requirements were examined and revised. It was an important meeting and my first reaction was one of excitement. Relief and gratitude as well that Peter had not given up on me; had chosen me over Jim Mason.

But by the time I got home that night I was less certain. It was ridiculous, I told myself. I'd been to numerous international meetings over the years; why should this be any different? It would only take me away from London for four days. But it was at the end of the school summer break and right before Lara started classes again. I knew what Adam would think: I was back to putting my career ahead of my family.

Was I? Wasn't it important that I find my feet again? I'd got the feeling that this was an opportunity that wouldn't be offered a second time; a chance for me to show I still had what it took to lead the department. It wasn't unheard of for a director to have only light clinical duties so he—or she—could focus on management. Heavens, was I really thinking it might come to that?

There was another reason for my nervousness about broaching the subject with Adam. The meeting was in New Orleans.

I DECIDED I WOULD AT LEAST RAISE IT AS A POSSIBILITY. I should have discussed it with Adam first, but I decided to treat Lara as the adult she almost was and include her from the beginning. She might be keen for me to go if I promised I'd at least see if Danny's grandmother still lived in the same mansion, and try and talk to her. If it made Lara happy, that might pacify Adam.

I waited until we were in the middle of dinner. I had no appetite anyway. No one spoke as I argued my case. That's what it felt like. As if I had to justify myself. They sat there, eating, as I talked. "I'd fly to New Orleans on Saturday and I'd have Sunday to find Savannah Leaumont's house again and see if she's there. Although she must be in her late eighties at least by now, so she mightn't be, I suppose." Lara and Adam had both stopped eating. "There's a welcome dinner for the meeting participants on Sunday evening and the meeting is all day Monday and finishes at midday on Tuesday. I can fly back to London on Tuesday afternoon, two days before you two are back at school."

"Surely there's someone else who can do it?" Adam said.

"Dad, don't be so negative," Lara said. "Mum's gotta go.

Otherwise that bloody Jim what's-his-name will lord it over her forever."

I tried not to choke on my pasta. Lara was practically hissing with indignation. Or perhaps something else.

"I can go with her. It's karma, don't you see? You said that when I was better we could do something special for my sixteenth birthday, and this is perfect. Mum and I can both meet my great grandmother."

"Don't get carried away. You can't just show up like that. The poor old lady might have a heart attack," Adam said. But he sounded just a little amused.

"Nah. She'll be blown away that she's found us. I've read about her. She's as tough as…as those ginger biscuits Finbar makes."

Finbar poked his tongue out at her.

"Perhaps I should see her first, just to make sure. Then we can all go to New Orleans later," I said, not daring to look at Adam.

"Please Mums, please? We could go a few days earlier so you and I could do lots of stuff together before you had to go to your meeting. We could go to blues clubs. You love blues."

Oh, it was so long since she'd spoken to me as if she cared. I knew she was being manipulative, but it was a start. Could I take her? Even if finding Savannah turned out to be impossible, even a disaster, it might bring Lara and I close again. I'd risk anything for that.

PART II

KATRINA

New Orleans, August 2005

CHAPTER 14

$\mathcal{N}$inety degrees, humidity seventy-five percent, and only eleven in the morning. My antiperspirant had given up before Lara and I had ventured out the door. The hotel had changed not one iota, and its air conditioning still didn't work. By the time we'd walked from Frenchmen along Decatur Street, looking for Danny's Piano Bar, strings of hair were sticking to my neck and my cotton dress wept beneath my armpits. Lara, in her shorts and T-shirt, looked every bit as hot. At least the clumsy plaster cast on her arm was gone, cut off four days before our flight. It had mended well and she was so diligent with her arm strengthening exercises that it shouldn't take long for her arm to stop looking like a white stick. No surprise that she'd got her way and we'd left London on Wednesday. We'd have six full days in New Orleans before our flight home on Tuesday evening, giving Lara 34 hours to recover from her jet lag before the new school year started on September 1st.

From the moment I booked our flights, Lara fizzed with anticipation. I fizzed with apprehension. Adam would never forgive me if Lara found it too much. Perhaps she would be too tired to start school so soon after we returned, but did it really matter? She'd been away for almost three months so another day wasn't going to make any difference.

I sighed. This wasn't getting me any brownie points with Adam. It hadn't helped when I'd decided to book us into the quaint 1850s Creole Townhouse in the French Quarter where I'd stayed so long ago. Lara was adamant that she didn't want to hang around in the fancy hotel where the neurosurgeons were staying. Adam thought she'd be safer there, lying about at the cookie-cutter pool while I was in my meeting, and not roaming unsupervised around the seamy French Quarter.

Damn Adam. Lara was already letting me in a bit. If this trip gave her back to me it would be worth any amount of Adam grimness. He'd get over it once we were home. And deep inside I felt that if my family were happy and normal again, my anxiety and panic attacks would disappear.

Lara was meandering along in front of me as we wove our way through the bustling market and the narrow cobbled streets, one of which was once the home of Danny's Piano Bar. We hadn't found the jazz club on Google, so likely it had some other name and purpose now. Lara was constantly stopping, peering into cluttered shop windows, fascinated, as I had been that first time, by the exuberance of it all. Now she had her hands cupped around her face as she tried to see through the thick glass of a small shop. I looked up at the sign as I reached her. 'Voodoo Magic' it said. I touched a patch of faded blue exposed by the red paint peeling from the door. This was it, I was almost certain.

Pulling Lara back from the window I nodded at her, my eyebrows raised as I pointed to the Voodoo Magic sign.

"Danny's Piano Bar?" she said.

I nodded again and she grabbed my hand. We both peered in the window. The usual skulls and other tourist junk, and a large sign proclaiming that psychic readings were available for forty dollars, no appointment necessary. "Let's get a reading," Lara said in a whisper.

"You don't believe in all that stuff?"

"I might. Anyway, perhaps whoever does the readings will know Savannah?" Lara had taken to calling Danny's grandmother Savannah as if they were already best friends.

I grinned at her. A spot of crystal gazing could hardly be any worse than all the therapy we'd endured. I pushed open the door, jumping when the life-sized witch hanging behind it let out a loud cackle. Plastic skeletons and gruesome masks dangled from the low ceiling, and a shadowy figure, engrossed in a book, was sitting behind a large desk weighed down by more books.

"Hullo," Lara said.

"Hi. What can I do for you?" The figure spoke in that slow drawl I was becoming re-accustomed to. A witch in the flesh. Lots of hair, wild and gray. Piercing blue eyes peered at us over half-moon glasses perched on a long nose.

"We were wondering about getting a reading," I said.

"And we thought you might know about Danny's Piano Bar," Lara added, no mucking around. "Mum thinks it used to be here."

"Gracious, that's going back a-ways. We've been here for, I don't know, maybe sixteen years. When did you last visit?"

"August, 1988, it was. So I guess it was sold not long after that," I said.

"Fancy you remembering exactly when you were here. It must have been a pretty special occasion, eh?" The witch's eyebrows got lost in her hair.

"You could say that. I don't suppose you know what happened to the owner?"

"Old lady Leaumont. I haven't heard that she's passed over, so I guess she's still with us. But she must be close to going over to the other side. Her son still runs a few night-clubs around town, and as far as I know they're doin' OK." Her tone was curious. "So what's your connection with her?"

I gave Lara a sharp nudge. "None, really. I met her years ago, and I knew her grandson. He used to sing here."

"Danny Leaumont, gravel for the soul." The woman chuckled. "I've still got some old posters with that on it somewhere. He was a sexy fella, all right. And they say he could sing up a storm." She peered at us, her eyes glittering. "I see him sometimes on dark, stormy nights. And hear him."

Lara gulped. "What do you mean you see him?"

I knew what her answer would be. She knew how to snare tourists.

"I live up above," the witch replied, flicking her head upwards. "Like I said, Danny takes a walk from time to time. Whatever happened to him didn't give him any rest. He's prowling around looking for peace, poor soul."

I stared at her, almost believing her. Would it be worth asking anything else about the Leaumonts? Sensible answers seemed unlikely.

"Cat got your tongues?" the witch asked. "I s'pose you think I'm talking twaddle. Sounds like you come from England. Folks from there don't know nothin' 'bout spirits."

"I'm sorry if I seem disbelieving," I said. "I've never had anything to do with spirits. I wasn't sure whether you were serious or just having us on."

"You can't see spirits if you don't believe in them. They're not going to waste their time with the likes of you." She winked.

"I believe you," said Lara.

"Ah. Would you like to see the poster?"

"Oh yes, yes, I'd love to," Lara said, and my pulse sped up. "Does it have a picture of Danny?"

"It does, in all his flame-haired glory."

I closed my eyes at the thought of seeing his face again. When I opened them the witch had risen from her chair. She towered above us, a beanstalk of a woman.

"We should introduce ourselves," I said, holding out my

hand. "I'm Georgia Grayson, and as you guessed I live in England, although I always thought I had a Kiwi accent. And this is my daughter, Lara."

The hand that grasped mine felt dry and bony. "Glad to meet you, Georgia, especially if you're a Kiwi. They're more my cuppa tea; not in Bush's pocket like the Brits." She cackled. "I'm Amanda Wilhelmina Katrina Thelma Damer, but my friends—here or on t'other side—call me Kat."

I laughed. "Hi, Kat. I like your name, and by the sound of it, your politics."

"Good. Now that we've got the essentials sorted, why don't you pour yourselves a brew while I look for this poster?" She nodded towards an electric coffee maker, its glass carafe half full of strong black coffee. The aroma reminded me that I hadn't fed my addiction since we disembarked from the plane.

Kat was shuffling around in the back of the room, scrabbling about in an old chest. She let out a yodel as she pulled out a cardboard tube and brought it over to the desk, extracting a roll of glossy paper. As she rolled it out, Lara caught the top to prevent it curling back on itself. Kat held down the bottom, and together we gazed at it in silence.

Then Kat spoke, her voice tinged with sadness. "That's him. He's the one who walks sometimes. He's got a face that's hard to forget, all right."

I could feel her eyes on me, and tried to get control of my emotions.

"Are you OK Mum?"

I swallowed as Lara touched my arm, her other hand still on the poster. "Yes," I said. "It's just a bit of a shock to see him again, so real and alive." My eyes devoured him, his body contorted around the song he was singing, his hair vivid red against the shadowy background. Green eyes flashed at us from half closed lids, and his mouth seemed to kiss the microphone he cradled in his hands.

"Here," said Kat, pulling out a chair, "Sit down. You look as pale as a ghost."

I sank down gratefully, but couldn't take my eyes from Danny. Lara was still standing, and I heard her quick breaths.

"I couldn't remember his face any more." I felt the sting behind my eyes.

"You loved him." Kat's voice was soft.

"A long time ago, very much. I had forgotten how much until now."

"Would you like to keep the poster?"

"Could we? I'd be happy to pay whatever you wanted for it."

"Now that's an offer hard to refuse," Kat said. "I can see I could take all you have, and then some. But you can have it for nothing. I'm thinking that if you take him away, he might stop haunting this place, and I could get a good night's sleep again."

"Are you sure? This is worth a lot to us."

"I'm quite sure. Instead, you can tell me what happened to him. I've always wondered why he was so unhappy. When I bought this building, the real estate agent told me that the old lady was selling it because her grandson had died in a tragic accident, and this place held too many memories. Apparently it was called Danny's Piano Bar after him. But you probably knew that."

"Yes." I watched as Lara slowly rolled up the poster, Danny's body disappearing bit by bit. First his signature bare feet and skinny jeans; then the sea-green shirt covering the slim body that I'd loved so thoroughly; the sensual lips that had all the women in his audience crossing their legs; the laughing green eyes that could see into my soul; and finally, the crazy crown of his flaming hair.

When I returned to the present, Kat had picked up my cup and was looking into it intently.

"What's the matter with my cup?"

"That's what I'm trying to find out," Kat said. "I'm reading your coffee grounds."

I laughed. "You're what? I've heard of reading tea leaves, but coffee grounds?"

"It's what you leave in them that's important; not whether you leave them in tea or coffee. Now quiet, while I concentrate."

"Read Lara's cup. She's a believer."

"No," said Lara. "Read Mum's first." I looked at her, holding her father's picture, her eyes filled with tears.

I nodded at Kat. The witch's reading would give Lara a chance to get herself together. It might even make her laugh. The minutes ticked by, and Kat muttered and frowned as she studied the cup. Then raising her head she said solemnly, "Are you prepared to hear what the spirits have to say?"

"I am," I replied, pressing my lips together. "Is this the forty dollar reading or do I get a better rate?"

"This is not a time to be flippant. And this is not my reading; I'm only the medium. This comes from elsewhere."

"What do you mean, elsewhere?"

"Only you can know what spirit you've been conjuring up. It is not for me to know your darkest thoughts."

"Right. So what does this spirit say?"

Kat pulled up a stool and sat facing me. Gazing into the coffee cup she began to speak, her voice strangely different—somehow huskier, and with her southern drawl barely apparent. "You've had great success in life and made money and friends, loved and lost and loved again, a beautiful daughter has been born to you, and you've traveled from your true home to live across the sea. But something inside you is deeply disturbed, deeply unhappy. You are embarking on a long journey to places even farther from home to seek answers." She paused, her body rocking forward. "I see a wild and fearsome challenge coming... it will test you like you've never been tested before… you must decide whether to face it or run away… "

Her voice died away and I opened my eyes. "Is that all?"

"It's all that I can see. Perhaps even the spirits can't see any further."

A shiver skittered down my spine. "That's a bit spooky."

"Ah, so you were entered by the spirit," said Kat, her drawl back again.

"You're really scaring me now." I attempted a laugh.

"It's always wise to be a little afraid of things we don't understand."

My hands were on my forehead, my fingers trying to massage away the rush of fear. "I think my jet lag is catching up with me; I feel a bit woozy. And this heat doesn't help." I pushed myself up from the chair. "Your turn, Lara."

She shook her head. "No, I've changed my mind. It's too creepy."

Kat grinned. "Well, you can always come back. I'll still be here."

I forced a smile. "It's been lovely to meet you, Kat. I'm not sure I believe your spirits, but they're fascinating."

"What will be, will be," said Kat. "If you need any more guidance, you come back and see me."

"Perhaps we'll drop by again before we leave New Orleans, even if we don't need any more coffee readings." Scrabbling in my bag I pulled out my wallet and extracted two fifty-dollar bills. "Here's something for your coffee fund. And thanks, Kat, for the poster and for the reading."

Kat waved my hand away. "I don't want your gold, Georgia. If I've helped you open your mind a little, then that's reward enough for me." She winked at Lara then grinned at me. "Mind, if you'd been a Brit, I might have taken your money. But a Kiwi? Never."

After wandering along Bourbon Street, listening to street artists and sharing a seafood platter in one of the numerous restaurants, we were back in our room by three o'clock. Falling onto our beds, we were asleep in seconds. Waking hours later, hot and sweaty and with my head pounding, I stumbled to the bathroom and drank three glasses of flat-tasting tap water before standing, eyes closed, under a luke-warm shower. After attempting to dry myself before the perspiration re-accumulated on my skin, I pulled on the thin T-shirt I slept in and collapsed back on the bed. Lara was still asleep, sprawled on top of her sheets in her pants and bra. Glancing at my watch I saw it was 7:00 p.m. and still Thursday, August twenty-fifth. No point in phoning Adam; it would be the middle of the night in London.

Perhaps I should wake Lara and we could go out into the hot night and find something to eat? I didn't feel hungry, but a long icy drink would be a welcome distraction. But I didn't have the energy to get dressed again and hadn't the heart to wake Lara. I quietly closed the bedroom door and sat on the sagging sofa in the small sitting room flicking through the myriad of crappy TV channels until I found some news. At first I thought the urgency in the newsreader's tone was simply the usual American hype. But gradually the words began to sink in as I watched the satellite images of the gray storm swirling around its central eye and almost obscuring the underlying map of Florida.

"Tropical Storm Katrina has been upgraded to a Category 1 Hurricane, and made landfall on the coast of South Florida, north of Miami between Hallandale Beach and Adventura at six-thirty this evening. Tropical storm warnings and hurricane-force winds are predicted to batter the Florida Keys as it moves slowly over the State. The hurricane has a well-defined eye on Doppler radar and has already spawned several tornadoes. It is on track to move across the Gulf of Mexico tomorrow, where it's in danger of increasing in intensity as it moves over the warm sea surface temperatures of the Loop Current, with a possible second landfall along the central Gulf Coast. Hurricane Katrina is the fifth hurricane of the 2005 Atlantic hurricane

season, and could build into the most devastating we have seen this year."

"Lovely," I said out loud. "Just what we need, a bloody big wind." I pulled on my jeans and a shirt and took the stairs to the deserted lobby. A youth with a serious crop of pimples came out of a room at the back.

"What's up, Missus? You need somethin'?"

"I just heard about the hurricane. What will happen if it gets to New Orleans—will you be evacuating the hotel?"

"Nah, we're always getting hurricanes here. If we got out every time, we'd never get nothin' done." The youth picked at a pimple.

"Is the manager here—or anyone else?"

"Nope, only me. Mrs. G. went off at seven o'clock, and I'm on until seven in the morning."

"That's reassuring anyway. I don't suppose she'd leave if she were worried. It sounds safe enough to wander around and find something to eat."

"Yeah. You'd better have a good feed." He gave me a sly wink. "Never can tell, might be your last."

ON FRIDAY, THE MINUTE WE WOKE UP, LARA TURNED ON THE TV. Katrina had weakened over Florida to a tropical storm, but had been upgraded again to a hurricane in the early hours of the morning, an hour before she reached the Gulf of Mexico. Poking my head out the window, I neither felt nor saw any signs of wind, but was confronted by a heat already oppressive. If the hurricane was going to affect New Orleans it was clearly a fair way off, so in the meantime we may as well see a bit more of the city. Last night, when Lara had woken, we had ventured outside and found a pizza joint, and this morning even Lara still felt too full for a big breakfast. A pastry and coffee in the hotel lobby supplied as part of the three star service was perfect.

"Now let's go and find Savannah's house," said Lara.

No putting it off now. That's what I'd promised her.

We took our time, ambling along near the Mississippi, checking out the markets and listening to the street music. We came upon the very bench where Danny and I had sat and talked the night we'd met; not that I told Lara that. But we sat there for a while watching the paddleboats. Then, licking ice creams, we walked up Poydras Street and along St. Charles Avenue, and caught the streetcar to the Garden District. With the help of a map in the tourist brochure I'd taken from our hotel, we found our way to Fourth Street, and there it was, Savannah's house, Danny's old home. We stood outside the closed iron gates and took it in. I could see the graceful mansion mesmerized Lara, and for me it was a time warp. The house was exactly the same, still crisply white in the humid air, the overpowering smell of tropical vegetation transporting me back to a bare-legged Danny, his messy red hair and faded pink T-shirt with its New Orleans Jazz Fest banner as vivid as a hallucination. For a moment I shut my eyes and sank into the feeling of his closeness. Then a miniature dog came running from somewhere on the street, yapping at these strangers on its patch, and the spell was broken.

"It looks a bit closed up," Lara said, her voice uncharacteristically nervous. Nothing moved in the house, and many of the shades were drawn—although I remembered that that was no guarantee of emptiness, but rather a way to keep out the hot August sun. "Well, we won't know unless we knock on the door," I said, grasping the latch fastening the daunting gates. My heart was pounding. What would I say if Savannah were home? Did she know about my part in Danny's death? Even if she remembered me, like the rest of Danny's family she'd probably want nothing to do with me.

Savannah Leaumont. I could almost see her sweeping down

the grand staircase. Perhaps she didn't live here anymore? What if she had died, or was in a home?

My hand fell from the latch and I reached down to pat the little dog, who seemed to have decided we were friends and not foe.

"Come on, what's the worse that can happen?" said my wise daughter, her tone determined now. She unlatched the gate and walked up the path to the door. The sound of the snarling lion's head hitting the brass panel on the beautiful door echoed through the house. We stood there, poised to… poised to smile? To introduce ourselves as long lost family? Nothing. No footsteps.

"Oh, she's not home," Lara said, those four little words trembling with her pent-up emotions. This had meant so much to her, more than I'd realized. And now she was going to be disappointed. She banged the lion against the door again, but there was no one there, or if they were they weren't keen to open the door.

"You lookin' for Miz Leaumont?"

We both jumped and spun around. The man was clearly the gardener with his gardening fork balanced across his wheelbarrow.

"Hi," Lara said. "Yes, we are looking for Mrs. Leaumont. Is this her house?"

"Has been for as long as I can remember," he said, "but she's not here. She's getting something done in hospital. Went in yesterday."

"Oh. I'm sorry. I hope it's not too serious?" I said.

He shook his head. "She had the other one done a few months ago and she was back on her feet in no time."

"The other one?" I asked.

"Her hip. They can replace them these days. Wear 'em out and they stick in new ones."

"Ah. Well that's good. Do you have any idea when she might be home?"

Another shake of the head.

"Do you know which hospital she's in?"

"Might be Memorial. Not too sure."

"Thank you. What a shame we've missed her." I could see Lara drooping by my side. "We might be back next year some time. Hopefully we'll be able to see her then."

"Mr. Luke usually comes by every few days. Do you want me to give him a message? He can pass it on to Miz Leaumont."

"Yes, we do," said Lara, before I could reply.

I frowned at her. "No, but thanks. We'll get in touch with her later when she's fully recovered from her surgery."

"Gosh, I'm so thirsty," Lara said. "I don't suppose I could get a glass of water?" Her hand was on the enormous front door handle.

"That's locked, Miss. There's a tap around the back but you'll have to drink from your hands."

"Oh. OK." She stomped down the steps and followed him around the back of the house. Little minx. I was hot, but my stomach had stopped churning. Goodness knows what Lara would have said if Savannah had been home. It was probably a blessing we hadn't come two days ago. Savannah might have been in hospital now with a heart attack instead of a hip to be replaced.

BACK IN THE HOTEL AROUND FOUR O'CLOCK, WE HAD COLD showers before turning on the TV. We didn't have to wait more than a second to discover the latest dire news.

"Hurricane Katrina is rapidly intensifying as it crosses the Gulf of Mexico, and experts are putting New Orleans directly in its path, with the chances of a direct hit forecast at ninety percent. The city is predicted to feel the full force of the hurricane by Sunday night or the early hours of Monday. This could be an unprecedented cataclysm, as eighty percent of

the city lies below sea level. Louisiana governor, Kathleen Blanco, has declared a state of emergency for state agencies. All residents should secure their properties immediately and make urgent preparations for a possible evacuation. Those who are able and have transport should leave New Orleans as soon as possible until the hurricane is over, and it is declared safe to return."

Why didn't I feel more apprehensive? Probably because I'd never experienced what a major hurricane could do first hand. The American media always over-reacted in situations like these. Going by the parties in the streets and some of the flippant comments we had overheard in the pizzeria last night, the French Quarter was clearly of a similar mind. But we'd better check what the hotel was doing, if anything.

I left Lara gazing at the poster of Danny and went down to the lobby. Mrs. G. was chatting to the porter and broke off when she saw me. "How are you, Dr. Grayson? Enjoying your stay?"

"We are, thank you. I thought I'd better ask you about this hurricane; we don't have too many in London." I smiled at her.

"It does look as if it might be a bad one. They seem to be getting worse every year." Mrs. G didn't look the least bit concerned.

"I heard on the news that the Governor had declared a state of emergency. Are people getting out of the city?"

"Some will be, but plenty can't or won't. Best to wait and see. We can't be getting out every time there's a hurricane. I think this is the third already this season."

"But on the news they seemed to think there was a ninety percent chance that this one will hit New Orleans head on, and that you might get a lot of flooding."

"They always say that. I s'pose they have to cover their butts," the pimply porter contributed, grinning broadly at me. "Don't worry about it. It will get a bit windy, but we're OK here."

"This hotel is awfully close to the river. Isn't that a concern?"

"It ain't never bin flooded before," the porter replied. "Anyways, it won't be here for ages yet. Chances are it will take a turn and end up somewhere else before then."

I reported back to Lara who seemed as unworried as pimple face. "Well, there's no point in getting in a tizzy. If the locals aren't worried by the media hysteria, why should we be?"

"You're right. But I'd better phone Adam. He's probably pulling his hair out."

He answered after the first ring, interrupting my greeting with a rush of words. "Georgia, thank goodness. I've been pulling my hair out. Are you all right? What's happening there?"

I tried not to smile but then realized he couldn't see me, so let it rip. "It's OK, Adam. Everything here is perfectly normal. You know Americans. They love to go over the top about these sorts of things."

"Haven't you been listening to the news? The hurricane is gaining strength, and New Orleans is directly in its path."

"If that looks like happening there's plenty of time to get to somewhere safe. In fact, the best strategy is to stay put inside."

"You should get out now while you can. It's not your city, so why even risk it?"

"Adam, for heaven's sake stop dramatizing. I'm perfectly capable of making sensible decisions about what to do and when. I'll decide tomorrow, depending on the latest information. If necessary we'll get a flight to Houston, or perhaps we'll rent a car and drive there. So calm down."

Adam was silent for a few moments. The tension crackled across the phone line. "Why can't you just get a flight home? Lara shouldn't even be there."

"Because we've just got here. If the hurricane does hit, it's only going to last a few days. Lara's so excited. We're going to Snug Harbor tonight." I could hear the irritation in my tone. I forced a more cheerful note. "You'd love it here. I'd forgotten how fascinating it is. History and romance pours out of every street, and the music is fantastic. There are musicians and street clowns and break-dancers on every corner, and they're all so good. We'd pay hundreds of dollars to see them in a theater in London. And the food is to die for; great for a seafood freak like you."

"What on earth is Snug Harbor?"

"It's the best jazz club in New Orleans. We're having dinner in its little restaurant first."

"Lara shouldn't be out so late. Have you forgotten she's recovering from a head injury? You know how exhausted she gets."

"We're going to the 8pm show and dinner before that. We'll be home in our little beds by 10pm. It's only a ten minute walk from our hotel."

"Let me talk to him, Mum," said Lara, almost snatching the phone out of my hand.

"Dad, it's Charmaine Neville tonight. She's the Queen of Jazz. She's phenomenal. It's the best birthday present I could have. The only thing that would make it better would be having you and Finnie here too."

I don't know why I bother really. Listen and learn, listen and learn.

SNUG HARBOR WAS AS INCREDIBLE AND INTIMATE AS I'D remembered. Lara's entranced expression alone made the trip worthwhile. She'd even stopped moaning about missing Savannah. Her next plan—which I hadn't agreed to—was to visit Savannah in hospital on Tuesday, after my meeting finished and before we had to get to the airport for our flight home. But I was a bit shaken up by Adam's concerns. If the hurricane were still a threat in the morning, I'd see if the meeting was still on schedule. If it were cancelled then we'd try and get a flight to Houston or Atlanta. Perhaps if Katrina blew herself out quickly we might even be able to return to New Orleans for a day and use the air tickets home to London that I'd already paid for.

What about that Kat, though? The wily old devil must have already known that the hurricane was coming; that's why she said I'd be facing challenges in a wild storm and I should stay and face it, or something like that. Perhaps we should stay. It would be a new experience for both of us.

I grinned. Wouldn't Adam love it when he discovered that I took more notice of a crazy old voodoo witch than him. Hope the old lady keeps safe. Her voodoo shop was even closer to the river than the hotel, and it didn't look as if it could stand much wind. Perhaps she'd escape on her broomstick.

CHAPTER 15

*A*ny hope that Katrina would miraculously disappear overnight was quashed next morning with the dramatic news, broadcast continually, that the killer hurricane was now a Category 4 with winds in excess of 140 miles per hour. And it was still right on track for New Orleans. At last my gut told me this was real, and it was time to get out. I phoned the hotel where our meeting was to be; as I expected it had been cancelled. Most of the neurosurgeons had already cancelled their flights; they'd not been due to arrive until Sunday.

There was a short queue at our hotel reception desk, the first I'd ever seen there. As I stood behind a large family—large parents and two large children, all eating large dough-nuts—I overheard them asking why their shuttle hadn't arrived to take them to the airport. Mrs. G, uncharacteristi-cally harassed, assured them she'd called it over an hour ago, and they would have to be patient. As they collapsed on some seats near the door, enormous bags stacked beside them, Mrs. G. greeted me with a wry smile.

"Have you decided to leave too, Dr. Grayson?"

"'Fraid so; it looks like the best option. It sounds as if it might be difficult getting to the airport." I nodded towards the family.

"Everyone has the same idea this morning. Perhaps you and your daughter could get a ride in the Bennetts' shuttle if it ever arrives."

"That would be great, if they could fit us in."

Mrs. G. chuckled. She'd apparently read my mind. "They're very roomy shuttles. You should be able to squeeze in. Hang on a mo' and I'll ask Mr. Bennett."

She returned a minute later. "That's fine. Goodness knows when it will turn up, but you'd better be ready."

"Thanks, I'll go and get Lara and our luggage," I said, surprised by the sudden stilling of the butterflies fluttering in my chest. I'd been trying to ignore them. While Lara threw her clothes into her case, I left a message on Adam's answer phone; it was three in the afternoon in London. I'd forgotten that today was Finnie's big cricket match at the end of their cricket camp. Adam had a policy of always turning his mobile off when we he was doing things with the family.

Half an hour later the loaded shuttle was crawling through the city, hemmed in on all sides by vehicles of every description. Most were going the same way, northbound to the airport along Highway 61, or towards Interstate 10 and away from New Orleans. Our driver dropped us two hundred yards from the main terminal entrance behind the backed-up traffic. The departure hall was jammed with stressed-out people and crying kids, and bidding a heartfelt goodbye and good luck to the Bennetts, we punched two bottles of water out of a dispensing machine and resigned ourselves to a long wait in the United Airlines queue. Lara was wilting, her red hair frizzy in the humid air and her eyes enormous above smudges of dark. The weight on my heart got heavier. Guilt, worry, fear.

It was two hours before I confirmed what I already knew; we would not be getting a flight out until after the hurricane.

Pushing our way against the thronging crowds back outside into the searing heat, we found a shuttle dropping off a load of hopeful passengers, and asked if we could catch a ride back into town.

The driver grinned at us. "You're goin' the wrong way, doncha know."

We climbed into the shuttle. "We figured it might be better than hanging around here. Can you suggest a nice hotel that's likely to stand up against all hurricanes? The one we've been in had hopeless air conditioning and we could do with a cool room if we're going to sit this out."

"Hard to say, but any of the big hotels should be all right. What about the Park Plaza? That's survived a few almighty blows. I'm headin' there now to pick up some folks."

"That sounds fine, thanks. Hopefully we'll be able to get a room if everyone else is leaving."

With most traffic going the other way, the trip into the city was a good deal faster than the one to the airport, and we soon pulled up at the solid looking Park Plaza Hotel.

"Good luck," said the driver as I handed him a generous tip. "Enjoy the Big Easy in the big wind." He winked at Lara and she managed a grin.

"You too. Keep safe," I said, sounding a good deal more relaxed than I felt.

We pushed through the people pushing back to get into the shuttle, and stood in another queue at the hotel reception, fascinated by the mix of people milling about in various forms of dress with all manner of strange baggage.

"What are they all doing here?" Lara whispered. "They don't look like stranded tourists."

A woman sitting on a large bag, a cat next to her in a wire cage, overheard her. "We'd be better off if we were tourists," she said. "Most of us folk here have no way of leaving, and our houses mightn't stand up to a hurricane as bad as this one looks like bein'. It's better to hole up in a hotel until it's over."

The twenty minutes we were standing in the queue was more entertaining than Bourbon Street. Lara got talking to two girls about her age and I contemplated getting out my camera so I could share the strange sights later with Finnie and Adam. But I managed to control the urge. Snapping away while the locals worried about whether their homes would still be standing next time they saw them would definitely tag me as a brash tourist. We finally reached the desk, and when I inquired if there were any rooms left, the receptionist asked me if I was a doctor. I nodded, wondering what on earth about my current appearance gave this away, and was even more puzzled when she asked me for my letterhead authority from Tulane.

"Pardon?"

"You're a doctor from Tulane?"

"No, no: I am a doctor, but just visiting."

"I assumed you must be from Tulane University Hospital. They've worked a deal with us for their staff and families to stay during the hurricane. But you have to show something, like a page with letterhead, to prove you're one of theirs. So I can't give you the cheap rate, but we've still got some rooms at the rack rate."

"Thanks." I looked around. "Goodness, it's quite a crowd. I hope you've got in enough food."

"We hope so too. Folks usually leave as soon as the hurricane passes, so with luck that will be Tuesday at the latest. We'll get lots more guests tomorrow though, unless Katrina is good to us and turns away."

"Fingers crossed, although I suppose that means someone else will cop it." I watched the desk clerk tap away on his computer, hopefully finding us a hurricane-proof room with good air conditioning.

"I've got a twin on the fourth floor. That would be the safest bet. It's high enough so it won't get flooded, but not too high, so it won't sway about. And not too many flights of stairs if the power goes out. Also, it's got fairly small windows, so there'll be fewer windows to smash."

"Heavens, I'd never have thought of all those things." The butterflies began their fluttering again. "It sounds as if you've done this a few times before."

"Yeah, but this hotel is as solid as a rock. Just hunker down, and you'll be fine." The clerk pushed over the registration form. "Can you fill this in, and you'll need to pay the full room rate in advance. That's a policy we have for hurricanes. How many nights do you want?"

I considered for a moment. "Make it three. We have a flight out on Tuesday night." I handed over the completed registration form and my credit card.

"Thank you Dr. Grayson. Katrina will have moved on by then. Good job you have a flight booked though. Now here's your key, and a map of the area and the various sights around here..." He paused, and laughed. "You probably won't need that. Room 402. Take the elevators over there," he said, pointing. "You'll need to take your own luggage up; the porters are run off their feet."

"Not a problem." I thanked him, extracted Lara from her new friends, and we made for another queue.

On Sunday, we woke feeling remarkably chirpy. Last night after an excellent hotel dinner, we'd made the best of a balmy evening and strolled along Canal Street and through City Park. The clear sky made the prospect of the oncoming hurricane much less frightening. Hard to imagine Katrina was out there somewhere, wrecking a swathe of destruction as she advanced on New Orleans. On our return I had a gin and tonic in the hotel bar, and Lara had a non-alcoholic and very expensive cocktail. We obviously weren't the only people finding the hurricane hype somewhat surreal. The bar was buzzing, and everyone was having a fabulously good time. We dragged ourselves away from the blues band an hour before midnight, and took turns luxuriating under a high-pressure shower before falling deeply asleep on our blissfully comfortable beds in the air-conditioned room.

Even our phone call to Adam had been positive. Although he didn't sound too happy when I told him we'd failed to get out, he calmed down when I described our new sleeping arrangements, especially when I added that the hotel was listed on the National Register of Historic Places—a handy detail Lara had read out from the welcome pamphlet on the coffee table—and therefore had withstood one hell of a lot of hurricanes. Finbar talked to us as well, excited because they'd won their cricket match and he'd batted two sixes. He was envious though. "Lucky sod," he said to Lara. "I don't suppose there'll be another hurricane when we all go to New Orleans in December, on our way to New Zealand."

My eyebrows were up when I took the phone back from Lara and spoke again to Adam. "New Orleans in December?"

"Well, I did say we could all go some time, and Finbar seems keen. I thought it might make Lara happy given you weren't able to see Danny's grandmother. We could do a bit of advance planning and perhaps you could write to her first."

I felt the smart of tears behind my eyes. "I love you. I'm sorry about all this. But we're safe as houses so you don't need to worry. Lara's already made friends with some local girls staying here."

"Not sure safe as houses is the best thing to hope for. I'm glad you're in a solid hotel though. That one you started off in didn't look too sturdy."

I gazed down from our 'smallish' window on to a calm-looking city. I knew it would be stinking hot and humid outside our cooled cocoon. The streets below had few people on them. Perhaps we should go for a walk while we still could, and find somewhere in the French Quarter for a monstrous American breakfast?

Lara had turned on the TV to check the latest gloomy predictions about Katrina. Maybe it was a storm in a teacup and had died away in the night. No, she was on target to slam into New Orleans on Monday morning. A second rapid intensification had occurred at seven this morning, and Katrina was now a Category 5 storm. Extensive flooding of New Orleans was predicted as a result of the massive storm surges of up to thirty feet that would be generated by a hurricane of that size. This was rapidly becoming one of the most intense Atlantic hurricanes on record.

Ray Nagin, who we learned was the mayor of New Orleans, was due to report to a news conference at ten, so we decided to have breakfast in the hotel before venturing out. A pancake stack, maple syrup, two eggs easy over, bacon and tomatoes, all diluted by two large cups of coffee for me, and tea for Lara. We were glad of it as ballast when we returned to our room and had to stomach the next bulletin. Nagin called Katrina 'a storm most of us have long feared,' and ordered what was apparently a historic first—a mandatory evacuation of the city.

I wasn't too sure what that meant, but clearly we and a great many other people weren't going anywhere. We found ourselves glued to the TV, watching hyped-up news reporters interviewing people as they tried to get out, dreadful scenes of the devastation Katrina had wrought through Florida, and bird's-eye views of Interstate 10, now with the southbound lanes turned into northbound ones, packed with fleeing New Orleanians.

The Superdome was also filling up with the homeless, poor, and frightened, and already looked like an organizational nightmare. Apparently up to 100,000 New Orleans citizens had no car or means of personal transport to leave the city, even if they wanted to. Thank heavens we were safe here, and not stuck in the Superdome, or in endless hours of unbearably hot traffic jams and road rage.

At noon the National Weather Service reported that Katrina had been downgraded to a Category 4, still a catastrophic storm, with winds of up to 140 miles per hour and a storm surge of twenty feet. But a new warning had entered the mix. The levees in New Orleans, built to withstand a Category 3 hurricane, might be overtopped.

"All wood-framed low rising apartment buildings will be destroyed. Concrete block low-rise apartment buildings will sustain major damage, including some wall and roof failure. High rise office and apartment buildings will sway dangerously, a few to the point of total collapse. All windows will blow out."

Heavens, how will Mrs. G's little old hotel and Kat's Voodoo Parlor remain standing in this?

"Persons, pets and livestock exposed to the winds will face certain death if struck. Power outages will last for weeks. Water shortages will make human suffering incredible by modern standards. Once the tropical storm and hurricane force winds onset, do not venture outside."

Sitting on our comfortable hotel beds, the wind picking up outside, the message finally sank in. *This is actually happening. It's not a case of American over-reaction.* While Lara stayed glued to the TV, I paced the room, trying to focus my mind and think what we should do next. We were being told to stock up on essential supplies and water. Perhaps we should go out and find a supermarket and get some stuff, just in case? We should certainly get some spare batteries. We both had head torches but they mightn't last the distance if the power was out for the next few days.

The hospitals? Could I offer some help? Should I try and contact Stork at Baptist Hospital—has its name been changed to Memorial? The last time I'd seen Stork was at a Neurosurgery Conference in San Francisco about three years ago, and he'd seemed happy then in his job at Baptist —or Memorial or whatever it was called now—so he'd probably still be there. He was a seriously good neuroradiologist.

Those crazy days at Mass General. I hadn't thought about them for years. Stork Hamilton had been a slightly peripheral member of my close group of friends there, but his laconic southern drawl and wicked sense of humor had made him a welcome addition whenever he deigned to join us. Before the hurricane messed up our plans, I'd been wondering whether I should look him up. I knew Stork would be hurt if I didn't, and he'd love to meet Lara. But the thought of having to explain about my panic attacks was not pleasant. Bad enough knowing that the medical community in London, and probably elsewhere in the UK, was gossiping about me, without spreading the news internationally. Not that Stork would gossip, but somehow these things always got out sooner or later.

I sighed. Was it even worth trying to find him now? I wouldn't be much use as a neurosurgeon, given my incompetence label. But if legally all I was permitted to do was assist with general first aid, explanations mightn't be necessary. I could surely still manage that without going into panic mode. And Lara would be OK staying by herself for a few hours in the hotel. Last night at dinner we'd sat with one of the girls Lara had met in reception and her parents, and the girls had exchanged room numbers. The two of them could hang out together. Better than being stuck with me for hours on end.

So around two o'clock, leaving Lara with a gaggle of other teens in the well-stocked games room and armed with a map of the area and directions from the desk clerk, I started out for Memorial. The winds were definitely picking up as I walked the short distance to the sprawling hospital complex on Napoleon Avenue. The security guard at the main entrance was trying, without much success, to vet the steady influx of locals arriving in the hope of being permitted to shelter from the storm, and I managed to convince him to let me in.

Showing my London hospital ID card to a receptionist on the information desk, I asked her to page Dr. Hamilton, and sat down to wait. Not that I expected Stork to appear, given the chaos all around.

Less than ten minutes later there was a tap on my shoulder. Stork stood at least six foot three inches and was as skinny as a stalk; thus his moniker. His actual name was Bryce. His long, mournful-looking face topped by a halo of spiky, graying hair, belied his naturally optimistic outlook, an attitude that had not deserted him, even in this crisis.

"Georgia, my lovely." His grin split his face as he grabbed me and buried me in his hug. Pulling back he looked me up and down. "Nice of you to drop by."

"I thought I'd see how you guys could cope with a spot of wind and rain." I felt a smile crease my face; I'd almost forgotten the surge of warmth that seeing an old friend could generate.

Over a cup of dishwater coffee from the dispenser machine in the lobby, we rapidly exchanged news about our families, before getting onto the current chaotic situation. Stork's wife, Marcie, and his two kids, were also bunking down at the Park Plaza to ride out the storm. Stork did some consulting at Tulane University Hospital and had decided to take up their offer of cheap accommodation for staff families. He nodded towards the family groups milling around the lobby, many with dogs and cats and birds in cages.

"A lot of staff whose families can't get out, or don't want to leave, stay in the hospital buildings during hurricanes, but Marcie and I thought the hotel would be safer," he explained. "It's likely to get frantic here. Many of our medical staff have already left New Orleans, so we'll have our work cut out if Katrina is as bad as predicted."

"What's with all the animals?"

"I know. Bizarre, isn't it? The hospital will be full of pets as well as people. So much for hygiene." Stork's long face made him look as doleful as the beagle sitting in a cage a few yards away.

"Could I help?" I offered tentatively. "I realize I couldn't do much, given I'm not licensed in Louisiana, but my Massachusetts license is still current from the short courses in aneurysm surgery I've been teaching in Boston over the past few years. Perhaps I could assist with—I don't know—first aid, or even triage if that's permitted, if you have an influx of people with injuries after the hurricane."

"Hey, that could be helpful. If we do get in a pickle the State Governor will likely suspend state licensure requirements so out-of-state medical professionals can help out."

"I'll give you my mobile number and if you need me, just call. I'll find Marcie when I get back to the hotel. It'll be good to see her again. Lara and your two are sure to hit it off."

"Marcie will be glad of the company and some distraction from two cooped-up kids. I won't get over there this evening. We've just had a crisis meeting, and I need to stay on site until the hurricane is over, and we know we're on top of things. But with luck, we'll all be back to normal, bar a few broken windows and some surface flooding, by tomorrow night."

"So soon?"

"They're predicting it will have passed over by late Monday, but we shall see." Stork's beeper went and he pulled it out. "I've got to go, Georgia, but it's fantastic to see you. You picked the right place at the wrong time for your visit. It's a pity it couldn't have been under better circumstances; we could have taken in some good music."

I hesitated, and then spoke quietly. "Actually, I've been taking time off from surgery for the last few weeks. I had a bit of an overload meltdown. That's why I was shunted off here for the neurosurgeons' training meeting. Our director figured I couldn't do any damage sitting in a seminar room. But I'm still licensed in the UK as well as Massachusetts, and OK to do everything but neurosurgery."

Stork looked taken aback. "Gosh, that's rough. You always did work too bloody hard, and it's a tough specialization."

"It's been difficult, especially for Adam and the kids."

"I bet. But are you feeling any better?"

"My problem is understanding why it happened, and I think I'm getting a bit closer to that."

"I'm sure you'll get the better of it," said Stork. "Once Katrina's done her thing, if I can do anything to help I'd be happy to."

"Thanks. If we get a chance I wouldn't mind talking about it with you. It's too hard with the guys I work with in London."

"I can imagine. If we do need some non-surgical help, are you sure you're up for that?"

"Absolutely. I'm certain I can handle it; in fact I'd really like to help out. It seems wrong to sit on my backside. If I found it was too much for me, I'd tell you."

The wind and rain were picking up as I returned to the hotel with a bag of emergency supplies. Lara was back in our room, glued to the TV again. We located Marcie and we all had a rushed dinner in the packed hotel restaurant. By seven that night an early dusk had fallen over the city, now in the grip of howling winds and rain as Katrina edged closer.

There was no escaping the relentless weather updates from the TV monitors throughout the hotel. But by the time we returned to our room to phone Adam, getting him out of bed, I had some better news to report; Katrina's sustained winds had weakened slightly and the storm surge was now eighteen, not twenty feet. She was predicted to make landfall before sunrise as a Category 4 storm.

I did my best to keep my conversation with Adam light by telling him about Stork and his family, but we soon ran out of optimistic conversation, especially as we had to struggle to hear each other across the crackling line. After Lara's turn, she handed the phone back to me and I promised to call again as soon as we woke. Poor Adam, it was worse for him than us. He'd be too tense and fearful to sleep well tonight.

Peering through the window, in the watery streetlights I could just make out the trees below, bending double as gusts hit them. As instructed by the hotel staff, we pushed our beds as far away from the window as they would go without completely blocking the door to the en suite. As I was closing the curtains against the threat of breaking glass I heard a loud explosion, and saw a sheet of flame shooting into the air somewhere below. At the same time the room and the world outside was plunged into darkness. New Orleans—well this area anyway—had already lost its power, and the eye of the storm was still hours away.

Fumbling my way to the bedside table, I retrieved my head torch. Lara had just found hers and I sat beside her on her bed as the whole building shook every time a screeching gust of wind caught it. *At least we're not on the top floor.* The room was already heating up without the air conditioning, so we had cold showers by the wavering light of our torches and collapsed on our beds, uncovered and sweating, and a little bit scared.

CHAPTER 16

In spite of the whistling, roaring elements I fell into a fitful sleep, waking with a jolt in the pitch black as an explosion rocked the building. Scrabbling for my head torch I scanned the room, heart still in my mouth.

"What is it?" I heard Lara say.

Then I noticed the curtains billowing and moved cautiously to the window, my feet squelching on wet carpet. Pulling the curtains aside, I peered out. I felt a draught and my head torch glistened off streaks of water seeping in the edges and running down the window as the wall of rain thundered into it. The glass was pumping in and out like a live thing, and the windowsill was swimming. Lara grabbed my arm and I moved a little so she could look out too. Through the streaming rain I could see a multistory building lit up by flames engulfing it from below. But the Park Plaza was in darkness as I looked down and then up at the floors above me.

Praying that the window wouldn't shatter, we went back to bed. Lara turned on her stomach and squashed a pillow over her head, and I followed her example. And there we lay, hour after hour, trying to muffle the phenomenal noise of the hurricane as it ripped New Orleans asunder. With every almighty crash my heart rate accelerated and I held my breath, prepared to flee to the corridor if the window shattered or the wall collapsed. At last the room began to lighten, and creeping gingerly over to the window I peered down through the wind-blown rain. Was I still asleep and dreaming; perhaps I was in a boat?

Below me, surging along the wide avenue that yesterday had been Canal Street, a river of swirling water was pushed along by howling winds. I flinched as great chunks of wood, sheet iron, and heavy branches from trees fired through the air and crashed against buildings. Cars lay on their sides and even upside down, and power poles spewed at crazy angles across the flooded street, deadly looking power lines whipping in the wind and floating on the water. I looked over at Lara's bed. Her pillow had slipped off her head and she was lying on her back, fast asleep.

As the light strengthened, I gazed transfixed at the surreal scene outside. Through the gusts of rain I saw something crawling through the water and with horror realized it was a man struggling towards the hotel, grabbing whatever he could to steady himself as the wind threatened to blow him away. I picked up the hotel phone; surely they would send someone out to rescue the poor fellow? But the phone was dead. By the time I discovered my mobile was dead as well, the man had vanished.

"What's it like out there now?" Lara was sitting up, her eyes bleary.

"Terrible. The wind is wild and the road below is like a river. I think we should go down to the lobby and see if they have any idea how long it's going to last." I was pulling on my jeans and sneakers, and as soon as Lara was dressed I grabbed our door key card and with our head torches on we went out into the unlit corridor, joining a stream of people all pushing down the stairs to the lobby. Some were silent, others talked excitedly, and a few were crying hysterically. Already the lobby was full of people sliding and sloshing through water flooding across the floor. At the reception desk, harassed staff members were answering a barrage of questions, seemingly with no more idea of what to do than their guests.

Then a man in a security uniform jumped on the counter and shouted for silence. He finally managed to get the frightened crowd's attention. "There's no need to panic." He patted the air in front of him, using gestures that suggested anything but calm. "This is superficial flooding from the torrential rains, and now that the rain is easing off, the waters will dissipate quickly."

"Bullshit," a male voice shouted. "The fucking water's still pouring in. We should be getting outta here fast." His voice was joined by others, and the security guard waved his arms even more, his face red as he tried to make himself heard.

"The streets outside are flooded and you leave at your own risk. Once the winds have dropped, if you want to leave you can wade to the Superdome. The water is only a foot or two deep in most places. There'll be food and shelter there. In the meantime we'll be handing out cold food and drinks in the restaurant on the next floor. We have no electricity, and there are no working elevators."

"I'm fucking leaving now," shouted the same male voice.

"If you leave you won't be permitted back, as we can't cope with the numbers of people we already have. We'll do our best to ensure everyone's safety, but we can't guarantee it. Those of you who stay should remain in your rooms, if you can, to keep the stairwells clear." He pushed his cap off and wiped a hand across his forehead. Even from where I stood on the other side of the lobby, I could see the sweat pouring off his face. The only human sound now was the whimpering of a child; even loudmouth seemed to have got the message. Then a massive explosion rent the air, coming from outside somewhere.

"We're all going to die," a woman screamed. Others took up her frenzied cries as the crowd dissolved into chaos. Some people pushed back towards the stairwells; the remainder struggled towards the door to the street.

The security officer was shouting again. "No one is going to die. Please remain calm. Please remain calm."

The screams and cries abated, but the crowd was anything but calm. I heard my name and turned quickly. Marcie was making her way over to us, her children in tow.

"Georgia, thank goodness. I hoped you'd be down here. Are you all right?" Her blue eyes fastened on mine.

"We're fine. Had a wonderful sleep. How about you guys?"

"We're OK. I missed Stork though. He'd have sat on these two," Marcie said.

Lara was grinning at Marcie's children, who looked more excited than scared.

"Jamie, stop that." Marcie frowned at her son, who was jumping up and down, laughing as he splashed his sister.

"Yes, menace, stop it." Isabelle stamped her own foot down, spraying her mother and Lara as well as Jamie.

"Why don't we see if we can get any of this cold food they're supplying, before it's all gone?" I suggested, pushing away the sudden sharp longing to see—and touch—Finnie and Adam.

Marcie nodded. "That's what we need, gang. Stick close, or we'll get separated." She herded Isabelle and Jamie in front of her, and we all made for the back of the queue already forming at the bottom of the stairs.

"Is there a doctor here? We need a doctor, quickly." The frightened voice rose above the noise of the crowd, and I looked around and saw a man at the other side of the lobby waving an arm high in the air. I glanced at Marcie.

"I'd better see if I can help. You guys go and get some food. Lara, can you go with them? Grab me a bread roll or something. I'll find you later; if I don't, I'll see you back in our room." I was moving away as I spoke, hoping another doctor would be there before me. *Damn, I seem to be the only one.* The hotel was full of doctors' families, but presumably the doctors themselves were all manning the hospitals.

I squatted beside a woman half-sitting, half-lying, in the water sloshing on the floor. There was a greenish tinge on her dark, clammy skin and naked fear on her face as she tried frantically to take in another shallow breath. "What happened?" I asked the man who had called for help, and was now kneeling beside me.

"She's having a heart attack." He glanced around at the people closing in to get a better look. "Quickly, please, someone call an ambulance," he yelled, his voice hoarse.

My own pulse escalating, I focused on the woman's perspiring face. *Poor thing. I know exactly how you're feeling.* I took her firmly by the shoulders and concentrated on speaking calmly. "You're not having a heart attack. You just feel like you are because your breathing is too fast and shallow. Look at me and try to breathe as slowly as I am." I pressed my hand firmly against the woman's upper chest above her large palpitating bosom as I tried to sooth her, and called to the curious crowd, "Has anyone got a paper bag?"

A bag was thrust into my hand and I upturned it to get rid of a few pastry crumbs. I held it over the woman's mouth and nose. "Breathe in and out of this; that will stop your panicky feelings."

The woman grasped the bag with both hands, her brown eyes wide and terrified as they stared into mine. Her breathing slowed, her shoulders seemed to soften, and then her large frame began to shake, the soft rolls on her arms quivering and her lower legs, protruding from cut-off jeans, jittering up and down in the water. I gestured to the man beside me to help get the woman into a chair. "Are you her husband?"

"Yes, Ma'am, I am." His hoarse voice had a quaver in it now. "Thank our Lord you were here. She would have died..."

"No, she was in no danger of dying. She began to breathe too fast and that's what caused those dreadful feelings of panic. It truly feels as if you might die, but no one ever does."

Her husband seemed confused. "But she had terrible pains in her chest."

"Yes, that's common, and one of the reasons it makes people think they're having a heart attack."

"Will it happen again?"

"I don't know. It might do. If it hasn't happened before, it was probably a result of being in this frightening situation. She became very anxious and started to breathe quickly, and before she realized it she was hyperventilating. Just in case, keep a paper bag with you, and if it happens again get her to breathe into that; it'll bring her oxygen levels back to normal."

"Thank you, Miss." The woman's voice was a whisper. "I'm sorry for giving you trouble."

I smiled at her. Her skin looked much better, and her trembling was now only perceptible in her hands. "You've had a frightening experience. Believe me, it can happen to anyone, and it's good to know how to deal with it when it does." I turned to a hotel official standing anxiously beside us. "I don't suppose there's any hope of hot tea?"

"No, I don't think so. But I'll make sure she has somewhere quiet to lie down. Thank you, doctor—you are a doctor?"

"Yes, I am, just visiting from England."

"I'm the floor manager. We're grateful to you, doctor. Perhaps you could give me your name and room number in case we need you again."

"Of course." I returned his clammy handshake. "But you should see if there's a local doctor here. I can't do much being out of state."

"I realize that, but if there's no one else available..." The manager's voice tailed off. I could almost see the desperate thoughts flitting through his head as he viewed the disaster scene that, only yesterday, had been his elegant lobby. "At least the worst is over, and we haven't been obliterated by Katrina. This water should soon be gone, and then we can begin the big cleanup." The manager's raw sigh broke the hush that had overtaken the small group of people still crowding us. He raised his voice. "OK folks, the show's over. Let's clear the way so we can get this lady and her husband to a room upstairs."

I followed the crowds to the dining room and by some fluke found Lara quickly; her red hair stood out like a beacon. As the day wore on and the wind dropped, the atmosphere in the crowded hotel became almost jolly as the residents of N'Orleans realized they had survived the mother of all hurricanes. I shuddered as I looked around at the many families— from their dress and accents probably poor—who had taken shelter in the hotel. *What will you find when you return to your homes?* What were the chances of their houses standing against winds that had lifted the roof of the Superdome? —This gem had spread like wildfire through the crowds.

Back in our bedroom, we looked out on a blue sky, and below we could see the water rapidly clearing from the higher parts of the streets. People even wandered about, inspecting the chaos wrought by the winds. Marcie and the kids appeared; they'd decided to take a walk to Memorial and see how Stork had survived the night.

"Let's go with them," Lara begged, and I took no convincing. No doubt thinking a doctor might be useful to keep around, the floor manager readily agreed that we could all leave and return to the hotel later.

Amazingly, the wind had dropped to a pleasant, if stiff, breeze, and the water was rapidly receding from the streets. Houses with broken windows and missing roofs stood forlorn in their torn gardens, and the façade of one two-story house had been ripped off, exposing like a doll's house staircases and rooms, some still with furniture. Cars had been flattened under falling trees or blown into crazy positions across the roads. At one point we narrowly escaped a geyser of water that shot from a manhole, ten feet or more into the air. But the street outside Memorial Hospital was almost dry, although from the debris piled up next to the sidewalk it had obviously been flooded earlier.

Entering the Clara Street lobby, we were swallowed by a mass of people. Some appeared to be leaving and others had settled in groups on the floor or on chairs, surrounded by precious belongings, including the occasional rabbit or cat in a cage. The mood was generally upbeat, and plenty of laughter could be heard. One group sang hymns, accompanied by a woman with a guitar. Areas were roped off where large windows had blown out. Some had makeshift boarding over them, but others were still open to the elements.

Narrowly avoiding standing on a crawling baby, we made it to the information desk where two men in porter uniforms were struggling to deal with the muddle of people coming and going. Neither of them knew who Stork was, let alone where he might be, so Marcie disappeared up the nearest stairs on a mission to find him. Thirty minutes later she was back, Stork with her. He looked ten years older than he had yesterday—the bags under his bloodshot eyes not helping—but he grinned at Lara and me over Jamie's tousled head.

"Hi, Georgia. Thanks for looking after this lot. And a wild guess here, but I've got money on your name being Lara?" Stork's eyebrows rose.

"I am. Mum's told me all about you."

"Hmm. Well, I could tell you a thing or two about your mum."

"How was it here last night?" I asked.

"Pretty bloody scary, actually. We've got lots of windows out and roofs off, and we've had rain pouring in everywhere. We lost all power early on, so it's been a nightmare managing the ICU patients. The generators are coping with all the essential services, but only just. Only two of the elevators are working and the phones—mobiles too—are out. And on top of all that the place is full to the brim with evacuees. Most of them ended up in the corridors last night because so many windows were blown out. Heaven knows how the kitchen is feeding them all."

"Have you got enough medical staff?"

"No, not by a long shot. A lot of doctors have left town, and everyone here is exhausted. None of us got any sleep last night."

"You could help out, Mum," said Lara.

I felt a flutter low in my stomach—*excitement?* "Is there a way I can help without going against your licensing regulations?"

"No one cares about licenses right now," Stork said. "It would be jolly helpful if you could do a round with one of the junior residents, especially with the neurosurgery patients. All the Memorial Neurosurgery Attendings were either on holiday or at a meeting in New York when Katrina decided to call. So you could give specialist advice and the neurosurgery resident could act as the official doctor."

I turned to Lara. "Are you sure you'll be OK at the hotel without me for a while?"

"Duh. I'm sixteen, mother."

"She can help me entertain these two," Marcie said, her gaze straying to her kids squatting down by a cage with a cat in it. "Stay as long as you're needed. Poor Stork looks as if he could do with some help. If you can't get back to the hotel tonight, Lara can stay with us. We've got two adjoining rooms so Jamie and I can have one and Lara and Isabelle the other.

"Thanks Marcie." I looked up at Stork, towering above us. "Tell me where to go."

"I'd better check it out with the CEO first, just to cover you." He turned to Marcie. "Can you guys get back to the hotel by yourselves? I can't leave; there's still so much to do before it gets dark again."

"We'll be fine, honey." Marcie stretched up to kiss her husband, and he cupped her face in his hands and gazed in her eyes for a long moment before kissing her very gently and very lingeringly on the lips. The bridge of my nose tingled and I squeezed shut my eyes. *Adam and I used to be like that. Can we ever be like that again?*

"Come on kiddoes, time to go," Marcie said, looking flushed.

I shook my thoughts away and fished in my pocket for my hotel key card. "Here, Lara, take our room key."

"What about you? Won't you need it if you get back late and I'm with Marcie?"

"I thought I could stay here. Is that possible, Stork?"

"Sure it is." He winked at his wife, then turned back to me. "You'll have to bunk on a mattress in my office with me though."

"Good grief, that's a lot to ask. But if you promise not to snore…" I fished around in my shoulder bag, and pulled out a fat wallet. "I've got my Massachusetts Practicing License with me if the hospital needs some ID."

WITHIN THIRTY MINUTES, IDENTIFIED BY A CODED WRISTBAND, I was in the corridor outside the sixth floor Intensive Care Unit, listening to a tired junior neurosurgery resident as she summarized the case histories of the patients they hadn't been able to discharge before Katrina hit. The patients, many attached to beeping life-support equipment and a few to noisy mechanical ventilators, were crowded side-by-side in the corridors and other common areas. They'd been shifted there last night when the large glass windows in the adjacent ICU shattered, covering the unit with glass. The crowded spaces also housed other less critically ill patients from wards damaged during Katrina. Pauline, the resident, who looked not much older than Lara, was struggling to keep the frightened and distressed patients as safe and comfortable as possible.

On our bed round, we had difficulty hearing each other over the dissonant sounds of the monitors, pumps, and ventilators, and the worried voices of family members who were trying to still the patients' fears in spite of their own. We arrived at the bed of an elderly woman, whose labored breathing could be heard even above the racket. She lay motionless, her weathered, wrinkled arms lying outside the white sheet, an IV snaking from the inside of her right wrist, and an emerald ring adorning a thin brown finger on her left hand. From the end of her bed I could see her long, white hair, but her face was obscured by the covers stretched over a cradle that spanned her from waist to knees. She had no one with her, and Pauline flipped through her notes.

"I don't know this patient. She was brought in from orthopedics early this morning and I haven't even had time to say hullo." Pauline's shoulders slumped; she was close to tears.

"Take your time," I said quietly. "You've been doing an amazing job. No one is expecting you to be able to do everything. Why don't I look at her notes?"

I saw Pauline's shoulders straighten a little, and her eyes closed briefly behind her glasses as she took some deep, shuddering breaths. She managed a tremulous smile as she handed me the file. "I lost it there for a minute. I'm so tired…"

"As soon as we get through here you should take a few hours sleep. I can manage by myself for a while." I began to read the summary page at the front of the file.

Mrs. Leaumont is an 89-year-old woman who underwent a total right hip replacement on August 24th. Prior to her surgery she was an exceptionally healthy woman for her age with no major risk factors and no previous significant medical problems apart from a total left hip replacement in February of this year. Her recovery from that was excellent.

As I scanned down the page, the patient's name slowly penetrated my buzzing thoughts. Of course, I'd known who it must be. I was going to meet her after all. I checked the patient label at the top of the page.

Savannah Leaumont; DOB April 12th, 1916.

CHAPTER 17

My eyes blurred as I took in the rest of the label: *Fourth Street, Garden District. Next of kin: Luke Leaumont.* For a second I didn't move, didn't breathe, didn't think— and then I slowly turned the pages until I came to the most recent entries in the old lady's file. I waited until the words on the page stopped moving. They'd been written by a nurse at ten this morning.

Elderly woman previously recovering satisfactorily from hip replacement transferred from orthopedics at 9:30am and requiring close monitoring because of concerns about her rapid heart rate of 119 and breathing of 25 times per minute. Assessment by resident requested.

"Let's check her over," I said, moving to the head of the bed. Pauline wheeled over a screen, and did her best to conceal the old lady from the other patients nearby. *Kat, you old witch. This is your best trick yet.* Mrs. Leaumont was lying with her eyes closed, her chest rising and falling rapidly under the pale blue bodice of her cotton nightgown. My throat ached as I looked at the lined face, her coffee skin contrasting with the pure white hair flowing defiantly from a central part to lie untidily on the pillow. She still possessed the fine beauty I remembered.

"Mrs. Leaumont?" My voice was louder than I intended. "Can you hear me?"

Her eyelids fluttered open, and she looked up at me, her dark eyes sunken and unfocused. "Yes," she said, croakily. Her breath caught as she spoke.

"I'm the doctor and I'd like to check your heart, if that's all right?" I said, leaning close to her.

"Yes." She blinked and seemed to look at me more intently. My heart was in my mouth. "You're not Dr. Sullivan. Why isn't he here?"

"Your own doctor isn't able to look after you for a while. Do you remember there was a hurricane last night? The windows in your ward were blown out, and you were brought over here to the ICU so we could keep a close eye on you."

"Oh, I do remember. Is the hurricane over yet?"

"Yes, it is, and luckily it doesn't seem too bad. But I'm afraid the hospital is short of medical staff, so that's why you've got me to look after you. Is that all right?"

"Yes, thank you, I don't mind." Her eyelids fluttered and closed.

I used my watch to check Savannah's breathing rate—twenty-six breaths per minute; still too fast. Borrowing Pauline's stethoscope, I positioned it on the old lady's chest. Her lungs sounded clear, and I could detect no heart murmurs or abnormal beats, but her heart rate of 122 was too rapid.

"You're having some trouble with your breathing," I said, as I handed the stethoscope back to Pauline.

Savannah—Lara's habit of calling her Savannah had infected me—Savannah opened her dark eyes again. "I do feel a bit short of breath."

"Is there a portable oximeter here?" I asked Pauline. "And can you check her temperature and blood pressure?"

"I'll go and see what I can find." Pauline rushed off.

Poor girl. But she was looking slightly less fragile, probably because she no longer had to take sole responsibility for twenty-five critically ill patients. Turning down the covers I gently examined Savannah's hip wound. It was healing well with no obvious infection, and her legs weren't swollen. Pauline arrived back with a small battery-powered oximeter, and I attached it while Pauline took the patient's temperature and blood pressure. Damn, her blood oxygen saturation was too low; eighty-nine percent. It should be up around ninety-eight percent.

I smiled at my new patient. "Pauline and I will take a look at your results and then we'll see if we can help with that rapid breathing of yours. We'll be right back."

Moving along the corridor, away from the crowded beds, we discussed our findings. Savannah had no fever, but her rapid breathing and accelerated heart rate, along with a relatively low blood pressure and low blood oxygen saturation, suggested that she might have a pulmonary embolus. "So, what should we do now?" I asked Pauline, unable to stop myself from using even these desperate circumstances as an opportunity for teaching.

Pauline rose to the occasion and answered confidently, "We need some more tests: a blood gas to get a precise reading of her blood oxygen, and radiology at least. Then a respiratory therapist would give her any supplemental oxygen she required using a nasal cannula, and we would start her on blood-thinning medication, perhaps by an intravenous pump."

"Well done. But I don't think any of those diagnostic procedures are going to be feasible any time soon." I surveyed the chaotic scene before us. "We need to go ahead on what we have, and give her oxygen and blood-thinning medication via injection. We'll have to keep a careful eye on her breathing and blood oxygen saturation. That's about the best we can do."

"Right. I'll set that up." Pauline looked almost happy. "Do you want me to tell Mrs. Leaumont?"

"No, I'll do that. You get the oxygen set up and see if you

can locate this medication." I wrote rapidly in the patient notes and handed the file to Pauline to authorize as the licensed medical practitioner, before returning to Savannah.

"Hullo again." Her eyes snapped open and I smiled at her.

"Hullo," she said, her voice surprisingly clear. "Have you decided what's going on with me?" She seemed almost amused in spite of her labored breathing.

"I think so. Your wound is healing nicely, so that's good. But you might have a small blood clot that has traveled from your leg to your lungs as the result of your surgery; it's quite common after a hip replacement. It's important to treat it without delay, so we're giving you some oxygen to help your breathing, and an injection that will thin your blood and stop the clotting."

"I thought that's what you got on long plane trips?"

"Some people are at risk of embolism in that situation as well."

"It seems unfair that I'm not even flying somewhere exotic. At least that might have compensated for all this carry on." Her eyes twinkled.

"Ah, but think of how much easier it will be to run around, now you've got a new hip," I countered. "Exotic places aren't much use if you can't walk about and explore them."

"That's true. Don't mind me, I'm just a grumpy old woman," she said, her amused expression back. "I'm very grateful really. But I need to get home and see if my house is all right."

"I know you must be worried, but first you have to get yourself properly better"—I looked around me—"although I agree that's a tough ask in this situation."

"Oh well, it could be worse, I suppose," Savannah said, her breathing rasping in and out.

"Do you have any family in New Orleans?"

"My son Luke is here. I think he came in and saw me this

morning—I'm a bit confused. Perhaps it was last night. But he had to go and check on the house, and he has his own family to look out for."

"Perhaps he'll get back in later today." I turned as Pauline appeared, wheeling the oxygen equipment, a nurse behind her with a covered bowl. I touched Savannah on her shoulder. "I'll come back later. When the nurse has given you the injection, try and get some rest."

"Thank you, doctor, I will." Her Southern drawl transported me back seventeen years.

The remainder of the day flashed past as I checked patient after patient. A more senior resident had arrived soon after we'd left Savannah's bedside, and I'd sent a relieved Pauline off to find somewhere to sleep. Fortunately, none of the other patients in the crowded unit had developed any serious complications, and everyone appeared stable on their current medications. The main problem was the unbearable heat. Without any air-conditioning and with the temperature outside in the nineties, it must have been close to one hundred degrees in the hospital. Family members sponged down burning patients with cold water, and staff stripped down to the minimum they could wear and still stay decent. I considered transforming my jeans into shorts by hacking around the legs with scissors, but decided the more they covered the better, given the filth accumulating everywhere—especially in the toilets.

I had barely a moment to think about my strange meeting with Danny's grandmother, except to feel relieved that Savannah hadn't recognized me. How much she knew about my involvement in Danny's death, I had no idea, but given her poorly condition the last thing I wanted to do was upset her. I kept an eye out for Luke. Danny's uncle. Not that I had a clue what he looked like. I wasn't sure whether I'd approach or avoid him if he did show up. But as the afternoon wore on, Savannah remained alone.

I was feeling better than I had for months. I'd slipped back into my old habits without a trace of anxiety. It was like coming home. There was a moment when I felt my heart beginning to race, but within seconds it steadied as I focused on the patient in front of me. Janet McKenzie was a twenty-six-year-old woman who had been admitted to Memorial on Saturday, in labor with her first child. Feeling extremely unwell and with her contractions five minutes apart, she experienced a sudden unbearable headache within an hour of arriving and became confused and drowsy.

A probable subarachnoid hemorrhage precipitated by her labor was diagnosed, and she was rushed into theater for an emergency caesarean section. The baby was delivered full-term and healthy, and within two hours of the delivery, Janet's confusion and drowsiness had resolved, and she become conscious and alert. She had no focal signs, and subarachnoid blood was confirmed in her CSF. A fifteen-millimeter anterior communicating artery aneurysm was observed on an MRI brain scan, and she had been scheduled for surgery on Sunday. The impending hurricane had put paid to that, and the surgery postponed until after the hurricane had passed. Now any surgery was impossible, given the outage of power, the disappearance of neurosurgeons, and the impoverished nursing and theater staff.

Patrick, the senior resident, had come from internal medicine and had no experience of neurosurgery, let alone the treatment of cerebral aneurysms. His relief was palpable when he discovered my specialty, and he watched intently as I examined Janet and pronounced that I was satisfied she was in no immediate danger. She was still alert with a Grade 1 subarachnoid hemorrhage, and delaying the clipping of the aneurysm was a reasonable approach in the circumstances.

Brad, Janet's husband, sat on the bed trying to comfort her. Sobbing quietly, she lay with a wet towel across her eyes in an effort to reduce her throbbing headache, afraid for her newborn baby who was being cared for in the better-staffed and less crowded obstetrics ward. I advised an increase in her pain relief, but otherwise she was on the same suite of medications I would have had her on herself. I stayed at her bedside after completing my examination, carefully answering the anxious couple's questions. I could almost see Janet's swollen breasts and empty arms tingle as she begged me to let her feed her baby. Writing a quick note for Brad to take to Obstetrics, suggesting that the child be brought to her mother for each feeding, I was surprised by a tingle behind my eyes. *I must be tired, or getting soft. I've been away from patients too long.* I handed over the note, smiling at Brad as I explained he would need to sit with Janet while she was feeding their daughter so he could alert the nurse immediately if Janet felt unwell. *As if wild horses could drag him away.*

WHEN A GRINNING STORK APPEARED AT MY SIDE AND GAVE ME permission to knock off, I glanced at my watch in surprise. "Good heavens, eight o'clock. I hadn't realized it was so late. How's your day been?"

"OK I suppose, although I've had better ones. But I'm getting a bit peckish, and if we don't get to the fourth floor where they're hopefully still handing out fodder, we might miss out altogether."

"Mmm, you're right. I was wondering why my stomach was making all those strange noises. Patrick's back from a break, and I think everything's under control here." I pushed away a strand of hair stuck to my cheek.

"Right. Let's go check out with Patrick and see if you can be spared for the rest of the night. Georgie-girl, you've been bloody marvelous." Stork draped a long arm around my shoulders and gave me a quick hug.

"No problem; I've enjoyed it. I'm not too good at holidays." I realized as the words left my mouth how callous I must sound.

"No, you never were, I seem to recall." Stork appeared unfazed by my thoughtless remark. "Hopefully tomorrow we'll be able to transfer most of our patients to hospitals that haven't been damaged, so you'll be able to get back to your lovely daughter and on with your R and R whether you want to or not. At least your neurosurgeons' tedious meeting has been cancelled."

I forced a smile as the little bubble of buoyancy in my chest fizzled to nothing. "I'd love to help for as long as you need me. I'll have to at least check on some of my patients tomorrow."

That evening after I'd given up trying to get through to Adam, I went with Stork to the staffroom. I leaned back on the sagging old couch in the crowded room, and looked about at the disheveled, exhausted people around me who even now, in the midst of the chaos and tragedy of Katrina, were still excited about their work and at one in their mission to see their hospital through this. Closing my eyes, I visualized a tap deep inside me opening and letting out a trickle of warm honey, filling me up. Oh, how I needed to get back to my own life—not only to Adam and two back-to-normal kids, but to my patients, my theater, and my colleagues as well.

Once the tired doctors and nurses had expended their excess adrenalin, they wandered off, presumably to wherever they had managed to find a bed, couch, or a mattress on a floor. As Stork and I began our trek to Stork's sixth floor office in the Napoleon Medical Plaza Building, where earlier that day Stork had hauled in a second mattress, I asked him if he'd mind a quick detour to the ICU corridor so I could check on a patient. Stork shook his head, then grinned. "What was I thinking, that you'd have gotten slack with age?" Using head torches, we wove through the hot, smelly passageways and stairwells, trying not to step on the bodies lying, trying to sleep, in every space that was not littered with glass and other debris.

Finally we reached the makeshift ICU. It was dimly lit by the ceiling lights powered by the big generator systems, and it seemed strangely quiet without the babble of voices, in spite of the cacophony of noises made by the ventilators and monitors. A nurse was sitting reading at a small desk at the end nearest us, her dark skin glowing in the light from her headlamp. She jumped when we appeared beside her, but calmed quickly when she saw the long frame of Stork, clearly a familiar sight.

"I thought you might be looters," she whispered. "We've been warned to be on the lookout, especially where we have lots of drugs, like here."

"Sorry, June," Stork said. "It's spooky in here. Shouldn't you have someone else with you?"

"I do. There's a junior resident on as well, but she's gone off for a break."

"This is Georgia Grayson," said Stork, as I moved into the halo of light. "She's a neurosurgeon visiting from England, and she's been helping out on the ICU today. She wants to check on a patient before we get some sleep."

"Hi, Dr. Grayson." June sounded a little shy. "I've been hearing about how wonderful you've been from Pauline. She's on again tonight."

"She's doing an amazing job," I said, smiling at her. "She needed a sleep though. Is she OK?"

"She says she's fine now; well as fine as anyone is in this situation."

"Is it all right if I check on Mrs. Leaumont? I won't wake her if she's sleeping."

"Of course you can. She had a visitor; her son I believe. He left about an hour ago. But she's much better. Her oxygen saturation is up to ninety-five percent and she's breathing more easily."

"That's a relief." I looked at Stork. "I'll only be a few minutes."

"Take your time; I'll keep June company for a bit." He parked himself on the corner of her desk.

I reached Savannah's bed and looked down on her sleeping face. As June had said, she was breathing steadily, although she still had her oxygen connected. In the dim light she looked younger, and I could almost see the striking woman of seventeen years ago, entertaining me in her elegant Garden District mansion. I swallowed as Danny came, unbidden, into my mind. How bizarre it all was, Danny's grandmother here under my care. *She'll come through this, Danny, I promise.*

Giving myself a metaphorical shake, I went a little further down the corridor, searching for another patient amongst the ghostly shapes. I finally found her bed, moved further along from where I had last seen it. Janet was lying quietly, her sheet pushed off her hot body and a damp facecloth on her forehead, but her eyes were wide open. When she saw me, she managed a wobbly smile.

"Hullo, Janet. Why aren't you asleep?"

"I was lying here dreaming about my baby." Janet's eyes watered.

"Is she OK?" I asked, alarmed.

"She's absolutely perfect. The nurse brought her to me to feed for the very first time this evening." Janet's tears were flowing freely now, and for the second time that night I swallowed a lump in my throat.

"That's wonderful. Absolutely wonderful. I hope I can see her tomorrow."

"Oh, yes you can. I can't wait to see her again, but they said she'd be better off in Obstetrics tonight."

"I'm sure they're right," I said, looking around the crowded space. "And you should take the opportunity to get some sleep as well. I'll ask the nurse to bring you a sleeping pill."

"Thanks. I know I'll dream about her anyway."

"And the sooner you get to sleep, the sooner the morning will come." I smiled as I remembered how often Adam and I had said that to our children before a special day. "I'll see you tomorrow."

"OK. And doctor?"

"What is it?"

"Thank you."

"It's a pleasure, Janet." I moved quietly away, and got my emotions back in line by the time I reached Stork.

We set off for the hike across the enclosed catwalk to Stork's office. Stork gave me a towel and a toothbrush he had thoughtfully commandeered from the hospital stores, and in the women's bathroom I brushed my teeth vigorously and wiped my body all over, using clean, cold water from one of the full buckets that had been put in there, in preparation for Katrina's havoc. Returning to Stork's office, I discovered that even a mattress, pillow, and sheet on a cramped floor could feel luxurious, and within minutes I was asleep.

WAKING AROUND FIVE-THIRTY, I SAT UP AND STRETCHED MY stiff, aching body. Stork was still deeply asleep on the other mattress, squashed into the small floor space. I peered out the window at the mess left by the floodwaters below, but the street looked dry. The new sun was coloring the tops of the trees still standing, promising a blue day after the nightmare of Katrina.

The cleanup would be a massive task. Surely they would want me to stay and help? I'd beg, if I had to. Lara had seemed happy enough, keen in fact, for me to help out. Goodness only knows how long it would take for all the hospital services to be restored, and evacuating all the patients to fully functioning hospitals would be a logistics nightmare. Well, it would be if something like this happened in our London hospital. Hopefully I'd be able to do something useful. I flexed my neck and rotated my shoulders, releasing the tension in my tired muscles. I could feel a big smile creasing my cheeks—those muscles hadn't been used too often lately. Sad that it had to be in this horrific situation, but at least New Orleans had not been as devastated as predicted. And I was damn well entitled to this unfamiliar warming glow of satisfaction, back doing what I loved after so long away.

As I stepped over Stork on my way to the door, intending to perform at least minimal ablutions in the bathroom, Stork opened bleary eyes. "Mornin', Georgia." His voice was hoarse with sleep.

"Oops, didn't mean to wake you. I was just off to the bathroom."

Stork yawned hugely. "Man, I'll be glad to get back to my own bed tonight. How's it looking outside?"

"Lovely day so far. Should help the cleanup. Let's hope there's food somewhere. I'm ravenous."

Twenty minutes later, in the makeshift kitchen on the fourth floor, we queued behind a straggle of amazingly cheerful people, presumably relieved that they had survived the storm, and keen to get back to see how their own homes had fared. We were rewarded with a Styrofoam cup filled with grits, scrambled eggs and a sausage. As we stood to one side savoring the strange mixture, one of the residents I had met the previous evening came over to us, looking worried.

"Hi, man, what's up?" asked Stork.

"I've been trying to drive to my house, but couldn't get far. There's a torrent of water rushing across Claiborne Avenue, and the water is rising all over. I think one of the levees must have broken."

At that moment a man came hurtling through the door behind them, screaming hysterically. "We're flooding. All the levees have broken and there's only one way out of the city. We're all going to drown."

The security guard rushed to reassure him, but the crowd shifted uncomfortably, voices rising anxiously as parents hustled their children back through the door.

"Jumping catfish, that's all we need," Stork said. "Let's go to the Admin Centre and see what they know."

When the three of us reached the emergency command center, a number of disaster team members were already gathered around the enormous conference table. We soon learned that there were reports coming through about multiple breaks in the levees. The entire city was likely to be flooded, with water unable to escape from the low-lying city. Memorial had been sheltering more than two thousand people who would now have to be evacuated as soon as possible, before the roads became impassable. Once the street outside the parking building flooded, it would become impossible to drive out of the garage.

The biggest worry was that the hospital generators would fail if the water got too high, and if that happened the hospital would plunge into darkness and we would lose all the elevators and refrigerators. The ICU equipment now running on generators and batteries wouldn't hold out for long, so getting the ICU patients evacuated was a priority.

It was decided to use a triage system to evacuate the sickest patients first, with the 'Do not resuscitate' patients given the lowest priority. How the evacuation was going to happen wasn't clear, but a contingent of the National Guard was sheltering in the hospital, and presumably would be able to get the patients out by road.

The next few hours passed in a rush of adrenalin as Patrick and I, along with two nurses, listed the ICU patients in order of priority, getting together their charts, MRIs and X-rays, and pushing their beds into some sort of ranking system in the corridor. Worried family members assisted our efforts, fanning patients and wiping them with wet facecloths, trying to keep them hydrated and calm as the heat soared above one hundred degrees. Every so often, someone would appear with more dire news of flooding. By eleven that morning the streets around the hospital were filling up with water, and by one o'clock they were impassable. No one could get out of the garage now, and evacuation was dependent on boats and helicopters that would have to operate from a rusty helipad on the roof that hadn't been used for fifteen years.

CHAPTER 18

It was mid-morning when Stork appeared and pulled me over to the vacant nurses' desk. His face was gray, and I could see the anguish in his eyes. The same fear was haunting me. Without thinking I put a hand up to his cheek. "How are you coping?"

"I'm worried about Marcie and the kids. There are shocking reports coming through about Park Plaza hotel. Apparently it's badly flooded. I'm trying to organize a way to get them out of there."

"How are you going to get there if the flooding is too high?" My heart was racing.

"A security guard mate of mine is calling in some favors with some guys who are motoring around picking up people struggling to get through the water. It's rising fast. They promised that they'd do their best to get back to the hospital after they've dropped off the people they already had in their boat—god knows where they dump them, somewhere out of the floods where they can bake in the sun with thousands of others waiting for buses to get them out of this monster disaster. Our lot will be better off here. They'll give me a lift to as near as they can get to Park Plaza. I could have a go at getting there on my own two pins, and I will if they don't show up. But this way will be faster and I'm praying that they might return and pick Marcie and the kids up and bring them back here."

"I'm coming with you."

"Thanks sweetie, but no. You're needed here. I'll be fine. I'll bring 'em all back before you can say stone the crows. Don't worry about Lara, she's her mother's daughter, and to top that, she's got red hair." His lips wobbled into a tired grin.

"I'm coming. Give me a minute to tell Patrick. He'll have to manage without me for a couple of hours."

"You never did take any notice of your betters. I hope you can swim."

WE HAD TO WAIT IN THE LOBBY FOR ABOUT HALF AN HOUR before the boat returned, already with four wet and frightened people huddled in the back. We climbed in and the guy on the outboard puttered through the filthy water, out into the steaming sun, and into Clara Street. The water stank of gasoline and sewage, and everywhere I looked there were people hanging for dear life onto bits of wood or iron roofing piled high with their belongings. Boats stuffed full of people were ignoring cries for help, and broken power lines were all over the place, almost certainly alive. Three times we slowed and the other boat man and Stork dragged people over the side. There was no way I could assess them to see if they needed urgent medical attention, but they seemed OK. One of them was even laughing—hysterically or with perfectly understandable relief, I couldn't tell. It took a lifetime to get to the Park Plaza hotel—via a route unrecognizable to me until we were halfway along the choppy river that was Canal Street. The boat sidled up to the towering buildings and the boatman handed Stork a coil of green rope he'd hauled out from under the seat. "This is your stop. Take this and tie your family together before you try wading through this shit," he said. "There are some nasty currents, and if you get separated it will be a bugger to find each other."

"You couldn't hang around a bit could you? We might find them straight away," I said, almost getting on my knees.

"Sorry, hon. If we can we'll cruise back this way after we drop the next load off, but you're gonna be a while in there."

"Thanks Joe. You're a good man," Stork said, grabbing my hand as I wobbled to my feet. "We'll wade back if we don't see you, so don't worry too much. Thanks for the rope."

The water was up past my waist and we slogged towards what I had now realized was the main entrance to the Park Plaza. Stork grabbed my hand again and we pushed towards the doors. They were closed tight and we shoved our faces to the glass and peered inside. It was dark but there was enough light coming in the windows and door to see that it was deep in water, furniture floating aimlessly about, no people in sight. We pushed and pulled on the doors but with the floodwaters on both sides we had no hope of getting them open wide enough to squeeze through. We waded along the front of the hotel and around the side, and looking up saw people hanging out windows, their screams and shouts lost in the noise of motorboats and helicopters. Stork pointed to a window no more than twelve feet above us, its black center framed by broken glass. A brilliant green creeper snaked up the wall of the building, its leaves shining in the sun.

"I can get up there." Stork looked around. "Find something solid that I can use to smash away that glass near the sill."

"Then what will we do? How will we ever find them in there?" I was cold with terror.

"Ah, this will do the trick." He held up a piece of wood about eighteen inches long and bashed it against the wall. "Not rotten, anyway." He stuck the wood in the band of his sodden khaki pants, draped the coil of rope across his chest, and grabbed the creeper. I could see him fumbling around under the water with his feet, trying to get a foothold. "You stay here and I'll find them and we'll get back out this window. Easy."

"I'm coming too."

"You have a very small vocabulary, Georgia. You'd be more help staying here. They'll need a hand to get down from the window."

"Get up there and I'll follow."

It wasn't hard to find footholds on the creeper and Stork had done a good job smashing and flattening the glass. He hauled me in and I felt a sharp pain as my diaphragm scraped across the remains of the glass. I looked down at my ripped T-shirt, a small ooze of blood spreading out from a graze beneath it. "Oops, sorry," Stork said, then grinned. "Your first war wound."

We were in a bedroom. The floor was squelchy but not flooded. We switched on our head torches and pushed open a door into a black corridor. I checked the door number: 104. I needed to get to 402. Although surely Lara would be with Marcie? We could hear muffled shouts and helicopters, but the corridor was silent, too silent. We found a door with EXIT STAIRS marked on it.

"What was Marcie's room number?" I said. My voice was swallowed by the walls.

"515," Stork said. "Let's get up these stairs and find your room first. If they're not there or in 515, then we'll think again."

The corridor outside the stairs on Level 4 was spookily quiet given that there must have been fifty people sitting and lying on the floor in the dark. A few circles of light shone here and there and one girl I nearly tripped over was reading a book by the light of her weak torch.

"Lara," I yelled. "Lara Grayson?" A few people looked up

and a baby began to cry. I'd probably woken the poor little thing. We pushed our way to 402 and found the door hanging partly open. I shoved it and the light hit me as I looked inside. The window was smashed, and the carpet saturated and littered with glass and leaves and even branches. I could see my suitcase in the corner, but not Lara's. Stork spoke over my shoulder. "She'll be with Marcie. Let's get to Level 5."

There were more people in the Level 5 corridor, and when we found the door with 515 on it, there they were, all four of them, sitting and lying on the Queen bed that had been shoved as far away from the smashed window as possible. Isabelle was the first to move, and nearly knocked her father flying. And then Lara was in my arms and we were both crying like babies.

Stork ordered everyone to change their shorts for long pants, a cunning plan designed to protect legs from some of the filth and oil and sharp objects we were about to wallow through, and we returned to the exit stairs, the bodies in the corridor barely moving as we passed them. We found the window again and this time padded the glass that was left with towels we found in the bathroom. I went first, then the three kids, with Marcie and Stork last. The water had risen up to my chest, and Jamie was dog paddling to keep his head above water. Stork hoisted him onto his back and we wrapped the rope around them and tied it before roping the rest of us together in a long chain; Isabelle, Marcie, Lara and I. I almost wished I'd remembered my camera.

Stork began to push through the water. He was the only one who had a hope of finding the way back to Memorial. Every step had to be negotiated; the road or whatever we were walking over was an obstacle course. We all tripped again and again, and if we didn't find our feet quickly, struggled to keep our heads above water before we swallowed any of the disgusting sludge. We stopped and shuffled about so that Marcie and Isabelle could wade side by side, holding hands, with Lara and I doing the same behind them. Luckily we'd left enough slack in the rope. Our balance was considerably improved as a consequence and it wasn't so lonely.

Lara screamed as a body knocked into her, floating face down, the shirt billowing like a sail. A small dog swam past me, its feet paddling furiously, its black beads of eyes terrified under a straggly wet fringe of hair. I pushed my own hair out of my eyes and my hand was covered with a slick of oil. I realized it was everywhere, the upturned cars spewing and leaking into the mix. Toilet paper and shredded clothing and god knows what else were caught on buildings and festooned entire trees that were smashing and swirling through the water along with everything else. If we made it to Memorial without head injuries or drowning, we'd probably die of some gross disease. Boats sloshed past, uncaring about the wash they were sending over us and the other people floundering around in this sewer. I felt something touch my hand where it gripped Lara's just above the water. I screamed as I jerked our hands in the air and a black snake writhed its way between us. Lara's eyes were like saucers as we watched it glide out of sight.

"Was that a snake?" she said.

I nodded, my heart still pounding.

"That's the first snake I've ever seen outside a zoo," she said. "Finbar will be so jealous."

It seemed we'd been gone for days, but it was only two-thirty when we finally dragged ourselves up and onto the loading bay of Memorial, willing hands pulling us to a dry surface and untying our ropes. Stork collapsed in a long heap on the floor, and for a few minutes none of us seemed able to speak. Perhaps we were catching our breaths, perhaps we knew that if we tried to say anything, we'd start wailing and never stop.

Stork finally sat up, breaking the spell. "Christ, Jamie, you need to go on a diet. You weigh a ton."

I looked around. There were spotlights pointed at the loading bay where the water was washing up and back, up and back as boats motored past without even slowing down. I looked down at myself, wrinkling my nose in disgust. We needed to get cleaned up somehow, and feed the kids. And I needed to get back to help with the evacuation of my patients. Time for reflection later.

Stork shepherded us through the stifling hospital to the McFarland Building next door and by some magic found an empty bedroom with four beds on the fifth floor. We decided that he and Marcie and their two kids should sleep there and Lara and I would stay in his office. He raided one of the hospital linen rooms and found small-sized hospital issue pajamas for Jamie, and green scrubs, complete with theater booties, for the rest of us. Lara and I took ours, and armed with a large bottle of disinfectant, a box of plasters, some soap and a handful of flannels, slogged wearily back through the dark corridors to Stork's office. We proceeded to cover the floor and benches of the bathroom I'd used before with oil and filth as we stripped off our disgusting jeans, T-shirts and sneakers. At least they'd protected us from the worst of the oil and other unmentionables. There was still water in the buckets, not the best color but bloody good to wash in. "New women," Lara said, making use of the mirror to admire her fashionable outfit, and we returned to the McFarland Building where our lanky hero offered us dry bread rolls, hard cheese and a blissfully large bottle of orange juice, all scrounged from the fourth floor kitchen.

I looked over at Lara, sitting on the floor with her back to the wall. Her hand holding her bread roll twitched as her eyes closed and her head dropped on her chest. She was exhausted. I closed my own eyes for a second. Oh, for a nice clean bed and a very long night. I opened them again as Stork lowered his long body down beside me. "When you've eaten that, you're needed in the ICU. Apparently the ancient helipad has been deemed ready to welcome any rescue helicopter brave enough to land. There's going to be a very long queue for seats."

"Are there helicopters coming that can take ICU patients who can't sit up?"

"Search me. I bloody well hope so. But when they do come they won't hang around, so you need to start getting your patients up there now."

I hauled myself upright and saluted as Stork stood up too. "Right sir, I'll be my way." I looked over at Marcie, sitting with an arm around each of her tired children. "Can Lara stay here for a while? I'll collect her later or you can dump her on the bed in Stork's office if she gets too stroppy."

"I'll put her to bed as soon as you go. Don't worry, she'll be fine. We're all fine now," she said.

I smiled my thanks and stretched up to kiss Stork on his bristly cheek. "Thank you," I murmured.

CHAPTER 19

*P*atrick and Pauline were both working like slaves when I got to the ICU, cooling down patients and getting charts and drugs together for the impending evacuation.

"Thank goodness you're OK," Pauline said, hugging me. "We've been so worried."

"We're all fine, but it's a nightmare out there. The water's still rising. The sooner we get everyone evacuated to somewhere Katrina hasn't destroyed, the better."

Patrick nodded. "Well, we have some good news. They've found an easier way to get stretchers up to the helipad than climbing the stairs to the top of the building. There's one elevator working that can get patients down to the second floor where there's a crawl-hole from the boiler room through to the second floor of the parking garage. From there a truck can drive patients up the ramp to the ninth floor, and then they only need to be carried up two flights of stairs to the roof."

"Two flights, is that all." I tried to smile. "Better than carrying them up five flights from here I suppose."

"One of us should go and check out the route before we take our first patient. I've no idea if the crawl hole will be big enough for a stretcher; if it isn't we'll need to come up with another way to get our sickest patients to the helipad."

"I'll go," I said. "Can you give me rough directions? It should be a doddle after getting from Park Plaza to the hospital without being bitten by a snake."

I made my way down the stairs to the Clara Street lobby where there must have been over a hundred people staring out at the rising flood waters. On different levels in the parking building across the street, others leaned over waist-high concrete ramparts, gaping at the flooded city below.

There was a sudden disturbance in the crowded lobby, and I saw a young woman with a baby in her arms force a path towards the steps. A nurse rushed over and grabbed her arm as she stepped into the filthy, swirling water that drowned the pavement.

"Stop! You can't go down there," she yelled. "It's far too dangerous."

The woman turned and shrugged her off. Her face was white under damp, lank hair and her baby squirmed and whimpered. "Leave me alone. I'm getting out of here. I have to find my husband and my other kids." Tears flooded the mother's face.

"Where are they?" The nurse was still trying to pull her back.

"They went to the Superdome, but I came here because my baby was sick," she sobbed. Before the nurse could stop her she stepped waist-deep into the black water and, holding the now screaming baby up high with both hands, walked across what had been the side walk. The crowd let out a gasp as the water rose high on her chest. Holding the child aloft, she pressed forward.

A hush fell over the crowd as they realized what was

happening. A young guy, barely a teenager, pushed his way to the steps and within seconds had reached the young woman's side. I saw him talk earnestly to her and then she turned around and let him help her back to the hospital steps and up to the lobby floor, now relatively dry. The combined sigh of a hundred people rumbled around the lobby as the nurse and the boy hustled her off with her screaming baby.

I took in great gulps of the humid air as the enormity of the situation hit home. Trying to orient myself so I could find the boiler room, after two failed attempts I found a security officer who pointed me in the right direction. Some medical staff were already there, grappling with neonatal intensive care units with their tiny incumbents. The cots, piled high with charts and equipment, had to fit through a four-by-four foot hole in the wall. I began to assist, and found myself on the other side of the hole, on the second floor of the Magnolia Parking Building.

After helping to lift two of the baby units onto the back of a pickup truck, I grabbed the hand one of the men held out to me and levered myself up beside him. Steadying a unit with one hand, with the other I gripped tight the battery bank running the unit's life-giving equipment, and concentrated on keeping my balance as the truck wound and lurched its way up the ramp to the top of the building. From there we had to carry the neonatal units up some steel stairs to the roof and then through a fifty-foot covered catwalk that sloped up to the helipad. We parked the babies behind a line of others, all waiting for an ambulance helicopter that was especially equipped to take the bulky units. Where to was anyone's guess. Someone told me they would probably end up in the Women's and Children's Hospital in Lafayette.

I squeezed past the nurses and babies and the desperate family members standing with them, and onto the helipad. It was a decrepit looking platform, balanced on steel beams high in the air above a blacktopped, pebbled roof, with a death-defying drop around the sides. Catching my breath, I turned around slowly to take in the 360-degree view of the drowning city. My stomach was churning—whether from the dizzy height or from horror at the scale of the disaster laid out before me, I couldn't tell. I could see the Superdome, darker patches showing where parts of the roof had been ripped off, the massive building surrounded by water.

Rumors were rife around the hospital that the situation inside the Superdome was at crisis point, with thousands of frightened people stranded in stifling conditions. Poor, sick, injured, crazy, criminal, the very young and the very old were crowded together with New Orleans families and stranded tourists. With little food, water, or medical aid, and with the situation showing no signs of improving, the refugees' fear and anger was turning to rage. It was hard to know if rumors of fights, shootings and rapes were true, but in such dehumanizing conditions anything was possible. I shuddered as far below I watched ant-sized human beings push boats, mattresses and anything that would float, through the chest-high toxic waters. One thing was horribly clear; this mess would get a whole lot worse before it got better.

As I was herded back to the catwalk, a helicopter circled overhead. I saw the words 'Arcadian Air Ambulance Service' emblazoned on its flank as it finally made a skillful landing on the helipad. Screwing up my eyes as the blast of wind from the blades filled the humid air with dust, I heard the shout of relief coming from all sides. I grinned at a nurse cheering right next to me. She raised a fist in the air. "At last, praise the Lord. That's the first chopper that's landed. Now we can get these babies outta here."

Feeling in the way, I returned to the ICU corridor. Then came the long, drawn-out task of shifting each of our critically ill patients to a stretcher, keeping them attached to their battery-powered equipment, and getting them through the obstacle course to the catwalk. There we parked them behind the even sicker patients waiting for a helicopter. Each trip took at least forty-five minutes and sometimes twice that. The heat in the hospital must have been well over one hundred degrees, and it was a relief to reach the catwalk where some of the Plexiglas windows on the sides had been smashed to let in a breeze of relatively cooler, ninety-degree, outside air.

I'd been checking Savannah regularly throughout the day. My treatment of the old lady's pulmonary embolism had been successful and her signs were healthier now, but, given her age, she had been triaged for evacuation as soon as the most critical of our ICU patients had gone. She was holding up well and seemed unafraid for her own safety, in spite of being alone and unable to get hold of her son. I'd told Lara in a moment of closeness, when we where scrubbing the oil off our arms, that her great grandmother was in the ICU under my care. She'd looked almost disbelieving for a moment but then her belief in karma came to the fore. "Mum, I must see her. She doesn't need to know who I am, but I have to meet her. What if she dies and I never get the chance? I can pretend I'm a volunteer nurse aide or something." I'd been relieved that Lara was asleep when I left her with Marcie, but now I was worried. Savannah might not last until we returned to New Orleans. Surely Lara had a right to meet her?

I told Patrick I was going to find some food, and check on Lara, and to leave Mrs. Leaumont in the Unit until I returned. We'd take her up to the helipad then. Patrick nodded; we all had our favorites and he knew she was one of mine.

Thirty minutes later I was back with Lara, looking the part in her green scrubs and bouncing with anticipation. We handed Pauline the bag of dry bread rolls and cheese I'd got from the kitchen, and introduced Lara to the team, saying she wanted to volunteer. No one even raised an eyebrow. She wasn't the only outlier; many of the patients had one or more family members with them and they were a godsend.

We found Savannah's bed, lit by a battery-powered lamp. Her eyelids were closed and I touched her on the shoulder. She smiled when she opened her eyes and saw me. "Hullo doctor," she said, her voice stronger than it had been earlier.

"Hi there," I said. "Are you ready for a helicopter ride? It's your turn to take the obstacle course to get you there." I'd described the complicated route to her earlier.

"I'm ready. I wish I could tell Luke though."

"We'll leave a message at the nurses' desk for him. Now I want you to meet Lara. She's going to help me push your stretcher." I turned to beckon Lara to my side, and she swiped her arm across her eyes and rubbed the tears from her face. My eyes instantly filled and I blinked furiously.

"Hullo, Mrs. Leaumont," Lara said, coming and standing close to me. I could feel her shaking. "It's lovely to meet you."

Savannah held her hand out towards Lara and she took it in hers. I stepped back, trying to get myself under control. "Where did you spring from?" Savannah asked. "You're far too pretty to be stuck in this gloomy place."

"I'm, I'm…" She glanced around at me and I stepped forward again.

"She's my daughter," I said.

"Are you a doctor too? You look far too young."

"No, I just wanted to help out."

"Well dear, thank you. Your mother has been wonderful to me. I'm not surprised she has such a kind daughter."

Patrick loomed out of the dark and into our circle of light. "Time to go, Georgia. It's nine o'clock, and the word is that the helicopters will stop flying soon to give the pilots some rest."

We set off for the hole in the wall, Lara and I taking turns to push the stretcher and wheel the stand with its oxygen supply still connected to the old lady. Using our head torches to light the way, we negotiated our path to the elevator and through the pitch black and increasingly desperate hospital, chatting to Savannah about Finbar and Adam and our home in London, careful not to let slip our connection with New Zealand. When we reached the catwalk forty minutes later, it was almost clear of waiting patients. Savannah would be one of the last to leave today.

The ICU's most critically ill patients had already gone. During the day we'd suffered two deaths that in normal circumstances could probably have been prevented. With the morgue completely submerged and no refrigeration for the bodies, corpses were being held in the chapel. I shuddered to think of the conditions in there if this continued for much longer, especially as the air conditioning had long ago ceased functioning.

There was no point in bringing any more of our ICU patients up to the helipad at this late hour, so we had a good excuse to wait with Savannah. This was one small thing we could do for Danny. It was only an hour before midnight when we pushed her stretcher over to the tired porters standing ready to lift her into the waiting chopper. The old lady looked up at us when Lara gently touched her hand. She reached up and patted Lara's hair. "Beautiful," she said, her eyes filling with tears. "My grandson had hair like yours."

Lara sniffed. "Did he? What was his name?"

"Danny. My Danny boy. You have eyes like his as well. I think you're my lucky charm." She pulled on Lara's hand and my daughter bent down and her great grandmother kissed her on her forehead.

"Goodbye, Savannah," Lara whispered, and kissed her on her worn cheek.

A tired-looking porter grabbed the oxygen stand. "We have to get her loaded quickly. The chopper won't wait around."

"Where are they taking her, do you know?" I asked him.

"Probably to Lafayette. All the hospitals nearer are full, but she might still get in there. She's a lucky lady. This is the last chopper tonight."

I looked down again at my most precious patient. "Take care now, and I'll try and follow you up when everything has settled down here. If your son is able to contact us we'll make sure he looks for you at Lafayette first."

"And you take care too, doctor. Thank you, and God bless," she called, as she was lifted into the chopper.

Holding hands, Lara and I watched as it rose in the air and circled once before whirring off into the black sky. Below we could see fires burning randomly around the flooded city. The numerous choppers that had been flying above New Orleans all day, rescuing people stranded on the tops of buildings and evacuating other hospitals as well as ours, had vanished from the sky, taking their racket with them. The air was bereft of the normal tropical noises that made the nights here so enchanting. No cicadas chirping or owls hooting. No cars on the streets, no music in the French Quarter, no voices raised in laughter as lovers wandered hand-in-hand by Old Muddy. As the tired staff on the roof dispersed, desperate for food and sleep, the eerie silence was broken only by a lone gunshot.

DESPERATE FOR A TOILET, WE PICKED OUR WAY THROUGH sweaty bodies lying restless and miserable in the dark corridors and stairwells. *Where are the ladies loos when you need them?* We pushed through the door of the nearest men's bathroom, and I tasted bile as I was confronted by the putrid smell of an open sewer. Holding our hands over our faces, we stepped gingerly through the urine and vomit splattered around the waterless urinal. Retching, we peered into the toilet cubicles, their floors swimming with loose excrement. Selecting a toilet that was slightly less full, I squatted over the disgusting bowl, trying not to let it touch my clammy thighs.

In the ICU corridor my nose twitched gratefully as it smelled the faint sanitized hospital odor. I took in a great gulp of air and grabbing some antiseptic wipes from the dispenser, passed some to Lara. We scrubbed our hands and faces, then wiped the bottoms of our already damp and filthy booties. June was on night duty again, and Lara perched on the corner of her desk as I collapsed on the chair beside it.

"Gosh, you two look worse than I feel." June's eyes were black holes in her dark face. "You'd better get yourselves mattresses somewhere and have a bit of shut-eye. Tomorrow will be here all too soon, and it'll all start again."

I rubbed my gritty eyes. "You're right. We're absolutely whacked. Everyone seems blessedly peaceful here though."

"Yes, now all those noisy ventilators have gone. You've done well to get the critical patients evacuated."

"Is there anyone you want me to see before we go?"

"No, I don't think so. Although your subarachnoid hemorrhage lady was a bit upset before. Janet, isn't it? She wasn't feeling too good, but I think she's just frightened that she and her baby mightn't be able to get out. I gave her a sleeping pill."

I groaned. "Poor woman. What a time to have a hemorrhage. I thought about getting her evacuated today, but she was stable, and I was concerned about the stress of getting her up to the helipad in this heat, and then the helicopter flight with that aneurysm not clipped yet. Perhaps we'll be able to evacuate her by boat tomorrow."

"Where will she go?" Lara asked. "She needs to go somewhere she can have her surgery soon, doesn't she?"

"That would be best, but goodness knows where. All the hospitals near here are chock-a-block, and I don't suppose there are many neurosurgeons with free space on their operating lists."

"Couldn't you do it if you went with her to some hospital that still has a working operating theater?" June said.

My stomach knotted. "I probably shouldn't even be doing this general medical stuff. I do have a Massachusetts's license from a stint of guest teaching I do every year in Boston, but as far as I'm aware that doesn't permit me to work here. Certainly not to operate."

"Surely it's OK in this crisis," June argued. "Given the bloody mess the city's in, I can't imagine anyone would care who does what. Although Nagin and Blanco and bloody Bush are all so wrapped up in their petty rules and regulations and keeping control of their own little empires, I wouldn't be surprised if they allowed a young woman with a new baby die rather than allow a top neurosurgeon from England operate."

My eyebrows rose. "Heavens, June, where did that all come from?"

"From the reports that have been coming through today. Sixty thousand folk are holed up in the Superdome without any real chance of being evacuated any time soon, and people are dying there. There are looters and shootings and heaven knows what, and no one at the top seems to know what to do. It's criminal." She banged her fist down on her desk, angry tears gushing from her eyes.

"Hey, it will be OK." I got out of my chair and put my arm around her. June turned and burrowed into my breasts, her shoulders shaking. "What will become of our beautiful city?" she whispered, as I rubbed her back.

"Nothing will ever sink New Orleans. She'll come through this horror and be even stronger than before." Even as the placatory words come out of my mouth, I knew I was talking bullshit. It was hard to see how any city could recover from this—especially one built in such a crazy place.

June sat back and blew her nose loudly. "Sorry about that; I'm so tired and worried. My family has lived here for generations. For us, there's nowhere else."

"Oh June, that's terrible. Is your family safe, do you know?" Lara asked.

"I pray they are. Our house is in the Ninth Ward, and that has been completely submerged as far as I can work out. Thomas and our three kids went to the Superdome on Sunday, when I came here." Her tears were starting again. "I haven't heard from them since we parted, and with all that's going on at the Superdome, I'm so frightened."

"I know, I know. I can't imagine how scared you must be feeling," I said. "And here you are being strong for everyone else. But you've got to hang on to the thought that they'll be fine. How about I stay here tonight and you try and get some rest? I'll take Lara back to Stork's office first and be right back."

"You're a honey, and thank you. But I had a nap this afternoon, and anyway I'd rather be here with something to do than lying about thinking." She straightened her back and flashed her white smile at us. "Off you go. You need some shut-eye so you can evacuate the rest of our patients tomorrow."

Swallowing the ball of whatever was stuck in my throat— tears perhaps for June, loneliness for Adam and Finbar—I grabbed Lara's hand and we stumbled like zombies through the maze of corridors, stairwells, and catwalks to Stork's office. I heard Lara's stomach grumble. *Gawd, we can't possibly be hungry.* The stench was enough to put a blowfly off food. Now my stomach rumbled. *Yep, we're just a touch peckish.* In Stork's office, there on his desk were two granola bars, two oranges and a large bottle of beautiful crystal clear water. Lara read out his note. "*Sleep well, angels. Tomorrow the sun will shine again and we'll all get out of here. xxx.*"

The phone on Stork's desk was still dead. What I'd give to hear Adam's voice. But there seemed no chance of that until we somehow got out of New Orleans. Adam must be out of his mind with worry. My parents too, if he's told them.

Lara was already on her mattress and I dropped heavily onto mine. Alone with my thoughts at last, my emotions almost overwhelmed me—the desperate scenes I'd witnessed today, Lara's face when Savannah kissed her, Adam and Finnie, probably glued to the terrible news as it was repeated endlessly on the BBC. Rolling onto my stomach, I let my tears soak quietly into my pillow.

e were woken at eight by Stork, dressed in crumpled scrubs with theater clogs on his feet. A few days of stubble and a generous black eye made him look even more gaunt than usual.

"What's the situation in Memorial today, do you know?"

"I've just come from the early morning crisis meeting. The lower floors are under water and the floods outside are up to eight feet deep. Apparently the water hasn't reached the first floor. That's where the ER is, so they're going to try and evacuate by boat from the ER ramp, as well as by chopper. Goodness knows where to. But the hospital is desperate. We're running out of food and water, and the chapel is stashed high with bodies. The bathrooms are overflowing and a major health hazard. We're praying that the National Guard will start evacuating us today."

Lara groaned and opened bleary eyes.

"Hi gorgeous," Stork said, as she sat up. "Ain't this a fabulous mother-daughter experience? Some folk pay good money for this sort of adrenalin buzz. Are you ready for another day of bonding?"

"Bloody right I am."

"Lara, language," I said. "Just because you got covered in oil yesterday doesn't mean it is OK to swear like a mechanic."

"Says you who never swears. I'm going for a pee."

"How is your lot?" I asked, as she disappeared.

Stork rocked his hand back and forth. "Better this morning but both the kids woke up with nightmares last night."

"Heavens, I'm not surprised. But they've got the best parents. They'll come through it once you're out of this horrific situation."

"They will. And we're the lucky ones. Those poor bastards still in the hotel, and in the Superdome..." Stork screwed up his face and was silent for a moment. Then he seemed to pull himself together, and when he spoke his voice was thick with anger. "And the Ninth Ward has really taken a hammering; there'll be a huge loss of life. Someone's going to swing for this."

PAULINE MET US AS SOON AS WE ENTERED THE ICU CORRIDOR, a worried expression on her drawn face.

"Georgia, thank goodness you're here. We didn't know how to get hold of you. None of our pagers are working, so we couldn't even page Stork."

"What's the problem?"

"It's Janet McKenzie. We think she's had another bleed."

"What makes you think that?" I saw the screen around her bed.

"She had a sudden severe headache about thirty minutes ago, and became drowsy and confused, but she responds to her name and seems to know she's in hospital. She keeps asking for her baby."

I turned to Lara, who had insisted on volunteering her services again. "Can you ask Betsy, the nurse on the desk over there, if there is anything you can do to help out?" I could see she was on the verge of asking if she could follow me, and I shook my head. "You can't tag along when I'm with patients I'm afraid. But you could probably keep some of the other patients company; the ones who don't have any family with them. Check with Betsy first though."

"OK. I hope Janet's going to be all right." Her face was screwed up with worry.

"Me too. I'll catch up with you later. Please don't overdo it though. If you start to feel tired, can you find your way back to Stork's office?"

She nodded and trotted obediently over to the nurses' desk, and Pauline and I made our way to Janet's bed.

"Is her husband here?" I asked.

"No, we don't know how to get hold of him. But he'll be here soon, I'm sure. He'll bring the baby in for feeding."

I moved around the screen, nodding to Angela, the nurse by Janet's bed. Janet was lying on her back, whimpering, a wet towel over her eyes.

"Hullo Janet," I said, touching her gently on the hand. "It's Dr. Grayson. I hear you had another bad headache and you're not well again."

Janet's whimpering turned to sobs and she turned on her side, away from me.

I moved around the bed and squatted down. "I'll give you something to help with the pain in a minute, but I want to check you over first. Is that OK?"

Janet's sobs hiccupped to a stop. "Where's my baby?" she whispered. "I want Brad. Where is he?"

"Your baby is fine and Brad will be here with her very soon. Now I'm going to take this cloth from over your eyes."

"My eyes hurt, it's so bright," she sobbed, keeping them closed and covering them with her hand.

"I know. Let's turn you over on your back, and then try and open your eyes for me, just for a minute."

Janet complied, and taking the torch Pauline handed me, I quickly checked her pupils. Her eyes immediately closed again.

"Janet, can you tell me where you are?" I said, speaking loudly.

No response.

"Janet, open your eyes and tell me where you are," I said again, my voice firm.

Janet's eyes opened. "Baptist hospital," she whispered.

"That's what all the locals still call Memorial," Angela said.

"That's good, Janet. Now tell me what day it is."

"I don't know. Sunday I think."

"Can you remember what happened in New Orleans?" I asked, as Janet's eyelids flickered and closed.

"It's flooded," Janet whispered. The tears trickled from beneath her tightly shut eyes.

"Do you remember why it flooded?"

"I think we had a hurricane."

"That's right. But it's over now. Can you tell me what the hurricane was called?"

Janet was silent, except for her quiet sobs.

"The hurricane had a girl's name. Do you remember what it was?" I persisted.

"No, I don't know," Janet whimpered.

"It was Katrina. Do you remember now?"

"Yes—I don't know. I have such a dreadful headache, I can't think."

"You're doing well, Janet. I'll give you something for your headache in a minute. Do you remember how you were feeling before the headache?"

"No. I just remember it happening like it did before. I was feeling all right, just lying here waiting for my baby, when I was bashed on the head with a sledgehammer again. I thought the ceiling must have fallen in and hit me. It's so bad. Please give me something to stop it." Janet was crying in earnest now.

"Pauline will sort that out right away." I nodded to Pauline. "Now I need to check you over to make sure everything is OK. I'll be as quick as I can."

I completed my neurological exam and the Glasgow Coma Scale in record time, and helped Janet sit up so she could swallow the pain-relief pills Pauline had managed to find. Janet began to retch and Angela quickly shoved a bowl under her chin, catching most of the vomit that exploded from her mouth. As the nurse wiped her pale, sweaty face and helped her to lie down again, Pauline and I moved away from the bed.

"She's got no focal signs and her Glasgow Coma Score is thirteen." I kept my voice low. "We need to get her to a hospital where she can have that aneurysm clipped. She's had a lucky escape with this second bleed, but if she has another one her chances of surviving are slim."

"Where can she go?" Pauline seemed about to burst into tears. "She's just had her first baby. We can't let her die after she's got through all this."

"We'll get her out of here, one way or another. Can you go up to the helipad and find a doctor who has some authority? Explain that Janet must get to a hospital with a viable neurosurgery theater as soon as possible, and she'll need an Air Ambulance."

"OK, I'll go right now." Determination replaced her momentary lapse into despair.

I returned to Janet's bed, and, taking the cloth the nurse had been soaking in a bowl of cold water, squeezed it out and laid it back over Janet's eyes.

"I don't want to die. Who will look after my baby?" Janet's voice was blurred with pain.

"I know you feel bad but you're not going to die. You've had another little hemorrhage, but you're doing well. We're trying to organize air transport to a hospital as soon as possible, so we can get you sorted out."

"But where's Brad? What about my baby?"

"If he doesn't arrive in the next fifteen minutes I'll get someone to go and find him. He's probably with your baby. Have you decided what you're naming her yet?" I wanted to take her mind off her more pressing problems.

"I think so. We were going to call her Maybelle after my mother, but Brad thought we should call her after the hurricane. What was it again?"

"Katrina," I reminded her.

"Oh, yes. Do you think we should call her Katrina?"

I saw Janet's mouth curl up a little at the corners, and smiled at her. "She has certainly earned that name."

"What's happened? What's the matter?" Brad sounded scared as he appeared around the screen. Handing his baby to the nurse, he knelt on the floor beside Janet's bed. "Honey, are you OK?"

"I think so," Janet croaked. "Where's our baby? Is she all right? I've had another awful headache." The words tumbled out. She pulled the cloth from her eyes and squinted at Brad.

"Our baby's right here, and she's fine. But what's happened to you?" Brad glanced across at me.

"I'm afraid her aneurysm has bled again, but she's doing quite well and we're going to try and get her to a hospital outside New Orleans today so she can have the aneurysm sealed off. Then she'll be safer."

The baby had begun to mewl. The nurse rocked and hushed her to no avail.

"Can I feed her?" begged Janet.

"OK. The nurse can help you; I want you to keep lying flat and as quiet as possible. If you start to feel worse you must stop feeding straight away. The baby can always have a bottle until you're well enough to breastfeed her again."

I nodded at Angela, and the nurse laid the child across her mother's chest.

"I'm going to see what arrangements we can make to get you out of here. Brad, if you need to ask me anything, I'll be at the desk."

"But I can't leave without Brad and my baby," Janet wailed.

"I'll do my best to get all three of you out together. Now you stop worrying and leave it to us. Your job is to stay quiet and nurse that hungry little girl."

PAULINE WAS BACK THIRTY MINUTES LATER, LOOKING somewhat happier. "The doctor in charge on the helipad was lovely. She said to get Janet up there as soon as possible and they'll put her on the next chopper. Brad and the baby too. She doesn't know when one will come though; they have to take what they can get. Once they're in the air they'll have to go to the nearest hospital that can take her."

"Good work, you." I almost cheered, but thought I'd better keep it to a grin. *The show isn't over 'til the fat lady sings.* "We'd better get Janet's chart and her MRIs together. They'll need everything; they mightn't have MRI or radiography facilities available at short notice. No other aneurysms were evident when they did the angiogram, so it's almost certain to have been a re-bleed of the anterior communicating artery aneurysm."

"Lordy, I hope she's all right." Pauline sighed. "She's so young. It seems so unfair."

"If she's OK during the chopper ride and they can operate soon, somewhere, she'll have a good chance." I mentally crossed my fingers and toes.

"Oh, and the doctor up there said you will have to go with her. They can't risk her going without a specialist, and they haven't seen any ambulance choppers yet today. She'll probably have to be evacuated in a military chopper and they don't even have paramedics on them."

"Curses. There's a lot more to do here. But I guess she's right. I wonder if I'll be able to return on the helicopter?"

"I asked her that and she said you'd have to play it by ear. Apparently the choppers don't know what hospital they're going to next, so you might end up somewhere else. If I were you I'd stay with Janet wherever she ends up; we'll probably finish evacuating everyone here today anyway. Patrick and I can manage the rest of the patients."

I looked along the corridor at the remaining few beds. "You're right. Surely there'll be a major evacuation effort today. Stork thought they'd be getting a lot of people out by boat as well." My gaze caught Lara, sitting by Barry, an overweight middle-aged man who'd been recovering from a heart valve replacement when Katrina hit. He was one of the healthiest patients in our care, and as a consequence would be one of the last to go, along with the sickest patients, the ones with 'Do Not Resuscitate' on their charts. Two of those had already died. "Cross fingers the helicopter will take Lara as well. Stork and Marcie have enough on their plates without having to look out for her as well."

"They're big helicopters," Pauline said. "They'll squash her in somehow. Do you need to go back to Stork's office to get anything? Your toothbrush? I can get Janet's charts together and Patrick should be here soon."

"I've got my handbag here," I said. "I don't think we'll bother wading over to the Park Plaza right now to collect our suitcases. Goodness knows if we'll ever see those again." I hit my forehead with my fist. "Damn it, our passports are locked in the safe in our hotel bedroom. I should have thought to get them when we were on our rescue mission."

I went over and tapped Lara on her shoulder. Barry managed a smile, his face white and sweating. "This girl of yours knows more about N'Orleans jazz than I do, and I was born here."

"She doesn't know much about anything else though. Lara, I need to go with Janet when they evacuate her, so you have to come too. We're booked on the next helicopter out." I smiled back at Barry. "You should be getting out too, some-time today." *I hope.*

With the massive fuel tanks under water, most of the generators had now run out of fuel, plunging the hospital into darkness and halting the remaining elevators. Getting Janet down to the second floor via the stairwells was going to be a serious mission. Fortunately Patrick had arrived, and after a quick discussion we decided we would leave Pauline in charge of the remaining patients. Patrick, Brad, Lara and I would take turns carrying Janet's stretcher from the sixth floor up to the roof, five flights of stairs, rather than using yesterday's route, which had relied on taking the now defunct elevator down to the second floor to access the crawl-hole into the parking garage. The two of us not on stretcher duty would light the way through the dark, sweltering, stinking stairwells, carrying the baby and Janet's important charts and MRI scans.

I left a note for Stork with the nurse, said goodbye to the staff who were still slogging their guts out, and hugged Pauline. We'd become friends, real friends. I took a last look at the ICU corridor. So familiar. I felt a crazy affection for it and for this old hospital. Would it be scrapped, like the Do Not Resuscitate patients? The tears I held back weren't only tears of relief; they were tears of thanks as well; gratitude for a nightmare that had reminded me how much I loved working with patients, and not with their files.

Most of the refugees remaining in the hospital were now down on the second floor, waiting to be evacuated by boat from the ER ramp, or transported by truck up to the helipad. So the stairwells were almost free of people, but the smell of fear was everywhere. It was fifty minutes before we finally puffed up the steel stairs to the catwalk. The mood there was despairing and the heat almost unbearable. Twenty or so patients sat quietly on chairs and boxes, or on the filthy ground, their eyes closed. Most of the sickest had been evacuated the day before, but there were still some dialysis patients waiting. Without dialysis for four or more days they were growing weaker and more lethargic with every long minute. Two porters were moving people aside as they smashed in the remaining Plexiglas windows, allowing a small breeze to waft through the confined space.

Patrick shook Lara's hand and then extended his hand to me. "Good luck, Georgia. I can't thank you enough for all the help you've given us. We couldn't have saved as many people without your expertise, especially the neurosurgery patients." He glanced at Janet, nursing her baby.

"I'm glad I could help. It seems wrong to be leaving when there's still so much to do; I feel like a deserter." I reached up and kissed him on his stubbly cheek, and he straightened a little. "I can't begin to tell you what it has meant to me, being part of your team. It's me who should be thanking you. If you ever get to London, or want a job there, I hope you'll let me know. We could do with staff like you, and Pauline too. Please tell her goodbye and thank her; she's been phenomenal, and June too." I sniffed, and managed a shaky smile. "I'm going to miss you all so much; I feel as if I've known you for years."

As Patrick disappeared down the steel steps, I wove through the queue to the front of the catwalk and onto the helipad. Spotting a woman who appeared to be in charge, I explained about the urgent need to evacuate Janet, Brad, the baby and Lara and I. The woman was clearly doing an amazing job in spite of her obvious fatigue and the hot and dusty conditions on the helipad. How on earth she'd managed to keep everyone calm and focused so that the evacuation could proceed safely I couldn't imagine. And now here she was, giving me the warmest smile, as if nothing was wrong, or could possibly go wrong.

"Good, I've been expecting you. Your nice young resident told me all about your mother with the brain hemorrhage. Poor mom and poor baby. What an entry into the world." She sighed, genuine sympathy in her eyes, in spite of the tragedy all around her. Then she continued, her voice measured.

"Get your patient and her family and your daughter to the front of the catwalk, and I'll put you on the next chopper that has room to take you. Unfortunately the Arcadian Air Ambulance doesn't seem to be evacuating from here today, and in order to make the airspace over N'Orleans safer, our smart government has stopped all private helicopters from helping out in the evacuation." She grimaced and looked to the heavens. "So now we're relying mainly on military choppers, and so far only two have arrived, so I don't know how long you'll have to wait for one that can take a stretcher."

I made a quick decision. "Janet can manage in an ordinary seat if we can carry her aboard. Apart from a Foley catheter from her emergency caesarean on Saturday night she hasn't any other tubes and bits of equipment attached to her. And the father can carry the infant—she's absolutely fine. A right little cutie."

"That's great. Hopefully you can get to the Thibodaux Regional Medical Center—it's an acute care hospital with neurosurgery facilities, and only about sixty miles from here. It seems to have been spared any serious damage from Katrina."

With the help of a nurse on duty in the catwalk, we made our way to the front of the queue. A couple of people glared at us as we pushed past, but most seemed to realize that Janet was sicker than they were, and that the newborn infant needed to get out.

Ninety minutes later a military helicopter hovered above us and decided to land. The nurse and I somehow managed to push, pull and carry Janet up the narrow steps into the chopper, followed by Lara, then Brad with the baby. Janet's charts and scans were shoved in after us. A dialysis patient squashed into the remaining seat and the door closed, dulling the noise of the whirring blades. Lara grabbed my hand as we lifted straight up into the sky, hurtling our stomachs into our mouths. Far beneath, the brave Memorial staff waved from the helipad, and, below us, as far as the eye could see, rolled a sea of horror.

CHAPTER 21

The chopper circled once before heading southwest, away from the drowning city. To the north I could see Lake Pontchartrain, now seemingly extended south and east in a great sweep of filthy water to join the Mississippi. Ol' Muddy was truly muddy now. The French Quarter sat on the edge of the lake, but City Park and the Fair Grounds were completely under water. Tall buildings poked out everywhere, and I could see tiny figures on top of some of them. To the east the roofs of the houses of the Ninth Ward seemed to float in the lake, surrounded by all manner of boats and debris.

I twisted in my seat as I felt a tap on my shoulder. The co-pilot was holding out his headset, indicating that I should put it on. Settling it over my ears I adjusted the mouthpiece.

"I'm trying to contact Thibodaux Regional," the pilot said. "If I can get them, you'll need to explain about your patients and see if they have room for them. Good luck."

"OK, thanks," I shouted into my mouthpiece, hardly able to hear myself over the noise of the chopper. The crackling in my headphones became a man's voice identifying himself as the Thibodaux Regional Medical Center Air Evacuation Control Officer. Was this important-sounding title a recent invention or permanent? The latter alternative suggested that the hospital was well prepared for mass evacuations like this. The pilot was introducing me as the doctor in charge.

"Hullo. I'm Georgia Grayson. We have a young woman and her four-day-old infant in the chopper. The woman suffered a subarachnoid hemorrhage during labor and her baby was delivered by caesarean section. The aneurysm re-bled this morning before it could be clipped, so she urgently requires neurosurgery because of the risk of it bleeding again. She's stable now, but we need to get her on land as soon as possible. The infant is full-term and healthy. Over."

"Good grief, that sounds bad," said the Air Evacuation Control Officer, sounding reassuringly human. "We're full up, and I doubt you'll be able to get a neurosurgeon here to oper-ate. Where else have you tried? Over."

"You're it, I think," I yelled. "We need to get her down. Can we at least bring her there until we can find a hospital that can operate? Over."

"Who am I to deny her a chance? What is one more, and how much room can an infant take up anyway? I'll blame you if I get into trouble. Over."

"Thanks. And we also have a patient who hasn't had dial-ysis for four days. Over."

"Bring them all; we'll fit them in somehow. We'll meet you with wheelchairs at the helipad. Or do you need stretchers? Over."

"One stretcher for Janet, please, and a wheelchair. Over."

"Right-o. Anything else? Over."

"No, that's it for now. Over." I wanted to whoop.

"OK, doc. Over and out." The crackling stopped as the headset went dead.

Giving the co-pilot the thumbs up I handed back the headset and repeated the gesture for the benefit of the other passengers. Brad had one arm around Janet, and was cradling the baby in his other. *Poor guy. What a way to learn about father-*

hood. Janet had on a pair of non-functional headphones to protect her aching head from the noise. She had fed her baby just before the helicopter arrived and the infant was fast asleep, blissfully oblivious to the drama around her.

I indicated to Brad that I could take the child to give him a break, and he handed her over carefully before stretching his arm in relief. Holding the warm body wrapped in a still-whitish shawl, I gazed at the innocent face. Her rosebud mouth was making sucking motions and I could see her eyes move under her closed, almost transparent eyelids. *So tiny.* My heart fluttered and without thinking I bent and kissed her downy forehead. I had a sudden flashback—holding my own new babies, feeling that total surrender to them. I turned and smiled at Lara, and she touched the infant's cheek.

"I wonder what life will bring you, sweet little Maybelle Katrina," I murmured, under the noise of the helicopter. "All good things, I hope. You've had enough drama already to last a lifetime."

Below us now was a storm-battered, watery landscape, but no longer an infinite lake. I could see a town ahead, and to our south stretched the marshy swamp country bordering the Gulf of Mexico. Even from this distance the enormous waves that still pounded the Gulf were evident. Minutes later the helicopter was circling the hospital, and then we were on the helipad.

"THANKS, DUNCAN." I SHOOK THE HAND OF A LARGE BLACK man with a big smile. Lara and I had been taken to see the Air Evacuation Control Officer while the hospital staff admitted Janet, her baby, and the dialysis patient.

"No problem, doc. We can treat the dialysis patient here, but I'm not sure about your aneurysm lady. After I talked to you on the radio I got hold of Donald Matheson—he's a neurosurgery resident—and he told me that he and Karen Jenkins, the only neurosurgery attending in the hospital, are already overloaded with a list of acutes; mainly traumas that are still being evacuated here. When Katrina hit we were already low on neurosurgeons—two were in New York at a conference and one had left for Houston for the weekend. Until they can get back, Donald and Karen are it."

"Thank you for taking them in, anyway. Janet really shouldn't have been flying and I wanted to get her into an Intensive Care Unit as fast as possible. If we can keep her still and quiet, she'll hopefully stabilize and not bleed again until we can get her somewhere where she can have the surgery. Or perhaps when things settle down a bit here your neurosurgeons will be able to operate?"

"We'll do everything we can to help," boomed Duncan. "And the pair of you look as if you could use a shower."

"With actual hot water?" Lara said.

Duncan nodded and grinned at her.

"That would be bliss. Any chance we could borrow some clean scrubs?" I asked.

"I can do better than that. This whole town has been billeting evacuees, and we have a heap of folk willing to help." Duncan picked up a wad of paper from his cluttered desk and scanned a list of names. "Tell you what, you two and the young woman's husband can stay at Cheryl and Louie Ryan's place. They're good friends of mine and they haven't got any billets yet. They've got two spare bedrooms and they don't live far from here. Cheryl's about the same build as you guys, so I bet you can get some high-fashion rags from her." Duncan winked at Lara. "I'll give them a call and before you know it, you'll be smelling like roses again."

"It sounds like heaven. I'll see if Brad's ready to leave his family for a while." I rubbed the dry, itchy skin on my arm, the sensation of hot, clean water sliding over it impossible to imagine. "I don't know if it would be possible, but is there any chance I could use a phone to call my husband in London? I haven't been able to contact him since Sunday and he'll be frantic with worry. My mobile is still dead."

"Lordie, he will be worried. Use my secretary's phone. You might have a bit of trouble with an international call; the system is overloaded and a lot of our lines are down. But give it a go."

Duncan's secretary managed to connect me to London and disappeared out the door, telling us she was desperate for a cup of coffee. Lara collapsed on a chair, her face pale with exhaustion. Thank goodness Adam couldn't see her like this.

But it was Finbar who answered on the second ring. "Hullo?" he said, his dear voice bringing me to instant tears. "Hullo? It's Finbar here." He sounded upset.

"Finnie darling, it's me. It's Mum."

"Mum?" I could hear his shaky intake of air and some little squeaks and hiccups as he tried to say something.

"It's all OK sweetheart. We're fine; Lara and I are both fine."

"We thought you might be… might be drowned. Dad has been trying and trying to find out where you are and no-one would tell him."

"Finbar, is that Georgia?" I heard Adam's voice getting louder as he came closer. Then Lara pulled the phone off me. "Finnie, it's me. We're still in America but we're out of New Orleans and we truly are perfectly OK. There were no phones working or anything working and this is the first time we've been able to call you. Finnie, don't cry, it's all right, we'll be home soon." She was sobbing so much I could hardly make out her words.

"Dad, Dad, I'm sorry we couldn't phone you before but we can now and we have so much crazy stuff to tell you." She turned to me. I was hanging onto her arm, straining to hear Adam's voice. "Here's Mum," she said and pushed the phone, wet with her tears, into my hand.

"Adam?" I managed, before I choked up.

"I'd almost given up. I thought we'd lost you both." I heard his shaky intake of breath and then silence as we both struggled to compose ourselves.

"Are you sure you're all right? Where are you?" he said, his voice trembling.

"We're good, love. We're fine. This is the first time we've been able to get a phone connection out. We've just been evacuated to Thibodaux; it's about sixty miles inland from New Orleans, and has escaped most of the damage and flooding. We were evacuated from Memorial Hospital by helicopter to a hospital here."

"I thought you said you were OK? Is it Lara? Why are you in a hospital? Don't keep anything from me, Georgia. I can't stand it."

"No, it's not us. Lara and I were helping to evacuate patients from the hospital in New Orleans and we got a ride in the helicopter because they needed a doctor to look after the patients. There are still thousands stuck in New Orleans with no escape. We were lucky to get out."

"Thank heavens. Trust you to get involved in hospital evacuations instead of looking after yourselves."

"It's a long story, but it's OK. Lara has been incredible. I am so proud of her."

"Tell her I'm proud of her too. And you. I'm proud of you both."

I swallowed. "You should see us. We're dressed in filthy theater scrubs because our clothes got soaked, and we stink. The lovely people here at the hospital have found a family who are going to take us in, and clothe and feed us. Evacuees we are now."

"That's good. We're not having you back unless you're clean. When do you think you can get home?"

"God, Adam, I have no idea. It's chaos here and how easy it will be to get flights and where we can even get them from I have no idea. I'm too tired to even think about it yet."

"I'll start looking and book you on the first flight I can that's going from anywhere near there."

"Thanks, darling. That would be a relief. Find out the possibilities but don't actually book anything until I find a way to retrieve our passports. They're locked in the safe in our hotel room."

"You didn't think to take them with you?"

"Adam, we had no chance to think about taking anything with us. The Park Plaza is flooded. If it's a while before they can be retrieved, then we'll have to wait. It will still probably be faster than trying to get new ones."

"I thought Park Plaza had stood up to hundreds of hurricanes?"

"Not Katrina. She's broken a lot of records. And lives."

For a minute I thought Adam had been cut off, but then he spoke again. "I'm sorry. I'm so bloody relieved that I'm being stupid. I'll check out how long it will take to get urgent replacement passports for the two of you, just in case."

"Thank you. And do check out possible flights for us if you can; that would be an enormous help. But we can't hijack this phone any longer; it's the main line out of the hospital. My mobile needs charging but I think it's OK so I'll be able to phone you from that soon. I had my trusty handbag with me, so I amazingly still have my wallet and credit cards. Never again will I keep our passports secure by locking them in a bloody safe."

WE WERE ACCORDED GRACIOUS SOUTHERN HOSPITALITY IN THE Ryans' pleasant suburban home, and felt one hundred percent better after hot showers, hair washes, and a huge feed. Brad looked rather lost in Louie's clothes, but the pretty cotton dresses and matching sandals that Cheryl had taken from her own wardrobe for Lara and me were close to perfect. Lacy bras and matching panties were part of the package. It was the first time I'd taken on board that Lara was almost my size now.

"And I've got plenty more—I love pretty things—and another dress that will look much better on Lara than me," Cheryl said. "Lucky you're both about my size, minus a few inches around the hips."

It had been a few years since I'd had any underwear that matched, and as I checked out my grazes and bruises in front of the mirror, I decided that when I got home I would go on a lingerie shopping spree.

Cheryl also lent us her car. It was five that evening before Brad and I returned to the hospital, leaving Lara asleep on one of the twin beds in the room we were sharing. I checked on Janet who was feeling more comfortable in a crowded intensive care unit, her baby in the obstetrics unit nearby. Then I found my way to the OR Suite, hoping to find Karen Jenkins. I located her, a tall, middle-aged woman, in the small staff room. She'd just finished an operation and greeted me wearily, indicating that she had heard about our arrival. Pouring two coffees from the electric coffee maker, she told me, without emotion, that she didn't have long. Donald was already prepping their next patient for surgery. He would be the fifth patient she'd operated on without a break, and the second patient today with a gunshot wound to the head. How I felt for her, so exhausted and no end in sight. The last thing she needed was an aneurysm to clip.

Karen collapsed in a chair, stretched out her legs, and pulled the cling-wrap from a pile of sandwiches she extracted from under a cloth on the table. Taking an unenthusiastic bite of her sandwich, she made a face and then looked over at me. "You're a neurosurgeon, I hear."

"Yes, in London. I was in New Orleans when Katrina arrived, and helped out with the evacuation at Memorial."

"Duncan tells me you have a Massachusetts medical license? How come?"

"I was a senior resident at Mass General years ago, and for the past five years I've been back there for a few weeks every year to teach a specialist practicum in aneurysm surgery. So I've kept my Massachusetts license current." My heart began to pump as I realized what Karen was thinking.

"That's what I'd heard. We can get you a neurosurgery theater and an excellent theater nurse later tonight, if you can cope with a senior resident from general surgery as an assistant. Maurice is clued up, though, and he did a stint in neurosurgery as a junior. As for me, after my next op I have to sleep. I've been operating straight for twenty hours, and so has Donald. And tomorrow it all starts again." Karen yawned, emphasizing her point.

"You mean you want me to clip her aneurysm?" I tried to sound calm.

"Why not? Seems the obvious solution to me. She could hardly have a better surgeon for the job." Karen's face expressed her surprise.

"But I'm not licensed in Louisiana," I reiterated, trying not to sound relieved.

"So? Who's going to worry about that? Not me, that's for sure. Anyway, apparently Blanco—she's the Louisiana Governor—is about to suspend all state licensure laws for medical professionals, so we can use the services of anyone we can get while we muddle through this mess." Karen poured herself another coffee. "She hasn't done it yet, but she will, and it will probably be retrospective when she does. So you should operate tonight, given it's an acute. The CEO here said he'll take full responsibility if there are any questions."

For a moment, while Karen was speaking, I felt the familiar churning in the pit of my stomach. Then my head cleared and I knew I could operate—knew without a shadow of doubt that I wouldn't have a panic attack. I could feel the grin splitting my face as I answered the exhausted neurosurgeon. "That sounds good to me. Is it possible to get another MRI on my patient? I have the MRI and angiograms following the initial hemorrhage, so I can go ahead on those if necessary, but I'd prefer to get a follow-up scan, given her rebleed."

"I don't like your chances, but I'll point you in the direction of neuroradiology and you can ask them. But you need to see the CEO first; he'll have to check your credentials to make sure you're not an imposter." She grinned back at me. "Do you have any ID? We've got our IT systems running, so it's easy to check on your Massachusetts license."

"I've got it with me in my wallet. And can someone show me your theater? If I could meet the theater nurse and go over what I'll need, that would be good."

"No problem. Maryanne's an experienced neurosurgery theater nurse, so you'll be fine. She could practically clip an aneurysm by herself. She's due back at seven-thirty this evening, so come back after you've seen the CEO and neuroradiology. The theater will hopefully be ready for you by nine tonight, so that will give you time to get your patient scanned and prepped." Karen yawned again. "But I've got to get back in there now, for—thank the Lord—the last victim before I get to have some shut-eye." She rose, still chomping a sandwich, and extended a hand to me. "Thanks so much. I do appreciate your help. Sorry I'm not being very sociable. Any other time I'd be in that theater with you learning all I could from the expert."

"It's a pleasure," I said, the adrenalin already racing through my body. "It will be good to get back. I've missed it."

"That's the trouble with we surgeons. Can't even have a little holiday without pining for the scalpel," she said over her shoulder as she exited the room.

I SANK INTO THE WELCOMING MATTRESS AND SMILED UP AT THE dark ceiling. It was four in the morning, Lara was snoring softly, and my mind was buzzing. Yawning, but not very convincingly, I extended both arms above my head and pushed my legs towards the base of the bed. Closing my eyes, I visualized every vertebra, every bone, every muscle and tendon in my body. The buzzing became a hum, and my limbs softened. I relaxed my lips but they sprang back to a smile. The thoughts started twirling again, taking not a jot of notice of my poor tired head.

I shouldn't have had that tea. When Brad and I had arrived back at the Ryan's house, a pajama-clad Louie had got up and made us tea and toast. He was such a sweetie. Lara and Cheryl heard us and joined in; it was almost a party. Everyone at the hospital had been so helpful, and they had taken Janet and Brad and their hurricane baby to their hearts, in spite of the fact that their hospital was overflowing and they were all run off their feet.

I screwed my eyes shut and took in a delicious breath and held it. I'd called Adam before I finally came to bed; it was nine in the morning in London. Thursday, September 1st. Finbar's first day back at school. Adam had told him he could stay home if he wanted to—Adam had 'compassionate' leave from the university and had decided to extend it so he could check out passports and flights—but Finbar had bounced off, practically doing cartwheels along the road to his bus stop. When I told Adam about the aneurysm clipping, at first he seemed almost not to believe me. Hardly surprising. I could barely believe it myself. But then it sank in, and he sounded as choked up as I felt whenever I thought about it.

The operation had gone like a dream. A good dream. Not a single glitch, no flutter of anxiety or panic. No one in the OR could possibly have had any idea that only a few weeks ago I couldn't hold a scalpel steady. It was as if I'd never had a panic attack. I'd slipped straight back into my old confident surgeon self from that moment when, talking to Karen, I knew, just like that, that it was over, done with. The panic attacks were a thing of the past. From that moment on, that I might fail or even falter barely entered my head.

And I felt cautiously confident that this was not simply a temporary cure born of the crisis situation I'd been faced with. I sighed, and gave my head a little shake. Humility I'd learned, that was for sure. No more taking my skills for granted. Sarah's voice came floating back to me: *Even when you get control of your panic attacks, you should always be on the alert for occasional relapses.* In future I'd watch out for early indicators—a reluctance to take on certain operations for no good reason, for example. But my lips wouldn't stop grinning. Right now a relapse didn't seem remotely possible. And at least now I had some good old therapeutic strategies to fall back on. Heaven forbid that I would need them for more panic attacks, but they might come in handy for other problems. I smirked into the dark. Was I finally a psychotherapy convert?

Rolling over, I wound back my thoughts to the perfect hours in the Thibodaux OR, and luxuriated in each step of the surgery, the images still vivid in my head. Using the hospital's handsome cutting-edge operating microscope was a joy, and dissecting my way into the sylvian fissure and along the carotid artery to the bifurcation felt like poetry. More delicate dissection, and there it was, the large, bi-lobed aneurysm at the anterior communicating artery complex. A few tense moments, and then I closed a nine-millimeter straight clip securely across the neck. Oh, the whoosh of glorious satisfaction I'd felt at that point. Not so long ago that minor accomplishment would have made it just another good day at the office. Tonight it had felt like reclaiming my life.

And then the closing. I'd especially enjoyed doing that myself. In London I usually left it to David, but the familiar dance had been a sort of closure for me: stitching up the dura; fitting the bone flap back and covering it with Gelfoam before securing the clips with two bio plates; suturing the temporalis muscle back in its rightful place after inserting a suction drain; and finally suturing the galea and stapling the skin before applying the dressings.

I stretched again, my whole body throbbing as I re-lived the mix of achievement, and relief, and plain, old-fashioned happiness that had filled me up during that last half hour. Lying in bed in this house far from home, I almost whooped out loud like a kid on a roller coaster, barely managing to contain myself. But Lara, bless her, needed her sleep. I reached for my wallet on the bedside table and slipped out my favorite photos. I kissed the one of Lara and Finnie frolicking happily in the snow in Austria last winter, and then gazed at the photo of Adam, taken years ago when he was much younger; when we found it impossible to keep our hands off one another. *How could I hurt you so? You're everything to me.* My long ago love for Danny hadn't even been in the same ball-park. Our love affair had been so brief we'd hardly had time to get to know each other. "I'll be home soon," I whispered to the photo, "and I'll show you how much I love you." With Adam's smile in my head, I finally slept.

It seemed as if I'd only dozed off when my eyes opened on a bright room, strong sunlight filtering through the blind and seeping in under it, setting the dust motes dancing in the strip of light across my pillow. Lara's bed was empty. I could hear traffic outside the window and the sound of a radio somewhere in the house. I checked my watch. Gracious, eleven already. In the big kitchen I found Cheryl and Lara at the table with an enticing-smelling plunger of coffee between them.

"Morning, Mum," Lara said, her face looking rested at last.

"How ya doin' babe? Sleep well?" added Cheryl.

I dropped a kiss on Lara's head. "I did sleep well, thanks, brilliantly. As you can see from my late appearance." I poured a coffee. "Where's Brad? Isn't he awake yet?"

"Wide awake. Louie dropped him off at the hospital about nine o'clock, on his way to work. He was anxious to see his wife and baby. I don't think he slept much, poor boy."

"I'm not surprised. He's had a few exciting days. But I'm sure Janet is going to do well now."

"He told us what a marvelous job you'd done. He couldn't believe how Janet was awake and talking to him so soon after the operation. He was all cut up, just telling us about it." Cheryl's expressive face made no secret of her own feelings.

"Wait 'til you meet their little daughter. She's a real cutie," Lara said.

"I'd love to, and to meet Janet as well. When d'you think she'll be well enough for visitors?"

"P'raps later today; I'll let you know," I said. "She would love having a visitor to admire her baby."

"I love little babies. It's about time my two started their families." Cheryl moved over to the pantry. "Now, what can I get you for breakfast? Or perhaps it's brunch by now. Pancakes?"

"Don't tempt me. I can make some toast; that will be fine. I want to get to the hospital to make sure everything is OK."

"You phone the hospital and check, while I whip up some pancakes. They're what I'm famous for, and they won't take me a minute. Lara, can you manage a few more?"

Lara groaned. "I wish. But I couldn't eat another teeny mouthful."

I patted my stomach. "You've twisted my arm. Who knows what crises might happen today? I might need them."

I FOUND JANET STILL IN THE CROWDED INTENSIVE CARE UNIT, propped up in bed, a rakish bandage skimming her right eye, and her baby at her breast. Brad was by her side, sleepy and content.

"Hullo there, you three," I said. "I would have been here earlier, but I slept the sleep of the dead last night."

"That's good, Georgia. Brad told me that you were operating on me half the night. You must have been exhausted." Janet's expression was still heartbreakingly fragile as she looked up from her infant.

"Actually, I didn't feel tired at all. That was half the problem; it took me a while to fall asleep even when I did get to bed." I looked at Brad. "I bet you're done in."

Brad yawned. "You're not wrong. But I don't care. It's so good to be out of that hell hole and for Janet to have come through this." His tender gaze made Janet blush. "And we have our perfect daughter."

"Your cup runneth over." I smiled at the little family.

"It does. But I might go back to the Ryans' house soon and have a nap."

I looked down at Janet. "Have you decided to call her Katrina?" I asked, gently touching the baby's downy head. I caught Janet's rapid glance at Brad, who nodded at her.

"Brad was telling me about your daughter's dreadful accident. I can't remember too much about yesterday but I remember how sweet she was to me. Is she completely better now?" Janet asked, her face pink.

"She is. She's well on the road to full recovery and she adored your baby. She'll be in later, hoping for a cuddle."

"I'm glad. I can't imagine how awful it would be to have something like that happen to your child." She snuggled her contented baby closer. "Brad and I wondered if you'd mind if we called our baby after her? Lara is a lovely name, and if it weren't for you, our daughter mightn't even have a mother."

My throat constricted. I could see that Janet was close to tears. "I'd be honored. And I know Lara will be too, when you tell her."

"Oh thank you. That's wonderful. And thank you for fixing me." She reached for Brad's hand.

"Yes, thanks, Georgia. Thank you for everything." Brad couldn't stop grinning.

"Hey, guys, enough of the thanks. I just did my job. You two did most of the hard work."

There was a soft popping noise as baby Lara released Janet's nipple and turned her head away from her mother's breast. She opened her blue eyes wide and stared at me.

"And young Lara too of course." I touched the baby's soft cheek. "She did a good bit of the work as well."

"She surely did," agreed Brad. "Lara Katrina Maybelle McKenzie, welcome to the world."

After I'd checked Janet over, I took the stairs to the operating suite. Karen wasn't there, but I made myself at home in the small staff room, chatting to one of the nurses who had been in the theater last night, and had just come on duty again. It felt almost like being back in the neurosurgical tearoom in London. Before I'd finished my first cup of coffee, Karen appeared, her second procedure of the day finished.

"Georgia, great to see you. I hear that your op went swimmingly, and your patient is a box of birds."

"It did, thanks. The theater staff were superb, and your theater was a dream to work in. That operating microscope is quite something. I'll be putting in a request for the same model when I get home. Not that I'll hold my breath; we're not due for an upgrade for another two years."

"It is good, isn't it? And we've got a great team. P'raps you should think of coming here permanently," Karen said, her eyebrows arching skywards.

"I'm not sure my family would thank me. It might be a bit hot here for us."

"A tad warmer than England I guess. Perhaps I'll go there. I could do with a change."

"If you're serious, I'd be happy to help. You can surely work hard, that I know."

"Mmm. Katrina hasn't given me much choice over my work hours. But you're the famous one this morning. The whole place is talking about your amazing surgical skills. Maurice is thinking about changing his specialty from general surgery to neurosurgery after assisting you last night."

"That's praise indeed," I said, wondering if the glow I was feeling showed on my face. "I hope he's serious. We can do with all the neurosurgeons we can get." I took a deep breath. "Karen, I'd be happy to help out for a few days until you get on top of things. When will your other neurosurgeons be back? You and Donald can't go on by yourselves at this pace for much longer."

"Could you really? That would be awesome." Karen's smile transformed her tired face. "We're expecting the others back tonight or tomorrow, but even then we're going to be pushed."

"Phew, that's a relief. I thought you might think I was being a bit presumptuous. Tell me what I can do to help." I could feel the old excitement building inside me.

"You're on. You can start with the two traumas that came in this morning from the New Orleans Convention Center. Did you hear that there are about 20,000 sheltering there, and apparently Michael Brown—he's the FEMA head—and the Homeland Security Secretary weren't aware of it until today? It's a crazy thing to say, because broadcasters on CNN and FOX were pleading for help yesterday. But now it's been declared unsafe and unsanitary, like the Superdome, and they're going to try and evacuate it. There are dreadful reports of violence and shootings—rapes, too, apparently. The two traumas just admitted both have serious head injuries with bad depressed skull fractures. They were apparently in the same fight, on different sides. Are you up for that?"

"I am. Absolutely. Is it still OK for me to be operating on my Massachusetts license?

"You bet. These are still emergencies." Karen shook her head. "Believe me, you're not the only doctor working here on an out-of-state license. The sooner Blanco gets her act together and sorts it out so you can all work officially, the better."

"Are the patients already in prep?"

"One is, one isn't. Come with me and you can check the first guy in prep, and then scrub up."

I PHONED ADAM EVERY DAY. HE'D DISCOVERED THAT BOOKING flights was not easy, and that getting new passports would take at least a week, and then he had to post them to us. I told him I was thinking of driving back to New Orleans and getting our old ones. I was sure that if I explained the situation to whoever was in charge of the cleanup at the hotel, the passports would still be in our room. There was nothing essential in our suitcases other than my computer and Lara's iPod, but if we could rescue those as well, that would be a bonus.

"Not Lara though," Adam said. "I don't want her going back there."

That was fine by me, I didn't want her seeing the horrors I knew would be everywhere. But I did want to catch up with Stork and Marcie and make sure they were OK.

"I bet your Mum and Dad were happy to hear your voice," Adam said. "You should give a few more of your fans a call. Sarah has called here every day. And Sonja. Peter phoned yesterday and asked me to pass on to you that you're needed back at work. You've been cleared for surgery again.

He thinks you should be able to manage in a sterile London theater. He asked me to remind you that the Director applications are due at the end of the week, but he's giving you a few extra days to get yours in."

"Do you think he means it? Do Sarah and Simon think I'm OK to operate again?"

"I'm sure he means it. So I suppose it's been discussed with all the appropriate people. They can hardly deny what's in front of their noses; especially as it was on the BBC news that one of London's own neurosurgeons had flown in on her unicorn to save New Orleans' sorry butt."

"Very funny. But I'll take it." I squeezed my eyes shut, and let it sink in. "It's so bizarre. I came here with my career on hold and my daughter miserable because of me, and now…" I heard Lara's laugh on the other side of the kitchen door. "My luck seems to have turned, all because of a disaster that's destroyed thousands of lives and a beautiful city."

Mulling over our conversation later, I told myself I should feel happier. No more feeling useless, no more therapy. The Directorship once again a possibility. Lara and I communicating better than we ever had. I think she was even proud of me. Adam and I still had a way to go, but he really did seem to want me home. Yet there was still something missing. I wanted to pretend it didn't matter; shut it out of my thoughts as I had for so long. But it hung around, niggling and squirming. What had really happened that night? How had I known Danny's body would be at the bottom of the Pa?

CHAPTER 22

As the days flashed past, my confidence grew, and not once did I feel a hint of anxiety or panic before or during surgery. We were worried about Savannah, but with Duncan's help I discovered that she had indeed been taken to the Woman's and Children's Hospital in Lafayette. She'd been suffering from a bout of pneumonia but was slowly recovering, and her son Luke and his wife had been staying in Lafayette and visiting her daily. Janet continued to do well and was on track for discharge. She, Brad, and Lara's diminutive name-sake planned to make a fresh start in Houston, Janet's home-town. Their rented house in the Seventh Ward and all their worldly goods had been destroyed, first by the hurricane and then by the floods, and Brad said that if they never set foot in New Orleans again, it would be too soon. Katrina was being hailed as the worst natural disaster in US history. Even more disturbing was the US response to it—also the worst in the country's history.

By Monday, September 5th, one week after Katrina hit New Orleans, I felt as if I'd been on staff at Thibodaux Regional Medical Center for months. The predicted suspension of State Licensure laws governing medical professionals had been issued by Governor Blanco the previous Friday, evaporating any misgivings I had about practicing without a Louisiana State license. All the missing neurosurgeons had returned now and most of the flooding had subsided in New Orleans, so I made plans to drive there and rescue our passports and suitcases. Adam had booked us back to London on a flight leaving from Baton Rouge on Friday, but if I couldn't get our passports we'd have to cancel until Adam had organized new ones and got them to us via the very uncertain post.

I'd been in contact with Stork and Marcie who now had mobile coverage; their house in Uptown New Orleans had suffered some storm damage, but it was not too bad, and they were determined to stay in the city to help with the massive cleanup. I empathized with their decision; I too felt the pull to return. The Big Easy had become more than simply a connection to my past—the Memorial ICU and its staff and patients were never far from my thoughts. I decided to rent a 4WD—in case of damaged or flooded roads—and drive to New Orleans, leaving Lara with Cheryl and Louie. She'd wanted to come of course, but even if Adam and I had been OK with that, the authorities wouldn't be. Mayor Nagin had issued a complete evacuation of the city, with only people involved in the cleanup, health, or other essential services being permitted in. I was going to flash my medical credentials and say I was joining the medical teams. So by eight on Tuesday morning I was ready for the road, Cheryl not managing to hold back her tears as she hugged me tightly, and Lara giving me a High Five and a "You go show 'em, Mamma." She'd picked up a few Deep South expressions over the past few days.

The drive from Thibodaux to New Orleans, which in normal circumstances would have taken not much more than an hour, took me nearly three hours. From about thirty miles west of the city I was stopped three times at checkpoints where I had to show my physician ID. At the final checkpoint I only got through after the armed soldier phoned Stork, who assured her that I was a bona fide medic coming to work as an emergency doctor.

I felt shell-shocked as I drove the final stretch to Stork's house in Carondelet Street—along Napoleon Avenue and St. Charles, through streets that looked as if a bomb had hit them. Cars abandoned by the curbside sported smashed windows and no wheels. Gas tanks had been forced open, and some still had hoses hanging out, abandoned after the gas was siphoned off. Trees were down everywhere and rubbish littered every street. Two bodies lay like bloated dolls in gardens no longer shrouded by fences.

After much hugging and tears, I presented Marcie and Stork with some cold ham, a selection of dairy products, and some battered vegetables I'd bought in Thibodaux. We were soon sitting down to what the children declared was the first proper feed they'd had since before Katrina. We adults sat up late into the night, exchanging stories of our experiences after Lara and I had flown away from Memorial. Stork's recounting of the unbelievably putrid smells that now pervaded the city had us in fits of laughter. Not that stories of dead, bloated animals, overflowing trash cans and spoilt food rotting without refrigeration in the soaring temperatures were funny, but as Marcie remarked, wiping tears from her eyes, if you didn't laugh you would never stop crying.

Best of all, Stork set me up on his computer. I could hardly believe that the Skype connection worked and I could not only talk to Adam and Finnie, but see their faces as well. The two weeks since we'd parted at Heathrow Airport, Adam and I still so unsure of each other, seemed like a lifetime. The horrors of evacuating Memorial, the excitement of operating again at Thibodaux, and the good friends Lara and I had made at both places, poured out of me. My two boys listened intently, asking only the occasional question as I unburdened myself. On my computer screen I could see the concern on Adam's face as I talked.

"Be careful, won't you," he said, when Finbar had escaped, leaving his dad to his goodbyes. "The news is full of all the dreadful things happening there; murders and rapes and awful stuff. And you look terrible…"

"Thanks," I said, trying to smile.

"You know what I mean. You're on edge. You snap at me for the least little thing. And you're still thinking of applying for that bloody directorship."

"That's unfair. I'm tired, obviously. But I'm not on edge, as you put it. Peter has given me until the Friday after I get back to get my application in, so he clearly believes I can do the job." I swallowed, determined not to show how upset I was.

"You'll no doubt do exactly what you want to do," Adam said.

"Bully for me," I answered. "I'll phone you when I get back to Thibodaux." And I clicked the Skype connection off and dissolved in tears.

Next morning, declining Stork's offer to go with me, I found a tortuous route to Savannah's house. I drove first along Magazine Street, the main road that ran parallel with St. Charles Avenue and formed the riverside boundary of the Garden District. The scene was much worse here. The fires that had raged uncontrolled through parts of the Garden District had left many of the beautiful old houses as charred ruins, surrounded by the blackened skeletons of their ornate iron fences. My horror escalated as I drove slowly towards Fourth Street and turned north along it, passing street after deserted street of despair. At last I drew up at the house Lara and I had been to twelve long days ago. Getting out and locking my vehicle in case there were looters still on the prowl, I looked around. There had been no fires here, but the garden was littered with branches and an enormous old magnolia tree lay across the path just inside the gate, now hanging open on its hinges. Looking up at the house I could see the top story sagging and shutters torn off one broken window. At least two windows on the lower level were smashed, one with a tree branch through it.

I climbed over the trunk of the magnolia, and stepping around glass and debris reached the front door. It stood ajar. Damn, it looked as if looters might already have been here. My heart thudding, I pushed the door open wider and went inside. The house had an unpleasant musty smell, but at least I couldn't detect the putrid odor Stork had described so graphically. Perhaps no one had opened the fridge yet.

Memories flooded me as I gazed at the grand staircase rising from the dim entrance hall, shivering as the ghostly image of Savannah floated regally down it. Moving silently to the partially open door of the formal dining room, I pushed it inwards and peered into the gloom. I froze as I saw a man, his back to me, reaching up to a large picture above the fireplace —a portrait of Danny, his bright hair glowing in a ray of sunlight filtering through a broken window.

My whole body vibrating with rage, I sprang forward, grabbing the man by both arms. "Leave that alone," I screeched, fury pounding through me. "How dare you steal these people's belongings."

The man swung around, arms flailing, the panic on his face rapidly replaced by anger. "Hang on, let me go," he boomed. "Who the hell are you, anyway?"

"I'm a friend of the family," I snapped, trying to regain my grip on the man. Shit, I'd seen this man before somewhere. I dropped my arms. "Who are you?"

"This is my house. What do you think you're doing, walking in here?" The man glared at me.

"No," I groaned. "You're Leroy, aren't you?"

The man's eyes opened wide. "How did you know that?" Anger still distorted his face.

"I thought you were a looter, about to steal Danny's portrait." I looked up at his image smiling down at me. "He looks so alive," I said softly.

"And you are?" Leroy's expression relaxed a little.

"I'm Georgia Grayson. I knew Danny. I was Georgia McKinlay then. I was with Danny just before he died. He showed me a photo of you and his mother." I offered my hand. "I am so sorry, Leroy. I saw red when I saw you there. I had no idea you were in New Orleans."

Leroy took my hand and gave it a squeeze. "Good grief. What on earth are you doing here?"

"How long have you got?" I said, suddenly feeling desperate to sit down. Relief, that's what I was feeling.

"Come on through to the kitchen and I'll see if I can find a wine or a beer. I'm not game to open the fridge, but there might be a bottle or two in the pantry. Thankfully I've managed to get some odd-job men to come in this afternoon to clean out the fridge and block up the broken windows and a hole in the roof."

"Have you had any looters?" I asked, following him to the kitchen.

"I'm afraid so. I only arrived from New Zealand yesterday. My mother's in hospital and until she gets home I won't know for sure what they've taken. They've made a pigsty of her bedroom, so they might have got some jewelry. And some silverware has gone from the dining room, but not Danny, thank goodness. That portrait is precious to Mom."

Leroy fumbled around in the dark pantry and after a few moments hauled out two bottles of Budweiser's. "Aha, the bastards didn't find these at least. Probably too dark in there to see. We haven't got any power yet. Hope you like beer. Do you want a glass?"

"No, I'll do the Kiwi thing and drink from the bottle," I said, grinning at him. We sat at the big table, and again the memories flooded back.

"So, spill." Leroy leaned back, his expression curious.

I looked at him, remembering Danny's treasured photo of his parents. Leroy was still a fine looking man, his skin the color of Savannah's—or the color I remembered it being seventeen years ago—his tightly curled black hair snowy white now, and his brown eyes still kind in his craggy face.

"The short version is that I was here in New Orleans for a work meeting and got caught up in Katrina," I began. "Believe it or not, your mother was amongst the patients I looked after when I was helping out at Memorial—I'm a surgeon—and I organized her evacuation to Lafayette. Then I got evacuated and I've spent the last few days assisting at the hospital in Thibodaux. I managed to contact the Lafayette hospital and ask about your mother. She's had a rough time with the pneumonia on top of her hip replacement, but the doctors are pleased with her progress; you probably know that? I was concerned about her house, so now that I'm back in New Orleans for a few days I thought I'd check on it. I've been here before; back when I first met Danny. That's when I first met Savannah. "

"I've heard a few strange tales since I arrived but that takes the cake. It's a small world, eh!"

"It does seem to be."

"I bet Mom was surprised when you reappeared in her life."

"I didn't tell her who I was. I didn't want to remind her of Danny."

"It never really disappears, does it?" Leroy murmured. "That thought that he is still here, somewhere. That he'll appear any minute; walk through the door with his crooked smile and light up the room."

I saw my own grief reflected in Leroy's dark eyes. "I'll never forgive myself for Danny's death. Never. You have to know that." My voice was barely more than a whisper, but I could see Leroy tensing.

"It wasn't your fault. It wasn't anyone's fault. It was just one of those terrible tragedies that we pray never happens to us."

"It was my fault. We had a dreadful argument and then he ran out in the storm and..." I sat for a minute trying to collect myself. "How could I have thrown him out like that?"

Leroy looked at me, sympathy in his eyes. "You can hardly blame yourself."

My head was in my hands. Minutes must have disappeared before I looked up at Leroy. "Danny's mother blamed me. Why don't you?"

"It's a long time ago. You had a terrible time after his death, I know that. We were all a mess. His death almost destroyed Fiona. She had to be quite heavily sedated for a while." Leroy gazed into space.

"I'm sorry," I said, but Leroy didn't seem to hear.

"I always felt bad that we didn't keep in touch with you and your parents. But Fiona couldn't cope. I was afraid for her. We left New Zealand and came back here to N'Orleans. John—our son—had a good job in New Zealand and didn't need us any more."

"But you're back in New Zealand now?"

"Yes, for the past ten years. We had a little restaurant in Queenstown and we didn't sell it when we shifted to N'Orleans. Had a manager look after it. So we run it ourselves again now. I fear it must be in my blood." A smile lit up his handsome face, and I found myself smiling back. "We turned it into a Creole restaurant and changed its name to 'Danny's Piano Bar.'"

I blanched. "For Danny."

Leroy nodded. "For Danny. Mom sold the original here in N'Orleans after Danny died—after that, she didn't have the heart to keep it going..." His voice faded, and he seemed to be somewhere else for a moment. Then, shaking his head, he continued. "It was my son's idea really, to rename our Queenstown restaurant in memory of Danny. He began his professional singing career there, you know. When he was at secondary school he used to do a gig on Friday and Saturday nights. Not the main gig, but when the band or group we had playing took a break."

He went to the pantry and scrabbled around inside, bringing two more bottles of beer back to the table. "Fiona wasn't very happy about us calling it Danny's Piano Bar at first, but she gradually got used to the idea. We even have a piano." He handed me a beer. "And we've got a great poster on the wall of Danny from his N'Orleans days. Actually, that painting of him you thought I was stealing"—the corners of his mouth curled up—"was painted from that same poster. Mom commissioned the painting after Danny died."

"And your mother is still involved in her nightclubs? She's quite a character."

"She is that," Leroy agreed, affection warming his voice. "My brother Luke does most of the management nowadays, but even at 89, Mom still keeps her eye on things."

"Do you know how her clubs fared in Katrina?" I asked.

"Structurally they're fine. One's in the French Quarter and another on the West Bank. They've been spared the flooding, thank goodness. But whether the French Quarter will recover from this, who knows? I can't see the tourists flocking back for a long time," said Leroy, his voice gloomy.

"If there's a city that can rise again, surely New Orleans is it," I said, thinking as I uttered the words that it didn't look good, if the incomprehensible incompetence of the evacuation response was anything to go by.

"I don't know. N'Orleans has survived a lot of history, but never anything as devastating as this. We all know it's a crazy place to build a city, but it's here, and that's that. It's not as if it can be built somewhere else, nice and dry and safe. I pray it doesn't get rebuilt according to some ghastly modern plan." Leroy shuddered. "I can't even begin to contemplate it disappearing, so we'll just have to restore it, sweet and slow, like a good, spicy jambalaya."

For a time we sat in companionable silence, the devastation outside on hold. I sipped my warm beer, savoring the bitter taste on my tongue and feeling strangely at peace in Leroy's company. Even the feeling that Danny and his grandmother were there in the big kitchen was comforting.

"And you?" Leroy's voice jerked me back to the present. "Do you have a family? Children, I mean."

I looked at him. Was this the moment? "Yes, two. We— Adam, my husband—and I have a daughter and son. Lara and Finbar. Lara's here with me actually. Not here but staying in Thibodaux."

"Lovely names. How old are they?"

"Lara recently turned sixteen, and Finbar's twelve."

"Ah, nearly grown."

I shivered as I saw the sudden change in his expression.

"She must have been born not long after you and Danny were together…" Leroy's voice petered out, and I nodded, not attempting to hide my tears. He got up and walked over to the open window, staring out.

"She has Danny's red hair and green eyes," I said. "She's always wanted to meet you."

Leroy turned around, his face white. "You were pregnant when Danny died? Why weren't we told?"

"My parents didn't know either; not until I'd been in hospital for weeks. When they did find out they said that Fiona —you and Fiona— wanted nothing to do with them or me, and they thought it best to leave things be. I was really sick, depressed, for a long time. They were worried that you might want to get joint custody of my baby—and she was all that was keeping me from madness. And you'd left New Zealand. I'm so sorry. You had a right to know."

Leroy shook his head as if he was trying to kill something terrible inside. "Your parents have never told you."

"Told me?"

"Perhaps it's not my place, but you're a grown woman and I am so sick of secrets and cover ups."

"What?" I whispered. Was this the truth at last about why Danny was up on the Pa that night?

"I don't suppose it matters now after all these years. But you deserve to know the truth." Leroy sat down opposite me, his eyes sad. "This is going to be hard to hear, Georgia. I'm sorry."

"Please. Whatever it is, I want to know."

"Fiona and your father had an affair. Before you were born."

I stared at him, this man who looked so kind, my head refusing to take his words in. "My father and Danny's mother? Dad had an affair?"

"Yes. Fiona realized who you were when Danny told us about you; when he told us your surname. She was distraught. Seamus—your dad—had hurt her terribly. He got her pregnant and Fiona thought he'd leave your mother for her. But he wouldn't. I can understand that; your parents had a one-year-old son."

"My brother," I said, suddenly missing him, missing him so much, wanting him here with me, looking after me as he always did when we were kids.

"Seamus was a fool—sorry—but he was a fool to have a fling with a pretty young girl and be so bloody careless about contraception."

"Did Mum know?" My mouth was so dry I could barely get the words out.

"Your mother knew about the affair. That's what Fiona told Danny and me. Your mother was the one who insisted Seamus give Fiona up; discard her is how she saw it. He discarded her and their child."

"Did Mum know Fiona was pregnant?" I was aching for her, my gentle mother.

"I don't know. I think so. You'll have to ask her or your father about that."

"You must hate Dad. I'm sorry."

Leroy shook his head. "No, I don't hate him. I prefer to forget he exists. But I don't hate him. He gave me my son. John. Danny's big brother. I would have liked to keep thinking some random surfer with no name fathered him; that's what I thought until Danny showed up and dropped the bombshell that he was in love with you, and Fiona realized who you were and told Danny. Told us both that John's father was your father."

"But why did she have to tell Danny? Why? Why then? She'd kept the secret so long. Why would she do that when he was so happy? When we were so happy?"

Leroy shook his head. "I'm sorry, Georgia. She was hurt and angry. Danny being so joyful about you; so in love…that you were planning on getting married as soon as you could organize it …it brought it all back. She didn't know what she was saying. She told Danny that if he stayed with you, married you, you would never be welcome in our home. There was a terrible scene. I was as shell-shocked as Danny but I tried to calm things down, get Fiona to see that her affair with Seamus was all so long ago and she needed to give you a chance. That it wasn't your fault. But she wouldn't, couldn't hear me."

"And Danny put her first. Put his mother's selfish demands before his love for me." The blood was pounding in my head as I stumbled from my chair.

"That's my fault," Leroy said. "Danny told his mum that nothing would stop him marrying you, and that if Fiona couldn't handle that and welcome you into the family, we'd never see him again. I got him alone and tried to talk him out of such a drastic response. I was afraid for Fiona, her mental health. She adored Danny, and she was terrified that she would have to tell John the truth after all those years; that his father was Seamus and not me, and that Seamus was also the father of the woman Danny wanted to marry. She was afraid of losing John's love, losing his respect, as well as being forced into ongoing contact with Seamus and your mother, especially if you and Danny later had children."

"So you convinced Danny to reject me. Why couldn't he tell me the truth? Instead of lying to me and telling me he wasn't sure any more about us and we should separate for months."

"He reluctantly agreed with my suggestion, that's why. I suggested that he delay your marriage plans for a year or so, to give Fiona time to get used to the idea. I hoped that down the track a bit we could work out a way for Fiona to meet you so we could get to know you as a person first before Fiona had to get her head around the two of you marrying. I hoped she would gradually come around to at least welcoming you into our family, even if she refused to have anything to do with your parents. If she stayed resolute then Danny would have to decide whether to stick with his decision to break off all contact with us if you married."

"Why didn't he tell me that? I would have understood. I would have understood and we'd never have had that terrible fight." I was sobbing into my hands and then felt Leroy's arm around me. I opened my eyes and looked up into his face, his gentle eyes, seeing Danny there. I felt a tiny pressure on my back and then I was being held tight and close.

"Georgia, Georgia, don't blame Danny. He told me you adored your father and would be shattered if you found out he'd had an affair and fathered a child as a result. I'm guessing that's why he didn't tell you the truth. He was not much more than a kid himself. He didn't have the wisdom to know that the truth is always best, however much it hurts. So many secrets, so many lies. Danny was trying to protect you; he loved you so much. Seamus and Fiona though, me too, we didn't have the excuse of youth."

"I believed him. I thought he'd decided that his career was more important than me, more important than our love. All that bullshit about us having a long-distance relationship so I could establish myself as a neurosurgeon and he could take up the offer with RCA after all. That's what I thought it was. Bullshit. A weak excuse so he could get rid of me. That's why we had that terrible fight and he went out into the storm..." I pulled away from Leroy. "I should have told him I was pregnant. Do you think that would have made a difference?"

"You already knew you were pregnant?" Leroy said, the shock in his voice making me cover my eyes. I was shaking so violently I almost missed the seat of the chair as I collapsed down on it.

"I was so angry with him," I hiccupped. "I didn't want him to stay with me because I was pregnant. I wanted him to stay with me because he loved me. I should have told him. I should have told him the truth. He might have stayed with me then. He might have told me about Dad and Fiona and why he was so upset. We would have cried and comforted each other and been happy about the baby and told you all to go to hell." I took in a shaky breath. "And he would never have gone out in the storm and he would never have died."

"Don't think like that. It was a tragic accident."

"I upset him so much with my anger and hurt...and he was already destroyed by his mother...do you think he couldn't deal with it and, and..."

"Don't, Georgia. You of all people are not to blame. Danny wouldn't have taken his own life, I'm sure of it. He was upset and wasn't watching his step and slipped. That's what the police report concluded."

"But we don't know. We'll never know for sure. Between us we sent him to his death whether it was accidental or not."

"I'm so sorry, Georgia. I shouldn't have interfered. All I could think about was losing Danny if he married you and Fiona refused to see you. He's my son. I didn't know you. And you were the daughter of the man who got Fiona pregnant, and fathered John."

"Did Dad know Fiona had married you? Would he have guessed who Danny was by his surname?"

Leroy shook his head. "No, he didn't know Fiona's married name." He got up from his chair and moved back to the window. He stood there, his shoulders hunched, looking out at Katrina's destruction. After a while, seconds, minutes, I don't know, he turned around. "Your parents found out who Danny was after he died. They had flown back from Australia the same morning we arrived in Auckland and wanted to meet us, I suppose to say how sorry they were. You were in the same hospital as Danny was—as his body was. That's where we met your parents; outside the hospital morgue. They cut my boy up to see why he died. Your parents were as upset as we were; they'd just been to see you. You were in the psychiatric ward. They hadn't seen you for more than a year and by the time they saw you, you were so disturbed you were heavily sedated. It was terrible, terrible. Seamus recognized Fiona straight away. I don't know if your mother did."

His voice croaked to a stop and I sat there, looking down at the table, trying not to think.

"I made us all go to the hospital cafe and sit down. It didn't help. We were all too upset." Leroy was crying. We were both crying. I heard his chair scrape against the floor as he sat down again.

"I loved Fiona so much. I still love her," he said. "Before Fiona went to Great Barrier Island we'd been together for a while, but we'd broken up. Fiona broke us up, not me. I'd never stopped loving her from the moment I first saw her. But she wasn't sure she felt the same. So she went to the island— her mother had a cousin living there—to sort herself out. Then she came back to Auckland and told me she was pregnant. She said the surfer had gone back to the US the day after they'd had a one-night stand after a drunken party. I believed her. I knew she didn't love me as much as I loved her but I couldn't live without her. I thought I couldn't anyway. I was very young.

"Fiona was desperate to leave New Zealand. We got married as soon as we could and the next day flew to N'Orleans and stayed with Mom. When John was born I took him as my own son. No one knew. Not Fiona's parents, not my family. They all thought he was mine. My name was on his birth certificate, so he never knew I wasn't his biological father. He still doesn't know. But Fiona told Danny. She told him that if he married you, she would have to tell John the truth and she would lose him too. It doesn't make much sense, I know, but she wasn't thinking straight. None of us were."

"What did she have that was so… so addictive that neither Dad nor you could resist her." I hadn't meant it to be a question but Leroy answered me anyway.

"Danny looked like Fiona. He had the same charisma. Perhaps that will help you understand." Leroy went over to the pantry and brought out a bottle of red wine. He poured two glasses without even asking me if I wanted one. We sat there and drank it. There was nothing else safe to drink and we were both pouring sweat.

"Why didn't Mum and Dad tell me? They must have known it would help me make some sense of why Danny rejected me." I could hear my ragged breathing as my words stuttered out.

Leroy shrugged. "Perhaps they were afraid that if they told you, you wouldn't cope, given how unwell you were."

"Almost catatonic for a while apparently. Why was I so badly affected? I can understand terrible grief, but I'd never had any mental instability before."

"Who really knows the human heart? But I imagine that's why your parents decided not to tell you; all they wanted was to have you back whole. Not give you another burden." He poured himself a second glass of wine and gulped down a mouthful. "But I wish they'd found a way to tell Fiona and me that you were pregnant. Danny's child. That might have made all the difference to Fiona. To me too. Our granddaughter."

We sat in silence for a while, each lost in our thoughts.

"It's a terrible, terrible thing when your child dies before you," Leroy said, his voice breaking.

"Yes, it is." I closed my eyes against the image of Lara's bruised body lying in A & E. "I can't even begin to think how dreadful it must be."

"Fiona suffered from awful depression for years after Danny's death. When our children were young, she was so vivacious, so happy. She grew to love me, and our kids were everything to her. She still has the occasional bad patch, but mostly she keeps it under control with medication."

I walked over to the window. I felt a sudden jolt as I saw the tangle of fallen branches and a sheet of iron caught low in a tree, still standing, but stripped of its finery. Plastic, cardboard, paper and other debris littered the garden and flapped gently in the soft wind on this lovely summer day. Lost in the agony that had hidden inside me all these years, for a while I'd forgotten Katrina. I turned away from the devastation outside and looked at Leroy, a man facing still more tragedy—his city in ruins, his mother old and unwell, and no doubt his family's nightclub business in serious jeopardy. And now he had the added burden of telling Fiona that Danny had a daughter.

"Will you stay here?" I asked him.

Leroy started, as if from some dream. "I haven't thought that far ahead," he said, sounding weary. "But I'll stay until Mom is on her feet again, and we've got this house mended." He gazed around as if seeing, not the normal-looking kitchen, but the chaos outside. "I'm not sure Mom will be able to live here by herself anymore." He paused. "What do you think, Georgia?"

"It's probably too early to say. But I read her medical notes, and the orthopedic surgeon was pleased with her hip replacement. So I don't think that will hold her back once she fully recovers from the pneumonia."

"She has a live-in companion and a daily cleaner and a gardener anyway. I guess they left before the hurricane hit. Let's hope they want to come back," Leroy said. "And Luke and his family will be coming home to New Orleans soon. But I'll have to return to New Zealand, at least for a while. I left in a mighty hurry. I have excellent staff, and Fiona is there to keep an eye on the restaurant, but if I'm going to be away for an extended period I'll have to find a manager."

"I need to think about all this. I can't take it in. I have to talk to my parents before I do anything else."

Leroy nodded. "Be gentle with them, Georgia. Whatever they did, however wrong it was, I'm sure they did it out of love."

"Lara is on a mission to meet Danny's family. That was one of the reasons we came here. Do you think…"

"Not yet. Not yet. One day perhaps we'll meet her. But we all need time."

"Will you give me your address in Queenstown? I don't want to lose you again. For Lara's sake."

"Of course." Leroy took the notebook I extracted from my handbag and scribbled in it. "Are you going to contact Fiona? Can you give me a few days to tell her first?"

I nodded. "I'm sorry, Leroy. None of this is your fault. Danny loved you so much."

Danny's father opened his arms and held me until I had no more tears.

CHAPTER 23

I leaned back in my seat, desperate for sleep. My flight from Baton Rouge to Boston gave me six hours. But sleep didn't come and I peered out the window of the Continental Airlines jet as it flew away from the shattered landscape. My stomach contracted as I caught my reflection in the 'plane window and saw a hint of Lara. How I wished I was with her now as she winged her way home to London. But I had to finish this, and the only way to do that was to confront Dad. Mum too. She wasn't entirely blameless, keeping Dad's secret from me all these years. I clamped my eyes shut and forced myself to think of something—anything—else.

Seventeen days since we'd landed in New Orleans, but it felt like months. I'd driven back to Thibodaux yesterday, passports and suitcases on board, preparing myself for an argument with Lara when I told her I was going to New Zealand to see Mum and Dad, but that she was going home. She took it like a lamb. Poor kid had had enough excitement; she wouldn't admit it but she was homesick for Adam and Finbar, and even school. Adam hadn't even tried to discourage me from changing my plans and flying to New Zealand. I'd intended to tell him about Dad and his affair, but it was too hard. Too raw. Secrets and lies. I'd tell him later after I'd talked to Mum and Dad.

And I had to tell Lara the truth. After I'd come to terms with it. Somehow I had to find out, remember, whether I was with Danny on the Pa. Being rejected by Danny—I can understand how hurt, how angry I was—but ending up seriously disturbed in a psychiatric ward? Panic attacks ever since? It made no sense. There was something more terrible that I'd repressed. Did Danny slip? Why was he even up there? What if I had something to do with it? Is that what I've blocked out all these years?

I took the cup of coffee from the steward and ripped the plastic from the sandwich. Outside the window gentle white clouds floated in a calm blue sky. Down below New Orleans became further and further away. Would I ever go back? Take Lara? Would she ever see Savannah again? Her father's Piano Bar? Would she ever meet Leroy?

Fiona?

Yesterday, after Stork had pulled a few strings and got the police to get our suitcases and passports from the cordoned-off Park Plaza, we'd walked around the French Quarter, and for a small moment the swarm of angry bees buzzing in my head calmed down. The voodoo shop was locked, but still standing. Even if Kat had ended up in the doomed Convention Center or the Superdome, she was a survivor. Mrs. G too. Her hotel was deserted, but other than smashed windows it had also escaped obvious damage.

I was desperately looking forward to the next three days. I needed a space to think before getting to Auckland. Stork had tracked down Harry's mobile number, and he'd asked me to come and stay before my plane left for Auckland on Monday night. Something else to feel guilty about. I knew full well why I'd avoided Harry all these years—the same reason I'd never returned to Great Barrier Island since Danny had died. Too scared of my memories. *No more denial.*

Lucky Harry, living in that wonderful beach house. It was a surprise to hear he'd given up orthopedics, but being a family doctor would have its compensations, and Caroline and the kids were probably much happier living on Cape Cod than in an apartment in New York. Harry had sounded almost the same; perhaps a bit more serious. It would be good to see him. We'd had a lot of fun, back then, when we were young and immortal.

PICKING UP A RENTAL CAR AT THE AIRPORT, I JOINED THE steady stream of traffic heading out of Boston. With only a quick coffee stop in Hyannis I made good time, and nearly shot past the short no-exit side road leading to the shore. There, set apart from two other houses and facing the windswept sand dunes and silvering sea was the lovely two-story house, shingles brown now with time and weather. The green paint on the shutters and window boxes had faded, and the trees and shrubbery hugging the house had matured, giving it an overgrown look. The moss-covered stone chimney liberated a wispy spiral of fragrant wood smoke into the mild September evening, and the windows glinted a welcome in the luminescent evening light.

The door opened and Harry came towards me. For a second I felt shy, but then he held his arms open and I fell into them. Emerging from his bear hug I pulled back and looked at him. He was looking back, and as our eyes met our laughs collided in mid-air. Harry had lost most of his hair, his face was lined, and his once slim frame had thickened. *I must look so much older to him too.* Then, within seconds, the changes time had stamped on my old friend vanished and the Harry I remembered was standing there.

"You're still gorgeous," he said, and I felt his fingers tipping up my chin. "Slim as ever, and all that lovely hair." He took away his warm fingers and my eyes watered as I saw the wry expression on his face, so dearly familiar.

"I always was the better looking of the two of us, and the older we get, the wider the gap grows," I said.

"And still modest, I note. Damn it, Georgia, it's good to see you. Come in and see the old house." Harry took my hand and pulled me in the door.

"I can't believe I've left it so long." I looked around the big kitchen, still much the same. "I love this place. It feels so—I don't know—homely, I suppose. I didn't realize I'd missed it so much."

"You're a busy girl, and the Cape is not exactly a weekend jaunt from London." The same old grin split Harry's face.

"I know, but to tell you the truth, I've been in Boston for a few weeks almost every year for the past five years, teaching a course at Mass General. I could easily have made time to come over here for a weekend. I hadn't even realized that you lived here now, but I could have found out."

"Never mind, you're here now. Make yourself at home while I brew some coffee."

I moved over to the antique dresser, picking up a photo that peeked over the piles of paper on its surface. "Caroline looks wonderful," I remarked, gazing at the smiling woman with a youngish teenager on each side of her. "And it's easy to pick the parents of these two." The girl was a younger version of Caroline and the boy a dead ringer for the Harry I'd known when we were at Mass General. An intense longing for my own kids tightened my throat. I swallowed. "You guys are the perfect American family."

"Not so perfect anymore," mumbled Harry, as he set the coffee pot on the table.

I replaced the photo and sat down. *I should have twigged that all wasn't well. Trust me to put my foot in it straight away.* I sipped my coffee, waiting for Harry to explain further.

"Caroline walked out six months ago. She took the kids with her."

"Oh Harry, I had no idea. What happened?" I screwed my eyes up as a pain stabbed at my temple. "Sorry, Harry, it's none of my business."

"It's OK, Georgia. I don't mind talking about it. In fact it's all I ever seem to do." He rubbed his hand over his balding scalp. "Basically I messed up once too often. One little flirtation that went too far, and Caroline found out about it."

"Gosh. How awful. Is she, is the new girlfriend still around?"

"No, she wasn't ever serious—that's what's so stupid. Why I'm so stupid, I mean."

"Do you think Caroline might come back?"

"I kept hoping for a while, but when the kids were here last month they let slip that she has a boyfriend who seems to be serious—like he sleeps there every weekend."

"That must be hard to deal with. I guess you'll get used to it in time though." I tried to think of a less fraught topic. "How long were you practicing in New York?"

"Ten years—I joined a private practice there after we got married. Caroline didn't want to leave, but my practice got into financial trouble. The competition in orthopedics was ridiculously intense, and the liability cover we needed became impossible for us to service. So when my partner retired, I opted out as well." Harry grimaced. "The orthopods who took it over are doing fine; my heart simply wasn't in it. I got quite depressed near the end."

I heard the despondency in his voice.

Harry took a few gulps of coffee. "So we decided to change lifestyles completely, and came here five years ago. The community was crying out for a doctor, and Mom and Dad had retired to San Diego, so the beach house was sitting here empty. That made a difference, given our financial situation. I did a few courses to get me up to speed on family practice, and that's about it."

"And being the local doctor; are you happier?"

Harry's face relaxed. "I love it. It's not the easy option by any means, and in some ways it's harder work than the New York practice. I do house calls, work seven days a week quite often, and even deliver babies sometimes. And twenty percent of the time I don't get paid. But everyone is genuinely grateful, and getting to know my families well is pretty special. A few folk have gone cool on me since Caroline left, but surprisingly most people seem to have forgiven me, or at least don't let it affect their attitude towards me as their doctor. Not that they have much alternative." He looked glum again.

"I'm envious," I said. "Living in this sort of a place, and having that intimate relationship with your patients."

"The trouble is, it will never make up for losing Caroline and the kids." His blue eyes looked almost black. "Take it from the expert, Georgia, and never allow yourself to succumb to temptation. No way is it worth it."

I caught the shine in his eyes, and looked away, Adam's distraught face hovering behind my eyes.

"Not that that's likely. You always were too good to be true." He grinned, the Harry of old again. "We had some bloody good times back then, didn't we just. Remember the sexy Danny?" His grin evaporated as fast as it had appeared as he caught my expression. "Sorry, that was thoughtless. I'd almost forgotten you two were serious for a while. I only found out that he'd died because there was a bit about it in Music Review. I was gutted for a while. For you, more than anything. I did write to you. But you probably didn't get my letter. I couldn't find your folks' address, so I sent it care of Auckland Hospital."

"I can't remember if I got it or not. I couldn't face answering letters, so I might even have thrown it away. I was in a terrible state for months, but I should at least have let you know."

"Don't be silly. It doesn't matter. I'd just wanted you to know I was thinking of you. Danny was a good guy, in spite of his charm."

"What do you mean, in spite of his charm?" I asked, not knowing whether to be irritated or amused.

"Calm down, girl. I was trying to be smart. All I meant was that charming, sexy fellows usually make my fists itch, but Danny seemed almost unaware of his charisma. A pity really. I'd have liked an excuse to hit him."

My eyebrows arched upwards. "Whatever for?"

"I was jealous as hell, that's why. Surely you realized?"

"Over me? You're kidding. I thought I was just one of the guys to you."

"You were so besotted by lover-boy, nothing else penetrated your pretty head."

I scanned his face. He must be having me on. Nope. "Heavens Harry, I'm sorry, I had no idea. You were so easy to be with, and I thought you were in love with Caroline. And there was me filling your ear with my love-sick raves."

"Anything was better than nothing. I survived my broken heart, and once you went back to New Zealand I got over you pretty darn smart—decided Caroline was my true love after all—so don't go getting too big a head."

My shoulders relaxed and I grinned. "No hope of that. But why on earth did you organize Danny and his band to entertain at your 30th birthday? Here's me thinking you were playing cupid."

"I was, I suppose. There was no way around it; you were in love with the guy and you were miserable. I wanted you to be happy, or at least find out if he and you were for real. A bit of me probably hoped you would discover he wasn't as hot as you'd remembered, and you would fall into my arms." He leered, but not very convincingly.

"You had a lucky escape. Imagine the stress if you'd got married to a neurosurgeon."

"Right. Back then all I could think about was how sexy you were." Harry grinned and then frowned. "Christ, we were bloody relieved when you sent us that Christmas card out of the blue, telling us about Lara and that you'd met Adam."

"I'm sorry, Harry. I was so thoughtless, leaving it for so long. Caught up in my own pain. It wasn't only you, and it wasn't just back then. I've been so self-centered, cutting Adam out, not taking Lara and Finbar home very often to see Mum and Dad." I swallowed, but the tight ache in my throat didn't budge. "I know I can't make up for all of that, but I'm going to change. Try and be less selfish from now on."

"You're forgiven. I never blamed you anyway. Caroline and I felt for you. You should remember your old saying—I think you inherited it from your father—do you remember? You used to say that guilt was a pointless emotion. I've tried to tell myself that plenty of times over the past year, believe me."

"I'm not so sure about that now. It sounds like an excuse for bad behavior."

"Bugger. I might stick with your dad's advice for this weekend at least. Seems to me soul searching is not all it's cracked up to be."

"Do you think you and Danny would have stayed together if he hadn't had that dreadful accident?" It was after dinner and we'd both had a few wines.

"No," I said, my voice sounding a tad strained. "He'd already decided to leave me. Actually, Danny's part of the reason I returned to New Orleans after all these years. I've been having problems myself, and I've been seeing a therapist. Apparently the mess I'm in stems from my guilt over Danny's death, and not facing up to it."

"What exactly happened? The accident, I mean?"

Strangely I found I could say the words. "He fell from a cliff after we had a terrible fight. We'd planned to get married and stay in New Zealand and he flew south to where his parents lived to tell them. When he got back he'd completely changed. Told me he wasn't ready for marriage and wanted to go back to the US and take up a contract he'd been offered with RCA. I was so hurt and angry that I didn't tell him I was pregnant. I chucked him out. The weather was terrible and I didn't care. Next morning I found his body, but I can't remember whether I was with him when he fell. The more I think about it the more I feel scared that I might have, I don't know, pushed him because I was upset or angry, I don't know. Or perhaps it was suicide."

"You've been thinking this stuff all these years? Gosh, Georgia, that's horrible." Harry banged his coffee cup down on the table.

"Apart from Adam and my therapist, you're the only person I've confessed to."

"How did Adam take it? You two are all right? Please tell me you are. I don't think I could stand it if you weren't."

I nodded. "I think we're going to be OK. It's been touch and go though. How Adam has put up with me, I'll never know. But he has, and I think I've come through the worst of it. Being in Katrina helped. Put my trivial problems into perspective, I suppose. Adam has been so worried about me that I think he's almost forgiven me for my shitty behavior."

"Make sure you don't take that for granted," Harry said. "He sounds like someone to hang on to."

"He is. He's such an incredible father. And he loves Lara to bits. As much as I would give anything for Danny not to have died, even if he hadn't left me we could never have been as happy as Adam and I have been all these years." I was silent for a moment. "I know it's tough being married to a neurosurgeon. I'm never there when I'm needed. I don't think

Danny would have coped very well when I had to put my patients first."

"He probably realized that, and that's why he broke off your relationship." Harry raised his eyebrows. "It did seem too perfect—and too quick—to last."

"Perhaps." I raised my coffee cup. "And Harry, my dear friend, here's a promise to you. I've never been unfaithful to Adam, and I never will be."

Over the weekend our intimacy grew, and it felt as if, for the first time in seventeen years, I'd found a friend I could talk honestly to about anything. Or nearly anything. I could sense that Harry shared my feeling of closeness. Poor guy, he'd been starved of friendship for too long. We found we had so many things in common: our passion about medicine; the raw emotions our relationship upheavals had exposed; our children; and even our fledgling fears about growing older.

I had any number of friends in London, but apart from Sonja, most of them were also professional colleagues, and our conversations were never really personal. This time with Harry uncovered another precious part of life that I'd been missing. When I got home I'd put a lot more effort into nurturing the friends I already had, and take the time to make new ones.

DURING THE WEEKEND HARRY HAD BEEN CALLED OUT ONLY A couple of times, but on Monday he reluctantly returned to work. After breakfast, as he was leaving, he mentioned that he had an old LP record I might want to listen to. He looked worried, and feeling a sudden apprehension, I asked him why.

"Last night I decided it would be wrong not to show it to you. I just hope it doesn't bring you more grief."

"Harry, you're making me nervous. What on earth is it?"

"I'll leave you to find out for yourself." Harry buffed his

polished scalp. "You'll find a pile of records in the cupboard by the stereo; it's in there." I felt the touch of his lips on my cheek and then he was gone, leaving me with the breakfast dishes and an unsettling quiver deep in my chest.

After forcing myself to clear away the breakfast things, I pulled the stack of old LPs from the cupboard and sat on the floor to go through them. All sorts of good stuff: blues, folk, jazz, even the occasional sugary musical. What was I looking for? It was obviously some record that was going to bring back memories, presumably of Danny, but what on earth could it be? He'd never had the chance to make a recording before I dragged him away from his shining career, so it couldn't be that.

Aha, this must be it. I turned over the old LP; a live recording made at Snug Harbor; Harry and I had gone there before we'd rocked up to Danny's Piano Bar. Harry was a funny old coot. Why would he think this would upset me?

I opened the lid of the fancy-looking modern record player and placed the LP on the turntable, childhood memories flooding back as I carefully positioned the needle on the edge of the vinyl. I closed my eyes as the needle found its groove, the crazily dancing forms of my teenaged friends leaping in my head. Adam and I should buy one of these new old-fashioned stereos so Lara and Finbar could experience this pleasure. Or would they? Without the memories, would it still be this evocative? Opening my eyes, I continued to flip through the record stack, my uneasiness vanquished by the jazz that shimmered from the high-tech surround speakers.

I almost flipped right past it but the flash of red hair caught my eye. My heart somersaulting, I pulled it free. With eyes blurred I stared down at the cover. *Danny Leaumont: Live at Danny's Piano Bar.* And there he was, seated at the grand piano in his sea-green shirt, the black face of his bass player barely visible behind him and the skinny young drummer peering over his drums. Feeling drunk, I turned it over and read the blurb on the back. It was printed over a photo of the club's iconic blue door, framed by a massive oak tree, its sinuous, moss-dressed branches arching through the star-pierced dark.

Danny Leaumont was a popular draw card at 'Danny's Piano Bar' in the French Quarter of New Orleans. In January, 1987, soon after returning to New Zealand to visit his parents, he died tragically. This recording was made live at the Piano Bar the week before he left New Orleans and released posthumously six months after his death. Danny Leaumont has left us a musical treasure, rich in its breadth: blues, jazz and ballad. As rough as the bark of a Live Oak, as immersing as the rain that soaks our skin as we lie beneath it, as warming as the sunlight dappling its deep shade—here is a voice that will make you dance or dream or weep—a voice that, sadly, we will not hear again.

Still in a daze, I lifted the needle from the record still spinning and replaced it with Danny's final performance. I lay on the floor and closed my eyes, his voice transporting me back. It was a wonderful recording and I felt myself smiling as I heard the lewd comments from some hecklers and Danny's smart replies. And then he said he'd come to his last song and the words of 'Danny Boy' washed through me, my Danny's grainy voice somehow sounding perfect, even in a blues club in New Orleans. As he presumably left the dais, the stamping, clapping and calls for more were tumultuous. The sudden hush was broken by his oh so dear and sensual voice.

"Thank you friends. And yes, I do have an encore. If you hadn't wanted one I would have sung it anyway." A burr of laughter from the crowd. "This is, for me, a special song, and it is the last one I'll sing here for a while…" I heard a break in his voice as the tears pushed against my eyelids. "A song for the people I love most in my life—my family and especially Savannah Leaumont, my grandmother, who I know will keep Danny's Piano Bar sizzling until I return. But Georgia—my love, my future—most of all I sing this for you."

I lay, unmoving, long after the haunting notes of 'Georgia On My Mind' had floated out the window to be swallowed by the sea. In the late morning I found myself on the beach walking aimlessly through the dunes, possessed by bittersweet memories—the joy of that magical Cape Cod weekend and the pain that our brief happiness was destined to bring to me, to Adam, to Fiona and Leroy, and now to Lara. So many people who loved Danny and who missed him when he never returned.

"WHERE DID YOU FIND IT?" I ASKED HARRY THAT NIGHT OVER dinner.

"It was an amazing fluke. I was in New Orleans a few years ago, and couldn't resist browsing through bins of second-hand records. Caroline had just given me the new turntable so I was always looking for gems. I nearly had a heart attack when I saw Danny's record."

"He never told me. I wonder why?"

"I bet he was going to surprise you; present the record to you when it came out."

The heavy fog filling my head softened. "Perhaps he was. I'm going to find a copy so I can give it to Lara."

"That copy is yours," Harry said. "On the condition that you bring your whole family to stay here one day. Before your kids grow up."

"Thank you. Somehow I knew that coming here would be healing." I grinned. "But a large G&T would be even more healing. Enough of all this deep and meaningful chat."

Harry's mouth turned down. "Even a G&T is beyond me now. Half a bottle of wine is about my limit if I want to stay awake and be in a fit state to tend to the Cape Cod aristocracy tomorrow." Then a smile changed his face as he put his hand on his heart, and in a tune that was clearly made up on the spot, warbled, "But, Georgia, my sweet Georgia, all I need, all I need, is your smile…" His warbles lapsed into speech. "And if the fastest way to get there is by plying you with G&Ts, I'm your man."

Early next morning, a cold mist hanging over the sea and my head surprisingly clear, I sank into Harry's bear hug. We'd promised each other that in future we'd spend time together whenever I visited Boston. As I was about to get into my car, Harry handed me a photo.

"I thought you might like this," he said, a catch in his voice. "Caroline snapped it the morning after my thirtieth birthday party, as you and Danny were coming back from your walk on the beach."

I gazed at the photo, a little yellow around the edges but the colors still true. In it Danny and I strolled towards the photographer, not touching or looking at each other but laughing at the camera. Our feet were bare and I was carrying my sandals in one hand. My other hand was brushing my wind-tousled hair from my eyes, and I was glowing with health and happiness. My blue jeans were rolled up to mid-calf and I had on a white, polo-necked jersey. Danny had on his dress-up jeans from the party the night before, and his green shirt was crumpled, the sleeves rolled high. We both looked so very young. And inside me was the tiny beginning of Lara.

I looked at my friend, the tears that I'd held back finally in my eyes. "Oh, Harry. This is a memory worth keeping."

Harry gently touched the image of Danny's face. "They shall not grow old as those that are left grow old," he murmured. "Age will not weary them nor the years condemn."

PART III

DANNY

New Zealand, September 2005

CHAPTER 24

The welcome home dinner Mum had prepared so lovingly made it impossible to voice what I needed to say before I could begin to relax. Andrew and his family were there as well, and I was bombarded with questions about Katrina. I found myself trying to make it humorous, but that didn't prevent Mum's tears as I described the rescue mission—complete with snake—from the Park Plaza to Memorial. Dad's eyes were suspiciously shiny as well, but I hardened my heart, and when I finally fell into bed, exhausted from the long plane journey and too much emotion, my sleep was far from restful.

It was 10am when I staggered into the big kitchen for breakfast; Mum and Dad had long since finished theirs. But they kept me company at the table while I picked at the bacon and eggs Mum put in front of me, before I gave up, excusing my poor appetite on jet lag. "I need some fresh air." I said. "It's such a lovely day. Dad, let's drive down to the beach and have a long walk."

I saw Mum's face fall and felt mean, but I needed to confront Dad first. I wasn't sure I would be able to talk about this with Mum. How could I blame her? She'd had to deal with Dad's affair; Leroy seemed to think she'd known about it for years. Then came the shock of discovering who Danny was and who his brother was, and her fear for me in the psychiatric unit, and on top of all that finding out that I was having Danny's baby. How she and Dad were even still together was mind blowing.

Dad of course suggested we all go for a walk, but Mum, sensitive as always to my moods, declined, saying that she had things to do, and it would be lovely for Dad and I to have some time together.

"I'LL DRIVE." I TOOK THE TOYOTA KEYS FROM DAD. I NEEDED to be in control, and I knew that if I sat in the passenger seat I'd somehow feel like a child again. Seeing the sign to the beach I turned the vehicle sharply and parked on the strip of grass bordering the sand. Dad opened his door. "Let's sit here for a bit," I said, the blood thundering in my ears.

Dad pulled the door shut again and we sat in silence, separated, it felt, by an ocean of lies. I fixed my gaze on the calm blue waters dotted with the occasional white sail.

Finally Dad spoke into the void. "Is something wrong, love? It must have been horrifying, what you've been through. I guessed there were things you didn't tell us last night because it would have upset your mum and Andrew's children."

I took my hands off the steering wheel and shoved them under my thighs. It didn't stop them trembling but at least it wasn't so obvious.

"Are you all right?"

Dad's words penetrated the red fog filling my head and I swallowed. "No, I'm not all right. Dad, I know about you and Fiona. That you had an affair." I forced myself to look at him, this man I had loved all my life.

He was staring straight ahead, out the window, his face gray.

A slow burn coiled through my body. "How could you do that to Mum? Was it a one-night-stand? Some boozy night in the pub while Mum was at home with Andrew?"

"How did you find out?" Dad said, his voice a croak.

"I met Leroy, Danny's father…" I stopped, my head burning. "I met him in New Orleans. I went to see if Danny's grandmother's house had been damaged in Katrina, and Leroy was there. He was sick of all these lies and he told me. Told me that John, Danny's brother, was your son. How Fiona was so upset, so upset because you had got her pregnant and then abandoned her and her baby. After all those years I finally knew why Danny changed his mind about marrying me. After seventeen fucking years."

"I'm sorry, love. I didn't want to upset you."

"Upset me? You knew how upset I was that Danny rejected me. How could you think it would be worse if I knew it was because he'd found out that his brother was your son, and he didn't want to cause his mother any more grief?"

"I didn't think about it like that. You were so sick; you don't realize how sick you were. We were scared to tell you. Your mother thought it would send you back into that terrible state and you'd never come out of it."

"But I was pregnant. Pregnant with Danny's child. How could you keep that a secret from Danny's parents?"

"By the time we knew you were pregnant Fiona and Leroy had left New Zealand. Fiona had made it clear she never wanted to hear from us again. We talked about it, about trying to track down a contact for them… but we decided to leave it be. Having Danny's baby inside you was all that was keeping you from…"

"From what? Say it. From what?"

"From staying in a psychiatric institution for ever. We didn't know if you would even want to live if you had to give up that baby. What if Fiona and Leroy wanted to take her from you? To make up for losing Danny?"

"That's ridiculous. How could they? I was her mother."

"You were very, very unwell. What if they'd used that to get custody?"

"You were her grandparents too. Even if I ended up in the psychiatric ward forever, you could have taken her. Shared her even with her other grandparents." My hands escaped from under my body and bashed the steering wheel.

"Fiona hated me. It was terrible, that meeting at the hospital. I didn't trust her. Your Mum didn't trust her. It wasn't only grief for Danny; it was as if the past, her and me, it was if it had all just happened. If she could have hurt me by causing trouble over your baby…we couldn't risk it." Dad's hands shook as he gripped them together in his lap.

"Why didn't you tell me when I was well again? It would have been terrible but I would have coped because I had Lara. And at least I would have known why Danny rejected me. Why didn't he tell me the truth? Why didn't he tell me that night instead of dying like that?" I covered my face with my hands, Danny's face in my head. I felt Dad's hand on my back and jerked it away.

"We didn't understand. I'm sorry. I don't know what else I can say."

"Why didn't Mum tell me? Did you stop her? Did you stop her because you were so ashamed?"

"No, of course not. I *was* ashamed, but Hannah and I talked about it . We talked about it many times, but we always ended up thinking it would be worse for you to know than not to know. How could it help? Lara was a beautiful little girl; she saved you."

"So you think I should keep your nasty secret from Lara?"

In my peripheral vision I saw Dad nodding. "Why tell her? What good can it do?"

I turned my head and looked at this shriveled copy of my father. "Lara wants to know her father's family. She wants to know who she is. Don't you think she deserves to know the truth? Know her other grandparents? Her Uncle John? Doesn't he deserve to know who his father is?"

Dad's sigh shook through his body. "Lara will get hurt. You can't risk that. Fiona didn't want anything to do with us. She made that clear."

"Well, I'm going to Queenstown to see Fiona, and I'll ask her if she's changed her mind. Leroy is going to tell her. He probably already has. I think she'll want to meet Danny's daughter. Of course she will. John has two boys. Lara's her only granddaughter. "

"No, Georgia. Leave it be. You don't know Fiona. I don't think she's stable. How will Lara feel if Fiona doesn't want anything to do with her?"

"If that happens, I'll decide then what I should tell Lara. But I think I'll tell her the truth, however painful it is. If I don't I'll be as bad as you and Mum."

"Did Leroy want to meet Lara?" Dad said, his voice so small I could barely hear him.

"He will, I'm sure of it. He was shocked when I told him about her. He's a lovely man and when he has got over all the terrible stuff that's happening because of Katrina, I think he'll want to meet her. He'll be a wonderful grandfather for her, I know it."

Dad flinched and my tears welled up. I sat there, my head down, my body shaking. "Dad, I didn't mean it like that. I'm sorry. I just meant… you're her granddad; you're a wonderful granddad. I just meant…"

"I know what you meant. It's all right. It's all right love. Perhaps you're right. Perhaps Fiona will want to meet her, and then she'll have two more grandparents."

"And another uncle and two new cousins. Your grandsons." I blew my nose, and my hand found Dad's. We sat in silence for a while and then Dad stretched, his body creaking as he moved in the cramped space. "Do you think we could have a bit of a walk on the beach before we go home? I don't want Hannah seeing us upset like this."

I nodded, sick to the stomach with the sour air in the car.

WE WALKED FOR A WHILE IN SILENCE. THE SEA HELPED, AND the smell of the salt in the air. I breathed in and out, in and out, *re-lax, re-lax* as we walked, and my thoughts and body gradually calmed.

"Dad, why did you have an affair? I always thought Mum was the only one for you."

"Your mum and I were going through a difficult patch when I met Fiona. We were struggling financially. Hannah had to stop working after Andrew was born, and she became pretty depressed, stuck in the house all day. I think her work as the community nurse had kept her sane. I had had too much to drink when I first met Fiona. She was staying with Rachel; you remember her? She ran the Tryphena store. She was Fiona's second cousin or something like that. I suppose I was attracted to Fiona because she was so carefree and beautiful, and she really seemed to like me. I didn't realize how young she was, not that that's any excuse."

"So how old was she?"

"She was nineteen..."—Dad hesitated—"and I was thirty."

"Hell, Dad, how could you? How did Mum find out?" I tasted bile as anger burned my throat.

"I don't know. Hannah must have sensed it somehow. She asked me if I were in love with someone else, just like that, and I broke down and told her everything. I think I would have soon, anyway."

Oh Mum, I'm sorry.

"But I still loved your mother. I never stopped loving her. I can't explain it. I couldn't understand myself then, and I still can't understand how it all went so wrong."

"How long? How long was it going on?"

"A few months, six months, that's all. I told Fiona it was over and she left the island. I never saw or heard from her again until we met her and Leroy at the hospital after Danny died."

"But you knew she was pregnant."

Dad took in a deep breath. "She wasn't even sure about that. She'd missed one period, that's all. Even if she were pregnant I hoped she might get an abortion."

"Abortions weren't even legal then. How could you ask her to do that?"

"I'm not proud of myself. I knew it was possible to get abortions safely if necessary. I would have supported her if she'd wanted that; made sure it was safe."

"Really?" I heard the sarcasm in my voice. "Did you think about leaving Mum?"

"No, of course not. If Fiona had kept in touch and told me for sure that she really was pregnant and was keeping the baby I'd have supported her and the baby financially. Perhaps I could even have had some contact with the child; I don't know."

I felt a twinge of pity as I saw the pain shadowing Dad's dark eyes. Then I steeled my heart. "You're lucky Mum didn't throw you out."

"You don't need to tell me that."

We'd reached the end of the beach and without speaking we turned and started back. My anger had burned away and left only sadness—for Mum, for Leroy, and even for Dad and Fiona.

"When we met Fiona and Leroy after Danny died, she never even asked about you." Dad mopped at his eyes with his handkerchief. "I suppose that was the only way she could cope. Anyway, she told us they were taking Danny's body back to Queenstown for cremation, and then they were leaving New Zealand and I was never to contact her again."

I stole a glance at Dad, my heart squeezing as I saw his anguish. "She'd just lost her son and thought I was to blame. Perhaps I was?" I whispered.

"That's silly talk, Georgia. Any blame is Fiona's and mine. And even that isn't entirely fair."

His hand clasped mine, so much frailer than I remembered it, and I tensed, and glanced at him. His face was raw with grief. Who was I to criticize his love affair with Fiona? If she had been even a little like Danny I knew how difficult it must have been to resist her. And how could he ever have imagined that I, not yet even born, would meet Fiona's son and then go right ahead and fall in love with him?

I squeezed his hand. "I'm sorry, Dad. You can't blame yourself."

"I never knew John, never even knew what he looked like, but at least I know he's alive and well. I wonder if he and Danny were close? It must have been terrible for him when Danny died."

"Oh Dad, they were close. Danny often talked about him; all the stuff they did together when they were kids. Danny showed me photos of him, of all his family. They looked alike. John and Danny."

"I would have liked to have met him, at least once, when he was grown, even if he didn't know who I was. And your Danny; I wish we'd met him. I wish it had all been different."

"Fiona should have told you when John was born. If she had, I think Mum could have handled it," I said. "She should have told John right from when he was a boy that Leroy wasn't his biological father."

"It's not considered right to keep these things—biological

parentage—from children nowadays, I know," Dad said. "But back then everyone thought it for the best. And perhaps it was. That way John was free to love Leroy as his true father—the man who brought him up and gave him everything."

"But it can't be like that for Lara. She's always known Danny was her biological father, and it hasn't stopped her from loving Adam every bit as much as I love you," I said.

"Still? Do you still love me, Georgie-girl? After all this?"

I nodded, too full to speak. Then Dad's arms were around me and mine around him.

BACK IN THE TOYOTA, I HESITATED, AND THEN TURNED TO Dad. "Would you like to see a photo of Danny? My friend Harry gave me one of him—Danny and me actually—taken when we were in the States. He looks so like John, it would give you an idea."

I heard Dad's sharp intake of breath. "That would be wonderful, wonderful. I had given up all hope of ever knowing what he looked like."

I fumbled in my handbag and pulled out my wallet. Zipping open the compartment I slid out the photo of Danny and me on Cape Cod and handed it to Dad. He sat for a long time, his eyes never moving from the photo. A tear dropped onto Danny's face and he gently wiped it off.

"He's the male version of Fiona when she was young," he murmured. "He looks a little older, but he has that same wonderful alive look. Such joy on his face, so beautiful." He looked at me and his smile took years off his age. "And look at you. You were a pretty young thing back then. Still are, of course."

A trickle of warmth seeped into my cramped heart.

"Thank you, Georgie-girl," Dad said, reluctantly handing

back the photo. "So young to die. I thought I understood how Fiona must have felt when she took him home to cremate him, but I understand better now—now that I've seen him. It must have been like cremating herself."

That night, in my girlhood bedroom, I wound the sheets into a tangled mess, determined not to give into the weakness of a sleeping pill. I heard the toilet flush and then the creak of the bed in Mum and Dad's room. I wasn't the only one sleepless tonight. It had been tough on us all facing the end of the secrets and cover-ups, justified for so long in the name of love. Reaching over to the bedside table I fiddled with the dial on the ancient transistor radio. A mellow male voice told me to 'stay tuned to your all-night easy, easy listening show.' That should put me to sleep.

"And who could be easier on the ear than Joe Cocker?" the voice crooned.

"Anyone but him." My words hit the wall opposite and bounced back. Joe Cocker's voice, entangled, it seemed, forever more with Danny's, was about as easy as ECT. I flicked the dial again—and then turned it back. *Georgia, Georgia…*The rough voice slipped through my mind, sweet as honey.

And while in the master bedroom my parents struggled with their own nightmares, I lay on the narrow mattress that had soaked up my adolescent dreams, and wept for Lara.

A clear sky provided magnificent views as the plane followed the Southern Alps, their highest peaks still capped with white, all the way to Queenstown. But climbing down the steps onto the tarmac I was already regretting my decision to delay my return to Great Barrier. Fiona would almost certainly refuse to talk to me.

The taxi wound its way along the shores of sinuous Lake Wakatipu with the perfectly-named Remarkables forming its dramatic backdrop, their upside-down silhouettes mirrored in the deep, dark waters at their feet. I drank it all in, memories flooding back. I loved this part of the country, so familiar from long ago weekends away from my medical studies at Otago University.

After booking in at a lakefront hotel I wandered around the small town center, not much changed over the years. Some of the restaurants had new names and probably new menus, but the old favorites were still there. I found the iconic Cow Pizza Barn in the same place and discovered that the pizzas and the huge stone open fireplace were as soul warming as ever. Feeling mellow in spite of the vague unease that was almost normal for me now, I wandered down another of the narrow streets looking for a jazz club I remembered from the past. But before I got far, I saw the sign on the stone face of a restaurant I didn't recall. *Danny's Piano Bar*. I'd known I would stumble across it soon—the town was too compact to hide much—but it still took my breath away.

My heart thumping, I strolled past it and glanced in the window. It seemed quite busy for a Sunday night with a number of tables occupied, and I walked on. *Re-lax, re-lax.* Turning, I retraced my steps, but this time I pushed open the door and went inside. *What if Fiona's here, acting as hostess? I don't want to meet her in a public place.* A baby grand piano sat silently in the corner, but before I had time to take in the framed poster on the wall behind it a young waitress bustled over. I mumbled some query about whether they were open on Monday, and when the girl wandered off I sauntered casually over to the piano and looked up at Danny. My vision blurred as I thought of Leroy, standing in his mother's house in the ruin of New Orleans, looking with love at the same picture. Then Dad's face flashed through my head and I turned away, my stomach churning.

The next morning I puffed up a steep street behind the town, stopping at the unassuming wooden house where Danny had spent much of his childhood. I didn't have to ask the woman who answered my knock if Fiona Leaumont lived here. Lara was drawn in every detail of her striking features and red hair, even though Fiona's hair was faded now.

"I'm Georgia Grayson. I knew Danny, and I met Leroy in New Orleans last month." I half expected Fiona to slam the door in my face, or to pretend she had never heard of me.

Her face blanched, and I saw a flicker of fear in her eyes before she pulled herself taller. "I wondered when you'd show up," she said, her voice flat. "You'd better come in."

She led me into a surprisingly spacious kitchen with large windows looking out over the astounding scenery below, and pointing at a chair by the table she turned her back and busied herself making a pot of tea. Neither of us spoke until she'd placed a mug in front of me and sat down herself.

I poured some milk into my tea from the jug Fiona pushed towards me and took a long swallow, spluttering the hot tea up again. Pulling a tissue from my handbag I mopped my chin.

"What do you want?" said Fiona, glancing at me and as quickly averting her faded green eyes.

"I thought it might help to talk."

"Help *you*, you mean. Why should I help *you*?" she said, a brittle edge to her flat tone.

"Help us both." I kept my voice gentle. Fiona looked as if she might slide under the table any minute. "We both loved

Danny, and Leroy told me how badly you suffered after he died."

"I'm not interested." Her eyes glistened and she blinked rapidly.

"I never understood why Danny stopped loving me after he visited you. But I know now; Leroy told me, and I talked to Dad."

Fiona's nostrils flared. "They had no right to tell you."

"Leroy told me because he was tired of secrets and lies."

"So you know now. I hope it makes you happy." Her voice was flat again.

I tasted the bile that burned my throat whenever I let the truth creep into my thoughts. Swallowing, I forced myself to speak evenly. "No. It makes me sick. I have to face telling Lara."

Fiona seemed to crumple and she grasped the table. I pushed her mug of tea towards her. She held it in both hands and took great gulps. I waited until she'd put the mug down before I spoke again. "Has Leroy told you about Lara?"

"You should have aborted it."

"How can you say that? I loved Danny. I wanted our baby. Danny didn't tell me that John was Dad's son. Nor did my parents. Until Leroy told me I had no idea." I forced myself to ignore the red haze hovering behind my eyes, and leaned over and covered Fiona's hand with mine. "Stop blaming yourself, Fiona. Danny wouldn't want that. He loved you."

"I should never have named him Danny. It jinxed him, me, all of us."

"What do you mean?"

"I called him Danny because 'Danny Boy' was Seamus's favorite song. That was what he was singing in that pub on Great Barrier when I first saw him. That's why I fell for him. I would have named my first baby—his baby—Danny, but I was too angry."

"I'm sorry Dad didn't stay in touch and help you when

you had John," I said. "He said he wasn't even sure you were pregnant. I know that sounds like an excuse. It probably is."

"He rejected me and asked me to leave the island. He never really cared about me; it was all a bit of a buzz for him, that's all. He made it clear he would never leave his wife. Even if I'd known for certain that I was pregnant it wouldn't have made any difference to Seamus. He already had a family." Fiona pushed herself up from her chair, her face a ghostly white against her red hair.

I steeled myself to look at her, and watched a single tear slide down her cheek. Should I spare her any more? Damn it, no. If I didn't confront her now, I'd never know.

"Why did you take it out on Danny?" I wanted to scream, but I kept my voice low. "Why did you stop him marrying me?"

Fiona stared at me, every plane of her face tense. "I couldn't stand the thought of him marrying into your family. What if you had children? I'd have had to see your father. I'd have had to share my grandchildren and my son with your parents. Why should I? Hadn't Seamus hurt me enough? What about John? He would find out. He didn't deserve that. He thought Leroy was his father." Fiona's face seemed to cave in, and she clamped her hand over her heart.

"Will you tell him now? He's Lara's uncle. His children are Lara's cousins."

"I thought I was protecting Danny," Fiona whispered. "I didn't want him to become part of your family. I thought he'd go back to New Orleans and forget you. You had no right to take him away from his career. But you took him away forever."

I shook my head as a blackness descended, blotting out Fiona's face. When my head cleared, I found my voice. "Lara deserves to know you and Leroy. You're her grandparents. She looks like you. Would you like to see a photo?"

Fiona shook her head. "She won't want to know me when

you tell her I stopped Danny marrying you. I've got two grandsons. John's boys. I don't need a granddaughter."

THE NEXT DAY I DROVE ALONG THE LAKE TO THE START OF A hiking trail that I'd often walked when I was a university student. For the next four hours I pushed myself hard, and after a picnic lunch began the hike back, feeling more at peace than I had for six months. Perhaps next summer we'd bring Lara and Finbar down here and spend a week doing some of the walks.

Back in Queenstown, too tired to be bothered with decisions about where to eat, I had an early meal at the hotel. Feeling rejuvenated, I walked along the lakeside in the evening light, seeing Danny as he might have looked back then—a teenager in a small town, bouncing stones across the lake surface. If only I'd known him at that age; known him because his brother was my brother and we were all family.

Damn their shame and selfishness. How hard would it have been for Fiona to have found a way to tell Dad he had a son, tell Leroy the truth, tell John and Danny when they were little? Then the ripples from the past wouldn't have destroyed us. Danny would be alive, perhaps with children of his own. I blinked back tears; angry, sad? Perhaps both.

Yet such wonder came out of it. If Danny and I hadn't met as strangers and fallen in love, there would be no Lara. And that was unthinkable.

I thought of Danny alone above the baby grand in the bright and airy Danny's Piano Bar here in Queenstown, so far away from his steamy, smoky nightclub in his beloved New Orleans. In the narrow street I'd wandered into, almost without thinking, I stood again outside, looking in. Tonight the restaurant was buzzing, with every table full. Through the open door I heard the piano and glimpsed a dark-haired man at the keys, his head close to the microphone as he crooned out a song. Above him, from his softly lit frame, Danny smiled at me. Then a young couple tumbled out the door, their faces glowing, and the door shut behind them.

When I checked out of my hotel next morning, the concierge handed me an envelope. "A woman came in early asking if you were staying here," he told me. "She said she didn't want to disturb you."

In the taxi carrying me back along the lakeside to the airport, I opened the envelope and looked at the two photos it contained—one of two small boys with cheeky grins and red curly hair standing beside the gates of Savannah's home, and the other of a forty-something man with less hair, still red, and his arms around two kids, both with that same curly red hair. The stone wall behind them was the same as the stone wall in Danny's Piano Bar here in Queenstown. The note was brief and unsigned. *Seamus wanted to know what his son looked like. These are for him. I hope you can forgive him.*

CHAPTER 26

Standing on the deck of the catamaran I watched a pod of dolphins surfing in the wash that skimmed off the forward floats. Every few minutes, with perfect timing, paired dolphins would peel away and arc their graceful bodies high into the air, turning in flight to expose their creamy undersides, small dark eyes shining and mouths curved in a laugh at the humans hanging over the deck railings. My spirits lifted, chasing away the hollowness in my stomach that had dogged me from the moment I'd boarded the boat.

Now the island was looming up ahead and the catamaran seemed to dance across the calm blue of Tryphena harbor. I peered down through the clear sea, sun captured in its folds like a watermark. The boat glided, motor stilled, alongside the rackety wooden wharf. Taking deep breaths of the salty, gloriously clean air, I concentrated on the scene around me. It was all so familiar. The usual eccentric collection of people of all ages cluttered the wharf, along with dogs, rusty cars, and muddy four wheel drives. I watched as with much shouting and throwing of ropes the gangplank was tied into place and quickly tested by a group of rowdy surfers, unable to wait another second to get to the next wave.

I grinned as I spied Sam. The old chap was still meeting the boat with his battered van. There were always a few passengers who needed to get somewhere on the rugged island but hadn't taken into account the paucity of public transport. Sam had seemed pretty old when I was in my twenties, so he must be in his late seventies by now.

Well, here goes. How hard can this be?

"Holy Moly, if it isn't young Georgia," Sam said, flicking his head. "Haven't seen you around for a bit. Thought you'd deserted us for good. You still a brain doctor?"

"Yes, we live in England, but I'm back for a short break." I clambered into the van.

"You wouldn't have made much money doing your fancy doctoring on the Barrier. We're all as healthy as rabbits." Sam skillfully turned the van around in the small space as I pulled fast my seat belt. "And breed as fast as rabbits too," he added, as three small kids raced in front of the van, followed by their bare-footed mother, an infant swaddled to her chest with a tie-dyed shawl. "Unless you have some good cures for hangovers? You might find some work here then."

I laughed. "'Fraid not."

"Never mind. It's good to know you've done so well. I know your old man is chuffed about what you've achieved. Not bad for the kid of a fisherman from the Barrier, eh?"

"Well, I had a go at fishing but never caught anything. Being a doctor is easier." I looked at the road winding ahead. "Living here when I was a little kid was pretty special, but I suppose going to school in Auckland was good for me too—gave me more opportunities. I've been lucky. And I certainly couldn't have done it without Mum and Dad's support."

"That's for sure. But you've made them proud and good on you. Will they be over to keep you company? What about your own family?"

"No, I'm here by myself. My parents and my brother and

his family are in Auckland, and Adam and our two kids are in London. But we'll all be coming over in January."

The road meandered along the curves of the shore and through the small settlement of Tryphena, strung out along a necklace of bays. "I'd forgotten how beautiful it is. And not too many people about. I guess you're hoping for a bumper crop of tourists after Christmas?"

"Yep. Gotta make a living somehow, 'specially with the cops and their fancy drug squad from Auckland snooping about with their helicopters and ripping up all the marijuana crops." Sam glanced over at me and winked. "Not that I'd have a bar of that, but it's a bit of extra cash for some of the younger ones."

"Dad tells me the local population is decreasing."

"Yes, it's about 800 now and most with no jobs." Sam chortled. "Still, better to be jobless and on the bones of yer bum here than in the big city, eh? At least when it's sunny."

Chugging up and over the bush-covered backbone of the long island, I held my breath as we reached the highest point before the descent to the east coast. And there it was, laid out before me—endless surf beaches separated by rocky head-lands—next stop, Chile. Coasting down past an idyllic beach where land prices were now affordable only by the well heeled, we stopped in Claris, where, in the solitary shop, I purchased a few supplies to supplement the food stashed in my suitcase. Over a bridge spanning the clear amber of a stream as it wandered through the swamp, jagged silhouettes of hills hazy in the distance, and around a headland to a smaller, curved surf beach. A lone surfer swooped effortlessly towards the shore, diving off before he hit sand and then powering out to the back again.

At last we pulled up beside a farm gate marking a rough track that wound its way across a paddock before disappearing into the dunes. Sam jumped out of the van. "No decent road over to your place yet—not good enough for my old bomb anyway. I'd give you a hand with your stuff, but there's fishing to do before nightfall. Can you manage?"

"No problem." Paying Sam his thirty dollars and waving as the van turned and rattled back down the road, I pushed open the gate, the old wood warm on my hands. Wandering along the track, hauling my suitcase along behind me, I lifted my face to the sun and breathed in the salt-infused air, perfumed with grass and cow dung. Comic long-legged pukekos grazing on the paddock scattered, squawking, as I approached. I could hear the soft booming of the surf muffled by the sand dunes, and skylarks singing high in the blue before dropping to earth.

The going became harder as I left the track and took a shortcut straight up the dunes. Puffing slightly as I breached the top, I gazed across the soft folds of white sand, their pale green grasses shivering in the sea breeze. As I watched each wave break on the beach below, the roaring of the surf separated into a regular sequence of crashes. Sinking to the sand I absorbed the familiar sights, sounds, and scents of the most glorious place on earth.

After a while I reluctantly got up and almost ran down the next dune, my suitcase bumping along behind me. And there was the house basking in a grass hollow, its back to an enormous pohutukawa tree. I went over to the garage and peered through the filthy window. The Landrover was still there, and still covered in mud. I scrabbled for the house key under one of the old pottery crocks jumbled by the garage door. My fingers quickly located it—its hiding place hadn't been changed in my lifetime. Even if I'd forgotten where it was, almost anyone on the island could have enlightened me.

The house was little changed on the outside, although the solar panels and enormous solar water cylinder on the roof were new—well, new to me. Dad had warned me that the house had been dragged, kicking and screaming, into the modern world with 12-volt power, hot and cold running taps, and even a shower, all courtesy of the solar paraphernalia on the roof. Mum had even got her wish—a gas stove to supplement the time-intensive wood stove.

I unlocked the back door and stepped into the simple rectangular room with the wood and gas stoves, kitchen sink, and cupboards at one end, and, at the other, the big open fireplace with old easy chairs pulled cozily around it. I sniffed. Still that musty smell of old wood smoke tinged with a tang of rat activity—hopefully in the ceiling and not in the house. Going over to the fireplace I examined the various assortment of peculiar junk on the massive mantelpiece—flotsam and jetsam found on the beach. There were some new finds but all the old treasures were still there.

A wooden table took up half of one long side of the room, with a sweep of floor-length, faded navy-blue curtains covering the wall of windows behind it. I slid the curtains back from the generous expanse of glass and the dim room lit up, the seascape stretching out before me. Opening wide the French doors, I stepped onto the broad wooden deck. The scented air filled me up as I took in the sweep of dunes stepping down to the wide crescent of white sand, the dark green and silver of the gnarled pohutukawas on the edge of the dunes, then all the blues of the sea and sky. How could I have forgotten how wonderful this place was?

I closed my eyes and breathed in slowly, in out, in out, before I dared look the other way. The Pa was still there, jutting out into the white-capped ocean. Though it seemed benign now, its flax-covered flanks shining, I knew that was a lie. The almost forgotten fortifications built by the Maori who lived there 600 years ago still held their violent memories. I shivered as a stray wisp of cold air whipped across the deck.

An urgent pressure in my bladder led me outside the house. Thank goodness Dad hadn't succumbed to a flush toilet. Our ancient doorless long-drop facing out to sea had a million dollar view. And the house still had no telephone and no mobile coverage. Exactly what I needed; a few days of total isolation from the outside world.

THE MORE I PACKED INTO MY DAYS THE LESS TIME I HAD TO think, so I snorkeled—clad in an old wetsuit that I could still squeeze into—fished off the beach, and kayaked around the coastal bays, setting a single crayfish pot in a spot that had once been lucky. In the evenings I indulged myself with lonely meals of barbecued crayfish, green-lipped mussels, and on one evening, an iridescent snapper caught from the kayak. After dark I picked through the old books and magazines that crowded the bookshelves. When my head fell to my chest and my eyes closed, I stumbled to bed, sleeping deeply for a few hours but invariably waking before dawn, my thoughts churning and my grief raw again. Only with the return of the sun was I able to banish my sadness for a few welcome hours.

Not until the fourth day did I walk to the north end of the beach. I had to force myself to look up at the grassy track winding through tall flax to the highest point of the Pa—the track Danny would have taken on his last journey. I couldn't see the sheer cliff on the far side where the Pa dropped into the sea, and my racing pulse told me I wasn't ready to go there yet. Perhaps I would never be ready.

At seven o'clock every evening I telephoned Adam from the public phone box thirty minutes fast walk along the still unsealed road. It was eight in the morning in London and after my long days filling in time I was frantic to hear Adam's deep voice. But I couldn't tell him about Dad and Fiona. I rehearsed the words I would use, but it didn't help. They stayed in my head. Another secret.

The second week brought rain and I climbed the ladder to the low-ceilinged attic, brushing away the thick swaths of cobwebs and rat turds to find the box of stuff I'd stored there before Danny died. Hauling the box downstairs I put the envelope on top to one side and sorted through my old photo albums, my eyes watering from the dusts of time or from some emotion escaping through cracks in my depression. The albums chronicled years of happy holidays where Mum and Dad looked younger than I was now. I gazed for a long time at a photo taken on my first birthday and wondered how my parents could look so happy, so soon after Dad's affair. Was it all an illusion, the happiness I remembered? The happiness I thought Adam and I had, our children had?

When at last I reached the bottom of the box I picked up the envelope and put it down again. Photos I'd put there so long ago, before I knew they would have been better destroyed. Realizing the rain had finally ceased, I went on a strenuous run. It was not until many hours later, another solitary meal over, that I found the courage to look at the photos. But their power to hurt had been diluted by the pictures I'd seen of Danny so recently; rather, his striking looks and the tragedy of his early death were simply confirmed yet again. Then I pulled Danny's LP record from my suitcase and spun it on the old record player. Lying on the couch in the dark, covered with the same throw I had wrapped around a shaking Danny on the last night I saw him alive, I listened to his husky voice. Deep within me the tears began and kept coming until I was filled with them. With no one to hear me and no one to worry about my mental state, I let go and wept and wailed until I was empty.

The next day I was exhausted but a little less depressed. That evening I phoned Adam slightly later than usual, knowing it would be 8.30am in London and Finbar and Lara would have left for school. I finally felt strong enough to tell him about Dad's affair and Fiona's ultimatum to Danny. Adam was shocked into silence, but he pulled himself together and told me firmly that it made no difference to anything all these years later. My dad was no worse than any other fellow who cheated on his wife. Just bloody unlucky.

I was relieved by his reaction, although I knew he'd be reeling inside. He didn't want me to hang up, and tried to get me to talk about normal things, like how cold the sea was and what I was having for dinner. Then he did his best to cheer me up, chuckling as he described Finbar's new venture—playing his guitar and singing old rock 'n roll songs with two of his friends. As I stood alone in the dark phone box listening to him, I could feel my heart swelling in my chest.

"That's what I miss most about you," I whispered when he'd finished his story.

"What? What do you miss?" I could hear the love in his voice, his laughter gone.

"Hearing you laugh in the dark."

I LEANED BACK IN THE OLD ROCKING CHAIR ON THE DECK, A coffee by my side and a novel in my hand. The Barrier was at last working its magic. Danny's decision to go along with his mother's demands and reject me...what that said about his love for me... how I reacted... why he climbed the Pa... was I there?—those thoughts still haunted me. But mostly I was able to bring myself back from the brink of another bout of depression by using the cognitive behavior therapy strategies Sarah had taught me. Looking at myself in the mottled mirror above the sink I would repeat the trite phrase we had come up with to 'reset' my faulty thoughts: "If I can mend a brain, how hard can it be to heal the hole in my heart?" I still found such a simplistic strategy difficult to take too seriously, but at least it made me smile. I even tried the same strategies to help me with my struggle to forgive Dad.

I looked up in surprise, my musings shattered, as a motorbike skidded to a halt in a cloud of sand and the pillion passenger climbed down, pulling off her helmet and shaking free her curly hair.

"Nice spot you have here," she yelled above the still puttering engine. She bounced up the steps and threw her arms around me, then burst into tears.

Wiping my own eyes, I finally extracted myself from her hug and held her at arms length. "I don't believe this. What on earth are you doing here?"

"That's a nice welcome, I don't think," Lara said, her tears over. She grinned. "Here's me come all this way and all you can do is stand there with your mouth wide open."

The motorbike rider deposited her backpack on the steps. He raised a hand to me and winked at Lara. "Looks like you've found the right place. I'll leave you to it. But don't forget about the band at Claris Club on Saturday night. If you need a ride, give me a call." With that he got back on his bike and with a roar, was off in another cloud of sand.

"You certainly know how to arrive in style," I said. "I suppose your father and Finbar are hiding around the next sand dune, about to spring out?" I almost expected this to happen.

"You wish. Afraid you only get little ole me." Lara looked around and let out a whoop. "What an awesome place. How dare you keep it from us all these years."

I reached over and touched my daughter's cheek. "I know. I'd forgotten myself how very special it is. This is the first time I've been here since Danny's accident. But I promise we'll be coming here from now on."

Lara disappeared inside and I heard her exclaiming at the view. I dragged in her pack and set the kettle on the gas hob while she explored the rest of the house. At last, when I'd managed to get her to sit down with a cup of tea beside her, I discovered why she was here.

"Dad thought we needed each other. He reckoned it would do me good to have a holiday in the sea air and that having to deal with me would cheer you up."

"What about school?"

"I've done all that stuff from the first semester. I did it last year. It's only the last few months I missed. The others in my class are doing those beginning of term tests. I passed them all a year ago. So the form mistress told me I may as well stay home and get even more betterer." She grinned her old Lara grin, and my heart lifted.

"Seems to me your English could do with a refresher course."

Lara smirked. "Nah. I'm good. And Finbar's green with envy. I think he almost wishes he'd had a head injury too, so he could get off school."

"I'm surprised your father would have a bar of it after your long relaxing holiday in New Orleans." Lara's complexion was still rather pale.

"Ho, ho. You're the problem. Dad's worried sick about you. He sent me because he has a full-on teaching semester and he knows I'll sort you out." I could see Lara struggling to look unconcerned, but she didn't quite manage it.

"He's right. I already feel betterer. How on earth did you get a ride here on that motorbike?"

"I stuck my leg out and he picked me up." Lara gave me a quick kiss on my cheek. "Just kidding. Dad put me on the plane and I got to Auckland at dawn yesterday morning, and Granddad and Grandma picked me up and I stayed with them last night. Then this morning I got that funky little plane over here. I was shitting myself when it landed on the grass. I thought we were making a crash landing. Granddad had already phoned the woman in the airport office and asked her to organize a taxi to take me to your house. But she said a taxi would never get along the dune track and got her son to bring me on his motorbike. Cool, eh!"

"Very cool. That was nice of her and her son. Did you pay him?"

"I tried but he told me it was no prob, he was going this way anyway, and I could buy him a beer at the Claris Club on Saturday night."

"He did, did he? And I suppose you told him you were only sixteen?"

"Don't be tragic. As if."

"That's a long trip for a little girl to do all by herself."

"Watch it, missus," said Lara. "Any more lip from you and I'm gone."

We spent the day walking on the beach and talking, and in the evening I made dinner while Lara jogged to the phone box to call her father. Later, when she'd disappeared for the night into the old bunkroom that had once been Andrew's and mine, I poured myself a wine and relaxed by the fire. Then I opened the little box, wrapped in silver paper with lots of sticky tape and a less than perfect blue bow around it. Lara had presented it to me after dinner.

"A pressie from Dad. He made me promise not to open it, so all that sticky tape is not me trying to disguise a crime."

"As if you would. Thank you sweetheart. Never have I had a present delivered to me by a maiden on a motor bike…"

"Who has traveled 12,000 miles to get it to you. Dad owes me one," Lara said, her smile worth more than any present could possibly deliver.

My breath caught when I finally freed the pretty box from its wrapping paper. Inside, on a bed of cotton wool, rested a gold ring set with a dark blue sapphire nestled between two small diamonds. Beside it was a pair of earrings; delicate diamond studs with gold drops glowing with the same dark blue stones. I read Adam's handwritten note.

Darling Sapphire Eyes,

I never gave you an engagement ring, and I hope you like these. The ring is an eternity ring, and that's what I want, to be with you always.

Perhaps you will wear it whenever you're not operating. I never really doubted our love, but when I thought I'd lost you and Lara to Katrina, I knew that I could never be happy without you.

I send you Lara so you have time enough together to heal. I hope you find the courage to tell her the truth. I have no doubt at all that with your love she will be able to deal with it. After head injuries, hurricanes, snakes and assisting her mother while she saves lives, discovering that her parents shared the same brother will simply be another colorful strand to add rich-ness to her life experience.

All my love, Adam.

e spent our first full day together doing nothing. Lazing on the beach and in the hammocks on the deck, eating, and reminiscing about New Orleans, Katrina, and all our new friends. Lara confided that she'd been thinking about medicine as a career instead of a less certain future as a singer. I was both moved and strangely disappointed: moved because she said observing me with my patients had inspired her, and disappointed because of my own dream that one day Adam and I would be part of an audience brought to tears by her voice.

When I spouted the standard balanced comment of a standard balanced parent: "Medicine can be hard, but there are always jobs for doctors. A singing career is less certain, I suppose," she twirled around, tra-la-la-ing, and came to a stop with deep bow.

"So I'll be a singing doctor. Don't worry, Mum, it's months before I have to decide. I can do all the science subjects next year just in case I decide on medicine, although I think I'll have to do bloody math, so that might be the end of that dream. But at least there aren't any school subjects I have to do to become a blues singer."

That evening I got out Danny's LP and played it for his daughter. She sat on the floor and listened, mesmerized, as she ran her fingers over the photo of Danny on the LP cover.

"He's so groovy, Mum. And I love his voice. I wish I could sing like that."

"You are every bit as good," I told her, my throat constricting. "Your voice has some more maturing to do, but one day…"

"How awful that he died so young. All his wonderful career gone, just like that." Lara had tears in her voice.

"Darling, don't cry. It was a long time ago." I dropped to the floor beside her and covered her hand with mine.

"But it's so sad, and it makes me think of Tony," she hiccupped. "I know we weren't like you and Danny—I hadn't known him very long—but he was my boyfriend and I felt so bad when he got killed."

"Oh love, I know, I know." I held her until her sobs stopped. "I'm sorry I wasn't really there for you when you were trying to cope with losing Tony. I was too intent on my own problems to realize what you were going through, and that's unforgivable. I, of all people, should have understood how you were feeling."

Lara sat back and blew her nose on an already saturated tissue. "It's OK, Mums. You were going through it all again at the same time, over Danny. We should have helped each other."

"Am I forgiven?"

"Of course you are. I was so horrible to you and Dad, but you mainly. I was acting like a little kid. But I'm over all that now."

"I don't think you were acting like a little kid at all." I grinned at her. "Perhaps a stroppy teenager. But I'm glad we're OK again."

"Me, too." Her brow crinkled. "How can you ever go near that Pa, after finding him?"

"I've managed to walk to the Pa end of the beach, but as soon as I look up at it I freak out. I'm determined to climb it though, before I leave here. I hope it will bring back more about what happened that night, and I need to know."

"Granddad told me about it. The Pa I mean. How it is tapu and people shouldn't climb up to the top. But he said I should tell you that it is different if it is out of respect for someone who died up there, like Danny."

I raised my eyebrows. "Did he just. That makes it a bit less scary. When we were kids it was definitely a no-go area."

"Granddad knows these things. He told me lots about his ancestors. He said he and you and me and Finbar are all tangata whenua of Great Barrier Island. So when we do climb the Pa it's not as if we're tourists just doing it for fun. Our ancestors will be with us and we'll be doing it to honor Danny's memory."

"Well, I can hardly argue with that. What do you mean, when we climb the Pa? Do you want to try too?"

"I think that's partly why I'm here. So you and I can do it together. Dad said he'd be happier if I were with you." She looked down at her fingers, and picked at a nail. "Dad has been awfully upset. He tries not to let Finbar and me see, but I know. He hardly ever goes out any more with his friends, except to see Mike and Sonja sometimes. Just before I left they had a farewell party for that Irish friend of theirs, Julia. We all went." She slanted her eyes at me. "Dad thinks she's become a pain in the butt, always phoning about nothing. He said her poor husband couldn't stand her conniving, and went back to Dublin. Anyway, she's gone too now, back to Dublin."

"Her poor husband," I said.

"Yeah, that's what I say." Lara's grin was slightly wobbly. She held her hands up and inspected her nails. "Dad's lonely for you. So the sooner we climb the Pa and get back home, the betterer."

"I couldn't have put it betterer myself, sweetheart."

WE STARTED EARLY, AND WERE ACROSS THE STREAM AND AT the base of the Pa by eight. It was a perfect day, the surf rolling evenly in across a clear blue sea, and the flanks of the Pa covered in towering flax bushes, their long leaves shining in the sun and their spiky flower stalks a picture against the sky. Scrambling up the faint track to the saddle I breathed evenly, in out, in out, *re-lax, re-lax.* Lara came close behind me humming to herself, ready to catch me if I stumbled. A tui swept past us with a swish of its wings, its liquid call falling through the air. We watched as it landed on a black flax stalk and, delicately dipping its curved beak into a dark red sticky flower head peeking prematurely from its plump green bud, sucked out its sweet nectar. And then we were on the saddle, the long grass warm and comforting against my bare legs. We sank down into it and the memories flooded back. Happy memories of Andrew and I making huts up here as kids, picnics with Mum and Dad, scrambling down into the pretty stony bay on the seaward side and snorkeling in the deep clear pools. The last time I'd been here was with Danny on Christmas Day, 1988. I still hadn't realized I was pregnant. We were so very, very happy.

"Bliss," said Lara, lying back and throwing her arms wide. "Pure bliss."

"Mmm, it is rather," I agreed, lying down beside her, my eyes closed so I couldn't see the steep side of the Pa rising up on our left.

"Why don't we come back here? We could live in Auckland and come over here every holidays."

"It would have its charms, but what about all your friends in London? And there is the small matter of earning enough to pay for your and Finbar's exotic tastes."

"I know. It's not going to happen. You'll be even busier

soon when you're the Director of Neurosurgery," she said, her voice glum.

"I don't think that's going to happen either. I've missed the deadline for applying," I said, noticing how my body felt lighter as it absorbed the warmth of the sun and the scent of the grass.

"But you've worked so hard for it. Dad said they'd accept a late application from you. You're a star now after all the stories about what you did at Memorial. Don't let sleazy Jim beat you."

"You know, I don't think I want the Directorship any more. I'd rather spend more of my time with patients and in surgery, than stressing out about budgets. Let sleazy Jim have it, I say. Not that I want him as my boss, but I'll simply ignore him."

"Yeah! Good decision. You'll have more time with us then."

We sat up and celebrated with a High-Five. And then we saw them, a pod of dolphins, leaping and dancing through the sparkling blue.

I MANAGED THE FIRST PART OF THE ALMOST INVISIBLE TRACK to the top of the Pa without even my re-lax re-lax mantra. Lara's singing helped.

"I love to go a-wandering, along the mountain track," she bellowed out, behind me, and I remembered singing the same song on hikes with Mum and Dad when Andrew and I were kids.

"Come on Mum, sing with me. "Val-deri…"

"Val-dera," I warbled, panting as I scrambled around rocks and up and up.

Waltzing Matilda came next, and Lara never even muttered at my off-key rendition. I stopped perhaps twenty meters short of the top, trying to catch my breath, my heart pounding.

"Wow," Lara said. "Some view."

We could see the stream, estuary, and beach below us, the dunes rolling into paddocks, blue hills in the distance, and puffy white clouds floating in a blue blue sky. I looked back along the beach where the sea played gently on the sand. I nodded, my heart slowing down. I felt like congratulating it. It wasn't panicking, this heart of mine. It was simply recovering after some good healthy exercise.

"OK?" Lara said. "Why don't I go first now and check out the top, and you can follow?"

I nodded again. I didn't trust myself to speak. I watched her climb the last ten meters and suddenly it was back in my head, and it was Danny's body I was watching, struggling up to the top. I closed my eyes and clamped my hands over my ears to shut out the crashing sea and howling wind.

The sky has darkened and the rain is soaking through my T-shirt and shorts and the wind is screaming between the track and me. I'm on the ground, hanging onto grass and bushes, crawling my way further up, stones spinning off under me, rain running like a river down the hillside. The sea crashing on the rocks gets louder and louder as I crawl higher and higher. A jagged flash lights up the sky and seems to hit the massive rock balanced on the very top of the Pa. The place where the spirits of Maori chiefs leave this world for the next.

"Mum, are you OK?"

Lara's voice? What is she doing here with Danny? Another voice. "Georgia, Georgia. Stay away from the edge, we'll sort it out, stay away." Danny's voice. His hands grab my arms, he's a black shape in the darkness, I can't see his face, and I push him off me. I grab at the rock; it's between me and the cliff, the cliff that ends on the rocks and terrible sea so far below. The wind howls around the rock and tries to separate me from it and I crouch into it, my heart breaking. "You're lying, you're lying," a voice is screaming. My voice. "You never loved me, all you care about is your career. You've just used me."

"Georgia, be careful, it's dangerous, come away from the edge, we'll work it out, I'm sorry, be careful, come to me." Danny's voice shouting. I don't want to hear him.

"Leave me alone, leave me alone. I never want to see you again." I hit him and hit him, his body his face that I loved and can't have. I shove him hard and he comes back and his hands are hurting my arms and I kick out at him and I fall back but the rock isn't there and I'm falling, falling and the sea is roaring for me and I don't care, this is all that is left. It's scratchy and I've stopped falling but the sea still roars and waits for me.

"Georgia, Georgia, don't move. Stay still, hold onto the bush, I'm coming down to get you." Danny's voice. My hand grabs the bush and it pulls away and I see my hand grab and grab and then it clings and my other hand clings too. I cling to the bush, it clings to the side of the cliff, and the water pours down past me to the rocks below. My head is squashed in the prickly branches and I hear Danny. He is screaming my name, "Georgia, Georgia," and I think of him singing, Georgia, Georgia on my mind, and he loves me, he isn't leaving me, that's a dream, he loves me and I ran away from him but he came after me because he loves me and I am his heart and he is my heart and his baby is inside me and I mustn't hurt our baby. Danny is coming down to rescue me and our baby and it will all be all right. I lean my head back out of the scratchy bush and Danny's shape is climbing down the cliff to me. His foot slips and I scream and he is still climbing down, so slowly, so slowly, and I cling to the bush. A bolt of lightning jags across the sky and Danny's red hair is flying and I scream as his body, Danny's body, falls towards me and hits me as I cling to the bush and he's gone and I didn't stop him, I didn't catch him. I look down and can't see him, only the white foam as the waves pound on the rocks below. I have to go down to him but I can't, I can't, it's too steep and slippery and there are no more bushes to hold on to. I have to climb up the cliff and crawl down the other side and around the bottom through the stream and to the wild sea where it bashes on the cliff and find him, find my Danny before he gets too cold and the sea takes him away from me and our baby. One hand, grab that bush, pull up, the other hand, stretch up to the next bush, pull up.

"Mum, Mum, what is it? Open your eyes, hush Mum it's all right, you're all right, I'm here with you. Open your eyes."

Lara's voice. What's Lara doing up here in the dark and rain?

"Mum, Mum."

Don't shout. I can hear you. You shouldn't be up here, it's dangerous, Danny fell. He was trying to rescue me, I fell and he was trying to rescue me and now he's in the sea and I have to find him.

"Mum, what's wrong?"

The sun has come out, where am I, the rain has stopped, it's daytime and I haven't found Danny.

"Mum, Mum, say something."

Lara's arms are around me and she's crying. The rock is pressing into my side and I look up at it. I am lying on my back and the sky is blue above me with puffy white clouds. I turn over onto my stomach and see over the edge. The cliff drops away to rocks far below, the sea breaking over them but not wild any more. The vomit fills my mouth and I watch it spurt over the cliff and bury a white rock lily growing from a crevice.

"You scared me, Mum. You were screaming and saying things and calling out Danny's name. Did you have a panic attack? I'm sorry Mum. I couldn't help you. You crawled up here after me and I couldn't make you hear me."

I pushed myself slowly back from the edge of the cliff and around the big rock and sat there, my back against its solidness, looking down the track to the saddle and out over the stream and the estuary and the calm dolphin sea. In out, in out, *re-lax, re-lax*. I gripped Lara's hand and she wriggled even closer to me and we sat there, our hearts slowing, slowing, our eyes crying, crying.

I TOOK ANOTHER SWIG FROM THE DRINK BOTTLE LARA HAD pulled from her daypack. My thirst felt as if it would never be sated. We'd been sitting here for a while, an hour at least, while we calmed down. Lara had tried to get me to climb back down to the saddle but I'd wanted to stay up here, partly to get back my breath, strength, and sanity, and partly for a reason I couldn't quite grasp. I felt safe here in the lee of this rock; the last piece of earth Danny had been close to before being no more. I needed to tell Lara what I'd remembered, re-experienced. It had been so much more vivid, so much more real, than those times when Sarah had taken me back with the hypnosis she preferred to call deep relaxation. I needed to tell Lara all of it in case I lost it again. Sitting here in the warm benevolent sun, it was all clear to me. Even the small details seemed clear but perhaps I was inventing those. But I knew the sweep of my memory was true.

Danny had told me everything. He didn't lie to me, he didn't cover up, he didn't keep any secrets. He told me what his mother told him; that his brother John was my half brother and his mother was so upset that he thought we should delay getting married for a year to give her time to come to terms with it. It was me who hadn't been able to grasp it, who'd called him a liar, told him it was just a stupid excuse so he could get out of marrying me. I knew it was true of course; why would anyone invent such a terrible story? Why didn't I tell him I was pregnant? Why? Was I afraid he'd still put his mother's feelings first? Leave me like Dad left

Fiona? So I ran out, ran, ran, as far as I could go and that was the end of the beach. And there was the Pa.

I was nearly at the top before I heard Danny screaming through the wind at me from the saddle. I stood by the rock, not knowing where I could go next to get away from him, away from the truth he was forcing on me. I didn't want to die, I never wanted to die, I only wanted to get away, be in the wild storm where my pain could find company. I remember pushing him away, and Danny trying to pull me from the rock. I remember slipping backwards and falling. Danny falling. I remember somehow finding the strength to climb back up. I remember crawling, stumbling back down to the saddle, wading through the stream—it was so deep and wild—getting around to the cliff side of the Pa, finding him. My Danny. How long I was there before I must have stumbled all the way across the dunes and the paddocks to the road, I couldn't remember.

When I was done, when I had told it all to Lara as it played back to me, I felt the weight slither through me and imagined it rolling over and over as it disappeared into the sea far below.

"Mum, let's go down now. It's over. You don't need to cry any more."

"These are tears of relief. I've been so afraid that I'd blocked those memories because I caused Danny's death. Directly caused it. That I was so angry, so upset, that I pushed him, and he went over the cliff. Somehow, it's not so terrible to know that he fell trying to save me, and that I did all I could to find him, to save him."

"I get that," said Lara. "Totally. It was a horrible accident. If anyone was to blame, it was Granddad and Fiona. But it was so long ago, and all they did was fall for each other when they shouldn't have. I don't think we should blame them any longer. It's too exhausting."

"Sweetheart, I never meant to tell you about Granddad

and his affair with Danny's mother like this. I knew I had to tell you, and you'd want to know the truth. I was getting up the courage to tell you some evening when we'd had a nice day and a lovely dinner and were feeling happy and peaceful."

"This way was much better. Like a thriller."

"I know you're just putting on a brave face for me. We'll talk it all through more sensibly when we've recovered from today. It's a big thing for you to take on board. It's taken me a while to even begin to get my head around it."

"It's exciting. Now I've got new grandparents and an uncle and two cousins I never knew I had. And a place to stay in Queenstown and New Orleans. What's not to love?"

"We'll talk more about all that later, when I'm down on flat land."

"Uh oh. More intrigue. OK Mums. Let's get you down the mountain."

But we didn't leave the top of the Pa straight away. There was another reason we'd come up here. Not that I'd known this, but Lara had.

"Granddad told me that if we did come up here there was something we needed to see. He wouldn't tell me what but he said I had to look around just to the side of the rock for a hollow between some big flax bushes. Somewhere on the side looking towards the beach."

My eyebrows went up. "Perhaps he found some Maori artifacts there. He had a good eye for them." I scrabbled in my shorts pocket. "I discovered this in these old shorts when I put them on this morning. It's been here all these years. Thank goodness I didn't throw all my old clothes in the bin. I pulled out a small stone adze and gave it to Lara.

"It's beautiful." She ran her finger across the edge. "It's

still sharp after all these hundreds of years. Where did you find it?"

"Right here on the Pa. On the saddle that Christmas Day when Danny and I had our picnic lunch. He found it actually, and gave it to me. I was nervous about taking it away from here, but Danny convinced me that it was just one of many, and that whoever made it was probably one of my ancestors, one of my tupuna. That he would be happy to know it was with me, given in love." I shivered. "Perhaps if we had left it here none of this would have happened."

"You never did have a gift for logical thought," said Lara. "If none of this had happened, you and Danny would never have met and fallen in love, and made me, your fabulously talented daughter."

CHAPTER 28

I stayed in my sunny place while Lara fossicked about in the flax.

" Hey, Mum, I've found something. Come over."

Gingerly I made my way to where she was kneeling down, examining something intently. I felt fine though. No fast beating heart.

My eye caught a dull gleam in the grass and I dropped down beside Lara, pushing back the tangle of green growing over the sides of the dirty slab of stone, almost hiding it from view. Through the covering of time and moss that coated the surface of the bronze plaque set into the stone, I could make out fragments of words and numbers. A 'D' in curly script and a date ending in a '9'. The ache in my throat told me that this was what Dad had wanted us to find.

"It's for Danny," isn't it," Lara whispered. "It's a memory stone for Danny."

Ripping out handfuls of grass we scrubbed at the stone's face, but that quickly proved ineffectual and we looked around for something else to use. Then I felt a nudge as Lara pushed the adze into my hand. "This is why you brought the adze with you," she whispered. "Why Danny found it."

I leaned over the plaque and gently traced the flowing 'D' of his name. Lara pulled off her T-shirt and rolled it into a soft ball and scrubbed at the bronze. Gradually the moss and crusty soil came away, liberating an inscription still filled with the soils of time and hard to read. I put the adze to use again, perhaps 500 years or more after it had been last employed. It fitted perfectly into the rifts carved much more recently into Danny's memorial. We worked steadily, painstakingly scraping and freeing each letter and each number. Memories of happy times on the island, as a girl and as a young woman, with my family and with Danny, floated gently through my head. But no sad memories came to haunt me as Lara and I worked together, and I didn't try to read the words that our efforts were gradually revealing until we'd liberated the very last letter. The plaque shone dully in the sun now, the old-fashioned lettering standing out, finally free of its camouflage.

Danny Leaumont
April 1961 - January 1989
-Oh, Danny boy, oh Danny boy, we love you so-
Always remembered by
Georgia and Lara,
Seamus and Hannah.

Through my tears I heard a tui calling and then a voice as sweet soaring into the sky. Lara was standing, gazing out to sea, her hands crossed on her breast, her voice as pure and clear as the love that shone in her glowing face.

"Oh, Danny boy, the pipes, the pipes are calling
From glen to glen, and down the mountain side,"

As the plaintive words sang through my mind and lodged in my soul, I could hear Dad and Danny singing with her. Grandfather, father and daughter. And as she came to the last verse, I heard my own voice singing with them as I stood side by side with Lara and completed the circle.

"And I shall hear, though soft you tread above me,
And all my grave will warmer, sweeter be,
For you will bend and tell me that you love me,
And I shall sleep in peace until you come to me."

WE HAD OUR LAST SUPPER THAT NIGHT ON THE WEATHERED old table on the deck, the candles flickering in the still night. The meal was simple but delicious; fresh snapper with garlic and black pepper, sprinkled with grassy olive oil and barbe-cued in foil over the little fire outside, accompanied by part baked, part burnt potatoes done in the ashes, and a salad made from the straggly lettuces and bolting rocket in the vegetable garden—survivors of the mild winter. With our last bottle of sauvignon blanc, we drank toasts to Adam and Finbar, to our happy future together again as a family, and rather sadly to our little house and beautiful island.

"Here's to the Barrier," said Lara, clinking her glass with mine. "And Mums, here's another special toast; to the memory of Danny."

My throat constricted as I looked at my beautiful daughter in the candlelight, the red flames in her hair reminding me of Danny sitting at that very same table so long ago. "To Danny, may he rest in peace," I said, clinking my glass with Lara's.

After dinner we washed up, packed the last few bits of our belongings, and settled down in an easy silence in the two old chairs by the empty fireplace. It was not long before Lara, already half asleep, came over to say goodnight.

"Don't be late, Mum; we've got an early start in the morn-ing." Dropping a kiss on the top of my head, she disappeared into the bunkroom.

I lay back and closed my tired eyes. It must have been an hour or more later when I woke, uncomfortable in the lumpy chair. The only sounds I could hear were the quiet noises of the night—the distinctive call of a morepork before it swooped on silent wings to snatch an unsuspecting mouse, the occasional lonely cry of a shearwater flying from its day out at sea to its nesting site on the summit of Mount Hirakimata, the muffled rumble of breakers on the beach far below, and close by, the regular breathing signaling my daughter's sleep.

Pulling myself out of the chair, I tiptoed out the door into the gentle night. The moon was not yet up and the sky was black velvet punctured with thousands of stars. I looked up at the Southern Cross and its pointers, always the easiest constellation to find however dazzling the Milky Way. My bare feet made their own way to the beach, down the steep track they had known since babyhood.

The warming seas had encouraged luminescent algae to flourish, and in the black night it glowed and bloomed an eerie greenish-white in the breaking waves. I'd gazed on the unearthly sight many times in the past, but never before had it seemed so magical. The horizon lightened, and I ran down the sand to the very edge of the breaking waves, watching the perfect circle of the full moon rising majestically out of the sea, paving a silver path to my feet. The warm breeze on my face, fragrant with sea and grass smells, the briny taste on my lips, the low roar of the surf as it rhythmically immersed my feet in cold glowing foam, the black sea cut through with the ribbon of moonlight, and behind me, protecting the house where I'd been born, the Southern Cross. Yes, this was home.

Happiness, pure and sweet, flowed through me for the first time in many long months, and then I saw him. At first I thought it was a fleeting shadow falling across the silver path as a wisp of cloud passed in front of the moon, now riding well clear of the horizon. But then I saw the flash of a green shirt, and copper sparks flying from his hair as the moonlight set it on fire. In the sigh of the wind and sea I fancied I could hear his warm, husky voice, finally setting me free.

Let me go, Georgia, and take back your heart...

The whispered words faded as the moon slipped behind a cloud. When the silver path reappeared, he had gone, and I could no longer hear his voice in the wind.

EPILOGUE

LARA

Great Barrier Island, New Zealand
January 15th, 2010.

It is peaceful here on the hammock on the deck overlooking the bay. Mum and Dad are sleeping in their bedroom, and brother Andrew and Becky in the bunkroom. This year Danny's brother John and his wife and their two sons are in New Orleans, but they were with us here last summer. I can hear laughter from the tents on the grass to the side of the house where the rest of us sleep at night: Andrew's son and Finbar in one, Andrew's daughter and Lara in another, and Adam and I in the third. The permanently open doors of our tents look out across the sand dunes to the beach and the Pa.

It's a hot summer afternoon; this morning we exhausted

ourselves making our annual pilgrimage to the top of the Pa where we remember Danny as Lara sings. Always Danny Boy. Mum and Dad don't make the final climb with us any more; they manage to get to the saddle even though Mum is 79 this month and Dad is 80. They live here permanently on the island now, both of them busier than they ever were in Auckland, organizing community events, and joining in on numerous conservation efforts to preserve the island's rare birds, lizards and plants. Dad still keeps them fed on fresh fish and Mum supplies their organic greens from her raised garden behind the house.

We come over here every chance we get. I have more time since we moved home to New Zealand three years ago. My work as a neurosurgeon, one of five at Auckland Hospital, is as challenging as it ever was in London, but I have no desire to take on any higher role. The London Department only had to suffer under Jim Mason's command for a year before he tired of the endless meetings and resigned at the same time as I did. But in his case it was so he could make more money as a full-time private consultant. To my joy, Karen Jenkins, my dear friend from Thibodaux, applied for and won the Directorship, and replaced sleazy Jim with warmth, empathy and brilliance. In her Christmas letter she wrote that she still loved it, but planned to move sideways in another two years. When she retired at sixty, she would return home to Louisiana and find a place to settle close to a good crabbing estuary.

Adam is a full professor now at Auckland University, and Finbar begins his last year at grammar school in February. He is the captain of the First Eleven, and Adam never misses a game. And Lara. She flew through her repeat year of school in London, even passing math! By then she'd decided that a further school year wasn't for her; medicine had been a passing phase, but music stayed her passion. Savannah's reference probably helped her get admitted to the Bachelor of Music in Jazz Studies at Loyola University in New Orleans.

She was nearing the end of her degree now, and already sang three nights a week in Lara's Piano Bar. Savannah had bought Voodoo Magic from old Kat when she'd decided it was time to fly off on her broomstick to Florida, where her daughter lived. Lara and Leroy took charge of the renovations and turned it back to the moody club I remembered, but without the smoky atmosphere. The new name had not been Lara's choice; she'd wanted to call it Danny's Piano Bar again, but Savannah over-ruled her. "Time to move on," she said.

Savannah will be 94 later this year, and no longer feels spry enough to come to Great Barrier. She is well cared for in her Garden District home by Leroy and Fiona, who returned to New Orleans the same year as Lara went to live with her great grandmother.

Tonight is the annual Great Barrier Island concert under the stars, where all the locals gather and enjoy two hours of entertainment with the summer visitors. As always it will be colorful, and the range of abilities displayed by the performers staggering. Most of them can sing in tune at least, which lets me off the hook. And always there are a few special performers. It is not hard to attract top acts from Auckland and elsewhere in New Zealand. Who wouldn't want a weekend surfing and fishing on the most beautiful island on earth?

We were all seated on the grass in front of the canvas-covered stage before the first act came on; the children from Okiwi School with their Maori songs and a haka. Not a dry eye in the crowd after that start. Bands, dancers, budding opera singers, bluegrass, a folk duet, heavy metal, more Maori songs, a Beatles band. At 10pm the compere climbed back on the stage and waited until the crowd stopped their chatter.

"Right, we've come to the end of another great concert. Just one more special guest to end on." He waved his arm in our direction. "Seamus McKinlay, come on up here, you old bastard."

Dad got up from the folding canvas chair he was, as a nod

to his age, allowed to sit on, and walked up the steps. He looked mighty fine, tall and straight, his hair pure white but as thick as it had ever been. He looked down at us all, hushed in anticipation.

"Sorry, folks. You're not going to hear my old voice tonight. I'm passing the baton to my granddaughter. She's going to blow you all away. Come on up, Lara." He beckoned to Lara sitting in the grass next to me and she gave me a quick kiss on my cheek before she joined her grandfather at the mike.

I felt Adam's warm hand close around mine as my eyes feasted on her slim form, from her bare brown feet, to her faded blue jeans and sea-green shirt. She detached the mike from its stand, and as Dad sat down at the piano beside her and played a chord, she smiled her Danny smile and shook her Danny hair and said, "Mum, this song is for you."

And cradling the microphone like a kiss, she closed her green eyes, and sang,

"Georgia, Georgia…"

Her voice rose into the dark sky and through the stars and past the moon and settled on top of the Pa.

"Just an old sweet song
Keeps Georgia on my mind."

Dear Reader,

Before I became a novelist I had a different career— teaching, researching, and practicing clinical psychology and neuropsychology. Writing character-led fiction clearly involves some understanding of human psychology, but I have discovered that it also draws on my knowledge of psychology in ways that are so subtle that sometimes it is an editor or reader who discovers a theme in my story that I hadn't planned. Once it is pointed out, I can see how it grew out of the psychology of the characters and their interactions.

Reading novels also deepens our understanding of psychology, and comes with significant psychological benefits. The very act of reading prompts our imaginations to soar, more so than when watching a movie. With a book we need to imagine so much about the characters and locations, and this fires up complex systems in our brains. Apart from escapism, reading fiction has been shown to increase our ability to empathize with other people different from ourselves or with different views from ours, and allows us to experience other worlds, sometimes realistic, sometimes pure fantasy. It also gives us a way of 'rehearsing' situations and how we might react, respond, and feel, should we be faced with similar situations in the future. Reading allows us to go at our own pace, not the speed required by watching a similar story on a screen, and thus gives us time to think more deeply about issues raised by the story. Of course, many fictional characters show terrible judgment –that's part of the story—but we can learn from that as well. I shudder to think how the recent Covid-19 pandemic, when in its early stages, affected some readers of pandemic horror stories.

Thus the discussion topics that follow are going to be a little different from the questions typically found at the end of many 'bookclub' reads. With my psychologist's hat on (perhaps not a hat, but after all these years a permanent part of my brain) I have expanded some of my story-related questions into areas probably more suited to a workshop for psychology students! To discuss all of these could take a very long book-club session, giving little time for the other important function of bookclubs–a catch-up with friends. So pick one or two topics and leave the rest for your later contemplation. Indeed as seasoned bookclub readers, you will have no problem ignoring my discussion topics entirely if you have more fascinating byways to follow!

1. *Work-Family Balance*

(a) At the start of the novel, Georgia and Adam each had a full-time career. How well do you think they balanced their parenting roles with their careers? How fair was this? In an ideal situation, do you think factors like gender, age of children, the relative 'importance' of the parents' jobs (e.g.: teaching university students and conducting research versus saving lives, or significantly different salaries), the passion each parent has for their work, and how 'good' each parent is at parenting, should be considered when parents decide how to manage this balance?

(b) What about blended families and situations where children are co-parented by separated parents? How might these scenarios influence decisions about work-family balance?

(c) If you have been in a situation where one parent spends more time at work than the other, how did you and your partner, and/or other parent decide whose career was more important? Do you think same-sex parents might have a different idea of fairness than heterosexual couples? Why?

(d) By the end of the novel had the work-family balance between Georgia and Adam changed? If so, what factors played into this?

2. *Anxiety Disorders*

(a) At the start of the novel we learn that Georgia had suffered from episodes of anxiety for many years, that she believed she had these under control, and that her colleagues at the hospital weren't aware of this side of her. She believed that if they knew, this would damage her chance of being appointed the Director of Neurosurgery, a role that in the past had always gone to a man. Do you think her fear that she would be discriminated against unfairly if it were known she had an anxiety disorder was valid? Are men in the workplace treated differently than women if they have a mental health problem?

(b) Neurosurgery is a profession that, unlike many other medical specialties, is still dominated by men. It is seen as a 'tough' career and not one where the doctor can take time out to have a child, or go part-time. Thus women who want or have children tend not to choose it as their specialty. Do you think this point-of-view should be challenged? Can you think of demanding careers that were once closed to women who wanted to take time out for parenting, but where women are now both successful and accepted? Is there any career that requires total dedication to the work at the expense of family and other aspects of life?

With my psychologist's hat on: As part of their ongoing registration requirements, many 'helping' professions require regular supervision or mentoring. For example, for practicing psychologists this is expected even at senior career levels. Perhaps if this had been a requirement for all the neurosurgeons in the hospital were Georgia worked, she would have (and indeed should have) talked about her anxiety issues with her supervisor as they arose, and she would have been supported in the use of strategies to protect her and her patients from any consequences of an escalation of her symptoms. For example, she might have felt it appropriate to refer a patient on if she considered, for any reason, that she was not in the right frame of mind to treat that patient. Most importantly she would not have felt inadequate or embarrassed by this. Of course, if her anxiety escalated to levels that were unsafe long term, then she would be supported to seek further help and possibly a different career. Different careers suit different people. Professions that believe their practitioners should never require time out are ignoring what it is to be human, thus exposing clients to poor service or worse.

3. *Mother-teenager relationships*

(a) Georgia's relationship with Lara was more fraught than her relationship with Finbar. Part of this was due to the ages of the two children and the particular circumstances around Lara's biological father, but these factors aside, do you think the relationship between mothers and daughters is often more challenging than between mothers and sons? If so, why? Is there a similar dynamic between fathers and sons? How might this be different with same sex parents and their same and different gender children?

(b) Georgia and Lara arrived in New Orleans just before Hurricane Katrina hit. Living through this crisis brought them closer. Why do you think this was? How do you think it changed the way each thought about the other? Has the recent Covid-19 crisis or any other crisis or exceptionally difficult time you have been through with other family members changed the way you see or feel about them? Do you think their view of you has changed?

4. *Family Secrets*

(a) What was the original family secret, and how did it spread through the generations and become more damaging?

(b) If the child born of the affair between Seamus (Georgia's father) and Fiona (Danny's mother) had been Danny and not his brother, then Lara would have been the child of an (unintentional) incestuous union. Would this have changed your opinion of Seamus's unfaithfulness to Georgia's mother, and his treatment of Fiona? If you consider that scenario makes his behavior worse, how do you square this with the fact that Seamus could not have predicted who might be a future lover of his and Fiona's child?

(c) Given that Georgia was pregnant and psychologically fragile, do you think her parents were justified in keeping from her the fact that Danny's mother had borne a child by Seamus? If so, should they have revealed this secret later, once she was well?

(d) Who owns a family secret? To answer this, you might first need to define what a 'family' secret is. For example, is an affair a family secret if it does not result in a child or result in any other obvious outcomes that affect the wider family (such as a change in economic circumstances)? How can the family members who are at the center of the 'secret', or discover it, decide whether to tell other family members or keep it to themselves? Do all family secrets become less damaging or hurtful once the people at the center of the secret have died? If you discovered a significant secret that your now dead grandparents had and clearly didn't want others to know, would you feel it was OK to tell that secret to others in your family (or outside your family through a published memoir)? If you believed it might cause pain or shame to the living descendants, would this change your decision? What if you believed those family members were being overly sensitive? What if the family secret was something so terrible you believed that it should be brought into the open at any cost, and who would be most damaged by that cost?

e) Lara was an intelligent 16-year-old who had just survived Hurricane Katrina when she learned that her grandfather Seamus had been unfaithful to her grandmother and had, as a result, fathered a child, and that therefore Danny's brother was her uncle both through Danny and through Georgia. What did you think of her acceptance of this? Did it ring true? If Danny had been Seamus's son, how much worse do you think this would have been for Lara? Consider the well-adjusted teenagers you know; do you think they would be well able to cope with information like this, if they have a good self-image?

With my psychologist's hat on: Some journalists, supported by anecdotal cases, have suggested that men and women who are closely related but unaware of this are likely to be sexually attracted to each other. While there is no research-based evidence for this, there are increasing concerns about the practice of sperm donation when a single man's sperm is donated to many women, especially within a relatively small geographical area. Even when, as now common, the sperm donor's identity is known to the mother, she is unlikely to know the identity of other women who have used his sperm. Thus there is a small but increased chance of half siblings meeting and, not knowing they are related, falling in love. Do you see this as a problem, if they never find out they are related? How does this change if they have children? In today's world more and more of us are having DNA tests, making genetic secrets increasingly impossible. Should the rules around sperm donation be changed in some way so that teenagers conceived by sperm donation are informed of the names and perhaps given photos of all their half siblings? If so, how could this be achieved whilst still preserving their parent's wishes (and rights?) to privacy?

5. *Titles of Novels*

Book club and literary novels often have titles that are somewhat abstract, or intended to hint at a theme in the book. In Chapter 6 of *The Moon is Missing*, Georgia and her therapist make casual conversation about the clear moonlit skies in New Zealand, where Georgia grew up, as compared to London. Having read the novel, does the title make sense on a deeper level?

NEWSLETTER SIGN-UP

PLEASE SUBSCRIBE TO MY OCCASIONAL E-NEWSLETTER about living life on an off-grid island (the very one in *The Moon Is Missing*!); book reviews of books I love; and a little writerly news.

GO TO 'Jenni's Off-Grid Newsletter'
    (www.jenniogden.com/newsletter)

IF YOU ENJOYED *The Moon Is Missing*, please do review it on Amazon and Goodreads, or anywhere else where books are sold (a few sentences—or even just a rating—is all it needs.)

Then sample the first chapters of my award-winning debut novel *A Drop in the Ocean,* set on another island, this time on Australia's Great Barrier Reef. So far it has sold 80,000 copies and I'd love you to make it 80,001!

A DROP IN THE OCEAN

JENNI OGDEN'S DEBUT NOVEL

bout the book
Anna Fergusson runs a lab researching Huntington's disease at a prestigious Boston university. When her long-standing grant is pulled unexpectedly, Anna finally faces the truth: she's 49, virtually friendless, single, and worse, her research has been sub-par for years. With no jobs readily available, Anna takes a leap and agrees to spend a year monitoring a remote campsite on Turtle Island on Australia's Great Barrier Reef. What could be better for an introvert with shattered self-esteem than a quiet year in paradise? As she settles in, Anna opens her heart for the first time in decades—to new challenges, to new friendships, even to a new love with Tom, the charming, younger turtle tagger she sometimes assists. But opening one's heart leaves one vulnerable, and Anna comes to realize that love is as fragile as happiness, and that both are a choice.

"...EVERYTHING A READING EXPERIENCE SHOULD BE, endearing and enduring, time spent with characters who seem to be people I already knew."—**Jacquelyn Mitchard**, *New York Times* #1 best-selling author of *The Deep End of the Ocean*

"...ANNA FERGUSSON LEARNS THAT LOVE IS ABOUT LETTING go. Jenni Ogden takes us on a sweeping journey, rich with unique characters and places, moving backward and forward in time, to reach this poignant and heartfelt lesson."—**Ann Hood**, *New York Times* best-selling author of *The Knitting Circle, The Red Thread,* and *The Obituary Writer*

READ ON FOR THE FIRST TWO CHAPTERS...

CHAPTER 1

ON MY FORTY-NINTH BIRTHDAY MY SHINING CAREER CAME TO an inauspicious end. It took with it the jobs of four promising young scientists and catapulted my loyal research technician into premature retirement, an unjust reward for countless years of dedicated scut work.

That April 6th began in precisely the same manner as all my birthdays over the previous fifteen years—Eggs Benedict with salmon, a slice of homemade wholemeal bread spread thickly with marmalade, and not one but two espressos at an Italian café in downtown Boston. On my arrival at eight o'clock sharp, the elderly Italian owner took my long down-filled coat and ushered me, as he had for more years than I care to re- member, to the small table by the window where I could look out on the busy street, today frosted with a late-season snow that had fallen overnight and would soon be gone. He always greeted me with the same words: "Good morning, Dr. Fergusson. A fine day for a birthday. Will you be having the usual?" as if he saw me every morning, or at least every week, and not just once a year.

Perhaps the unusually deep blue cloudless sky, almost suggesting a summer day, should have warned me that something was not quite as it should be. But superstitious behavior is not a strength of mine, and after my indulgent breakfast I walked to my laboratory in one of the outbuildings of the medical school, taking pleasure in the crisp winter air and stopping to collect my mail—in this e-mail era, usually consisting only of advertising pamphlets from academic publishing houses—before entering the lab.

Rachel looked up from her desk with her hesitant smile and gave me a beautifully wrapped parcel—a good novel, as always, the thirtieth she had given me. One for every birthday and one for every Christmas. I have kept them all. "Happy birthday Anna," she murmured, not wanting to advertise my private business to the others in the lab. Two of my four young research assistants were already at work, hunched over their computers. The other two would be out in the field interviewing the families who were the subjects of our research program. Huntington's families, we called them.

The research I had been doing for the past twenty-four years—first for my PhD, then as a research assistant, and finally as the leader of the team—focused on various aspects of Huntington's disease, a terrible, genetically transmitted disorder that targets half the children of every parent who has the illness. Often the children are born before the parents realize they carry the gene and long before they begin to show the strange contorted movements, mood fluctuations, and gradual decline into dementia that are the hallmarks of the disease. Thus our Huntington's families often harbored two or three or even four Huntington's sufferers spanning different generations.

Thankfully I was spared having to deal with them; I have never been good with people, and especially not sick people. I didn't discover this unfortunate fact until my internship year after I graduated from medical school. But as they say, when a door closes, a window opens, and I became a medical researcher instead. Of course it took a bit longer, as I had to complete a PhD, but that was bliss once I realized that my forté was peering down a microscope at brain tissue.

So there I was on my forty-ninth birthday, looking at the envelope I held in my hand and realizing with a quickening of my heart that it was from the medical granting body that had financed my research program for fifteen years. Every three years I had to write another grant application summarizing the previous three years of research and laying out the next three years. Every three years I breathed a sigh of relief when they rolled the grant over and sometimes even added a new salary or stipend for another researcher or PhD student. I had become almost—but not quite—blasé about it. The letter had never arrived on my birthday before; I had not been expecting it until the end of the month. So I opened it with a sort of muted optimism. After all, it was my birthday.

"Dear Dr. Fergusson," I read, already feeling lightheaded as my eyes scanned the next lines, *"The Scientific Committee has now considered all the reviewers' comments on the grant applications in the 2008 round, and I regret to inform you that your application has not been successful. We had a particularly strong field this time, and as you will see by the enclosed reviewers' reports, there were a number of problems with your proposed program. Of most significance is the concern that your research is lagging behind other programs in the same area."*

I stared glassy-eyed at the words, hoping that I was about to wake up from a bad dream with my Eggs Benedict still to come.

"The Committee is aware of your excellent output over a long period and the substantial discoveries you have made in the Huntington's disease research field, but unfortunately, in these difficult financial times, we must

put our resources behind new programs that have moved on from more basic research and are able to take advantage of the latest technologies in neuroscience and particularly genetic engineering."

My head was getting hot at this point; latest technologies and genetic engineering my arse. Easy for them to dismiss years of painstaking "basic research," as they called it, so they could back the new sexy breed of researcher. No way could they accomplish anything useful without boring old basic research in the first place.

"A final report is due on the 31st July, a month after the termination of your present grant. Please include a complete list of the publications that have come out of your program over the past fifteen years. A list of all the equipment you currently have that has been financed by your grant is also required. Our administrator will contact you in due course to discuss the dispersal of this equipment. The University will liaise with you over the closure of your laboratory.

We appreciate your long association with us, and wish you and the researchers in your laboratory well in your future endeavors."

THE OTHER TRADITION I KEPT ON MY BIRTHDAY WAS DINNER AT an elegant restaurant with my friend Francesca. I could safely say she was my only friend, as my long relationship with Rachel was purely work-related, except for the novels twice a year. I was tempted to cancel the dinner and stay in my small apartment and sulk, but something deep inside wanted to connect with a human who cared about me and didn't think of me as a washed-up old spinster with no more to discover. Fran and I had been friends since our first year at medical school, when we found ourselves on the same lab bench in the chemistry lab, simply because both our surnames began with 'Fe.'

Fran Fenton and I were unlikely soul mates. She was American, extroverted, gently rounded, and 'five-foot-two, eyes of blue,' with short, spiky blond hair. I was British, introverted, thin, and five-foot-eight, eyes of slate, with straight dark hair halfway down my back, usually constrained into a single plait, but on this occasion permitted to hang loose. Fran was also, in stark contrast to me, married, with three boisterous teenagers. She worked three days a week as a general practitioner in the health center attached to the university where my lab was, and we did our best to have lunch together at least once a fortnight. I once went to her house for Christmas dinner but it wasn't a success; her husband, an English professor, found me difficult, and her teenagers clearly saw me as a charity case. But the birthday dinner was always a special occasion for Fran as well as me, I think.

When she read the letter she was satisfyingly appalled, and said "swines" so violently that there was a sudden hush at the tables around us. When the quiet murmur in the room had resumed, she reached over and put her small, pretty hand over mine. I felt the roughness of the skin on her palm and blinked hard as I realized what a special person she was, never seeming rushed in spite of the massive amount of stuff she did — including slaving over a houseful of kids. Her eyes were watering as well as she said softly, "It's so unfair. How could they abandon you like this in the middle of your research? What will happen to all your Huntington's families?" Sweet Fran, always thinking of the plight of others worse off by a country mile than people like us, whereas all I'd been thinking about was myself and how I'd let down my little team.

I blinked hard again and turned my palm up and grasped her hand. I'd been aware how close to tears I'd been all day, but of course I hadn't allowed myself to succumb; not my style at all. In fact my brave little team all remained tearless as I gave them the news at our regular weekly meeting, which just happened to be today. Rachel had disappeared into the bath- room for a long time as soon as the meeting was over, and when she finally reappeared looked distinctly red-nosed. That's when she told me that she would take this opportunity to retire and go and live with her elderly sister in Portland. Dear Rachel, loyal to the end.

Fortunately, the last PhD student we had in the lab had submitted her thesis a couple of months ago. I'd promised my four shell-shocked researchers that I would personally contact every lab that did research similar to ours and put in a good word for them. They had become quite attached to their Huntington's families, which is not a recommended practice for a research scientist, but was a characteristic that I'd learned was essential for effective field workers. Releasing four Huntington's researchers on to the market at once was practically a flood, but they were young and good at what they did and would surely get new positions in due course.

Fran was asking me about other grants, and I wrenched myself away from my gloomy reverie. Taking my hand back, I grabbed my wine glass and emptied it. "Not a chance, I'm afraid," I told her. "The fact is, I'm finished. God knows how I lasted as long as I did."

"Anna, stop it. It's not like you to be so negative about your research. You've done wonderful things. You can't give up because you've lost your funding. Researchers lose grants all the time; they just have to get another one."

"Trouble is, the reviewers' reports were damning. And they're right. I was lucky to have the funding rolled over last time. They were probably giving me one last chance to do something new, but I blew it. I simply carried on in the same old way because that's all I know. I'm a fraud. I've always known it deep down, and now I've been sprung." As all this was spewing out of my mouth I could feel myself getting lighter and lighter. I felt hysterical laughter burbling up through my chest, and I poured myself another glass of wine and took a gulp, all the while watching Fran's face as her expression changed from concern to shock. Then a snort exploded out of me, along with a mouthful of wine, and I put my glass down quickly and grabbed the blue table napkin, mopping the dribbles from my chin and dabbing at the red splotches on the white tablecloth.

Fran's sweet face split into a grin and she giggled. "You're drunk. Wicked woman. It's not funny."

"It's definitely not funny, but I'm bloody well not drunk. This is all I've had to drink today, and half that's on the tablecloth." I wiped my eyes. "Let's finish this bottle and get another one." We grinned at each other and then sobered up.

"So what now?" asked Fran.

I looked at her, my mind blank. My pulse was pounding through my whole body. I forced myself to focus. "I suppose I will have to apply for more grants, but you know how long that takes. I don't think I've got much hope of getting anything substantial."

Fran screwed up her face. I could almost see her neurons flashing as she searched for a miracle.

I tried to ignore the churning in my gut. "I'll be okay for a while. The good old Medical School Dean said I could have a cubbyhole and a computer for the rest of the year so that I could finish all the papers I've still to write." I swirled the wine around in my glass, and watched the ruby liquid as it came dangerously near to the rim. "Given that boring old basic research is no longer considered worthy, I wonder why I should bother, really."

"Is he going to pay you?"

"Huh, no hope of that. Although he did say that I might be able to give a few guest lectures, so I suppose I'll get a few meager dollars for those."

"Why don't you go back to clinical practice? You know so much about Huntington's disease. You'd be a wonderful doctor for them and other neurological patients."

"Fran, what are you thinking? You of all people know that I'm hopeless at the bedside thing and anything that involves actual patient contact. That's why I became a researcher."

"But that was twenty-five years ago. You've grown up and

changed since then. You might like it now if you gave yourself a chance."

"I haven't changed, that's the problem. I don't even like socializing with other research staff. You're the only person in the entire universe who I feel comfortable really talking to."

"Well you have to do something. What are you going to live on?"

"That's one of the advantages of being a workaholic with no kids. I've got heaps of money stashed away in the bank. Now at last I'll be able to spend it. Perhaps I'll fly off to some exotic, tropical paradise and become a recluse."

"Very amusing. But you could travel. At least for a few months. Go to Europe. It would give you time to refresh your ideas, and then you could write a new grant that would blow those small-minded pen-pushers out of the water." Fran sounded excited by all these possibilities opening out in front of me.

I could feel my brain shutting down, and shook my head to wake it up. "Perhaps I could take a trip." I pushed my lips into a grin. "Go and see my mother and her lover in their hideaway. Now there's a nice tropical island."

"Doesn't she live in Shetland? That's a great idea. You should visit her."

Fran didn't always get my sense of humor.

"Fran, it's practically in the Arctic Circle. I do not want to go there. And right now my mother and her gigolo are the last people I want or need to see." I rolled my eyes.

"Don't be unkind. Your mother has a right to happiness, and I think her life sounds very exciting. I thought she was married?"

"She is. And good on her. But she and I are better off living a long way apart." I yawned. "I can't think about all this any more tonight. And it's way past your bedtime; you have to work tomorrow."

Fran frowned. "I wish you didn't have to go through all

this. It's horrible. But I know something will come up that's better. It always does."

BUT NOT FOR THE NEXT FOUR MONTHS. I CLOSED UP—OR down— the lab, took the team out for a subdued redundancy dinner, and moved into the cubbyhole, where I put my head down and wrote the final report on fifteen years of work. Then I wrote a grant application and sent it off to an obscure private funding body that gave out small grants from a legacy left by some wealthy old woman who died a lonely death from Parkinson's disease. I had little hope it would be successful, as all I could come up with as a research project was further analysis of the neurological material we had collected over the past few years—hardly cutting-edge research. At least waiting to hear would give me a few months of pathetic hope, rather like buying a ticket in a lottery.

That done, I dutifully went into the university every day and tried to write a paper on a series of experiments that we had completed and analyzed just before the grant was terminated. But my heart wasn't in it, and I could sit for eight hours with no more than a bad paragraph to show for it.

Boston was hot and I felt stifled. Fran and her family were away on their regular summer break at the Professor's parents' cabin on a lake somewhere, and the medical school was as dead as a dodo. I used to begrudge any time spent talking trivia to the researchers in my lab, but now that I didn't have it, I missed it. Even my once-pleasant apartment had become a prison, clamping me inside its walls the minute I got home in the evenings. I was no stranger to loneliness, but over the past few years I'd polished my strategies to deal with it. I would remind myself that the flip side of loneliness could be worse— a houseful of demanding kids, a husband who expected dinner on the table, a weighty mortgage, irritating in-laws—it became almost a game to see what new horrors I could come up with. You, Anna Fergusson, I'd tell myself sternly, are free of all that. "I'm a liberated woman," I once shouted, before glancing furtively around in case my madwoman behavior had conjured up a sneering audience. If self-talk didn't work, or even when it did, more often than not I'd slump down in front of the TV and watch three episodes straight of Morse, or some other BBC detective series, and one night I stayed awake for the entire 238 minutes of Gone with the Wind.

When Fran finally returned from her lake at the beginning of August, I was on the phone to her before she had time to unpack her bags. Understanding as always, she put her other duties aside and the very next day met me at our usual lunch place. She looked fantastic: brown and healthy and young. I felt like a slug. It wasn't until we were getting up to leave, me to go back to my cubbyhole and Fran to the supermarket, that she remembered.

"Gosh, I almost forgot. Callum was mucking about on the Internet while we were at the lake and came across this advertisement. He made some joke about it being the perfect job for him when he left school, and I remembered how you said after you lost your grant that you should go and live on a tropical island." Fran scrabbled in her bag and hauled out a scrunched up sheet of paper.

"Fran, for heaven's sake, you know that was a joke. What is it?" I took the paper she had unscrunched and read the small advertisement surrounded by ads for adventure tourism in Australia.

For rent to a single or couple who want to escape to a tropical paradise. Basic cabin on tiny coral island on Australia's Great Barrier Reef. AUD$250 a week; must agree to stay one year and look after small private campsite (five tents maximum). Starting date October 2008. For more information e-mail lazylad at yahoo.com.au.

I looked at Fran in amazement. "You printed this out for

me? I think the sun must have got to you. Lazylad is looking for some young bimbo. And he wants to be paid to look after his campsite. What cheek."

"That's what I thought at first, but Callum pointed out that thousands of people would give their eyeteeth for an opportunity like this if the cabin were free. But that's the beauty of it; you can afford it. And wasn't your father Australian? You mightn't even need a visa."

"Fran, you're a dear, but can you see me on an island on the other side of the world, singing jolly campfire songs with spaced-out boaties?"

"Have you got a better idea? Or are you just going to continue to fade away in your cubbyhole?"

"No, I'm out of there as soon as I finish this damn paper I'm writing, and then I thought I might try my hand at writing a book." So there, I felt like adding.

Fran's face lit up. "A book? That's fantastic. What sort of a book? A novel?"

I started to laugh. "What happened to you up there at the lake? This is me, Anna. I haven't suddenly morphed into a normal person. I'm still the same old ivory tower nerd, clueless about people. No, I thought I might be able to write some sort of account of my experiences getting research grants and running a lab. All the highs and lows. Perhaps I'll discover where I went wrong." I could hear the gloom in my voice as the words came out of my mouth.

"But that's a great idea. And you'll need somewhere to write it." I could see the mischief in her eyes as she grinned at me.

"I know what you're thinking, and no, I do not want to live on a desert island at the end of the world."

"Oh well, worth a try. It wouldn't hurt to check it out though, would it?"

Two days later I composed a careful e-mail to Lazylad, not expecting a reply. Surely the cabin had been snapped up by now if it were such a dream opportunity. I got used to holding my breath as I turned my e-mail on each morning, scrolling rapidly through all the usual stuff looking for Lazylad, telling myself I didn't care. But the idea of going to Australia had got stuck in my head.

I had all but given up and stopped daydreaming about writing a book on a deck looking through the palms across an azure blue ocean, when there it was—a reply from Lazylad, who I later found out was actually called Jeff.

Thanks for e-mail. Been away sorry for delay in reply. Cabin still available if you want it. Photos attached. Island called Turtle Island (after the sea turtles here) and is a coral cay just above Tropic of Capricorn about eight hectares in area with a large reef surrounding it. A few eccentric people own houses here and that's about it apart from my small campsite. Only transport is fishing boat or charter. Cabin basic but comfortable, everything included. Solar hot water (roof water) and solar power for lights and computer, gas fridge and stove, no telephone. Satellite broadband from some locals' houses you can use occasionally in return for a few beers. One of the local fishermen brings supplies over about once a fortnight in his boat and locals can hitch a ride for a small fee or more beers. Fantastic snorkeling and diving, birds, turtles, etc. Weather always perfect (almost). If you are interested e-mail me your phone number and I'll call you when next on mainland to chat. Looking after campsite is a doddle. First come, first served (no bookings), take their money, and make sure the old guy on the island does his job of emptying the toilet and the rubbish bins. It would be good to get someone here before I leave for UK on 18th October so I can show you the ropes.

When I scrolled down so I could see the photos my hand was trembling. The first one showed a rectangular wooden building with what appeared to be an open front with a wide deck. A big wooden table and a few white plastic chairs, along with a heap of what looked like diving stuff—a wetsuit and flippers and a tank—sat on the deck. In the dimness of the inside I could make out a bed on one side of a partition and what looked like a kitchen on the other. The cabin was surrounded on three sides by trees with large leaves, and in front of the cabin was a sweep of white sand. The sand had something black on it, and when I zoomed in I could see it was a cluster of three large black birds just sitting there. The second photo showed a narrow strip of white sand, fringed by trees with feathery-looking leaves, and then the truly azure blue sea and sky. The last photo was like something on a travel brochure: a tiny, oval, flat island with green vegetation crowning the center and white sand around the edge, surrounded by blue. In the blue I could see dark patterns, the coral. I grabbed my pendant and brought it to my mouth. The last time I had seen coral sea had been when I was twelve years old, and I had thought then that I never wanted to see it again.

Chapter 2

I stood hanging on to the railing that ran round the bow of the fishing boat and looked at the white-and-green spot on the horizon. "Heavens, it's tiny," I said, obviously louder than I had intended.

"Don't tell me you didn't know?" I turned to see the weather-beaten face of fisherman Jack, who was kindly delivering me to my new home. Presumably his son was driving the boat while he took time off to chat. "Well yes, I knew, but it somehow looks a lot smaller than I'd imagined. I suppose it's the isolation of it in that great expanse of sea, rather than it being so small."

"Think of it as the whole reef." He leaned over the side

and nodded his head like a pointer. "Look, we're already over it; you can see the coral below now. The island is just the bit sticking out at high tide. So it's really a massive area." He grinned at me.

"Right. That's very comforting." I looked back to the island, which was getting marginally bigger. Not another island to be seen. Not even another boat. And then a dark speck appeared in the blue, weaving back and forth and increasing in size until I could make out a small dinghy. "What on earth is that boat doing?" I asked, pointing. "It looks as if it has lost control."

"Some would agree with you there. It's the turtle rodeo. I'll cut the engine when we get a bit closer in and you can watch for a bit. It's a sight not to be missed."

"What do you mean, a turtle rodeo? Surely people aren't allowed to ride turtles." I was shocked.

Jack chuckled. "Now there's a good idea. You hang on there and I'll get up to the wheelhouse and bring her closer." We turned towards the smaller boat and our engine went quiet. I could hear the screeching of the dinghy's outboard motor as it sped first one way, and then, in a mighty spray of water, turned back and then around again in dizzying zigzags. I could make out three figures, one standing dangerously near the bow. Suddenly the boat screeched to a stop, and the black figure at the front dove into the water as the engine was silenced. I held my breath as the figure disappeared below the surface. Minutes seemed to go by before the diver's head came out of the water right by the dinghy. He seemed to be carrying something—it looked like a large body. We were still too far away for me to see.

I remembered my binoculars and scrabbled for them in my backpack. It wasn't a body—well, not a human one—but a massive turtle that the man—I supposed it was a man—had clasped in front of him. I could see the big head and the front flippers flapping desperately as the people in the boat struggled to get ropes around them. The man in the water was grasping the shell, which was much wider than him. The others in the boat were leaning over the sides trying to grab the flippers, and then I saw them tying the poor thing to the side of the boat. They seemed to be measuring its shell. This went on for some minutes while the dinghy pitched and swayed—it was quite choppy—and then they untied the unfortunate creature and it sank below the surface, and I hope got well away. The diver was clambering back into the dinghy, and one of the others waved at us. Jack was standing beside me again, waving back at them. They started their outboard and made a beeline for us. Their dinghy did a sort of side-skid like a teenager in a hot rod as they reached us and pulled up short, their motor grumbling to a low putt-putt.

"Tom, gidday," Jack yelled. "Just telling this young lady about your rodeo. She thought she'd like to go for a ride on a turtle while she's here."

Cheeky sod. I wonder which he thinks is more amusing, the 'young' or the 'lady'?

"Hi Jack, any time, tell her. Does she want to come for a ride now?" the diver was shouting back, his black wetsuit glistening in the sun, his hair springing from his head in wet spikes. I tried to appear nonchalant as I stood there gripping the rail, my heart pounding as I looked down at the dinghy. I could see them all grinning at me, and I was glad I could hide behind the enormous pair of D&G sunglasses Fran had given me as a going-away present.

Jack's arm shot out and landed around my shoulders, pulling me towards him. I could feel myself tensing as his hot breath exploded on my cheek. "This is Anna Fergusson. She's going to be looking after Jeff's campground for a year." His free hand gestured sweepingly towards the dinghy. "And this daring fellow is our resident turtle whisperer."

The man in the wet suit dipped his head and raised his

hand in a desultory wave. "These are my two research assistants, Bill and Ben," he said, still grinning.

Am I meant to return their banter? "Hullo," I said creatively.

All three of them nodded at me and I tried to make my face look pleasant.

"So, do you want to come on board?" asked the diver. "We've about finished the rodeo for the day—one more turtle, perhaps—so we'll be back at the wharf by the time Jack's got your gear to your place. Blow the smoke out of your lungs."

"Thank you," I said, knowing how stiff I sounded. "But I don't think I'm dressed for it." I felt ridiculous in my long black pants and blue shirt, even with the top buttons open and the sleeves rolled up.

"No worries, another time maybe." His grin flashed again and his eyes crinkled in his young brown face. I smiled back at him without thinking. It was impossible not to. I realized I had taken off my sunglasses and our eyes were connecting. Then their motor roared and they sped away as I hurriedly replaced my glasses, hoping jolly Jack hadn't noticed the heat in my face.

THE SMELL HIT ME FIRST AS I STEPPED OFF THE SMALL WHARF and onto the brilliant white sand. A hot, dry, musty smell. Not unpleasant but definitely not lavender. Then the sound of birds, hundreds of them. I looked over to the green rim of trees bordering the twenty meters or so of sand; black- and-white birds were flying in and out, busy as bees. The heat rose up from the sand, and I was glad I had put a pair of shorts in my bag. I nearly hadn't, as my legs hadn't been exposed to the elements for at least twenty years. The shorts were another present from Fran.

Jack's son had disappeared into the interior of the island

as soon as we tied up, and Jack had already dumped my one suitcase and computer bag onto the sand. He was now carrying off armloads of banana boxes stacked three high, his biceps distorting a labyrinth of tattoos. Numerous food boxes, seven of them mine, food and supplies that had to last for two weeks minimum until Jack came back from the mainland with the next food haul. An old tractor with a trailer behind it was now chugging through the gap in the trees and down to the wharf, driven by Jack's son. I stood and watched as they rapidly loaded all the boxes, my luggage, large gas bottles, enormous tins with DIESEL written on the outside, and various other things onto the trailer. I made a weak attempt to help but was obviously in the way.

"Come on, I'll walk you to your cabin. Nick will drop your bags and food off in a bit." Jack walked towards the gap in the trees and I followed him, increasing my stride to keep up. He was a broad man, and must have been well over six feet. My feet felt hot in my well-worn hiking boots. I nearly tripped over a group of the busy birds that seemed to be chattering to one another on the sand. They were so pretty. A neat, soft black body with a perky white cap. Big black feet and a black beak completed them perfectly. Jack looked back as I stopped.

"They're white-capped noddy terns. Not so many here yet, but there'll be hundreds of thousands in a few weeks, and all these trees"—he waved a hand at the large-leaved trees we were walking through—"will be loaded with their nests."

"They're beautiful. There seem to be an awful lot here already."

"Wait 'til you see their babies. They must be the prettiest little birds alive."

We continued walking.

"The other bird we have here in the thousands is the wedge-tailed shearwater. Ghost shearwaters, we call them, because of the howling noise they make. Once they're nesting it's almost impossible to move without stepping on a bird or collapsing one of their nesting tunnels. Even sleeping is diffi-cult with the racket they kick up."

I felt a strange sensation in my belly and chest, a sort of bubbling. Excitement, that's what I was feeling. Pure excitement.

My cabin was even smaller than I had envisioned. "Mini-malist living" would be putting it mildly, but that was fine by me. I was a minimalist from way back. Jack stopped long enough to demonstrate the vagaries of the enormous and scarily ancient-looking gas fridge/freezer and the even older gas stove. Next came the shower, an ingenious contraption that involved filling a bucket with water from the taps over the large sink, hauling it up to the ceiling of the shower cubicle on a rope pulley, and then, by pulling on another rope, tipping it over so that it emptied its load into a funnel that filtered down to a large shower nozzle. The water that spurted from the taps was disgusting—full of black bits and smelling slightly off. Jack grinned when he saw my expression and suggested that I boil it before drinking it. The only fresh water on the island came from rainwater tanks fed by roof water thick with the drop-pings of thousands of birds, especially foul following a down-pour after a long dry period. I silently thanked Jeff—alias Lazylad—for his wise counsel when he helped me buy my food supplies on the mainland, especially his insistence that I fill two banana boxes with plastic bottles of drinking water.

The power came courtesy of two solar panels on the roof, stored in batteries under the cabin and converted from 12 volts to 240 volts by a humming piece of equipment in a cupboard. It hadn't even occurred to me that power might be a problem, so I felt a jolt of simultaneous horror and relief. Perhaps I could have coped without my iPod, but I would have had to turn right around and go back if I couldn't use my Kindle and computer. I had brought a universal plug adaptor with me, of course—part of my overseas conference travel kit.

Jack disappeared, and Nick arrived on his tractor, dumped my bags and boxes on the deck, and with a "See ya round, mate," roared off. I returned to the kitchen end of the cabin and opened the few cupboards and checked out the mismatched crockery, glasses and cutlery. A blackened kettle sat on the stove, and an equally blackened fry pan and a couple of battered saucepans hung from large hooks suspended from the low ceiling. I looked at the few photos stuck on the walls with tacks. One of them was a picture of Jeff and another man, both dressed only in shorts, standing in the shallow water, an enormous turtle between them. When I first decided to take the cabin, Jeff had been going to meet me there and show me the ropes, but then he decided to meet me on the mainland and introduce me to Jack, who did the regular supplies run once a fortnight. Jeff would be in Sydney now, and soon on his way to the UK and a trial run living with his girlfriend for a year. He'd told me all this while we shopped and then had fish 'n chips in a local café. I looked again at the faded photo and peered at the other man in it for a few seconds before realizing it was the turtle whisperer. He looked different without his wetsuit. Both men had that Australian look, rugged and brown. The turtle whisperer—Tom, I think Jack called him— had quite a lot of dark-blondish hair. I'd got the impression that it was black when I saw him earlier, because it was wet I suppose. He was grinning his infectious grin, and his dark eyes were almost hidden in the crinkles of his smile. Both men had nice faces, open and friendly. Tom's was sort of lopsided, but perhaps that added to his attractiveness. How old would he be? Jeff had let slip that he was thirty-five—the right age to settle down, as he put it—so perhaps Tom was about the same age. I'd meant to ask Jack why he called him the turtle whisperer, but hadn't in the end. I suppose it's another Australian joke because of this turtle rodeo thing he does—the exact opposite of a turtle whisperer, if you ask me.

I finally got around to emptying my case into the small wardrobe and tallboy. I thought about putting my shorts on, but decided on my light safari pants and a T-shirt instead. The shorts would have to wait until I'd shaved my legs; the poor things hadn't seen a razor since my student days. I went brown quite easily as a kid, so fingers crossed I still would, and the Australian sun wouldn't burn me to a cinder.

After burying my black trousers and blue shirt at the back of the wardrobe and swapping my boots for sandals, I felt much better. I unpacked the food boxes and squashed the packs of rapidly defrosting meat into the freezer box, and the other refrigerator stuff into the fridge part. I managed to find space in the few cupboards and on the open shelves above the sink for the rest of my food, and hoped it wouldn't soon be infested by god knows what creepy crawlies. I made a mental note to beg, borrow, or steal some plastic containers from somewhere. I had a few scary moments lighting the gas hob, but finally managed to boil some of the bird-shit water and make a cup of tea. It had a very peculiar taste but I was cautious about using my precious bottled water except for drinking it cold.

I took my cup of musty tea and a plate of biscuits and cheese out on to my deck—I was already thinking of it as mine —and sat in one of the plastic chairs. It was still and hot and all around me were scuffles and birds calling, and through a gap in the trees was the white sand and then the blue sea, now with bits of coral sticking up in it as the tide went out. I sat there not believing it was me, and that I was there for a year with nothing to do but write my memoir—not that anyone else would give a damn if I did or didn't, and right then nor did I.

What on earth would I do for a year? Surely the campsite I was yet to see wouldn't take much of my time? Luckily my Kindle was stuffed with at least sixty books and my iPod loaded with my favorite music. And I'd better at least make some attempt at the memoir just to keep my brain ticking over.

After a while I got up, reluctantly, and followed a sandy path around the side of the cabin and through some trees for about two hundred meters. Jack had told me the campsite was back there. And there it was, quite a large sandy, grassy area with trees all around but with a gap showing the beach and sea. A wooden building near the edge turned out to house a toilet that looked fairly unsavory when I looked down it, but didn't seem to smell. Thankfully I didn't have to deal with it. A man called Basil, whom I was yet to meet, apparently did the honors. On the outside wall of the toilet was a shower like mine. A little way from that was a large open shelter with a concrete floor and a wooden picnic table in the middle. A gas barbecue and a couple of gas bottles took up one side. A guttering around the roof of the shelter led into a pipe connected to a water tank on stilts, and at the base of that was a concrete tub with one tap. A notice stuck to the tank said that the water was undrinkable without boiling and to use sparingly.

All in all a very pleasant spot, but obviously not on the main backpacker trail, as there was not a single tent to be seen. Keeping an eye on this should be an easy job. I wandered out onto the beach, where even more coral was now exposed, and looked both ways. I thought I must be in the middle of the long part of the oval island. Looking to my right, back towards my cabin, I could see the wharf where we had landed, with Jack's boat and a few others bobbing alongside it. Jack had explained that there was an artificial deep water channel there that the original occupants of the island —that is, the European occupants—had made with the help of a few sticks of dynamite. In the other direction the beach stretched for a few hundred meters before disappearing around the corner.

The light had become softer and the blue of the sky had

taken on a sort of transparent luminescence. I glanced at my watch and was surprised to see that it was five o'clock. I'd already been here four hours. Basil could wait 'til the morning. Basil Brush. I grinned as an image of the unknown Basil, complete with bushy red hair and tail, flashed in my head. Perhaps all Australians have these sweet, old-fashioned, simple names. Bill and Ben the flowerpot men, Jack and the beanstalk, Tom, Tom the piper's son . . . Christ, I'll never remember who is who. I wonder when I'm going to meet Waltzing Matilda? That's if there are any females here. Not that I'm likely to have anything in common with them.

ACKNOWLEDGMENTS

This novel was my first attempt at writing fiction, and after years in the bottom drawer, has morphed into a very different book. Thank you to the editors who read drafts and gave me insightful and generous feedback: Lesley Marshall, Jenny Argante, Philippa Donovan and Rebecca Horsfall.

I devoured many newspaper and magazine articles, videos, and books about Hurricane Katrina and her human cost in my efforts to do justice to the people of New Orleans, and especially the medical staff and volunteers who put their own lives at risk to save others. I found particularly helpful and moving *Leave No One Behind: Hurricane Katrina and the Rescue of Tulane Hospital* by Bill Cary; *Code Blue: A Katrina Physician's Memoir* by Richard E. Deichmann, M.D.; and *1 Dead in Attic: After Katrina*, by Chris Rose. While I have been to New Orleans many times, pre and post Katrina, it is impossible to imagine what it must have been like, especially for the people who call New Orleans home. All errors and misinterpretations of the reality are my own.

Thank you to Brooke Warner, publisher of my debut novel, *A Drop in the Ocean*, to my sisters at She Writes Press, and to the many other writers I have come to know in this fascinating world of writing fiction, especially those generous authors who took time out from writing their next book to read mine, and pen a blurb. Your ongoing friendship, support and your books transform my solitary writing space into a team endeavor.

I look back with gratitude over my long career as a clinical psychologist, neuropsychologist and observer of neurosurgical operations. The experiences I survived during those years now provide much of the bedrock of my stories.

To my four children: thank you for teaching me about parenting when you were kids so that I could later write fiction about parent-kid relationships—and for continuing the lessons now you are adults! And of course, I thank John for putting up with my obsession with stories and books—my own and others' —for so very long.

Jenni Ogden and her husband live off-grid on spectacular Great Barrier Island, 100 kms off the coast of New Zealand, a perfect place to write and for grandchildren to spend their holidays. Winters are spent near a beach in Far North Tropical Queensland. Jenni's debut novel, *A Drop in the Ocean*, won multiple awards and has sold over 80,000 copies. As a clinical psychologist and neuropsychologist, she is well-known for her books featuring her patients' moving stories: *Fractured Minds: A Case-Study Approach to Clinical Neuropsychology*, and *Trouble In Mind: Stories from a Neuropsychologist's Casebook*. Please visit her author website (www.jenniogden.com), sign up for her e-newsletter, and friend and follow her everywhere!